Gallows Drop

By Mari Hannah

The Kate Daniels series

The Murder Wall
Settled Blood
Deadly Deceit
Monument to Murder
Killing for Keeps
Gallows Drop

Other novels

The Silent Room

Mari Hannah

Gallows Drop

MACMILLAN

First published 2016 by Macmillan
an imprint of Pan Macmillan
20 New Wharf Road, London N1 9RR
Basingstoke and Oxford
Associated companies throughout the world
www.panmacmillan.com

ISBN 978-1-4472-8733-9

A CIP catalogue record for this book is available from the British Library.

Typeset by Ellipsis Digital Limited, Glasgow
Printed and bound by CPI Group (UK) Ltd, Croydon, CR0 4YY

For Kate

1

Eight thirty-five a.m. October twelfth. Eerily quiet.

Mist hung like a thick veil over the countryside, a barren wilderness unchanged for centuries. Not a dwelling or barn in sight. Nothing to suggest civilization existed close by. Except it did: in the pretty village of Elsdon two and a half miles to the north. On any other Sunday morning, Detective Chief Inspector Kate Daniels would have marvelled at the view, in awe of the peace and tranquillity of the spot on which she was standing. She rode up here often from her Newcastle home, respite from days spent in a murder incident room, or worse, the morgue. Apart from the rustle of wind through surrounding vegetation and occasional birdsong, there was no sound.

It was ethereal almost . . .

Beautiful certainly . . .

Not today.

The body hung from the gibbet. A grotesque sight, it swirled in the breeze, head lolled to one side, tongue protruding, arms by its side, hoisted by a heavy rope, thick with grease and covered in muck, the kind you'd see in any garage or builder's yard. Her eyes travelled down the badly beaten torso, coming to rest on white footless tights, caked in blood.

Tragic.

A chill pierced Kate's detective armour. She shivered, forcing herself to look, unable to get her head around what had gone on here or why. That wasn't unusual. She often struggled to make sense of the grim truths she unearthed. Right now, she wished she were at headquarters, a mug of hot coffee in her hand, listening to banter between team members arriving for work: DCs Andy Brown and Lisa Carmichael sharing a joke; DS Paul Robson moaning about his kid waking him at silly o'clock. Even DC Neil Maxwell's exploits in the love department would be welcome this morning. Ordinarily they would make her cringe.

Oh God!

Something she'd seen produced a sudden flashback: a distinctive skeletal tattoo depicting the bones of the victim's hand, a clever representation of what lay beneath the skin.

Kate shivered.

She'd seen this kid before . . .

A boy . . . over sixteen . . . not yet twenty-one.

She shut her eyes, walking herself back in time to the bustle of a country show, its annual festivities in full swing. The memory was as vivid as it was recent. She saw flags and purple heather. Heard the sweet sound of Northumbrian pipes floating on the breeze. The laughter of children, the chatter of stallholders touting for business, a man's guttural voice, muffled through a loudspeaker . . .

'Well done, Becca Johnson, winner of the ladies' fell race, joining us today from New South Wales. It's a long way home, folks, so please put your hands together and give her a great big Northumbrian send-off . . .'

In her head, Kate heard applause, her thoughts swinging wildly between the present and the past. It was late morning when she'd arrived at the show. That much she knew. Light drizzle hadn't spoilt the occasion. It must've been almost twelve thirty in the afternoon before she'd spotted the boy with the tattooed hand larking about with mates. Or was it later?

C'mon, think!

Jo Soulsby had been standing next to her, clapping and smiling, happy in the knowledge that they were due some time off soon, their first holiday together in years – a chance to repair a broken relationship. Relishing the thought of an extended break – much-needed relief from a demanding job – Kate had mentally packed her suitcase and was already in the car on the way to Scotland's east coast. She'd simply had a gut-full of murder.

Her leave period was almost here . . .

Almost.

The event manager's voice forced its way into her head. 'Now, will the under-sixteens Cumberland wrestlers please leave the beer tent and make their way to the main sports ring.' A mischievous chuckle filled the arena. 'Only joking, mums and dads – they stopped drinking ten minutes ago. They're ready to start soon, so off you go and give them your support . . .'

Kate pulled up her sleeve to check the time. The watch she was seeing wasn't the one on her wrist. It was the one she'd worn the day before. She tried hard to remember where the hands were pointing when the under-twenty-one competitors took to the arena.

One o'clock?

Two?

The sound of an engine made her open her eyes and glance down the road to the vanishing point. A car loomed out of the mist and sped past, travelling way too fast for the icy conditions. On either side of the thin strip of tarmac, moorland grasses bent towards her in the breeze. They seemed to point accusing fingers in her direction, telling her: *not again.*

The thought forced her attention to the figure dangling in front of her. The boy was one of the wrestlers she'd seen yesterday. She was sure of it. His clothes were strewn on the ground – ripped from his body by the looks of it: denim jeans, a grey hoodie, a pair of well-worn trainers, the familiar Nike flash picked out in fluorescent green. He had a few quid and a bit of loose change in his pocket, according to crime scene investigators, but no mobile or ID.

No ID?

He belonged to someone.

Given the community nature of country shows it was a fair bet that his family had been in the crowd, like her, cheering him on. For all Kate knew they could have been standing next to her, smiled or spoken to her as their son squared up to his opponent. She imagined him alive, adrenalin pumping, enjoying the rush of the occasion, an opportunity to take centre stage and impress his mates – a chance to emerge victorious and claim a coveted trophy.

Poor sod.

'What's the sketch?' Detective Sergeant Hank Gormley stepped gingerly from the slab of stone he'd been standing on, the base of a Saxon cross that marked the highest point on the old drove road. In centuries past, it was the route down which cattle were driven to market in Hexham and Newcastle from beyond Scotland's border twenty miles away. No less violent then than now. This was an area fought over many times.

'You tell me,' Kate said. 'Looks like someone gave him a right going over before they finished him off. Who found him and when?'

'Witness's name is Tom Orde. He was driving by at dawn on his way to work. Thought it was someone's idea of a joke and stopped to take a photo. Don't worry. He had the good sense not to share it – except with the control room. Lucky for us he hates social media.'

Hank accessed the photos on his mobile phone, turning the device to face her. Against the grey mist, the gibbet stood out, black and forbidding. It would have drawn Orde's eye as if to say: *Look here.*

The image spoke volumes.

Hank shifted his weight from one foot to the other, a puzzled expression on his face. 'Why bring him here to string him up? Risky strategy if you ask me. Whoever did this would have been totally exposed to anyone driving by.'

Kate had no words.

Looking past him, she tried to ascertain what the scene was telling her. The answer was, not much. Or was it? When the gibbet was built, hangings were a public spectacle. Was that the case here? Was there a hidden meaning behind this macabre display? A message of some sort . . . If so, who was the intended recipient?

The police?
Someone else?

'There's only one certainty in play here,' she said. 'We can safely rule out suicide.'

'There must've been more than one involved,' Hank said. 'It would've taken some effort to hoy a rope over the cross-bar at the top, let alone winch him up there. I'm not sure I could do it. Not on my own, anyway. One of the lads found vehicle tracks beyond the fence.' He pointed to an adjoining field. 'They appear to be fairly recent. Small wheelbase—'

'Not a tractor then?'

'More like a quad bike – the tracks go off down there . . .' He indicated barbed-wire fencing that ran alongside the gibbet. Early morning dew hung off it like tiny jewels, the weight of the water making them drip onto the heather beneath. 'It could've been the farmer checking his boundary. The tracks have been photographed. I've requested casts and sent a couple of uniforms to search for an access point.'

'Ask Lisa to check out whose land it is.'

'Already taken care of.'

Kate nodded towards the CSIs. 'Tell them to cut him down.'

She noticed how drawn Hank was as he gave the order and took his mobile from his pocket. It worried her. Against her advice, he'd insisted on signing himself off the sick – too early, in her opinion. A villain they had chased to Spain put a bullet in his chest. She wasn't with him when it happened but saw it later on video. Leaving him single-crewed, exposed and vulnerable, haunted her as much as the shooting.

'You OK?' he asked. 'You look a bit pasty.'

She nodded, the memory receding. It was a question she should be asking him. She wasn't OK – far from it – she was still reeling from that case. Almost losing him had shocked her to the core, the experience acting as a stark reminder of how precious and fragile life was. She felt guilty too for having fallen apart in the middle of the case.

Not like her.

The truth of it was, her confidence had taken a dive long before they reached La Manga. Since then, details of the enquiry she'd tried so hard to forget had kept bubbling to the surface, picking away at her, a prompt, if one was needed, to take time off with Jo – if only to get her shit together.

If Jo were here, how would she read the scene?

Jo's expertise as a criminal profiler had played a crucial part in some high-profile cases over the years, but it was Kate's remit to find the person or persons responsible for this latest killing and bring them before a court of law. She was the one with a duty of care to the boy and his family, whoever they were.

As was always the way in the first few hours of a new investigation, she had more questions than answers. Already she felt the heavy burden to provide them. Her eyes drifted back to the victim as forensic personnel moved in to cut him down. Kate felt an urgent need to get the boy out of the cold. To lay him in a warm place and cover him up. Much as she'd like to, she couldn't do that. Protocol demanded that she step aside while others got to work.

Standing by as her instructions were carried out, she

reminded those doing the cutting to stay well away from the knot, even though, strictly speaking, it was the job of the crime scene manager to advise them. What she needed most was an estimated time of death; a preliminary examination would give her a rough timescale to work on.

'What kind of moron would do such a thing to a young man in the prime of his life?' she said under her breath.

Hank ignored her.

'Where the hell is the on-call pathologist?' he muttered, mobile stuck to his ear, his frustration on display. 'Goes without saying that we'd like Stanton if he's available.' Tim Stanton was trustworthy and expeditious. He got the job done with minimum fuss, didn't waste time on power play. Some Home Office bods delighted in making the cops feel like idiots. Not Tim. There were more important things at stake than bigging himself up to the Murder Investigation Team.

Hank's face dropped as he hung up.

Kate peered at him through rolling mist. 'I take it he's not available?'

'It's not that,' he said. 'They've allocated the SIO.'

'So why the long face?'

He looked at her.

'I'm guessing he or she doesn't meet with your approval,' she said.

'Or the rest of the team.'

'You got Cameron?'

'Worse. We got Atkins – a useless dickhead no one has any time—'

'*James* Atkins?'

'The one and only.'

The name sucked oxygen from Kate's lungs. She focused on keeping her back ramrod straight, her shoulders squared, but inside she was fighting a wave of nausea. Thankfully, Hank was busy issuing orders and hadn't picked up on it.

'I'm stuck with him for bloody ages,' he huffed as he turned to face her. 'Who takes a month off? It's not as if you're going to the southern hemisphere, is it? That I could understand – but Crail? Blink and you'd miss it.'

'I'm not off a month—'

'As good as. You'll be bored witless.'

No she wouldn't.

His tirade of objections faded out of her consciousness. As if she were reading a time-slip novel, Kate felt like she'd stumbled into a previous decade, a previous self, her mind on Atkins. As a young copper operating in a predominantly male environment, she'd been forced to adopt a tough persona and quick wit in order to survive against guys like him. She'd learned to be on her guard at all times, rarely disclosing anything personal. She might have come across as cold, but she'd rather have that armour than not.

Irrational? *Probably.*

Necessary? *Absolutely.*

Now her nemesis was back – persecution his specialist subject – and she wasn't looking forward to renewing their acquaintance.

'Kate?' Hank waved a hand in front of her face. 'You haven't heard a word I've said, have you?'

'Sorry . . .' She focused on the corpse, rather than meet his gaze. 'You'll have to cope without me this time. There's no way I'm cancelling my trip . . . Jo would kill me.'

She would too.

Leaving Hank to the mercy of Atkins wasn't ideal, but nothing was going to derail Kate's leave. She had one shot to make her peace with Jo – to decide, once and for all, if they had a future together. It was down to *her* that their relationship had stalled in the first place. She had an awful lot to make up for.

Hank had misread her silence. 'You know Atkins?' he asked.

She ignored the question by looking the other way. The victim was being lowered with great care onto plastic sheeting, the crime scene manager instructing his crew to erect a screen so the victim couldn't be seen from the main road. A tent wasn't necessary unless it began to rain, and none was forecast.

'You obviously have history,' Hank pushed.

'With Atkins?' Kate shot him a disparaging look. 'Not the kind you mean.'

He waited for her to spill but she clammed up. DCI James Atkins was not a man she wanted to mess with, talk about, or even acknowledge. He was shit on her shoe. She wouldn't waste a breath on him. Defiantly, she met Hank's gaze, her unwavering silence piquing his interest further. She made a move for her car. Their conversation was over.

2

'Eat up, Beth. It's getting cold.'

It was an order rather than a request, one Beth Casey wouldn't argue with if she knew what was good for her, except she didn't always and that caused her problems from time to time. She glared at her dad, wishing he'd remember he wasn't talking to his subordinates at work.

She took a sip of water. It was tepid and tasted vile. He'd not run the tap before bringing it to the table. Even worse, the fried breakfast on her plate was swimming in fat. The smell alone made her gag.

Holding on to her nausea, she asked to be excused, telling her father she wasn't hungry and rarely bothered with breakfast, never before nine thirty.

Here it comes.

She'd seen his black look.

'Eat,' he said. 'I'm not busting a gut to put food on the table so you can waste it.'

Beth looked away. Her hands felt hot and clammy. It was way too early to be up and about, let alone eating. She wished she were somewhere else, anywhere but here. It would never cross his mind that she'd prefer to bunk in with a mate or do her own thing. That she'd grown up faster than most kids. She'd had to – and that was down to him. She tried telling him she was watching her weight but he didn't listen. Once her father made up his mind, he rarely changed it.

Unaware of her gaze, he was wolfing down his food like it was the last meal of a condemned man.

Beth glanced around her. She hated the soulless ground-floor flat he insisted on calling an apartment. Situated on High Grove in the market town of Morpeth, it was a prestigious address, in keeping with his status, or so he thought. High Grope, her mum called it, mainly because *he* lived there, but also because of the top-of-the-range cars parked in the courtyard outside, bought with the sole intention of impressing the opposite sex. Their male owners, mostly bachelors, hardly spoke unless you happened to possess tits the size of Texas. Fortunately for Beth, she was born flat-chested.

'Can I go to my room?' she asked. 'I don't feel well.'

'When your plate's clean.' He eyed her over a coffee mug. 'And when it is, get dressed.' He used his fork to point at her. 'You can't sit around the house all day like that.'

'Fine!' She glanced at her food. 'I don't want this.'

'All right!' he said. 'Leave the fry-up. Eat some toast.'

Beth dropped her head, exhaling loudly. She hated staying over at his place. Thank Christ it was only a temporary measure while her mum was in hospital for yet more chemotherapy. As soon as she was discharged, Beth would be out of there like a shot.

She chanced another glance in his direction. At forty-five, her father was already grey, but the skin around his eyes was as smooth as a baby's. Hardly surprising. To get laughter lines you had to smile occasionally. He needed more practice.

Nibbling at the edge of a piece of toast, she continued to observe him. His size alone was enough to intimidate most people. Even sat down, he towered over her. Beth was built like her mum. Small – in every sense of the word – less then five feet, seven stones wet through, size six in clothes, three in shoes.

Another nibble.

His phone rang – a possible escape route.

Setting his cutlery down, he scooped his mobile off the table, his thumb jabbing at the call button. 'Atkins.' He listened for what seemed like an age. 'When was this?' He pointed at the toast in her hand, encouragement to eat, anger creeping into his voice as the call continued. 'Has she now? Well you can tell Daniels to stand down. I'm on my way in.'

Shoving his plate away, he stood up, still talking into the phone. Beth cringed when she saw the look in his eyes. Hatred wasn't too strong a word for it. In response to a question from the person on the other end of the line, he swung round, peering at the computer on the desk behind him.

'No,' he said. 'Nothing's come in. No, don't bother, I'll be there.' He ended the call, cold eyes on Beth. 'I have to go out.'

'What about your meal? You said—'

'I know what I said. Work is work. Don't worry about me. I'll get something at the station.'

'I thought you were off duty.'

'I'm on call.'

'Well, if you're leaving me on my own, why can't I stay home? I'm not a kid any more, Dad.'

'Then stop whining like one.' He pulled on his jacket, checked his pockets for car keys, wallet, fountain pen. 'You're not stopping in that house alone and that's the end of it. It's too isolated.'

'No it's not!'

'You think I want you here?' There was no humour in the question. 'If you must know, it was your mum's idea. You don't like it? Don't whinge at me. Take it up with her.'

Wounded, but trying not to show it, Beth taunted, 'What's the matter, Dad? Am I cramping your style?'

'Not now, Beth.' There was little warmth in the kiss he gave her. He walked to the door, paused before reaching it and turned around. 'If that call just now is as important as I think it might be, I'll be late. Don't forget to lock up, and don't answer the door . . . to anyone.'

As the front door clicked shut, Beth heard a ping as an email dropped into his inbox. In his haste, he'd forgotten to log off. She wandered barefoot across the room to his desk, pyjama bottoms dragging along the floor. Through patio doors that overlooked a tiny garden and car park beyond, she watched him pull out his mobile. He appeared to be accessing the email that had just come in. As he did so, it opened simultaneously on the computer screen in front of her.

Legs buckling beneath her, Beth sank down in his chair.

3

It had taken the best part of an hour to get to Morpeth police station. The town was just seventeen miles away, but they were hard miles on narrow, winding roads. The moment she arrived, Kate had brushed aside the message DCI James *I'm-in-charge* Atkins had left via Control and launched a full-blown murder enquiry. There might be only two more days until her leave period, but she was damned if she was going to stand on the sidelines while there was work to be done just to assuage his inflated ego.

Despite the gravity of the offence they were dealing with, it was a typical day for the Murder Investigation Team. Alerted by Hank at dawn, detectives had collected all the necessary documentation from HQ and driven to Morpeth to organize their new home. The incident room here had none of the cutting-edge technology they were used to, only a basic whiteboard. Thankfully, the software to run HOLMES – the Home Office Large Major Enquiry System – was up to date, as were the computers they'd brought along.

Kate scanned the room.

Her team had done their best to arrange the room the way it suited them. Everyone was flat out: many on the phone, organizing actions, documenting and processing information as it filtered in from Area Command. All in a morning's work for a bunch of coppers she was proud to lead.

'As soon as Forensics are finished with the rope, I want it identified.' She pointed at Maxwell. 'Neil, make that your number one priority. Get on to surrounding farms, industrial premises and builders' yards. Ask them to check outbuildings and garages. Let me know if any is missing. Lisa, do we know who owns the farm next to the gibbet?'

'The land is leased to John Edward Dodds. Local man. He's been farming there for years, apparently. Robbo sent a PC out to interview him.'

'I told her to look out for short-wheelbase vehicles while she's at it,' DS Robson said. 'It rained yesterday. Hank thinks the tracks he found are fresh.'

'Two birds, one stone, works for me.' Kate flashed him her best smile. 'Get in touch. Tell her I want the owner's name as well as the tenant. Let me know what gives.'

'Boss?' DC Andy Brown was approaching from the corridor. 'This came through from the morgue.' He handed her a scanned image depicting the tattoo on the victim's hand. 'There can't be many tattooists in the sticks. It's cleverly done. Want me to follow it up, see if I can identify whose work it is?'

'That may not be necessary.' Barring Carmichael, the squad stopped what they were doing and paid attention. 'There was a missing persons call last night,' Kate explained. 'Which means we may have an ID. I'm awaiting confirmation.' Her eyes landed on Carmichael, the picture of concentration, as always. She was studying the briefing sheet, a curious expression on her face. 'Lisa? Something wrong?'

Carmichael raised her head. 'It says here there was no mobile with or near the body.'

'Maybe the killer took it,' Andy Brown suggested.

Lisa frowned. 'Would they, when it could so easily be traced?'

'You'd be surprised,' Kate said.

'Can you even get a signal up there?' Maxwell asked.

'Good question,' Hank chipped in. 'I couldn't earlier. I got the odd email but my phone was showing "No Service" most of the time.'

'Still,' Kate said. 'I think it's safe to assume the victim had a phone. What kid doesn't these days?'

'Whether he did or didn't, I doubt he was on a contract,' Lisa cut in. 'Boys his age change mobiles on a regular basis. They're mostly pay-as-you-go. Which isn't a lot of help to us. If you give me a name and address, I'll get on to service providers—'

'No.' Kate shook her head. 'Let's wait for the parents to ID the body.'

Yelling from the corridor rendered the rest of her response inaudible.

Heads turned towards the racket.

The doors of the incident room crashed open. DCI James Atkins appeared, full of hell and bursting for a fight, a detective none of them recognized bringing up the rear.

Whoever he was, he seemed uncomfortable.

Atkins didn't stand on ceremony. 'A word.' He was looking directly at Kate.

'Something I can help you with?' she asked.

The eyes of her team were upon her, every detective in

17

the room anticipating trouble. Atkins was known through-out the force as the *Angry Man*. Not one of her lot would give him houseroom – unless ordered to. She hadn't yet told them that they were going to be stuck with him for the duration of her absence.

That would go down like a lead balloon.

Atkins returned their stares until they looked away. He turned theatrically, eyes boring into Kate, his shouty mouth in excellent working order. 'Somewhere less public, if you don't mind.' He nodded in the direction of the corridor.

Remaining in her seat, Kate eyed the stranger accompa-nying him. He was a tall, fit-looking bloke; immaculately dressed in a pinstriped suit, blue woollen overcoat and stripy scarf. 'I don't think we've been introduced.' She stood up slowly and held out her hand. 'I'm DCI Daniels.'

'DS Colin Grant, ma'am.' It was a firm handshake. 'Very pleased to meet you.'

'He's my bagman, newly promoted,' Atkins said. 'Lon-doner, so don't talk too fast or he'll never understand you.' He pointed at the crime scene stills in her hand. 'I think those belong to me.'

Kate handed them over.

'Shall we use my office?' she said. 'If the gloves are coming off, there's plenty of room to swing a punch in there.'

With the exception of Hank, MIT members were just about managing not to laugh out loud. Atkins' face was like thunder as he strode off. Kate gestured for the two DSs to fall in behind him. When Hank reached the door, he stepped aside, holding it open for Kate, winking as she passed through it.

Before anyone had a chance to take a seat, Atkins rounded on her. 'Mind telling me exactly what you think you're doing?'

'Doing?' Kate's eyebrows almost found each other. 'Can you be more specific?'

'With my case,' he said.

He hadn't changed a bit. 'It wasn't your case at dawn.'

'I'm the on-call SIO.'

'Control said you were incommunicado. That's code for AWOL, if you didn't know. It's Sunday. You being such a stud, I thought I'd give you a break in case you'd had a heavy date last night. Hank and I were at a loose end. The guv'nor asked us to deal until you showed your face. We were happy to stand in.'

Atkins glared at her, unimpressed with the sarcasm. It had taken her a long time to prove she could handle the flak he threw at her. Nowadays she relished the opportunity to suck it up and throw it back at him.

In a battle of wills, he'd never win.

'No need to get defensive,' she said. 'We're on the same side. I can assure you that everything has been handled exactly as it should—'

'Got a name, an address?' He was sifting the photos.

'We think the dead boy is Elliott Foster.' Kate could tell from his reaction that the name registered. 'If it is, he has no form. He's almost seventeen. Hails from Alwinton village. You can thank me later.'

'Blimey! That was quick.' Grant's appreciation received a scowl from his boss.

Atkins shifted his focus to Kate. 'Anything else?'

'Elliott was reported missing late last night by his mother. Both parents are on their way to ID the body. You want me to take that on? I'm happy to be around when they arrive.'

'No, I'll sort it.'

'Suit yourself. From the description of his clothing there seems little doubt it's him.'

'Where's Alwinton?' Grant asked. 'I'm not sure I know.'

'It's your business to know!' Atkins barked. 'Do your bloody homework or sling your hook. There's no room for slackers on my team.'

Kate's eyes were on the bully. '*You* know exactly where it is though, don't you?'

Atkins was still giving his DS hard eyes.

More embarrassed than flustered, Grant pushed a hand through his shiny blond hair, biting the inside of his cheek. If Kate was reading him right, he was stemming a desire to return to London on the next available train. His eyes shifted to Kate and finally to Hank, delivering a message to both of them: wherever he'd worked before, he wasn't used to being reprimanded publicly.

For a split second, Kate thought he might defend himself. Then, with no wish to get his head bitten off twice, he thought better of it. She felt sorry for him. Atkins' management style had always left a lot to be desired. He'd not get much out of his new colleague treating him like a rookie fresh out of training school. She'd been there once . . . and some.

The experience had blighted her life.

Hiding her aversion to Atkins, she focused on Grant,

wondering what had prompted his move north, letting him know he was among friends. 'Ours is a big county,' she said. 'It'll take a bit of getting used to. Satnav is a must. And make sure you have a full tank of gas. Petrol stations are few and far between.'

'Thanks for the tip, ma'am.'

'My pleasure.' Kate smiled. 'I was born and bred here, but there are still places I've not heard of. For your information, Alwinton is in the foothills of Cheviot. Think big sky, sheep, cattle and little else. It's God's country to some. Hell on earth to those without a soul.'

The newbie relaxed. 'Where exactly was the IP found, ma'am?'

'Half-stripped and hanging from Winter's Gibbet.'

His eyes widened. 'A gallows?'

'Yeah,' Hank said. 'We still hang 'em up here.'

The southerner smiled at the wind-up. 'Where can I find it?'

'The old turnpike road at Hollinghill – otherwise known as Whiskershiels Common. It's a few miles south of Elsdon village, around fifteen miles from the victim's home.'

'Who was Winter?'

'Good question.' Kate could see Atkins getting impatient. Ignoring his scowl, she elaborated, just to piss him off. 'The gibbet is an ancient landmark; aka Steng Cross. In the eighteenth century, the body of Thomas Winter was hung there, within sight of his crime, having been hanged proper at the Westgate in Newcastle. He'd murdered a local woman, Margaret Crozier, who lived at the Raw pele tower close to Elsdon.'

'Save the history lesson,' Atkins snapped. 'What do we know about Foster?'

'He's dead.' Hank enjoyed being flippant with assholes.

'I was about to ask *you* that,' Kate said, before Atkins had chance to respond. He used to live close to the crime scene. As far as she knew, his ex-wife still did. In small Northumbrian villages, most people were acquainted. She had a feeling that her counterpart was holding back.

Hank shot Atkins a sideways glance.

Grant too.

Neither had picked up on the flash of recognition that had crossed the Angry Man's face when the victim's identity was revealed. Kate saw it though – as plain as day – and now she had, she couldn't stop thinking about it. Like a game of blink first, her eyes never shifted from his. And still he didn't admit or deny knowing the boy.

She watched him carefully. If an eyelash had moved, she'd have spotted that too. 'Elliott Foster has no form,' she said. 'He was a good kid by all accounts, a prize wrestler.'

'Maybe someone was jealous of that,' Grant offered.

'Very likely,' Hank agreed.

Atkins snorted. 'Pity he couldn't wrestle himself out of this one.'

'That's not remotely funny,' Kate said.

'Am I laughing?' Atkins glared at her.

'Maybe you should show the victim some respect, given the fact that you're acquainted,' Kate said. 'Or is it his parents you know – his mother, perhaps? Anticipating a positive ID, my team made enquiries. She's an office manager for a Morpeth law firm, Haynes & Rice. The boy's father is a joiner at Jewson's in Hexham. There's one brother: Adam. Twenty-one. Currently on a tour of duty in Germany. His regiment deployed there six months ago.'

Atkins didn't thank her. 'I'll get in touch with his commanding officer—'

'It's sorted.' Kate said. 'He's standing by, waiting for my nod.'

'You've been busy, ma'am.' Grant was impressed, trying not to show it.

'I have a good team behind me,' Kate said. 'It's what we get paid for at the end of every month. Same as you.'

'There's an army base not far from the scene,' Atkins said. 'Is it operational?'

Kate gave him a pointed look. 'Soldiers equal trouble, is that it?'

'Just an observation,' he said.

Based on prejudice.

Atkins sifted the crime scene photographs. 'Whoever strung the kid up must be tough, remarkably so if the IP was struggling to get the rope from around his neck.'

'That assumes he was still alive,' Hank said.

Kate's eyes found the floor momentarily. It was an image she didn't want to think about but, now it was in her head, there it would stay, a permanent scar on her memory. She could almost hear the boy choking and gurgling as the ligature tightened.

'Winter's Gibbet has to be fifteen or twenty feet tall,' she said. 'Hank made the point that one person couldn't get him up there, not with muscle power alone. There would need to be more than one, or some kind of mechanical device or pulley. Even so, I'd be very surprised if this involves the military—'

'Why?' Atkins asked.

'The army are welcome in the area. They're also well paid. The military spend a lot of money, in Otterburn in particular. Surrounding villages wouldn't survive without them. They go out of their way to foster good relations and keep the locals sweet. There's no history of tension in the community, of squaddie-bashing either, otherwise I'd have heard about it . . .'

Kate paused. She wasn't about to be sidetracked, not when she hadn't finished probing into Atkins' knowledge of the family.

'Does the name Elliott Foster ring any bells with you?'

Atkins glanced at his watch, a deliberate ploy to avoid eye contact.

'C'mon, don't be shy,' she chided, not letting him off the hook. 'You're among friends here. There must be a reason you're not disclosing prior knowledge. We're all dying to hear what it is.'

'We'll take it from here,' Atkins said. He was not only dismissing her, he was disrespecting her, writing her off in front of her subordinates. It wasn't the first time, either. Kate wouldn't give him the satisfaction of knowing that he'd got to her.

'Have it your own way,' she said. 'Hank and I will assist until my leave starts. If you like I could interview our finder, Tom Orde—'

'I don't think so.' Atkins cut across her.

'You have another suggestion?' she asked.

'I'm not working with you. Period. I pick my own team.'

'Eh?' Hank took a step forward. 'This is a joke, right?'

Without moving his head, Atkins' eyes shifted to Hank. 'Was I talking to you?'

Kate kept her expression inscrutable.

Hank was incensed. There was nothing she could do or say that would stop him speaking out. 'Do you have *any* idea how much experience we have in murder investigation, *sir*?' He made his last word sound like an insult. 'Because if you have a problem with my DCI, I think we should get it out in the open, so we all know where we stand. Don't you?'

Atkins didn't answer.

He didn't give a shit what Hank thought.

Grant didn't know where to put himself. He was staring at Kate, expecting her to explode. It would be hard to miss the simmering hatred passing between the two senior officers. For her part, Kate had known perfectly well what was coming. It was useless trying to reason with an illogical man. The stand-off didn't last long. Turning her attention to the two detective sergeants, she asked them politely to leave the room.

4

Seconds out, round two.

Kate waited until the door closed before turning to face her adversary. 'I know respect for women isn't high on your agenda, but I'd be careful if I were you, Atkins. Whatever your personal feelings for me, I don't appreciate being undermined in front of my DS, not by you or anyone. As you witnessed, Hank has a tendency to take insults personally. He's very protective. Gallant even. Things might get out of hand.'

'That would be a real shame—'

'For you maybe. I'm afraid I couldn't guarantee your safety.'

'Assaulting a senior officer is a serious breach of regulations—'

'Well, when it comes to violence, you'd know.'

He laughed in her face. 'I'm quaking in my boots.'

It had been a long time since they last worked together, but she'd never forget the way he'd made her life impossible. As her immediate boss, he'd sent all the shit her way. Every detail no one volunteered for landed in her lap. He'd shafted her at every turn. Made sure she was dispatched to all the dangerous areas when, spookily, the crew was under strength and there was no one available to double up.

Do it, or I'll get a man to do it for you!

His sickening mantra had been the thing that drove her on. Working alone, she'd kept her wits about her, ensuring that his actions had the opposite effect to the one he was seeking. The tighter he turned the screw, the more fine-tuned her senses became to danger. His unjust treatment of her only served to earn her extra respect – it galvanized her colleagues into supporting her. Atkins was openly prejudicial. There was no subtlety in his malice. Everyone could see what he was doing.

It didn't break her then . . .

It wouldn't now.

Kate glanced at her watch. 'I haven't got time for your stupid games. Take my advice and pick fights you can win. Your secondment to MIT is temporary. It won't be made permanent if I have my way. We're a close-knit crew. We work as one or not at all.'

'How will I sleep?'

'How do you sleep?'

'Perfectly well, actually.' He was still grinning.

'I'm warning you, Atkins: unlike your long-suffering ex-wife, I won't tolerate your bullshit. I've got news for you: 1993 was a long time ago. I'm not a kid any more.'

'Is there a point to this?'

'There is and you'd better take note of it. You're already a pariah in this force. It wouldn't do your career any good if a certain item was to fall into the wrong hands now, would it?'

'You're bluffing.'

'You sure of that?'

He wasn't or he'd have come up with a response.

Kate savoured her advantage. 'Even without that happening, there's not much further to drop before you hit rock bottom. Oh, I forgot: you reached the basement years ago. How is it down there?'

He pointed an index finger at her. 'When I decide to come for you, Daniels – and I will – you won't know what hit you.'

'And to think I once looked up to you.' As he glared at her, she turned on her heel, sauntered to the door and calmly let herself out.

In the incident room, the team was waiting – with bated breath – to hear the result of her battle with Atkins. As Kate entered the room, Hank got up and walked towards her, his face a picture of indignation. Never in his career had he been so close to lamping a senior officer.

'You OK?' he asked.

'Are you?' Kate's smile reached her eyes, pushing away her distress. She acted calm, but her stomach was in knots as a result of the exchange. She'd thought, wrongly, that her days of having to deal with Atkins were over. Some years ago her former boss, Detective Chief Superintendent Bright – currently head of CID – had assured her that their paths would never cross again. And, so far, they hadn't. He'd approved Atkins' attachment to the department as a last resort, giving her the heads up that he wouldn't arrive until she'd gone on leave. Wise to that fact, Atkins obviously had other ideas. Checking his roster as soon as she got back to the office, she'd found out, via friends in admin, that he'd cancelled his own days off at short notice. There was no doubt in her mind. He'd done it to ensure that her last few days at work were unpleasant, if not intolerable.

Another smile directed at her loyal DS. 'You're such a softie, Hank.'

'The guy's a complete prick!' he said. 'Did you challenge him?'

'And say what? You heard him. It's his case. Let him get on with it.' Picking up her coat, she slung it over her arm and turned to face the squad. 'Keep up the good work, everyone. Hank and I will be out of touch for a couple of hours. We'll review progress when we return – whether the SIO likes it or not.'

The team accepted that as a victory speech.

Hank still wouldn't let it go. Yanking his jacket from his chair, he put it on and ran to catch up with her as she strode towards the exit. 'Who the hell does he think he is?' he said, pulling his phone from his pocket. 'Naylor will go spare.'

'No.' Kate stopped walking and turned towards him. 'Put that away and leave the guv'nor out of this.'

'And let the tosser get away with it?'

'Did you hear a word I said?' Her tone was harder than before. She lowered her voice a touch. 'I can fight my own corner, Hank. I don't need – or want – your interference. Is that clear?'

'Crystal.' Backing off, he put his phone away.

'Thank you. Now stop sulking and come with me. We've work to do.'

'Where are we going?'

'Alwinton.'

His smile was a thin disguise. Kate hadn't heard the last

word on the subject of Atkins. Not by a long chalk. Hank saw himself as her minder. He'd do anything she asked except lie down and let Atkins walk all over her. Not a chance. Trouble was brewing.

They used her car. His was an old banger, unreliable. Kate preferred to ride in comfort, with the benefit of technology, all-weather tyres and windscreen wipers that actually worked. Now autumn was here, conditions could turn nasty in seconds where they were going.

You won't know what hit you.

The threat played on her mind as she drove out of the station. Until she went on leave, she'd have to watch her back. Like a lot of angry men, Atkins was an unknown quantity, unpredictable in the extreme. All the more worrying to think that he was in a position of authority.

To hell with him.

Kate pushed the thought away as something even more worrying edged its way into her head. She'd noticed Hank rubbing his healing chest wound with the palm of his right hand.

'When were you going to tell me?' she asked.

'Eh?' He swivelled in his seat to face her. 'Tell you what?'

'That you're still having problems.'

'Am I?' Butter wouldn't melt.

'Do I look like a fool to you?' She nodded at his chest region. 'Still giving you gyp, is it?'

Taking his hand away, he shoved it deep into his trouser pocket. 'It's temporary. Residual stiffness in my shoulder. Nowt to worry about . . . and no need to go off on one.'

'It's my job to go off on one. You're *my* responsibility. What kind of boss would I be if I didn't take care of you? I could—' She stopped talking as a car came round the bend in the middle of the road. Checking her rear-view mirror, she maintained her position, making the driver slow down.

'You could what?' Hank asked as the two cars passed each other.

'I could make a call and tell the powers that be that you're unfit for duty.'

'Fill your boots,' he said. 'Can I see the nice nurse at HQ – the one with the great legs?'

Kate laughed.

Hank had a penchant for a pretty face, especially, though not exclusively, when the rest of the body was wearing a nurse's uniform. His wife was a theatre sister at the RVI. 'That sounded really pervy,' she said. 'Like a Maxwell comment.' Hank gave a pantomime wince at being compared to the office Lothario. 'I'm serious, Hank. You need to take care—'

'I'm fine!'

'Would you tell me if you weren't?'

'I'm not sleeping well, that's all.'

'They're called night terrors.'

'What?' It came out like an exclamation. Hank shook his head, irked by the suggestion that he wasn't coping. '"Night terrors?"' he repeated. 'Is that what Jo calls them? I call them wank words. Pardon the expression.'

Kate wasn't allowing him to laugh it off. 'They're perfectly normal after what you've been through.'

'Bollocks. I'm just a bit restless.'

She sang her riposte. 'You didn't answer my question.'

He followed suit: 'It doesn't deserve an answer.'

Dropping the subject, Kate drove on. She didn't want to pry and was hoping he'd confide in her eventually. Next time she looked, he'd shut his eyes. He wasn't asleep. Unusual for him. His ability to drop off in the car, no matter what sort of crime they were dealing with, was common knowledge. Nothing separated him from forty winks. A few miles on and he could bear the silence no longer.

'My problems are nothing to do with work,' he protested. 'If you must know, Ryan failed his exams. Ring Julie if you don't believe me. The upshot is, our highly intelligent son doesn't have the grades to get him into the University of St Andrews or anywhere else decent. He's blown it, Kate.'

Whatever Hank was hiding was prompting him to share family matters he'd ordinarily keep to himself. It was possible that he was telling the truth about Ryan, but Kate sensed there was more to it. For now, and for reasons known only to him, he was unwilling to share the extent of his problems. She'd have to wait it out.

She indulged him by playing along. 'Did you try clearing?'

'There's nothing there for him. He left it too bloody late to do the hard yards. Now the daft sod is sulking for England and upsetting his mum. I've been laying the law down, that's all.'

'And he doesn't like it.'

'Any more than I do.' He grinned, trying to lighten the mood. 'He'll get over it and so will I. Julie, on the other hand . . .' He didn't finish the sentence.

Kate let it go, positive in her own mind that he wasn't being straight with her. Earlier that morning, shortly after she arrived at the crime scene, someone had discharged a firearm nearby. The shot came out of the mist, echoing all around them. It was most likely just a farmer out rabbiting, but Hank had practically fallen to the ground in shock. Ordinarily he wouldn't have batted an eyelid; the fact it had shaken him up worried her. In a moment of madness she'd threatened to cancel her leave, only agreeing to go when he promised to take it easy. There was as much chance of that as there was of her making chief in a culture where less than 3 per cent of officers above the rank of superintendent were women.

Hank was still mumbling to himself, denying any health problems, making out he was as fit as a flea. 'Tell you what,' he said. 'I'll get Jules to give me a rub down when I get home. How's that?'

'Sounds like it'll have to do.'

'Seriously,' he said. 'I might be under par but I could still give Atkins a poke if he gets out of hand. Say the word and I'm on it.'

She turned her head. '*Don't* even think about it.'

They fell silent.

As miles and miles of stunning countryside rolled by, Kate felt his agitation grow. Not one to forgive or forget if anyone upset her, she knew he was going to hate working under a new SIO, especially one as objectionable as Atkins. Hank was close to Kate. Gunshot injury or not, Atkins would make it his business to pile on the pressure, just to make a point. The man was an arse.

As if he'd read her mind, Hank cut into her thoughts:

'Why do I get the impression that you're holding back on Atkins?'

She glanced sideways. 'So *you* can keep secrets and I have to tell all? That's not how it works.'

'I'm serious, what the hell is eating you?'

'How long have we known each other?'

He narrowed his eyes. 'What's that got to do with anything?'

'You should know that I only ever discuss individuals who are important to me. Atkins isn't one of them. Take my advice and let the matter drop.' She indicated, turning off the A696 towards the Northumberland National Park. Sensing that Hank was about to ignore the warning, Kate changed the subject with a comment that stopped him in his tracks: 'By the way, I was at Alwinton Show yesterday . . . and so was the victim.'

'What? Why didn't you tell Atkins?'

'He didn't ask.'

5

Beth Casey was hyperventilating as she drove her Fiat 500 deep into Border Reivers country. In such a vast area, even kids her age needed cars to get about. Like mobile phone signals, public transport was patchy and unreliable. She'd taken her driving test within weeks of her seventeenth birthday, passing with flying colours at the first time of asking, an achievement she was immensely proud of.

Not so her father . . .

Firmly of the opinion that she was too young and vulnerable to be driving on country lanes at night, it gave him another reason to moan. Was he mad? Her new-found mobility had made everything so much easier for everyone. Now she was no longer dependent on him for lifts, they saw less of each other and that suited her fine.

Three quarters of an hour later, she pulled gently to the kerb and sat in the car, staring up at the windows of Wansbeck General Hospital, the pictures on her dad's computer forcing their way into her head. Was Elliott here, she wondered, lying on a slab, being cut to pieces, having his organs weighed?

She shivered at the thought, a wave of nausea hitting her again.

She hadn't questioned her father about the photographs on his computer because he'd forbidden her to touch it. Even if she'd tried to explain that she'd only done so in order to put the bloody thing to sleep and save his battery, he'd have made an issue of it. How could she have known that the email would open up in front of her?

The pictures were hideous . . .

It couldn't be Elliott . . .

It couldn't . . .

It was.

Climbing from the car, Beth didn't bother to pay at the machine. She'd left her dad's house in such a hurry she'd forgotten to put her purse in her pocket. A parking ticket was the least of her concerns. In any case, any fine would be sent to her mum's address. He'd never see it.

The oncology unit was heaving, as usual. The stench of disinfectant, chemicals and death seemed to permeate her clothes the minute she stepped through the door. Even though she'd wash as soon as she got home, Beth knew it would stick to her skin for days. It always did.

Visitors hurried down corridors, pale and concerned – like her. Patients shuffled along, hanging onto mobile drips, limbs stick thin, skin all dry and scaly, eyes hollow, expressions haunted. It seemed as if everyone in the world had cancer in some form or another. If she was ever unfortunate enough to contract the disease – she'd been advised that she had increased risk – she'd rock herself off rather than rot away slowly with family standing around making ridiculous statements: You're going to beat this, you *are*, you'll be out of here in no time.

Gimme the means and I'll finish it. That's what she'd be saying. Even without cancer, the thought had crossed her mind. Guiltily, she thought about the pills in her bag.

'Hi, Mum, how are you today?'

'Better.' Diane Casey smiled.

Liar.

Beth hated the pretence. She offered some in return, keeping her tone upbeat. A BAFTA performance that was killing her. 'I'm an idiot,' she said. 'Forgot your orange juice. It's in dad's fridge. If you have any cash I'll go to the shop and get some, a newspaper too if you'd like one. Some fruit maybe?'

Any excuse to get out of there.

Beth stopped talking as her mum's eyes strayed past her, searching the nurses' station beyond to see if her dad was following on behind. Why she still cared was beyond Beth. They hadn't been an item for years. Apart from an odd flashback here and there, she couldn't remember the three of them living together as a family. Her father only began to take notice at the point of diagnosis, a good dose of Catholic guilt compelling him to visit now and then when he was kicking his heels with nothing better to do.

'What's wrong?' The question jolted Beth from her trance.

She looked at her mum. 'Sorry?'

They examined each other closely for what seemed like an age. Beth's faked preoccupation wasn't fooling anyone. With great effort, her mum leaned forward and stroked her cheek with the back of bony fingers, a touch so gentle it made Beth want to weep. She was of a mind to climb in bed with her for a hug, like she used to when she was a kid in that awful women's refuge, over a decade ago.

Safe haven, my arse ... He'd found them, hadn't he? Followed them along the road, begging for forgiveness for the umpteenth time. Not because he was sorry. Out of concern for his sodding job. Using her as currency. A daughter needs a dad. Pathetic.

'You've been crying,' her mum said.

'So have you.'

Regretting her words the moment they left her lips, more especially the harsh way in which they were delivered, Beth looked away, her eyes seizing on the next bay, where a well-dressed lady was visiting her daughter. Like Beth, she was doing her utmost to be cheerful. Not quite pulling it off. Beth guessed her age at around sixty. Behind that thin-lipped smile was the face of a woman with a broken heart.

Beth knew the feeling.

She continued to stare at the woman, her mood plummeting further. There was something terribly wrong with the picture. Like someone had cast characters in the wrong roles, or they were reading each other's scripts by mistake. They should swap places. Revert to the norm. Daughters weren't supposed to die before their mothers. That was never meant to be. It wasn't right. Beth wondered who would care for the woman when she grew old – who would care for *her* when her mother passed away. She felt selfish even thinking it.

'Sweetheart, what's wrong?'

Beth looked at her mum. 'Nothing . . .'

'Honestly?'

'I'm fine—'

'You and your dad haven't been fighting, have you?'

'No!' Beth lied. 'He might pop in later.'

Diane Casey's face lit up. 'He's in Ashington?'

'Morpeth. He was called into work this morning. Said it might be a late one, so don't count on it. I'll text him to bring you some juice if he's coming. If not, I'll bring it tomorrow.'

Beth would have loved to tell her mum why her dad was at work, to share her fears about her best friend, Elliott. She couldn't bring herself to utter the words.

Her attention shifted to events going on through the window. In the grey drizzle, people were going about their business: working, playing, generally having a laugh. Nurses too, despite having to care for sick people all day long. How they did it was a mystery to Beth. She was due some fun too.

The way things were going it was a long way off.

'You sure you're OK?' her mum said.

Beth managed a half-smile. When she was growing up, Elliott was always round to play. Her mum loved him, like the son she'd always wished for, but never had. To heap more grief on her in her condition would be cruel. Besides, her dad would surely have mentioned it if Elliott *had* been the victim. Wouldn't he? Beth must have got it wrong. She prayed she'd got it wrong.

6

Rubbing at the stubble on his chin, Hank flipped the sun visor down and peered into the mirror behind it. 'I could do with a hot shower, a shave, a change of clothes,' he said, flipping it up again, trying to iron out the creases in his suit. 'I'm hardly in a fit state to interview anyone, am I?' He made a meal of running his eyes over Kate's whole body. 'You either – no offence.'

'None taken, you cheeky bugger.'

'Not a good impression though, is it? Half asleep and dressed like a couple of bloody tramps. One glance and eye-witnesses will look for a begging bowl.'

'Murder is bloody inconvenient sometimes. Don't concern yourself. We'll be hard pushed to find anyone at home in Alwinton now the show is over. They'll be in the show field, all pitching in with the massive clear-up job. Sundays, especially this one, aren't exactly rest days when you live in the sticks. Farming communities are at it round the clock.'

'Like us then.'

'*Just* like us,' she echoed. 'What time is it?'

Checking his watch, he lifted a hand to his mouth to cover an enormous yawn, for which he apologized. 'It's quarter past roast beef and Yorkshire pud. I'm assuming Alwinton has a pub and they serve Sunday lunch. I'm famished.'

'They do. It's called the Rose and Thistle and we're not stopping to eat. I'll buy you a bag of crisps.'

'You're heartless, you know that?'

'So ask for a transfer.'

Hank feigned interest. 'Y'know, that's not a bad idea.'

'Better the devil you know, Hank. You might end up with Atkins permanently.'

He went quiet at this, his attention straying out the side window. Kate's eyes drifted in the opposite direction, to the valley, where pockets of mist floated above dewy ground even though the sun was doing its best to burn it off. She loved the Upper Coquetdale. She used to ride here often on her motorcycle, then on to Rothbury to meet up with biker mates for fish and chips, something she couldn't possibly mention to Grumble Tum sitting next to her.

The scenery was superb as the valley gave way to the Harbottle Forest and eventually a view of the Simonside Hills. The silence in the car was interrupted by the sound of a text message arriving. She gestured for Hank to take it. Grabbing her mobile from the dash, he read a partial message on the home screen without accessing the rest.

'It's for you.' His tone was bordering on hostile.

'I know that, you divvi. It's *my* phone.' Kate waited, assuming, wrongly as it turned out, that the message was from Atkins. Maybe he'd had a change of heart and wanted her to interview their finder after all. *Well, tough.* 'Are you going to tell me who it's from? Or shall we play twenty questions? What does it say?'

'It's from Fiona. She—'

'Give it here.' Kate snatched the device from his hand and

put it in her pocket to read later. Fiona Fielding was a gifted artist with whom she'd had a brief fling while she and Jo were pissing about, trying to decide if they were on or off, a situation that had lasted for far too long.

It was one night only with Fiona . . . but what a night.

A physical reaction to the memory surprised her. Kate could feel herself blushing. As curious as she was to know what the message said, she wasn't about to ask Hank to read it for her. He was sulking again. Having put in time and effort as matchmaker to her and Jo, believing them to be a perfect fit, he'd taken against Fiona, mistaking her for the competition.

It tickled Kate to see his reaction to a simple text.

Like an obstreperous teenager in danger of losing his pocket money, he crossed his arms, sulking. He liked Jo a lot. That was good. So did she. At times she and Jo had come very close, only to be ripped apart by circumstance, which was why their holiday was so important. What Kate needed, more than anything, was to distance herself from her job and concentrate on their relationship. Though she didn't know it, Hank's brush with death had been the trigger for a change in how she intended to lead the rest of her life.

'How much further?' he asked after a few more twisty miles. 'It's not even signposted.'

'You've never been to Alwinton?'

'I've had no reason to.'

'It's beautiful, peaceful.'

'Sounds a blast.' He was still brooding.

Finding his strop more and more amusing, Kate changed

the subject. 'I wish the council would sort out these bloody potholes. They've taken months off the life of my tyres.'

'How big is it?'

'The council?'

'Alwinton.' Not even a smile.

'Not very.' She began to laugh. 'At a guess, I'd say population of no more than around fifty or sixty – not that that makes our job any simpler. There were a lot of people at the show yesterday. It's the last show of the year, so hugely popular.' Easing off the accelerator going into a bend, she put her foot to the floor on a long stretch of road coming out of it. 'Folks come from far and wide. It'll be a nightmare tracing everyone. What we need is to find the show photographer.'

'Was there one?' Finally, a flicker of interest.

'Why don't you try and find out?'

'I'll call the *Chronicle*.'

'Look!'

Kate pointed through the window. On the left-hand side of the road a flock of black Welsh mountain sheep were grazing on land she assumed belonged to Holystone Grange, a nineteenth-century listed building that rose majestically above them as they sped by. Hank made a snide remark about her feeling right at home among the animals.

Pulling his mobile from his pocket, he made a call, immediately drawing a blank. After a short conversation, he hung up. 'They didn't cover the event,' he said. '*Should* have, but their reporter rang in sick.'

'They didn't send a replacement?'

'Too many events happening elsewhere, apparently.'

'The feature was pulled?'

He nodded. 'It was the least high profile. There was no one available to fill in at short notice. "Hardly earth-shattering news" was the way the editor put it. Now he's keen to know why we're so interested—'

'You tell him nowt.'

'I didn't!'

'Okaay. Don't scowl. I'm just making the point that he has a bloody big spade.'

Hank stared at the red battery indicator on his phone. 'This thing is dying. I need to charge it. Pull in at the next Internet cafe, will you? Unless . . .' He let the sentence hang, one eyebrow raised, eyes trained on the pocket that held her mobile.

Kate smiled. 'Use mine. You may as well, seeing as I have no secrets any more. Not that Fiona and I are up to any-thing . . .' She sensed doubt. 'We're not!'

'I believe you.' He clearly didn't.

'Er, hello? Private life. Best not go there, eh?' She handed him her mobile. 'Access to text messages is restricted until I say otherwise. Try my address book: Helen Compson.'

'Never heard of her.'

'Just one of the many women I'm sleeping with.' They were both laughing now. 'Relax, Hank. She's as straight as they come and happens to be the features editor at the *Hexham Courant*. Call her.'

'And say what?'

'Nothing personal. She'll have your balls in a vice if you do. Ask her if she was at the show. I happen to know she loves it. If she wasn't around in a professional capacity, she

may still have gone along or know someone who did. Don't
hold your breath. I certainly didn't see her.'

'Jo with you, was she?'

Kate felt her cheeks burning. He was spot on. Whenever
Jo was around, others tended to fade into the background.
Still grinning, he punched in Helen's number.

'Engaged,' he said. They rounded another bend, only to
find a similar snaking strip of tarmac in front of them. 'It
really is the back of beyond out here. You sure this place
even exists? We're not lost, are we?'

'Ha! You sound like a kid: are we nearly there yet? Have
you really never been?'

'Nope.'

'You must have. Everyone goes once.'

'After a journey like this, I bet not many go twice.'

She chuckled. 'Try Helen again before we lose the signal.'

Pressing the call button, Hank offered to leave the phone
on Bluetooth so it would play in the car.

'No, you deal with it. I need a few minutes.'

Hank listened as the number rang out. 'Can I disclose the
reason I'm calling?'

'Absolutely. Tell her it goes no further until I say so.'

'You trust her to keep her mouth shut?'

'I do.'

He raised an eyebrow. 'Two words: Gillian Garvey.'

He was referring to a journalist Kate had fallen out with
spectacularly over her mishandling of sensitive information
in another case, a point-scoring battle that took place in full
view of local and national press, not to mention Detective
Chief Superintendent Bright.

Not her finest hour.

'Not the same animal,' she said. 'So be nice. Helen's a friend.'

'I'm always nice!'

'I know.' Another chuckle.

Hank held up a hand as Helen picked up with a friendly, 'Hi, Kate.'

'Actually, it's Hank here. I'm her—'

'DS. I know. She talks about you often.'

'Does she?' Hank explained what he was after and why.

His voice faded out of Kate's head as she negotiated a tricky incline. After a short conversation, he hung up, letting out a long breath as he placed her mobile on the dash.

'No joy?' Kate glanced in his direction.

'Quite the opposite. She covered the event and has interviews, pictures – all we need. And she's prepared to share. She said she'd call you later. Can't talk now. She was with someone. Only picked up because it was you. *Are* you sleeping with her?'

Kate pulled a face. 'We're mates. Nothing more.'

He grinned. 'She said to tell you there was an ex-copper there – also taking pictures. Might be useful. Alan Tailford. You know him?'

'Vaguely. Nice chap.'

'Your mate seems to think he's a keen photographer.'

'Worth talking to then – make a note of it.'

The light seemed to leave his eyes.

'You OK?' Kate took in his nod. 'So why the sad face?'

'Elliott Foster won his bout.'

'Helen told you that?'

'Last thing she said. She's friendly with someone on the show committee. He emailed all the results hoping she'd put a piece in next week's paper.' Hank paused, Elliott's ghost wrestling with him one last time. 'There are times when being a copper sucks,' he said. 'Did you notice how much he looks like our Ryan?'

Kate hadn't made the connection. 'Is that what's bothering you?'

Hank sidestepped the question. 'The poor bastard wasn't in the limelight long, was he?'

'I knew I'd seen him yesterday.' Kate wasn't sure if the lad's win made her feel better or worse. She'd watched some of the Cumberland wrestling but, with Jo by her side, chatting excitedly about their vacation, she'd not been paying attention. She'd let the boy down. It wouldn't happen twice.

7

The village of Alwinton was ghostly quiet as they drove in. A stone-built garage was directly ahead, beyond which were the steep inclines that only yesterday played host to the fell racing for those brave or daft enough to enter. Even the stone bus shelter had a pretty display of geranium pots outside.

There was no one about as they stepped from the car. Kate heard a barking dog and caught a glimpse of a man on horseback. He cantered up the right fork of the road, disappearing before she had time to attract his attention, the sound of hooves on tarmac fading to nothing as she walked the other way.

As she'd predicted, practically everyone who lived in the village was busy with the fallout from the show. Those that weren't involved weren't answering their doors. A dark cloud had descended on this peaceful community. Kate knocked at several houses before deciding, against her better judgement, to enter the Rose and Thistle public house.

Hank's face lit up at the suggestion.

'You get a pint and nothing else,' she warned. 'No arguments, it wouldn't be right. We're here to chat with the locals, not feed our faces.'

He didn't try to change her mind. Despite their dishevelled

appearance, they were the public face of Northumbria Police. He understood that. No matter how low he was on fuel, he'd never bring the force into disrepute or show insensitivity to the bereaved. They were his first and only priority.

The barmaid eyed them as they entered, throwing a forced smile their way. She seemed visibly relieved to talk to strangers, a chance to escape the misery that pervaded the pub and do something useful. Bad news had spread quickly. From the look on customers' faces, it had reached every single inhabitant despite a press blackout until the victim's brother was advised of his death. In a technological age of texts, tweets and a host of other ways to communicate, it was nigh on impossible to stop the jungle telegraph.

Everyone, these days, was an unofficial reporter.

Kate knew the pub well. It was the focal point of the neighbourhood, usually full of fun and friendly banter. Why wouldn't it be? The view through the window was stunning, the best you'd find from a public house anywhere in the country. The purple heather on the fells was particularly vibrant today, inviting visitors to stop a while and take in its beauty. *Look at me, it seemed to say.* Not that the regulars were taking any notice. Most were staring blankly into their drinks. Uncommunicative. Even the dogs on the floor appeared depressed, indifferent to the smell of Sunday roast emanating from the kitchen; no human was remotely interesting in ordering.

Hank was practically drooling.

After a brief chat with the barmaid, Kate dragged him outside to carry on their mini house-to-house, confident in the knowledge that she'd not run into the dead boy's parents.

According to Control, ID was confirmed and they were still in Newcastle awaiting an interview with DCI Atkins.

Kate was about to discover that some of her information was flawed. A local dog-walker told her that Elliott Foster didn't actually live with his parents but with his maternal grandmother, who lived down the road. This piece of intelligence hadn't come her way.

That changed everything.

Picking up on the DCI's concern, the man pointed to a cottage where an elderly lady was sweeping leaves from her garden path.

'That's her?' Kate asked.

He nodded. 'Her name is Jane . . . Gibson. I don't think the news has hit her yet.'

'A grandparent's worst nightmare,' Kate said quietly, to no one in particular.

'Indeed,' the man said. 'She's a tough old bird. Different generation. Not one to let tragedy defeat her, if you know what I mean. Believe me, she's had her fair share.'

'Oh?'

'Husband died in an awful accident when she was in her forties. Eldest son committed suicide. Self-centred bastard shot himself in woods not far from here. Couldn't cope.'

'With what?'

'Buggered if I know.' His focus switched to the old woman. 'People say things come in threes. Until now I didn't believe them. I reckon she could do with a friendly face, a sympathetic ear. We've all been over, of course. You don't like to intrude though, do you? Between you and me,

I don't think she'll believe it's him until she hears it from the horse's mouth.'

Kate checked over her shoulder. 'You mean us?'

'Her daughter.'

Thanking the man, Kate asked Hank to finish up and drifted away, her stress level rising as she turned her attention to the boy's grandmother. Denial was a natural reaction for those unfortunate enough to be affected by homicide. Families often clung to the false hope that the police might be mistaken, even though it was very rare that anyone was asked to ID a body that didn't belong to them. Despite Control's claim that the boy was Elliott Foster, Kate called the morgue to confirm it.

'Formal identification is complete,' she was told. 'The parents are with DS Grant.'

The revelation made her angry. Consoling the family was no job for a newcomer. Atkins was a bastard. As SIO, he had no business delegating such a task. Seething, she punched in his number, but then hung up before he could answer, deciding to have it out with him face-to-face when she returned to the office.

Someone far more worthy needed her attention now.

As she approached the garden gate, Jane Gibson looked up, the rims of her eyes red raw through her spectacles, arthritic hands so tightly clasped around a stiff broom handle that her knuckles were white, almost protruding through her skin.

'Are you lost, pet?'

'No, Jane. I'm Detective Chief Inspector Kate Daniels. May we go inside?'

Realizing what was coming, the old lady pressed her lips together, trying to hang on to her emotions, her blue eyes turning icy, as if she blamed Kate for confirming bad news when it wasn't her place to do so.

Leaning the broom up against the wall, the old lady put a shaky hand out to steady herself. For a moment, Kate thought she might keel over but she recovered quickly. 'I don't know about you,' she said, 'but I could do with some tea, Inspector. I'd really like it if you would join me.'

'So long as you let me make it,' Kate said.

In the tiny kitchen, Kate put the kettle on and made tea in a flowery pot. Jane took matching china cups and saucers from an overhead cupboard, then moved forward, covering the teapot with a thick, woollen tea cosy. Homemade, it reminded the DCI of her late grandmother, long knitting needles held firmly under her arms, clicking away so fast a young Kate's eyes could hardly keep up with them.

'Come through,' Jane said.

Turning her back on Kate, she led the way into the living room, where a fire burned in the grate. Kate followed her in with tea on a tray, taking in photographs of Elliott Foster and another boy at various stages of development displayed around the room. This woman valued family above all else. Understandable if she'd suffered the losses suggested by the man Kate had met in the lane outside.

Wondering if the suicide of the victim's uncle was connected in any way to Elliott Foster's death, Kate sat down, parking the thought for later. Jane Gibson poked the fire, then settled in a well-used armchair, the motorized kind that had the ability to lift and recline. On this occasion, the facility was redundant.

She wouldn't be relaxing anytime soon.

In more recent photographs, the older boy was in military uniform. Assuming this to be Elliott's older brother, Kate wondered if he'd been told the grim news yet. She hoped he had and was on his way home to comfort Jane. It was unfortunate that he lived abroad. It might take forever for him to materialize. The old lady needed him now.

'I'm so very sorry for your loss,' Kate said.

Jane shifted her gaze to the mantelpiece. 'He'll be devastated.'

'His brother?'

She nodded.

'They were close?'

'Inseparable.'

'I'm an only child,' Kate said, for want of something more appropriate.

Jane forced a smile. 'Me too.'

They drank tea and talked about her youngest grandson, what kind of lad he was, a general chat about the things he liked to do outside of Cumberland wrestling: playing the guitar, basketball and fishing. When the time was right, Kate moved the conversation on to more personal matters, asking how he came to be living with Jane. The reason given was much as she expected: acrimonious divorce of parents, both of whom needed to work, leaving the old lady quite literally holding the baby – or, more accurately, two.

'Can I ask when you last saw Elliott?'

Jane's alert eyes flew back to the mantelpiece. 'About quarter to six yesterday.'

Following her gaze, Kate's eyes drifted slightly left of the clock where a silver cup sat proudly. 'Elliott came straight here after the show?'

Jane's eyes filled up.

'Take your time,' Kate said. 'There's no hurry.'

It was vital that she trace the victim's movements, but not at the expense of upsetting his grandmother. The fact that she'd seen him after he won his bout was helpful to the DCI, narrowing the gap between the end of the show and the discovery of his body.

'He went out straight afterwards,' Jane said quietly.

'Did he say where?'

'To see Richard.'

'And he is . . . ?'

'Elliott's best friend.'

'Do you know Richard's surname?' Kate took a pen and small notepad from her pocket and flipped open the cover, poised to take down a name.

'Hedley,' Jane said. 'He's a good boy. He lives in Elsdon.'

'Do you have an address by any chance?' She did and Kate wrote it down, along with directions to the house. On the way to Alwinton, she'd passed through Elsdon, a village she knew well. She looked up from her notebook. 'Did Elliott drive or take the bus?'

'He has a pushbike,' Jane said.

Kate scribbled:

FIND THE BIKE!

'I don't suppose you know the make and colour? It's just, there was no bike found near the discovery site.'

'Give me a moment.' The old lady stood up and walked across the room to a Welsh dresser on the far wall. She opened a drawer, pulling out photographs, handing one to Kate. It showed Elliott posing with his bike for the camera. 'He got it for Christmas off his mum,' Jane said. 'Extravagant, I know.' Her expression hardened. 'My daughter has a guilty conscience.'

Kate made a mental note to return to that. She was keen to concentrate on Elliott's movements before Jane Gibson tired of all the questions. 'What exactly did Elliott do when he came home?'

'Not much. He had a quick bite to eat and left straight after.'

'What kind of mood was he in?'

'A good one. Having won at the show, he was as high as a kite. Richard never made it this year. He was working and couldn't take part. He's a wrestler too. Elliott was keen to get over there and rub his nose in it.' Registering Kate's vigilance, the old lady paused. Backtracked. 'I didn't mean, you mustn't think . . . It was healthy rivalry, Chief Inspector. Nothing they would fight over. They've been as thick as thieves since junior school. Well, not thieves—'

'Jane, relax. I know what you meant.' Kate's mind sifted this new information. Jealousy was a motive for many a catastrophic falling out. So was greed. But Jane seemed so sure that the two lads were the best of friends. Kate's eyes drifted to the clock. 'Did Elliott tell you what time he was due to meet Richard?'

'Half past.'

'Half past six?' Kate asked.

'Yes, I think that's what he said. I wasn't paying attention. I was making him a sandwich and listening to the last few pages of an audio book. I prefer being read to now. My eyes get so dry.'

An image of white tights entered Kate's head. 'Did Elliott take a shower before he went out?'

'No. He was running late.'

'And that's the last time you saw or heard from him?'

Jane welled up again.

Her tears were all the answer Kate required.

Leaving Jane to grieve alone, having declined the offer of a family liaison officer, the DCI let herself out. She walked to the grassy area where she'd parked the car, several pairs of eyes fixed to her back as she moved towards her vehicle, her attendance in Alwinton already telegraphed to those at home.

She felt sorry for this small community. A larger one might absorb the grief of losing a young lad from their midst. Kate had the distinct impression that this one would not. People here would go on remembering, torturing themselves, suspicious of each other, until whoever killed the boy was found and punished. For some, life here would never be the same.

8

They drove back the way they'd come, with the intention of tracing Elliott Foster's best friend, Richard Hedley. Hank was alert but uncommunicative. Unusual. He liked nothing better than a good natter about life, their current case and office politics. Kate hoped he wasn't still fretting over the row with his son, or the injury woes he claimed he didn't have.

There was no answer at Richard Hedley's door.

Hoping to track him down, they separated with an agreement to rendezvous at the car after a sweep of village homes. When Hank failed to materialize half an hour later, Kate completed another circuit of the village before heading to the Bird in the Bush. As she'd suspected, he was propping up the bar.

From the threshold, she observed the room. Coats and hats hung from pegs on the wall to her right, above a church pew where weary travellers could rest and remove muddy boots. It was a long bar with a large flat-screen TV, wall-mounted, high above the head of the man serving the drinks. A row of tables and chairs sat beneath the windows and there was a pool table at the far end of the room. In terms of temperature, it was warm inside but the atmosphere was chilly. Like the pub in Alwinton, the mood was subdued.

'Where the hell have you been?' Kate whispered as she approached Hank from behind. 'I've been all over looking for you.'

He swung round on his bar stool. 'You should've called.'

'I did,' she said through gritted teeth. 'Couldn't get a signal.'

'Actually, I switched it off to interview a witness.'

Kate's ears pricked up. 'Witness to what?'

'Ah, now you're interested.' He held up a menu. 'You want a sandwich?'

'No. Get on with it, Hank. We haven't got all day.'

'There was a disturbance in the village last night.' Hank flicked his eyes to a guy standing with his back to them – a big man wearing a brown Barbour jacket and heavy-duty wellington boots, two Border terriers at his feet. Hank pointed towards a table in the corner, a suggestion that she should take a pew.

Kate nodded.

He held out his hand before she had a chance to move. 'He doesn't say much unless you're buying.'

'Get 'em in, then, and bring him over.' She handed over a twenty-pound note and walked away.

Hank ordered another round, then tapped his witness on the shoulder, asking if he minded stepping away from the bar for a brief chat with his boss. Nodding, the man picked up the fresh pint Hank placed in front of him, supped an inch of the amber liquid, nudged his dogs with his left foot and charted a course to a table near the window.

As he walked towards Kate, she noticed the eyes of other

regulars following him across the room, a few muted comments passing between them.

'This is DCI Kate Daniels,' Hank said.

The man grunted a hello.

Kate extended a hand. 'Thanks for your time, Mr . . . ?'

'Willis. Matthew.' Ignoring the proffered hand, he wiped his mouth on the sleeve of his jacket. 'People call me Stan.'

She didn't ask why. 'Take a seat.'

Willis had the expression of a deeply troubled individual. She wondered if he was a relative of the boy, but kept it to herself. She would raise it when the time was right. If she was any judge, the big guy was a manual worker. He had a weather-beaten face riddled with purple thread veins, a bulbous nose and cautious, if not unfriendly eyes. It was easy to form the impression that he was capable of losing his temper if riled. Or was he anti-police – like her old man?

'My DS tells me you heard a disturbance last night.'

A nod was all the answer she received. When Willis failed to elaborate, Kate leaned back in her chair, crossed her arms and waited. This was going to take longer than she had time for.

'You live in Elsdon, Mr Willis?'

'All my life.'

'Good. That means you're familiar with the place. I'm guessing it's fairly quiet round here. I bet you don't get much trouble out this way.' He didn't confirm or deny it. 'What exactly *did* you hear?'

'Not much.'

'I'm going to need specifics, sir.'

'Kids yelling,' he mumbled.

'So no biggie – is that what you're saying?'

Willis shrugged.

Kate exchanged an invisible roll of the eyes with Hank, an unspoken message passing between them. If she was buying this witness beer, she expected information in return, and would make damned sure she got her money's worth. Taking her cue, Hank put down his pint and took over. Kate was hoping Willis might respond differently man to man, but after a few more questions, it soon became apparent that she was way off the mark.

When she spoke again, her tone was clipped, her loss of patience on show. 'You're hardly pushing the boat out here, Mr Willis. I'm sure you realize that we don't have time to waste.'

'Me either,' he said.

'So why bother mentioning a disturbance unless you're prepared to talk about it? I may be wrong but the mere fact that you've spoken to my DS would suggest that you think it has something to do with the incident we're dealing with a few miles down the road.'

'Maybe.' Willis had almost downed his beer. If he thought he was getting another before he started playing ball, he could think again.

'What time was this?' Kate asked.

'Couldn't say. I'd had a couple of pints.' He noticed her checking out his wrist. 'Never wear one. I don't work a nine-to-five job. Time is unimportant to me. It was dark, if that's any use to you. There was a bit of a ruckus over by the church, that's all. It got a bit heated. If I had to guess, I'd say it was around sevenish.'

Kate peered out of the window, her focus on the spire of St Andrew's Church across the village green. Picture-postcard pretty, the sight reminded her of a school history lesson. If her memory served her correctly it was the same church where William Winter's victim had been buried long ago. Had Willis seen much from that distance in the dark?

There were a few streetlights . . .

Even so, it was a fair way.

Kate turned to face him. 'Inside or outside the church-yard?'

'No idea. I heard it. Didn't see it.'

'This was well after the show, I presume?'

'As I said, it was dark.' He glanced at her feet. 'You can't have city folks stumbling round in the dark, can you? Might spoil their pretty shoes.' Kate ignored the dig. Willis pushed a little further. 'Boots is what you need up here, not fancy footwear that's neither use nor ornament to anyone.' His eyes drifted towards the TV. 'Come to think of it, the news had just finished on that thing.'

'And you were where exactly when you became aware of it?'

He head-pointed towards the pub's main entrance. 'Walking out that door.'

'Going where?'

'That way.' His finger indicated south of the village.

Kate felt one of the terriers shift position under the table, rub its head on her calf and go back to sleep on her foot. Not surprising. The heat from the radiator was ridiculous. She was feeling drowsy herself. A publican's ploy to get his customers to drink more, she wondered, or merely a considerate landlord who knew how cold it was on the surrounding fells?

Her focus was on Willis again. 'That way is home, I presume?'

'Where else would I be going?'

'So you had no need to walk past the church?' Hank cut in.

'Why would I?' He said it as if the question had been stupid.

Kate took over again. It wouldn't do to aggravate a witness she suspected had more to give. Not yet, anyway. 'You didn't think it was worth having a word with the kids to take the heat out of the situation? I reckon I might have, to keep the peace, in case someone got hurt.' She paused, wondering if he'd done that. There were a few nasty grazes on his knuckles; recent too, if she wasn't mistaken.

'You're a copper,' he said. 'I'm not.'

'Not your business then?'

'Correct.'

She pointed at the scratches on his hands. 'Mind telling me how you came by those?'

'Occupational hazard.'

'Meaning?'

'Drystone walling without gloves.'

'You should be more careful.' Kate said. 'Did you watch television when you got home?'

'Don't have one.'

'OK, we'll leave it there, for now.' Turning to Hank, Kate asked a question designed to unsettle the local man. 'Do you have Mr Willis's address, should we need to interview him formally?'

Hank confirmed he had.

'Phone number too?'

'Don't have one of those either,' Willis cut in. 'That's why I didn't call the law.'

'One last question, if I may.' Kate watched for a reaction. 'Do you happen to know Elliott Foster?'

'I know his older brother better. He drinks in here when he's home on leave. He's a good kid.'

'But you do know Elliott?'

'Not any more.' Willis got up and left the table. He made his way to the bar without a backward glance. Hank saw off his pint, got to his feet and led the way to the door. The interview was over.

9

Kate let out a sigh and took her mobile from her pocket as they exited the pub. Her signal was weak. She called the incident room, hoping to speak to Carmichael before it died, her eyes on St Andrew's Church a hundred metres away.

She was in luck: Lisa picked up. 'Lisa, I'll have to be quick before my signal drops out. Check the incident log. I'm after reports of a disturbance, or any other suspicious incidents in or around Alwinton, Rothbury, Elsdon, Otterburn since two o'clock yesterday afternoon. I'll hold.'

'Why two?' Hank asked as they waited.

'The victim was alive at two. I saw him with my own eyes. It's what went on afterwards that interests me. I'm wondering why Elliott was running late to meet his friend.'

'You think something happened before he got to his grandmother's that continued when he reached Elsdon?'

'Maybe. Even long shots are worth checking out.'

The line clicked.

Carmichael was back. 'Can't find anything, boss.'

'Damn—'

'Owt else I can help you with?'

Kate looked over her shoulder at the pub's front door. 'Actually, there is. See what you can find out about Richard

64

Hedley.' She reeled off an Elsdon address. 'And check out Matthew Willis – aka Stan – who also lives in the village. Hang on, Lisa. Hank will give you the address.' Kate held out the phone.

Hank took it, spoke to Carmichael, then handed it back.

Kate lifted the device to her ear. 'Anything happening at base?'

'Nothing report-worthy.'

'I'll call you later, if I can. Service is patchy here. Sometimes it works, sometimes not. In the meantime, ask Andy to dig out a programme of events for Alwinton Show – and get hold of the names of the organizing committee. I want names and addresses of anyone and everyone taking part: volunteers, sellers, exhibitors, contestants, judges, dog owners and anyone else you can think of. I have a feeling we're going to need it.'

'Will do.'

'Thanks, Lisa. By the way, if you see Atkins, tell him the IP didn't reside with his parents. They're no longer together. From the age of seven, he lived with his maternal grandmother – Jane Alice Gibson. She lives in Alwinton. I've already spoken to her, if he asks. I'll write it up when I get in.'

'Will you be here in time for the briefing?'

'Yes. Gotta go. See you then.'

Ending the call, Kate scanned the village green, homing in on the oak tree with a circular seat around it. On rest days, she'd sat there often, eating a picnic lunch. She spoke without looking at Hank. 'We're standing less than three miles from the gibbet at the only spot where anything untoward was reported since Elliott was last seen alive by his grandmother, and before that by me and, potentially, thousands of others at the show. What does that tell you?'

'What do you mean?'

Now she returned his gaze. 'Doesn't it strike you as odd that Willis failed to report it?'

'Not really. You heard him. He doesn't have a phone—'

She pointed across the road. Directly opposite the pub was a phone box. 'That must be all of ten metres from where he was standing, allegedly.'

'Maybe it's dead.'

Kate crossed the road and peered in. 'It doesn't look dead.' She didn't open the door to lift the receiver in case she contaminated evidence. 'Dead or not, I want it examined and fingerprinted. 'Even if it is out of order, Willis could have used one of his neighbours' phones to call for help if he'd wanted to. What's wrong with him?'

'You're assuming he gets on with them. He's hardly Personality of the Year material, is he?'

'I can't make up my mind if he's being deliberately obstructive or if he's socially inept.' Kate strode off in the direction of the church.

Hank followed. 'Some people are like that. Relaxed with people they know, awkward with strangers. And they don't come much stranger than you.'

She grinned. 'Thanks a lot.'

'You know what I mean. He only spoke to me because I was in the pub, digging around, making conversation—'

'Buying, you mean.'

'Maybe, but even nice people don't call the law like they used to. They mind their own business and get on with it.

Have you seen a copper today, apart from me? I certainly haven't.'

'No.' Kate sighed. 'Makes me so cross to think the public have so little faith in us. You can tell that by talking to them. I mean, someone just found a kid hanging. As the nearest village to the gibbet, this place should be crawling with uniforms. What the hell is Atkins up to?'

Hank shrugged. 'Well, he's not here searching for a crime scene, is he?'

The phone rang in Kate's hand. 'Speak of the devil.' For a split second she considered ignoring Atkins' call, but answered with her name and rank, adding, 'I'm a little busy right now,' just to wind him up.

'Where are you?' he bellowed.

Kate moved the phone away from her ear. He already knew the answer, via Carmichael. She played along. 'Elsdon, why?'

'I thought I told you to butt out.'

'I have—'

'Have you seen Gormley?'

'He's with me.' Kate winked at Hank. 'He's still *my* DS until I go on leave. We fancied a ride out, a bit of country air while I hand over my cases. I'm in training for time off, remember?'

'Daniels, I'm warning you—'

She cut the call.

Hank grimaced. He'd heard every word.

Kate was damned if she'd give in to intimidation. During a long police career she'd been sworn at – even spat at – by scarier men than Atkins. Whatever difficulties she might encounter in her role at MIT, it wasn't like being single-crewed in a panda in the city's West End. Or wandering the dark alleyways of Newcastle Quayside on nightshift where any Tom, Dick or Hyped-up Harry could jump out of the shadows and plant her one because she happened to be wearing a uniform. Compared to them, Atkins posed little threat. Mouth Almighty he might be. That didn't alter the fact that he was a bottleless coward.

'What next?' Hank was asking.

She pointed at the church. 'We're going to have a stroll around. I won't rest until I do. Keep your eyes peeled for cycle tracks. Elliott rode here on a pushbike from Alwinton, according to his grandma.'

They entered the churchyard at the south gate and began searching inside the well-tended graveyard, having notified the vicar of their intentions. Kate insisted on it out of courtesy to him and his parishioners. She felt bad about being there, even worse that Atkins hadn't talked to the family personally, the very first thing she'd have done had she been the SIO.

Poor Grant . . .

Talk about a baptism of fire.

Weaving her way through the gravestones, looking for signs of a fight, she began to wonder if she might stumble upon Margaret Crozier's gravestone, the old lady who'd been cruelly murdered by William Winter all those years ago, before he was hung on the gibbet as an example to other ne'er-do-wells.

If her burial plot was there, Kate didn't find it. According to Hank it wasn't listed on the churchyard plan available to the public inside the entry porch. Perhaps it was one of the unmarked graves. After all, 1791 was a very long time ago.

Sending Hank to explore the perimeter, she continued to search alone, finding signs of recent footfall. No more nor less than she'd expect in a well-tended graveyard. She walked on: a few more graves, more inscriptions. None belonging to Margaret Crozier and nothing Kate could identify as the scene of a fight.

Hank called out to her, dragging her attention from the past to the present.

The expression on his face was enough to tell her that he'd had more luck.

Taking the gravel path out of the south gate, Kate turned right and right again, wondering if it was Elliott's bike that had caught Hank's attention. He was standing beneath an oak tree, his eyes fixed to a patch of grass beside the church's west wall, a good few metres of which had been disturbed.

He pointed at two cans on the ground. 'Half-full,' he said. 'So probably an adult – legal drinking age anyway.'

Kate glanced his way. 'Makes you say that?'

'Trust me, I'm a detective. I'm also a man. It stands to reason that I was once a boy.' He made a silly face. 'Kids don't leave beer because they've had enough. They drink the lot, squash the cans, maybe even hide the evidence in the long grass.'

'Unless they were disturbed by Willis leaving the pub.'

'Possibly.' Hank shifted his gaze to the roadside. 'There's another couple of cans over there, but those are empty.'

'Looks like they've been tossed from a car.' Kate transferred her attention to the ground in front of her. 'These two, I'm not so sure about. That turf look suspect to you?'

'You took the words out of my mouth.'

The area of grass they were viewing was totally flattened with deep gouges in what was otherwise a well-cared-for patch. One of the divots exposed a definite boot print. Careful to preserve what *was* there, Kate crouched down to observe it more closely. She pointed at a blue piece of paper with some writing on it nestled in the grass a few feet away.

'What is it?' Hank asked.

'Some kind of confectionery wrapper,' she said. 'And what looks suspiciously like a cannabis joint.'

Hank's eyes were on the hand-rolled cigarette end. 'You want it bagged?'

'No, leave it be. This is a crime scene. What kind of scene, I'm not too sure.' Kate retraced her steps to the south gate, then did a U-turn and walked back towards him. She spread her hands, signposting the grass beneath their feet. 'Why here?'

'What do you mean?'

'Why here?' she repeated. 'Why not over there?'

Hank was literally and figuratively scratching his head.

'There are no drag marks from either bench in front of the church. Assume for one minute that Elliott was involved in a fracas, why didn't he use one of them to sit on if he was waiting for someone? From there you can see anyone approaching, vehicle or pedestrian. It's a good vantage point. You've got Otterburn to your right, Rothbury to your left, the gibbet straight on.'

Hank conceded she had a point. 'Maybe he lied to his grandmother.'

'About meeting Richard Hedley?'

'It's possible. Maybe he was meeting a girl. He was a handsome lad. He'd proved how macho he was, winning his wrestling match, and he had prize-money in his pocket. That must've increased his pulling power. Quite a turn-on for girls, I reckon. When I was his age, I was in the police cadets. Notched up a few female friends myself when word got out I'd joined the force. Let's face it, local lasses are hardly spoiled for choice around here, are they?'

Kate remembered meeting Hank for the very first time, the effect he had on the opposite sex, how female colleagues talked about him constantly, peeved that he had a ring on his finger. Not that it bothered some. Any man in uniform was fair game. He was as popular with the ladies then as now. Lost in the memory, she was silent for a while, before her thoughts returned to the investigation generally, the area surrounding the churchyard in particular.

Something didn't add up.

'Whether it was Richard Hedley or someone else Elliott arranged to meet,' she said, 'why here, in the dark, in the cold, rather than at their house?'

Hank pointed at the discarded joint. 'That might explain it.'

Kate looked at the roach end, the blue sweet wrapper catching her eye again as it flapped in the breeze. Putting on her specs, she bent over to examine it more closely. 'Can you make out the writing?'

'Not without my glasses.'

Kate could just read it. 'Ever heard of a Diggers Bar?'

Hank shrugged. 'It's a new one on me.'

She chuckled. 'I can't believe they make a chocolate bar you don't know about. It's a digestive biscuit of some kind.' She didn't know it yet – she wasn't facing him – but his attention had strayed . . .

'Kate?' he said, trying to attract hers.

'Hmm . . .'

'Take a look.'

She stood up straight.

He was indicating a dark patch, a sticky substance, on a projecting stone about a third of the way down the church-yard wall. Kate knew blood when she saw it. If she was very lucky there would be skin there too, possibly even hair. The question was: whose was it?

'Get on the blower,' she said. 'I want a full forensic team out here.'

Hank made a crazy face. 'Atkins will go ballistic.'

'Do I look like I care?' She felt a flicker of joy, as good as if Newcastle United managed a win after the worst start to a season she could recall. At last, the investigation was moving in the right direction.

10

Beth Casey stared at the TV, hanging on to the presenter's every word, her stomach in knots. 'Police are urging witnesses to come forward following an emotional appeal by the boy's parents. Senior Investigating Officer of Northumbria's Murder Investigation Team, DCI James Atkins, has vowed to leave no stone unturned in apprehending those responsible. He is particularly interested in hearing from anyone attending Alwinton Show on Saturday . . .'

The image switched from the studio to an outside broadcast.

Her father appeared on screen, as handsome as ever with his best suit on, shoes bulled like a guardsman's. His name and rank popped up in a caption at the bottom of the picture, an inside location she didn't recognize, the press suite at the force's new HQ perhaps. He spoke directly to camera, the Northumbria Police logo at his back.

Behind his steely blue eyes Beth saw what others would not: a triumphant expression that made her bilious. He'd been waiting for this moment his whole life and was sure to make the most of it. It mattered not how *she* felt or how it might affect Elliott's family, so long as the great detective got his sound bites in and impressed those with the power to offer him the next rank.

'This senseless and callous act has robbed a family of a loving son . . .'

His words faded out of her consciousness. At least he had the decency to look sincere. He stuttered slightly, as if upset by the information he was trying to convey. It didn't last. Beth hated to think what might be going through the mind of Elliott's father, seeing him up there showboating. Her father didn't care about him. Didn't care about anyone but himself.

Beth forced herself to concentrate on the words coming out of his mouth.

'A team of detectives will be working round the clock to take your calls, so if you have any information, no matter how insignificant it may seem, we'd like to hear from you. We need your help to track down the perpetrators . . .'

Her father wandered into the living room as the transmission ended and the item cut back to the studio. 'If it were up to me I'd dole out some summary justice,' he said, slumping down on the couch. 'Give the lowlife scum a taste of their own medicine. The courts are far too lenient these days.'

'You're a hypocrite!' Beth blurted out.

Her father glared at her: *Be careful.*

'Were you even going to tell me?' Beth held his gaze rebelliously until he looked away. Of all the strokes he'd pulled, she couldn't imagine one more cruel or hurtful. Elliott meant the world to her and he knew it. 'Well, were you?'

She waited for a straight answer.

Didn't get one.

'You know I can't talk about work at home. I'm the SIO, for Christ's sake. What I do is highly confidential. It's not your business or anyone else's, until I say it is.'

'I'm your daughter!'

'Yes, and you might have been tempted to get on that phone of yours. Then where would I be?'

'He was my *friend*.'

'He's scum, like his father.'

'That was your fault.'

'The man's a bully, Beth—'

'And you're not?'

He had no answer to that and she went on the attack. 'The only difference between you and him is that you get away with pushing people around by hiding behind a warrant card. You think you're better than everyone else, but you're not—'

'That's enough!' He stood up, took a swig of his drink, and walked towards her. 'I don't know what you're allowed to do at home but, when you're in my house, you show respect.' He stopped talking when the landline rang. Snatching up the receiver, he kept his hand over the speaker, glaring down at Beth, who was holding back tears. 'We'll talk about this later, when you're in a better mood, OK? I have other stuff we need to talk about too.'

'I don't want to talk about other stuff.'

He lifted the phone to his ear, his eyes boring into her. 'Atkins.'

'Grant here, boss.'

'What do you want, a medal?'

'We have a positive result.'

'On what?'

'From the crime scene at Elsdon—'

'You're breaking up, I can hardly hear you.'

'Sorry, it's a bad signal.'

Beth strained to listen in.

The man raised his voice. He was talking against background noises, a police siren getting closer. He sounded hyped up. Excited almost. Like her dad whenever he had a breakthrough in a case. His voice was louder than was strictly necessary. He hardly needed a phone. And, as he continued the update, her father looked confused.

Beth thought she knew why.

'What are you on about?' Atkins yelled.

'Sir?'

'There is no bloody crime scene at Elsdon.'

'There is now. DCI Daniels found the scene of a disturbance beside St Andrew's churchyard.'

'So?'

'She organized a forensic team and pulled some strings. Some doctor or other – Matt West, I think she said. He owed her. She collected. Had him standing by at the forensic science laboratory. She couriered blood samples. He fast-tracked them. They came back positive to the victim. There's no doubt about it. We definitely have a match.'

Atkins exploded, his colour rising. 'What the hell is she doing?'

Beth turned towards the window, listening to more of the conversation than she should. Through his reflection in the window she watched him get more and more agitated. It was all she could do not to vomit there on the carpet. She ran upstairs to her room and locked the door.

They knew.

11

For a while, Elsdon village had been overrun with police cars and vans. Photographs and videos had been taken. Officers in full forensic kit had crawled on their hands and knees conducting a fingertip search. When they were done, they climbed into their vehicles and drove off in convoy to complete their work elsewhere, each collected item now on its way for forensic examination.

Kate lifted her hands to ward off an attack as Atkins strode towards her, spitting orders to anyone who'd listen. She'd seen him angry like this before and got in first before he could open his mouth. She spoke quietly and calmly, hoping to take the temperature down and avoid a public slanging match. She might have known it was a big ask.

'Don't be difficult,' she said. 'I tried telling you. You weren't bloody interested. What was I supposed to do? Stand around like a spare part for the next two days? As I said before, we're on the same side. I'll be out of your hair soon.'

'You just happened to be passing when this information fell in your lap, I suppose.'

'Pretty much.'

'And you felt duty bound to follow it up.'

'You're doing OK so far.' Elsdon was off the beaten track

in the middle of nowhere. They both knew that she'd done nothing of the kind.

'You expect me to believe that?'

'Frankly,' Kate said, 'I don't give a toss what you believe.'

Grant wandered up before the SIO said any more. Atkins turned towards him with a look that could kill a man. 'What?' he barked.

'Locals seem nervous, sir.'

'Welcome to the sticks.'

'Jesus!' Kate said. 'It's hardly the West End!'

The SIO scowled at her, his expression a throwback to an earlier time when she had no alternative but to let him call the shots.

He still thought he could scare her . . .

He was wrong then . . .

He's wrong now.

'Can I get rid of the tape, sir?' Grant was trying his level best to deflect yet another row. 'The locals are keen to reclaim their village.'

'Forensics got what they want?' Atkins asked.

'They're all done,' Hank replied.

Atkins rounded on him. 'Did I ask you?'

Grant stepped in between them. 'They've taken casts of all the necessary tyre tracks and footprints. Samples have been lifted, items of interest bagged and logged. There were various bits of debris found in the surrounding area. Hopefully, some of it'll be of use to us—'

'All of which may have been discarded moons ago,' Atkins countered.

'The vicar says not,' Kate added quickly. 'There's a group

of volunteers who litter-pick on a regular basis. They did so on Friday to ensure the village had its best face on. The show brings in many visitors from home and abroad. The locals like it nice.'

'Do they?' Atkins' tone was scornful.

Eyeing a group of hopeful villagers, Grant laid a hand on the police tape, itching to take it down. 'We've got all we need, sir.'

'Let's not be too hasty.' Atkins was looking for an excuse to throw his weight around.

Kate bit down so hard her jaw nearly locked.

She turned to Hank and Grant. 'Guys, give us a moment, will you?'

The two men walked away mumbling about a situation no one but Atkins had authority to change, unless Kate could talk some sense into him.

'You're wasting your breath trying to change my mind,' he said when the others were out of earshot. 'Until this lot start giving up their secrets, the road remains closed.'

'Why?'

'You have one "uncommunicative" witness—'

'Well, at least we *have* one. What do you have?' The question was rhetorical and Kate was already asking a second. 'Have you any idea of the inconvenience it will cause to people who live here if you leave the roadblock in place?' Again she didn't give him the opportunity to respond. 'Of course you do, you used to live here. Why are you being awkward? You won't find any rubberneckers here. These are law-abiding locals. Discreet. Don't tar them with the same brush as those you encounter in the city. They're worlds apart—'

'They're not so different. The road remains closed.'

'Give me one good reason.'

'Because I say so,' he barked.

Kate wasn't finished. 'Think of the logistics. Imagine the detour villagers will have to make if you leave a roadblock in place. It'll take them hours to get in and out. If you're so keen to play SIO, try acting like one. Stop and think, for once in your life. If you don't put yourself out to talk to locals and show some cooperation, they sure as hell won't talk to you. If you're not here in their midst, visible to them, you can't expect to be kept up to date with their thoughts and fears, the fact that there's a few bad apples around here – and there obviously are. In case it passed you by, there are no beat officers on the street any more. How long do you think it's been since a copper, or even a bloody PSO stopped by? Look around you. There's no CCTV. You're going to have to pull the stops out to crack this one. If you don't get along with the residents, you're not going to get along. Period. So use a little give and take.'

Hank was back.

'Willis now thinks the assault was videoed.'

'How come?' Kate asked.

'He remembers seeing a dot of light – may or may not have been a mobile phone camera.' Hank had addressed his comment to Kate, disregarding Atkins completely. The fact that he was technically in charge of the case didn't come into it. In Hank's book, respect was something you earned.

It went both ways, or not at all, a sentiment Kate agreed with wholeheartedly.

'I thought Willis heard but didn't see?' she said.

Atkins raised an eyebrow, a smug expression on his face. 'What was that you said about the good people of Elsdon? Do me a favour!' He shifted his focus from Kate to Hank. 'Be very careful, DS Gormley. On this enquiry, I'm your SIO. You'd do well to remember that. How many does Willis think were involved?'

Hank had no choice but to respond. 'A good few,' he said. 'Seven, eight. Interestingly, he heard a lass's voice among the lads.'

'Sounds to me like he's making it up as he goes along.' Atkins levelled his eyes at Kate. 'So much for your credible witness.'

He was smirking as walked away. With their eyes on his back, he pulled up sharp, pausing for effect. Then he turned around and marched back towards them. 'Just in case you're in any doubt,' he said, 'the roadblock stays.'

12

'Personally, I don't think he should be heading up this case.'
Kate got in her car and slammed the door, almost taking it
off its hinges. 'A, he used to live round here and B, he has
no respect and not the first idea how to speak to people.
He's completely unsuitable. The role of SIO requires tact and
diplomacy. Can you believe he let Grant see that poor boy's
parents?'

'Did he?' Hank was appalled.

Kate took a long, deep breath, her attention straying out
the passenger-side window. Atkins was on the village green,
arms crossed over his chest, staring back at her. 'Look at
him,' she muttered. 'What the hell is he doing?'

'Standing around with his thumb up his arse, as usual.'

'You're not wrong,' Kate said. 'He thinks the villagers are
imbeciles. They know it too. You can see it in their eyes. Can
you imagine someone like Matthew Willis talking to him?'

'No.'

'That's what I thought.' Kate's frustration was boiling over.
'Material witness or not, he'll clam up. And when he does,
we'll lose the only ally we have.'

Hank raised an eyebrow. 'Ally might be stretching it.'

'Talk to Willis again and see what you can get out of him

before Atkins wades in there, all guns blazing, losing ground. Subtlety is not a word he's familiar with.'

'He just left,' Hank said. 'Want me to hang around in case he turns up?'

'And leave you to the mercy of Atkins?' She shook her head. 'No DS of mine will be his whipping boy. No, you're coming with me. Disappear after the briefing and I'll cover for you.'

'To do what?'

'Your dream job.'

'Do I need a whip?'

'Behave! I want to know exactly what you can see from the pub in the dark.' Ignoring his hands joined in prayer and the silly grin on his face, Kate's attention shifted once more to Atkins. 'Think you can manage that without him getting wind of it?'

'I'm gutted you feel the need to ask.'

'Be careful, Hank. This is still his case and he will shaft you at the first opportunity. If it were mine, I'd be organizing a reconstruction. I know it's not done much nowadays, but you never know what gem you might come up with.'

'Works for me.'

'Yeah. Shame Atkins is too pig-headed to go with it.'

Pulling his seat belt over his chest, Hank was unable to hide the difficulty he was having. Kate was close enough to see the pain behind his eyes. Despite their busy schedule – they worked at breakneck pace during the first few days of an enquiry – she asked if he wanted dropping at home. He declined, changing the subject back to Atkins before she got stuck into him again. The subject of his injury was not up for discussion. He'd signed himself fit for duty and that was the end of it.

'Are you going to tell me why the tosser hates your guts?' he asked.

'Nice sidestep.' Kate continued to stare at him. 'Why won't you tell me what's wrong? And by the way, you can forget doing anything after the briefing. You leave Willis to me.'

'What for?'

'I'm not blind—'

'Like I said, I'm a bit stiff. Stop fussing, I was warned about it.'

'I've made my decision.'

'Kaaate—'

'You're off duty after the briefing. No arguments.'

'Not before you tell me what went on between you and Atkins.'

Kate avoided his eyes. 'He's a piece of work, that's all.'

'Bollocks. He's a lot more than that. I've seen you handle guys like him. None of them get under your skin like he does. Is it personal?'

'It's history.'

'Not from where I'm standing.'

Kate warned him to drop it. 'You keep your secrets and I'll keep mine. It makes my head ache just thinking about him.'

Hank backed off.

Kate softened her voice. 'Will you promise me something?'

'Of course.'

'If it gets too much, will you check out for a while? Why don't you go on the Pat and Mick while I'm on holiday? That way you won't have the extra burden of coping with the SIO from hell.'

'I'm not letting him freeze me out—'

'You saw what he was like with Grant. Believe me, you'll get all the shit jobs and work the most hours—'

'Fine, I can handle that. I want this case sorted.'

'He'll be gone as soon as I return from leave.'

'You going to talk to the guv'nor?'

'Damn right I am. I can't understand why he let Atkins anywhere near a murder case. Don't worry, he won't be kept on.'

'And if he is?'

'I walk.' Kate started the engine and pulled away.

Kate swerved to avoid a male pheasant strutting across the road with all the time in the world, the bane of her life when she was off duty on two wheels. Before she left the countryside behind, word came in that the search party she'd organized to find the missing bike had drawn a blank. It wasn't what she wanted to hear. She drove on in silence. That bike was evidence but the area was vast. She had no manpower to search every hedgerow.

Unless . . .

'I have an idea,' she said. 'I need to make a call.'

Hank looked at her. 'To whom?'

'The only person with the means to help us out.' She found a number and pressed the call button on the Audi's hands-free. Stewart Cole picked up after a couple of rings, his velvet voice filling the car.

'Kate, what a lovely surprise! It's been way too long. I'm in withdrawal.'

Hank rolled his eyes.

Cole was an all-singing-all-dancing action man. The force helicopter pilot – ex-army too. Someone who, if he lived to be a hundred, couldn't repay the kindness the DCI had shown him. After he had helped out on a previous enquiry to find a missing girl, Kate had put in a good word for him at HQ, getting him what Hank considered to be a 'cushy number' flying around all day, enjoying himself, while officers below went trudging in the thick of it. As a result, Cole was putty in her hands.

'Stew,' she said, 'I need a favour.'

'Name it.'

'Any chance you can do a zip round the area from Alwinton to Elsdon in that helicopter of yours? I have no authority to ask, but don't let that stop you if you're at the airport twiddling your thumbs. Can you assist?'

'Sure.'

'I have no paperwork.'

'I never asked for any. Wanna join me?' He knew she'd rather eat worms.

'I'd love to,' she lied. 'Unfortunately, I'm tied up.'

'Sounds promising. Gimme ten, I'll be over.'

'Behave yourself—'

'You're no fun.' He sounded genuinely disappointed that she wouldn't be joining him on the flight. 'What am I looking for exactly?'

'A trail bike. White. Expensive. Not sure what make or model. I suspect it's been stolen and may since have been dumped. I'm fairly certain my victim was riding it last night. I need it found.'

'I'll do what I can.'

'Thanks. I'm heading to the incident room. Give me a shout if you come across it. Owe you one, Stew.'

'I'll be sure to collect.'

Kate glanced at Hank, laughing into her hand as he stuck two fingers down his throat. He didn't like sharing her with Cole and acted like a jealous teenager whenever the three of them came into close contact. His ambivalence was not lost on the amiable pilot either. In fact, at that very moment in time, he was interpreting the pause on the line, putting two and two together, no doubt picturing Hank's reaction to the conversation.

'Tell your DS to wind his neck in,' he said. 'I assume he's there, joined at the hip, eavesdropping as usual. I swear he gets a vicarious pleasure from our relationship. We should invite him out to dinner soon, or round to the flat some-time. Let him see the chemistry first hand—'

'In your dreams, pal.' Hank made a face at Kate.

She laughed out loud, enjoying the banter.

'I'll get back to you.' Cole was chuckling as he ended the call.

'This isn't a bike theft gone wrong,' Hank grumbled. 'More likely someone was after Elliott's winnings, roughed him up and took the money.'

'And then hung him afterwards? You don't believe that any more than I do.'

'So what do you reckon?'

'Just because I'm the boss doesn't mean I have all the answers. I'm as clueless as you.'

'Well, whoever beat the shit out of him could easily have finished him off in Elsdon and dumped his body over the churchyard wall. So why didn't they?'

'Good question. The gibbet has to be significant.'

'Yeah, but how? Why?'

'Hold that thought, Hank. If Cole finds the bike, maybe it'll point us in the right direction.' Her phone rang. Not a number she recognized. She pressed a button on the steering wheel to take it.

'Daniels.'

'Grant here, ma'am.'

'What can I do for you, Colin?'

'I wanted to let you know that the victim called his mother at around seven o'clock last night—'

'He what?' Kate wondered why he hadn't mentioned this when she was at the crime scene.

Atkins.

'She said he sounded drunk or stoned. Between you and me, I didn't warm to Gayle Foster. She's a bit unfriendly. I've seen punters more upset losing their wallet than she is about losing her boy.'

Kate exchanged a look with Hank, wondering if Elliott had used the phone box nearby or a mobile. 'What about the father?'

'Graeme was the nicer of the two by a country mile. There's no love lost between them though. He lost it when she suggested their son was on something. Pooh-poohed the idea as ridiculous. Accused her of being out of touch with the lad in recent years, quote: too busy putting your own needs first. Unquote.'

An old lady's words jumped into Kate's head. 'Actually, that makes perfect sense. Her mother, Jane Gibson, told me that Gayle felt guilty for having shirked responsibility for his upbringing. Consequently, she showered him with expensive gifts at Christmas and birthdays, but hardly ever stuck around to pay him any proper attention in between.'

'Quality time was clearly not on her agenda.'

'Neither was motherly love, by the sounds of it. Have you fed this to the SIO?'

Grant hesitated. 'He won't listen to me.'

'You're his DS.'

'Try telling him that.' Grant stopped himself from going any further.

Kate suspected he was weighing up whether or not he could trust her. His caution was justified. He didn't know her from Adam. As an incomer to the force, it would be unwise to speak out of turn to the wrong person. Many had done so and lived to regret it. He'd made a judgement call by the time he spoke again. What he had to say didn't surprise her.

He cleared his throat. 'DCI Atkins has made it clear that I'm his gofer and that's all I'm good for. I may be young in service by comparison, but I know my stuff. I'm not used to being undermined. I'm beginning to think I made a big mistake coming here. If you don't mind me saying so, the man's a moron.'

'You can say that again,' Hank interrupted, throwing caution to the wind.

Grant hesitated. 'Sorry, I didn't realize you had company.'

It was Kate's turn to be cagey. She wondered if he was on the level or if Atkins had sent him on a fishing trip to elicit behaviour unbecoming of a fellow officer. If so, it wouldn't work. She wasn't about to slag him off on the phone and land herself with a blue form – a complaint she'd never be able to defend to Professional Standards if her words were being recorded.

Hank was unwise to have done so.

'Don't worry about it,' she said. 'You're among friends. Your opinions on DCI Atkins will go no further. Outside of that, they do matter, to me, to Hank and the rest of MIT. For the record, you haven't made a mistake in joining Northumbria, for yourself or your family. You know where I am if you need to chat.'

'Thanks, I appreciate that.'

'Was there anything else we should know about?'

'Actually, there is.'

'Go on.' Kate made an impressed face to Hank.

'I just got off the phone with the pathologist. The spliff you found at the scene didn't belong to the victim. There's zero evidence to support it. Given the beating he took prior to being moved to the gibbet, I was wondering if he might in fact have been disorientated, rather than pissed or high on drugs as his mother suggested.'

Grant had done well with the parents.

Kate liked his style. He was making a lot of sense. Her guts were telling her he could be trusted. He'd hit on

91

something important and she commended him for it. 'Excellent work, Colin. I'll be sure to mention it to those that matter.'

'Make of that what you will,' Hank said.

It was a dig at Atkins.

Grant thanked them and Kate ended the call.

13

It was five by the time they arrived at the incident room. MIT detectives had already been fed, watered and primed for a long briefing. The room was charged with the expectation of a difficult road ahead and Kate felt the adrenalin rush that accompanied every new case. She took the floor, her aim to share intelligence both ways.

Calling for order, she scrolled through electronic notes she'd made throughout the day on her mobile phone, a reminder of the many topics up for discussion. As she lifted her head to speak, the device rang in her hand, Cole's number flashing up on screen.

Apologizing, she turned away to take the call. 'Stew, tell me you have good news.'

'I do.' He sounded chirpy. 'Although I'd rather give it in person.'

'I'm a bit busy right now.'

'I can see that.'

Feeling a presence behind her, Kate swung round and came face-to-face with his deep-set eyes. Dressed in a flying suit sporting the logo of the Police Air Support Unit, he looked fit and tanned, as if he'd recently been on holiday. Travelling was his thing. As the former owner of a parachute training centre and CAA approved flying school, it had become a way of life for him. He'd flown around the world in the course of two careers: the Army Air Corps and, later, as a civil aviation pilot.

'Your bike is with Forensics,' he said.

'Where did you find it?'

'Fifty-four degrees north and—'

'In layman's terms, you pillock.'

Cole grinned, showing impeccable teeth. 'Exactly where you said it would be: a mile north of Elsdon on the Alwinton road.'

Kate frowned. 'I've driven that route twice today and didn't notice it.'

'You wouldn't have. It was in a ditch, propped up behind a drystone wall, hidden from view – I suspect, to keep it safe. It's a great bike. Perfect for taking advantage of the countryside around there. Anything else I can do for you?' He was flirting.

Kate felt herself blushing. 'What's your gut feeling? Was it carefully placed or hidden in a hurry?'

'It wasn't thrown over the wall, if that's what you mean.' He pulled out his mobile and showed her a photograph. The bike was properly parked, handlebars straight, wheels too. Cole was watching her closely. 'I can see the cogs turning.'

'Hmm. I was just wondering if it had been there all night or put there this morning. Anyway, thanks for finding it.' She glanced over his shoulder. The team were getting restless. 'You want to sit in?'

'Sure. Any excuse to watch you in action.'

'Don't get excited. This is nuts-and-bolts stuff.'

'Nothing earth-shattering to report?'

'I wish. Grab a coffee and take a seat.' As Cole moved towards the vending machine, Kate called for order, giving her apologies for the delayed start. 'We have a lot of ground to cover,' she said, 'so notebooks out. I have news.'

Conversations ended and the room hushed.

Kate waited for Cole to find a seat. 'For those who don't know Stew – that's the man with a onesie on – he pilots India 99, the force helicopter. He spotted the victim's bike from the air and that's the best news we've had all day, so put your hands together and show your appreciation. Stop frowning, Hank. If you want to play Biggles, you need to learn how to fly.'

A giggle spread through the room, along with a round of applause. Hank and Cole were laughing along with the team. That pleased Kate no end. She was hell-bent on the two of them making friends. Cole held up his plastic coffee cup, a gesture of thanks for the acknowledgement of his minor contribution.

The noise died, allowing her to move on.

'We need to ask ourselves why the bike was placed over a wall and concealed from view. It could be that Elliott was going somewhere, other than Elsdon, or was meeting some-one near the dump site and didn't need it any more.' She scanned the room. 'Spit 'em out if you have any thoughts on this.'

Brown held a pen in the air. 'It could have been a simple theft. Someone half-inched the bike and hid it for collection later.'

'You mean it's nowt to do with what went on afterwards?' Carmichael screwed up her face. 'Isn't that a bit far-fetched,

Andy? It's more likely someone Elliott knew stopped and offered him a lift.'

'Or even someone he didn't,' Maxwell said. 'He should've listened when his granny told him not to talk to strangers.'

'Neil has a point,' Robson said. 'He'd be knackered after wrestling all afternoon. If he was running late, he might have accepted a lift from someone he didn't know and bitten off more than he could chew.'

'They're good suggestions,' Kate said. 'We know for certain that he made it as far as Elsdon – the blood on the church wall confirms this.' She looked at Cole. 'Are there any houses near the stash site?'

'No,' he said. 'It's quite a hike to the nearest property.'

'That makes my suggestion a lot less likely then,' Andy Brown conceded. 'A thief would hardly steal a bike and leave him or herself miles to walk home.'

'I agree,' Kate said. 'Let's talk about the crime scene at Elsdon. There are benches directly outside St Andrew's Church that Elliott could have used if he was meeting someone. It would appear that he chose instead to sit on the grass to the west of the churchyard. It occurred to me that he might have been waiting for someone he didn't necessarily want to be seen with.'

'Or he'd already met them,' Lisa said. 'And they were both sitting there together.'

'Maybe he was hiding from someone,' Andy was keen to redeem himself. 'Or meeting a girl. Didn't Willis say he heard a girl's voice during the fracas?'

'That's a lot of maybes,' Kate said. 'Jane Gibson assured me he was meeting Richard Hedley. We can't be sure of that until we find him, so keep an open mind. She also said that Elliott owned a mobile but had no contract she's aware of. She hasn't a clue what type of phone it was but I gather he was in the habit of topping it up at a supermarket in Morpeth. Raise an action to check it out please, Lisa. We need to ID that female and the mobile might help us with that. I'll return to the phone in a second . . .' Kate took a breath, scanning the room. 'Andy, there's no longer any need to chase up tattooists. We have an ID, so reference it off. I want to talk about scene issues, the gibbet first. Neil, any news on the rope?'

'It's good quality,' Maxwell said. 'Made of natural fibres. It's nicked and frayed in places with signs of mildew, but not rotten enough to snap when hauling Elliott onto the gibbet. Otherwise, it's unremarkable. Any building supplier will stock it. Almost every farm will use it. We won't be able to trace it easily.'

'That doesn't mean we don't ask around,' Kate said. 'Mildew would suggest it's been lying around outside. Any reports of missing rope?'

Maxwell shook his head. 'Not so far.'

'Keep at it. Anyone have anything else to say on the rope before we push on?' Kate waited for a response. 'I'm not hearing much enthusiasm, boys and girls.' Carmichael and Brown had their heads together, some whispering going on. 'Was there something you wanted to share with us, Lisa?'

Carmichael looked up, her face turning pink. 'Have you ever read *The Gallows Tree*? It's a book on true crime and punishment in the eighteenth century, written by an ex-copper my granddad knew: Barry Redfern.'

'Never heard of it or him. Is it relevant?'

'I think so.'

'Go on.'

'I think we're right to work on the assumption that it would take a couple of offenders to haul a body up onto the gibbet.' She paused, making sure she had everyone's attention. 'The book I just mentioned refers to special lifting tackle being used to get William Winter up there. I'm not suggesting our killer nipped home for some . . .' She was still blushing. 'But when Hank and I were having a chat about tyre tracks at the scene, it struck me that if a vehicle was used, for example a quad bike, it'd be a piece of cake.'

Kate threw her an appreciative smile. 'I'd like to see that book.'

'I'll fetch it in tomorrow.'

'Help me out here,' Kate said. 'The farmer who works the land adjacent to the gibbet . . . did someone say his name was Dodds?' She took in a nod from Hank. 'He needs a visit. Andy, can you fix that up? Specifically, I want to know if he's taken a vehicle – any vehicle – near the gibbet recently, because, if he hasn't, someone else has. Take him to the field. Don't tell him where we found the tracks. Ask him to indicate where he was yesterday, where he was working every day last week. Let's try and come up with a chronological account of his movements while using a vehicle, and which vehicles he used, if more than one. The tracks haven't been there long. Did you pass Art A-level?'

Brown shook his head, suddenly on the back foot.

'Well, I'm sure you can still draw a rough sketch to share with the team.' Kate glanced at the murder wall. No new developments had been flagged up, a matter of deep concern to her. 'Is there nothing new from DCI Atkins?'

Blank faces stared at her from every chair.

'Does anyone know if he's spoken to Tom Orde? Unless you know something I don't, I'm not seeing any progress on that.'

And still there were no takers.

Kate tried to hide her irritation. It was basic procedure for an SIO to talk to the 'finder' as soon as they had spoken to the victim's family. Atkins had done neither. She wondered if he'd ever read the murder investigation manual. It crossed her mind that he might be bypassing the squad because of their close association with her. Team members were clearly as unhappy with the situation as she was. She moved quickly on, for no other reason than to control the unrest spreading through the room.

'Can I remind you all that Richard Hedley didn't make the show yesterday. Like our victim, he's a wrestler. Jane Gibson told me that her grandson was proud of his win and would want to rub his best friend's nose in it. A throwaway remark, but there may be some truth in it. We need to find him. And not only him. Has anyone heard from Adam Foster yet?'

The receiver, Harry, was shaking his head. 'Not so far.'

'Get on to his CO again. He should be here, supporting his grandmother. Remember, scene issues are key. Oh, and while I'm on the subject of Jane Gibson: her son, the victim's uncle, shot himself apparently. Have a look at it. I want to know why. This family have had one too many dramas for my liking and I don't like coincidences.' Kate let that sink in for a moment. 'Anyone have any suggestions, ideas or thoughts up to this point?'

'Can I mention Willis for a moment?' Hank asked.

'Please do.'

Hank got to his feet so he could see and be seen. 'He has several grazes on his knuckles, he says from drystone walling *and* he's a big bugger – big enough to haul a heavy weight with one hand tied behind his back. He's a bit cagey around the police, so you should all bear that in mind if you come across him.'

'Is he violent?' someone at the rear of the room asked.

'He's hard to read. Just be on your guard.' Hank sat down.

'Before we wrap it up,' Kate said. 'Listen carefully because this is important. Grant wasn't enamoured with Elliott's mother, Gayle Foster. The father, Graeme, is less objectionable, but there is animosity between the two. According to Grant, Elliott called his mother around seven o'clock. She says he was stoned. The father disagrees. With no evidence of drugs or drink on his body, Grant has put forward the suggestion that he was possibly concussed from having taken a beating. If that was the case, it may be pivotal to the enquiry. I don't want to jump the gun here, but if he used the phone after the altercation, either they let him go or he managed somehow to get free of them.'

'So who strung him up . . . and when?' The questions had come from Carmichael.

'Exactly my point, Lisa.'

'Are you suggesting someone returned to the scene to finish him off?' Lisa's alarmed expression was replicated on the face of every MIT member.

'All options are on the table,' Kate said. 'It's possible that the mob involved in the altercation outside the church took Elliott's mobile so he couldn't call for help, or maybe he was so confused he couldn't find it after the fight and used the phone box a hundred metres away. We haven't recovered the mobile yet. I've asked forensics to check out the call box and sent Grant to retrieve Gayle's phone for further examination. I'm not prepared to speculate until we have hard evidence. If luck is on our side, this may be an early breakthrough.'

Carmichael shifted her eyes to Kate's left, letting her know that there was someone standing in the doorway. The DCI glanced over her shoulder. Atkins was leaning against the doorjamb with his arms folded across his chest. She invited him in. He didn't move or say anything. No thanks were issued for conducting the briefing, no explanation for his absence.

'OK to end the briefing?' she asked. 'I'll update you in your office.'

He turned and walked away.

Kate watched him go, steeling herself for another round of aggro. Dismissing the squad, she followed Atkins from the room. She found him in his office with his feet on the desk. She didn't sit down and spent the next fifteen minutes updating him, finally running out of steam and patience, mostly due to his lack of enthusiasm. Sharing the same air with him made her skin crawl.

Resting his elbows on the table, Atkins made a steeple with his hands, his forefingers propping up his chin. 'Very impressive,' he said. 'As you're so keen to stick your nose in, why don't you cover the post-mortem? I'd do it myself, only I'm playing single parent this week. I gather the prelims are done. The PM proper should keep you out of trouble for the rest of the evening. I'm afraid it'll be a late one. There's a backlog of cases from an RTA on the Metrocentre bypass. They've got rather a lot on.'

'Fine,' Kate said. 'I had no plans this evening.'

'Then tomorrow you can give the house-to-house a hand. There's not a lot of information coming in. Easy last day before you go on leave.'

'That's a bit below my pay grade.'

'Shame.'

'You know what, I'll do anything to get out of here.' Kate never took her eyes off him. Not a flicker of emotion showing on her face. He was calling the shots. She had to suck it up. She walked out, leaving his door wide open.

14

Kate arrived at Elsdon at six forty-five, by which time it was almost dark. She stepped from the car with a smile on her face. Following her intervention, and one or two complaints from residents on grounds that it wasn't justified, Naylor had vetoed Atkins' decision to leave the roadblock in place – one more reason, if one were needed, for the SIO to lose his temper.

Crime scene investigators had beaten her there. An arc light was being used to illuminate the village phone box. Inside she could see a figure in a white paper suit and blue gloves: one of two CSIs, busy making a visual and photographic record of what was in there. The blurred windows suggested he or she had already dusted for prints. With a hood pulled tight around the head, it was impossible to tell if the figure through the glass was male or female. The other CSI had just finished taping off the surrounding area to prevent contamination.

Parking the Q5 outside the Bird in the Bush, Kate turned off the lights and leaned against the headrest with Atkins' voice ringing in her ears. There was no autumn moon and lots of cloud cover. Apart from the CSIs, there was no one else about. To her left, through the illuminated pub window,

she could see only one drinker and it definitely wasn't
Willis. Still, she decided to go in and see if he was there.

The publican hadn't seen him, so Kate had a word with
the sole customer present. 'Sir?' She held up ID. 'I'm DCI
Kate Daniels, Northumbria Police. Can I have a quick word?'

The man scanned her ID. 'Murder detective?'

'Yes. Have you got a moment?'

'This about Graeme Foster's son?'

'Yes, it is.'

'Horrible business.' The man held up his pint glass. 'Can I
get you one?'

Kate declined.

'Coffee?'

'Thanks, I'm fine.'

They moved to the same table Kate had been sitting at
earlier with Willis. This character was about the same build:
thick-set, with neck muscles Schwarzenegger would've been
proud of. Here in the sticks, men were built to last. This one
was dressed in an old pair of jeans and a tatty donkey jacket,
the like of which she hadn't seen in years. Beneath a beanie
hat, a pair of healthy, shiny eyes stared back at her.

'I'm Paul Dent,' he said. 'How can I help?'

He sat down opposite, proffered a grubby hand. It was as
rough as sandpaper. Kate noticed the fingernails were bitten
to the quick, ingrained with muck. She had him down as a
farmhand or forestry worker.

'Were you at the show in Alwinton yesterday?' she began.

'No, I was working.'

'May I ask who for?'

'I'm a sole trader supplying logs. I had a rush job on. My

lad went to the show. I picked him up here at around this time last night.'

'You were in here last night?'

'No. I'd had a couple of pints in here at lunchtime. I can't afford to lose my driving licence, Inspector. No transport equals no business. I have a mortgage to pay, a family to feed. I sat in my truck outside.'

'Very wise,' Kate said. 'When you say "around this time" can you be more specific?'

'I said I'd collect him at six thirty. He was late, as usual. Kids!' he grumbled. 'Who'd have 'em, eh? They grunt at you all week and treat you like a taxi on a weekend. You got any yourself?'

'I'm not here to talk about me,' Kate said, her clipped tone warning him that she was a busy professional with little time for chatty conversation. It would be hours before she was finished for the day. 'Were you outside the whole time or did you drive around looking for him?'

'I was here. I had a few calls to make. When my son arrived, he was a bit worse for wear, to be honest. The wife went ballistic and sent him straight to bed when we got home. He went too. Made a detour to the bathroom to hoy his guts up. Lucky it didn't happen in my cab – I'd have given the sod a thick ear.'

Kate smiled in sympathy. 'You waited where exactly?'

Dent thumbed through the window. 'Just opposite, where I'm parked now, give or take a metre or two.'

Kate glanced through the window where a hefty pick-up truck was parked in front of her Q5. 'Is that your Toyota Hilux?'

'Yeah, I could do with a new one.'

Kate's detective brain was working overtime. She was thinking how easy it would be to sling someone's bike in the flat-bed section of a Hilux, or pass someone off as his drunken son, when it might in fact have been the injured victim he was shifting. 'And you didn't enter the pub?'

Dent was shaking his head. 'Like I said, I waited in the truck. I like a drink, Inspector. If I'd come in for one, I'd have been tempted to have another. From what I could see from outside, there was only one customer in anyhow. Not someone I'm that keen on.'

'Would this be Matthew Willis?'

Dent smirked. 'You know him?'

'I spoke to him earlier today.'

'Not the most riveting company, is he?'

Kate didn't rise to the bait. 'Were there any other vehicles around at the time?'

'A few.' Dent wiped his face with his hand, stifling a yawn. 'Most of the show traffic was gone. It made life difficult all day. There were some windy drivers on the roads – doing thirty in a sixty limit – pain in the fucking arse. Slowed me down.'

'I can imagine.' Kate had witnessed it too, but kept that to herself. 'Do you recall any particular vehicles passing through the village while you sat waiting for your son?'

Dent thought for a moment. 'A catering van took the Otterburn road. I don't remember what kind it was. It was fairly large, like a burger van.'

'Any others?'

'Only one,' Dent said. 'It must've been about five or ten

106

minutes later. A Telford's coach pulled up. White. The Border Duchess written on its side. Fifty-five reg I think. Jedburgh firm seems to ring a bell, though don't quote me on that. A group of men and a couple of women piled out. I thought my lad might've hitched a lift. I looked for him getting off.'

'And did he?'

'No.'

'Did you recognize any of the passengers?'

'They weren't from round here.'

Kate raised her head from her notes. 'You're sure about that?'

'Positive. The divvis tried to access the pub from the side and had to come round the front to get in. They must've booked a meal in the pub cafe. That struck me as odd. I'm sure I saw a sign on the door to say it was closed on show day. I was envious – having worked all day, I was bloody starving. My lass is no contender for the *Great British Bake Off*, Inspector. I need a woman at home who does what she's supposed to and puts food on the table the minute I walk through the door. Mine's too busy with her yoga classes. Tasty though, I can't deny her that. Curves in all the right places.' He smirked at Kate, seemingly unaware that he was being sexist.

'So, the cafe was privately booked?'

'I guess so. Not open to regulars anyhow.' He gestured towards the landlord. 'Ask him.'

'I will. Anyone else?'

'Not that I noticed.'

'Did the coach just drop the strangers and head off?'

'No. The driver let them off, backed up and parked at the bus stop.'

Dent glanced through the window, then at Kate. She stood up, looking out at the stone bus shelter, her eyes travelling in a direct line from the pub to the church across the village green. If the witness proved to be reliable, the coach he'd seen would have blocked the view entirely. Was this why Willis couldn't see the melee from the pub doorway? She filed that thought for further examination.

15

Leaving the warm pub behind, Kate walked out into the fresh air and turned right. Dent's account of a coach being parked at the bus stop added credence to Willis's insistence that the fracas going on across the village green had been heard but not seen from the doorway. He might well have heard a female voice, but he'd have needed to clear the parked coach on his way home to have seen the 'dot of light' he suggested might have come from a mobile phone. Clearly, he had more explaining to do.

She knocked on his door, hoping to question him again before Atkins got to him. There were no lights on inside. She stepped up to the window and peered through the glass. With no TV and no phone, she thought he might as well have dispensed with electricity altogether. It didn't surprise her when there was no reply.

Kate scanned the village green, her frustration increasing as a car passed by. Since the roadblock had been lifted, Atkins should have ordered a stop on every single vehicle travelling through the village tonight. His failure to arrange it was a missed opportunity. The arc lights and CSIs were long gone, the phone box taped up to prevent further use. Dent's Hilux was still parked on the roadside.

Clearly, he was having more than two pints tonight.

Kate checked her watch as she neared her Audi. Ten past seven. She'd have to drive like a maniac to make the post-mortem on time. Turning left out of the village, she pressed a button on her steering wheel, speaking Jo's landline number into the hands-free, hoping she'd be at the other end to pick up.

Seconds later, she answered with a cheery hello.

'Am I interrupting something?' Kate asked. 'You sound breathless.'

'I've just been for a run.'

'Wish I had. How far did you get?'

'You know me. I'm an all-or-nothing kind of girl. I did our usual, the full length of Jesmond Dene, up and round Freeman Park and home again. In fact, without you there slowing me down, I ran a personal best.'

'I'm impressed.'

'Liar. What's up?'

'Nothing.'

'Doesn't sound like nothing; I can see your pet lip from here. Put it this way, you're a little underwhelmed for some-one about to go on holiday. Is it this awful hanging?'

'You don't miss much, do you?' An image formed in Kate's mind of Jo in Lycra, a towel hanging round her neck, skin gleaming with sweat, phone against her ear. Kate hadn't meant to sound flat. She apologized immediately. 'I just called to hear the sound of your voice and tell you I can't wait to get away.'

'Me too! Are you packed?'

'Not yet.'

'You did remember we're out with Emily tomorrow night?'

Emily was a psychologist friend from university. Jo had worked with her at HMP Northumberland on a Home Office initiative examining the treatment of dangerous sex offenders. Jo had taken a temporary secondment there, a break from her role as criminal profiler with the police and her main job as forensic psychologist at the Regional Psychology Service. On so many levels, it was a disastrous period for all three women, but that was history. Jo was now back where she belonged, working with the Murder Investigation Team.

'I haven't forgotten,' Kate said. 'I'll pack when I get home tonight.'

'Make sure you do.' Jo's jokey tone dissolved. 'Might I have seen him yesterday? The wrestler?'

'You might. Young lad. Distinctive tattoo on his hand.'

'Oh no! I do remember him—'

'Ohmigod!'

'What? Kate? Are you OK?'

'Yes, yes I'm fine.' Kate's eyes were glued to her windscreen. 'You will not believe what I'm seeing here: a tawny owl with a wingspan of three or four feet. It's flying along the road in front of the car. In all the years I've been driving, I've *never* seen that happen. It's really magical. Oh, he's gone. I wish you'd seen it.'

'I do too.'

The B road twisted this way and that. Finally, Kate reached the T-junction, turned left and put her foot down, the conversation returning to the case she was grappling with. 'I take it the hanging was on the evening news?'

'Radio,' Jo said. 'A DCI whose name I didn't recognize was appealing for witnesses *and* I bumped into Lisa on the way out of the station earlier.'

Kate slowed a little. 'I didn't know you'd been in.'

'I wasn't there long enough to chat. Besides, I knew you were busy.'

'Did you manage to deliver your report on the Curtis case?'

'That's why I was there. Lisa filled me in on your latest. Sounds nasty.'

'Aren't they all?'

'I didn't mean the case,' Jo said.

'Oh.' Lisa had said more than she ought.

'Why is this Atkins guy giving you grief? More to the point, why don't I know about him? I thought I knew all your secrets.'

'No one knows *all* my secrets.' *No one ever would.*

'Ha! Wait 'til we get to Scotland.' Jo dropped into a mock German accent: 'I have ways of making you talk, Ms Daniels.'

Kate was looking forward to some deep and meaningful pillow talk with Jo, but not on the subject of Atkins, even though sharing that particular secret would explain much to her former partner about the way she'd run her life. Kate had a valid reason for holding back on the history that existed between her and Atkins. She simply couldn't bear to be reminded of it.

'C'mon,' Jo pressed. 'Stop holding out on me.'

'What's the one thing we both dislike over everything else? And I'm not talking Marmite.'

'So, Atkins is a bully. That much I knew. Lisa was spitting bullets when I saw her earlier. I don't think I've ever seen her so riled. She reckons Hank is ready to sort him out—'

'He'd better not!'

'He won't.'

Jo's hesitation made Kate think that he might.

'Don't pull him about it, Kate. He might be busting a gut to give Atkins what for, but he's not going to risk his career over it. I shouldn't have said anything. Lisa asked me to keep it to myself and not bother you with it. Why don't you call in for a drink on your way home and you can tell all? Problems are best shared . . .' She let the sentence trail off.

Kate wound her window down. She needed air. 'I wish I could, but I'm due at the post-mortem now and I'm still thirty minutes away. It'll be late when I finish. Don't worry about Atkins, or me, I'm fine. How bad can it get? Tomorrow is my last day. The case will be his problem then.'

'You sure you can bear to leave the children?' Jo was referring to the squad.

'Are you kidding?' Kate stared out at open countryside, buoyed by the promise of more to come as they headed north across the border. 'Seriously, I can't wait.'

'I'm pleased to hear it,' Jo said. 'Are you sure you don't mind us taking Nelson? I could always ask Emily to dog-sit. She'd enjoy the company. I'm sure she wouldn't mind looking after him.'

'Don't be daft. It'll be fun – as long as he doesn't mind me sharing your bed.'

'I was rather hoping he'd have to get used to that.'

Kate said nothing. So aroused was she by the promise of intimacy she could almost feel Jo's hands on her skin, exploring every inch of her as they used to. If it were possible, she'd drop the fantasy and head over there for the real thing. The illusion dissolved, cold hard facts barging their way into her head. Within the hour, she'd be visiting the morgue; writing up the case in order to hand over to Atkins by close of play tomorrow. She knew one thing: there was a lot more progress on her list than there was on his.

'How far have you got?' Jo asked. 'With the enquiry, I mean.'

'Not very.' Kate wondered if the sudden change of subject was nervousness on Jo's part. A nifty sidestep. Neither of them knew what the future held. Maybe it was better that way. 'I have two crime scenes. That's never a good thing.'

'Lisa said the victim was assaulted in Elsdon and not at the gibbet.'

'Correct. I found out that he called his mother last night, pissed, stoned or in dire need of help, poor sod. Problem is, his mobile phone is missing.'

'Maybe he used someone else's or the public box. There *is* one.'

'Yeah, I know. I'm on it. His mother's phone will confirm where he made the call from and pinpoint the exact time. That'll help. If it *was* the call box, either before or after the assault, Atkins will have to trace callers via the people they rang and that'll take time.'

'Won't they just be strangers passing through after the show?'

'Probably. He'll still have to talk to them.' Kate dealt in certainties, not probabilities. Often it was some innocuous scrap of evidence that solved a case, something a potential witness had seen or heard that they hadn't thought valuable to the police. 'They may not even be aware of what's gone on locally,' she said. 'Anyway, that'll be Atkins' headache, not mine.'

16

The Home Office pathologist was female. Apart from her age, early forties, the woman was about as far removed from her *Silent Witness* foil – Dr Nikki Alexander – as it was possible to get. She had short cropped, dark hair, prematurely grey. She wore sensible black tights and what Kate could only describe as functional spectacles.

No designer frames here.

Kate apologized for her late arrival, explaining where she'd been and why. 'No offence,' she said, 'but I was expecting Tim Stanton.' He was her friend and longstanding colleague – the pathologist Hank had requested to cover the post-mortem.

The woman peered over the top of her specs, a mischievous sparkle in her eyes. 'None taken. Don't look so worried. I'm out of senior school. Promise.'

'I wasn't, I didn't mean—'

'Lighten up, Chief Inspector. I was joking.'

Kate relaxed. 'Sorry, it's been a very, very long day.'

'For you and me both.' The surgeon smiled warmly. 'Tim was called away at short notice. His kid fell off a swing in the playground and was taken to hospital.'

'Ed or Maddie?'

'Ah, you know the family?'

'Quite well.'

'Figures. He talks about them constantly.'

'Isn't that what all parents do?' Kate smiled. 'I bet it was Maddie.'

'Good guess!'

Kate was beginning to like the new surgeon. 'She's OK I take it?'

'She's absolutely fine, despite being kept in for observation. I gather she's sitting up in bed being spoiled rotten by her daddy, eating all sorts of crap and being promised more treats when she gets home. If I were her, I'd be throwing myself off the swing on a regular basis.'

Kate laughed, relieved to hear that Stanton's kid was none the worse for her ordeal. 'You've spoken to Tim?'

'He just got off the phone. Said to tell you that you're in good hands. I'm Su, Morrissey. It's good to meet you, finally.'

'Likewise, I'd shake your hand only . . .' Kate pointed at the surgeon's bloody scalpel and nitrile gloves.

'I've heard a lot about you, Kate.'

'All good, I hope.'

'Hmm, so-so.' Morrissey flashed a smile. 'Tim is very fond of you.'

'The feeling is mutual. You seem to have the advantage.' Kate hadn't seen her around or heard Tim speak of her.

'You mean he hasn't talked about me? I'm crushed.' Su was teasing. 'I got lucky after graduating. Spent the last ten years working for the Department of Pathology and Laboratory Medicine at UBC. I've not long been back in the UK.'

'UBC?'

'University of British Columbia.'

'You've been there since qualifying?'

Su nodded.

Deep in Kate's memory something stirred. 'Was Tim your tutor in Edinburgh?'

'Taught me everything I know – and some. When a position came up here, he called me, asked if I'd consider coming home to work for him.'

'Headhunted? I'm impressed.'

'I said yes immediately. My husband was ready for a new challenge too, so we jumped at the chance.'

'He's a Brit?'

'Canadian. Our paths crossed in Bamburgh. He was heading to Scotland. I was going the other way. My parents live on the estuary at Alnmouth. He claims he fell in love with me. I reckon it was Northumberland that stole his heart. He's longed for a house on that coastline ever since.'

'And now you have one?'

'We're rooming with my folks at the moment. Never ideal, but we're waiting for the right property to come onto the market.'

Kate pulled a face. 'Easier said than done. Once people buy up there, they stay put until the hearse arrives.'

'As I am finding out.'

Kate's eyes slid off the medic to the dead boy on the examination table. His body was well developed, more muscular than it seemed when clothed. The kit he was wearing had been carefully removed before her arrival and laid out on a nearby table for recording purposes next to the other clothing found at the scene. Later, each item would be bagged individually and sent for forensic examination.

'He took quite a beating,' Su said.

'Was he healthy, apart from these fresh injuries?'

'Physically he was in great shape.' She pointed at Elliott's head. 'I'm curious about these marks beneath his bottom lip.'

Kate put on her specs. 'What am I focusing on exactly?'

'You probably won't see them from there. Grab some kit and gloves from the dispenser and take a closer look.'

Kate took off her coat, tied her hair up and put on a paper suit and gloves before approaching the table. Suspended from the ceiling was a large magnifying glass. Su Morrissey pulled it towards her, looked through it and stepped aside, enabling Kate to take her place. The lens was brilliant. Through it, she was able to see instantly what the surgeon was getting at: a row of perfect circular marks at the top of the victim's chin, below an ugly swollen lip.

'Knuckle duster?' It was a guess.

'Possibly. Whatever it was, it was driven home with maximum effort to cause this amount of damage. He stinks of liniment. Can you throw any light on that?'

'He'd been wrestling shortly before he died.'

'I did wonder. The white footless tights were a bit of a giveaway, but it doesn't pay to assume anything.'

'Multiple bouts too, I'm afraid. That probably means you'll find a glut of DNA on his body, from his opponents as well as the offenders who assaulted him, assuming they aren't one and the same.'

'Hmm . . .'

Kate raised her head. 'Problem?'

'Wrestling explains the marks on his back, but there are none of the defensive wounds to his arms, wrists or hands that I'd expect to see if he'd been in a street fight. I find that odd when he could obviously handle himself, don't you?'

'Maybe the injury to his head was the first blow.'

'That is the obvious conclusion to draw. It wasn't a tap, that's for sure. It was violent enough to produce an acute subdural haematoma.'

'Catastrophic?'

'Haemorrhaging of the eyes points to strangulation. I need more time before I can offer a conclusive cause of death. If it's all the same to you, I'd like to confer with Tim. This is my first case here and I'm not rushing it.'

'I understand.' Kate meant it: many cases hinged on such evidence. 'You're the expert,' she said. 'The one who has to stand in court and justify an opinion to a High Court Judge. For me, dead is dead, Su. If the cause is murder, that's all I need to know.'

'What I *can* do is narrow down the time for you. He died some time between seven and nine p.m. I'm afraid that's as close as I can get without a magic wand.'

Not long after the fight but after dark, Kate thought. 'Thanks for your help – and welcome home. Keep in touch on cause of death – and give my regards to Tim and his family if you see them.' Ripping off her protective suit, the DCI dumped it in the bin and headed out.

17

Chris Collins' house was an end-of-terrace cottage on a quiet road off the busy main route through the village of Otterburn. Music was audible through the door when Beth arrived, a Kasabian track on full volume: 'Where Did All the Love Go'. When there was no response from pressing the bell, she stood beneath his bedroom window and screamed his name at the top of her voice. When that didn't draw him out, she texted him: **I'm outside.**

The music was cut, the window opened.

Chris's head appeared through it. 'What's up?'

What's up? 'Let me in,' she yelled.

On the way over there, she'd wondered if he'd heard the awful news. If she was reading him right – and that wasn't always possible – he hadn't got a clue. Her father's words jumped into her head: *You might have been tempted to get on that phone of yours.* Beth felt angry that he viewed her as indiscreet and thought so little of her. She'd never have blabbed to her mates. Never. She was only telling Chris to warn him. Someone had to.

'Fuck's sake,' she said. 'Open the door!'

'Let yourself in.' He threw down the key.

Retrieving it from the lawn, Beth fumbled it into the lock and entered the house. Dumping her coat on the newel post, she climbed the stairs slowly, wondering how to break the news. Chris was sitting on his bed, a pair of Beats headphones around his neck, a birthday present from his adoring mum, bought with an unexpected injection of cash into her bank account – a winning premium bond she'd had for years.

He looked at her, a question in his eyes: *What now?*

There had been so much to cry about lately.

Beth choked on her words. 'It's Elliott,' was all she managed.

His face dropped, eyes growing cold. He told her to give it a rest. They had argued about Elliott often. Chris had never been able to understand how close they were. He got riled every time he saw them together. Everyone knew it. How was that going to be viewed by the police?

Despite her best efforts to hold them in, her eyes filled with tears she was powerless to prevent. Pulling a tissue from her pocket, she dried her face and blew her nose. There was something of her dad in Chris. He'd been getting more and more argumentative in recent weeks, going off on one if she so much as mentioned Elliott's name. But when he saw how distressed she was, an apology tripped off his tongue, as it always did. It lacked any real conviction.

'Beth, I'm sorry,' he said. 'I'm just sick of him hanging around us. Every time we turn the corner, he's there. It's like we can't get away from him. I feel invisible when he's around. I know you've been friends for years, but we've got better things to talk about now, don't we?' He tried for a smile that didn't come off.

And still Beth couldn't get the words out.

'Don't cry.' Chris was more angry than upset. 'You know I hate to see you cry.'

'He's dead.' There, she'd said it . . . finally. 'Elliott is dead.'

'Yeah, right!' Chris dropped his head on one side, a grin replacing the guilt he was feeling for being such a prick over her friendship with Elliott. 'For a minute there, you had me going—'

'I'm not joking, Chris. I wish I was.' More tears sprang from her eyes, making dark patches on her light blue shirt. She was suddenly outside of herself, watching from somewhere on the ceiling, another wave of nausea hitting her. She wanted to sit down, but where? The room was a dump, as usual. Clothing strewn all over the place: on the bed, hung over his computer screen, most of it on the floor. How he could live in such a mess was a mystery to her. She needed order and calm to function. Even the smallest amount of visual chaos stressed her out.

'Haven't you seen the TV?' she asked.

'It's broken, I told you.'

'They found his body at Winter's Gibbet.'

'He topped himself?'

'No – I don't know. No one does. We have to go to the police.'

Her words hung in the air between them as the news began to sink in. Chris turned his eyes on the TV, an accusatory expression on his face, as if the dusty object had somehow let him down. Blood drained from his cheeks, turning his face the colour of the grey sheets on his rumpled bed. He didn't move to comfort her. He just sat there while she stood in the doorway, exposed and alone in her grief.

When she could no longer bear to stand, she moved towards him, sweeping an armful of paraphernalia out of the way so she could make a space next to him. She put a hand on his arm. 'We need to go now, Chris.'

He pulled away, twisting his body to face her, eyes filled with fear. 'I'm not going to the police, I've done nowt wrong—'

'I know, and I'll tell them that.' She didn't want to rile him further but he had to be told. Somehow she overcame her cowardice and found the strength to say her piece. It took all she had to get the words out. 'People saw us with Elliott in Elsdon. We can't hang around waiting for a knock on the door. It'll look like we have something to hide. Like you said, we've done nothing to be ashamed of. We can explain—'

'I said no!'

'Why not?' Beth could see she wasn't getting through. 'Well, if you don't call them, I will.'

'No. You won't—'

'I have to! My dad's a copper.'

'And he'll be looking for a scapegoat.' His mouth was a thin hard line. He tried to reason with her. 'Who do you think your dad will look at first, eh? You know what he's like. He'll end it, Beth. He's been waiting for an excuse to break us up. You'll be handing it to him with bells on. I'll never see you again. That's not what you want, is it?'

'Of course not!' She stopped weeping and took hold of his hand. 'We're not kids, Chris. My dad might try, but he knows deep down he can't stop us seeing each other, any more than your mum can.' Beth held his gaze. 'Don't try and deny it. She hates my guts—'

'She's not as bad as he is. He's been trying to put you off me from the very beginning.' His eyes grew cold, the nice Chris fading away, the not so nice Chris taking over again. 'If you tell him what happened he'll laugh his cock off. He'll have us followed. He's good at that. You said so yourself.'

'I told you that in confidence! Don't you *ever* repeat it!'

Chris backed off. 'Look, I don't want to fight.'

'Me either.' Beth squeezed his hand. 'We have to stick together now. Our parents can't order us around any more. If they do, we can leave. We can go to London or somewhere in the sticks where no one will find us. Anywhere you want.'

His eyes lit up. 'Let's go now.'

'No.'

'Why not?'

'My mum needs me. You know I can't leave now. Besides, running away is the worse thing we can do. We have to come clean, tell the police or my dad what happened. Tell them about Gardner and the others—'

'Oh yeah, that'll work.'

'What other choice do we have?'

'Don't push me. I can't think straight if you push me.' He rubbed a thin film of sweat from his forehead. One knee was moving up and down nervously. He was avoiding a decision Beth knew he'd have to make, sooner or later. She could understand him not trusting her dad but didn't want to think too hard about why he didn't trust the police in general. He might tell her something she didn't want to hear.

'Go home,' he said. 'I'll call you later. I need time to get my head around this.'

'We haven't *got* time,' she pleaded. 'I can't tell you why, but . . .' She paused mid-sentence, deciding not to bring her father into it again. It would only aggravate Chris further. He'd dig his heels in and refuse to budge. There was no scenario worse than seeing the two significant males in her life in a rage.

'Chris, listen to me.' She took hold of his hand again in the hope that he'd see sense. This time he didn't pull away. 'I won't lie. We could be in serious trouble. We could, but I'm begging you to do the right thing. We have no other choice.'

'I can't go to the law—'

'They'll understand. I'll go with you.'

Downstairs, a door slammed shut. Beth stood up, panic rising in her chest as his mother shouted '*I'm home!*' up the stairs. She was the last person in the world Beth wanted to see. Then it all went silent. Beth imagined her on the floor below, eyes fixed on the newel post, anger mounting when she saw Beth's coat. She'd be jumping to conclusions – the wrong ones – accusing them of impropriety before she knew the facts. The condemnation didn't take long to arrive.

'Chris, have you got Beth up there?'

'Please,' Beth begged. 'We have to go.'

'I said no.'

'Hello!' His mum thundered up the stairs. 'Chris? You in?'

Beth spat her words out, another rush of courage from somewhere deep inside. 'You're gutless, you know that?'

'You don't understand—'

'Yeah, I think I do.'

Chris's mum entered the room, stopping dead when she saw that they weren't screwing each other's brains out. Her expression was a mixture of surprise and indignation. Beth pushed past her and ran down the stairs, slamming the front door behind her. Clear of the house, she texted Chris:

You have an hour. If you don't get in touch, I'll make your decision for you.

18

On the way out of the city morgue, Kate was still thinking about the circular marks on the victim's face when a second text from Fiona Fielding arrived: **Speak to me, Kate. I'm lonely. X.** The DCI smiled. The earlier message had announced that Fiona was in town: **Fancy a meet? Grabbing a bite to eat or even a quick glass of wine? I'm rather hungry. ;)**

'If only that were possible,' Kate whispered under her breath, a smile spreading over her face. In Fiona Fielding speak, 'hungry' had connotations that had nothing to do with food. It meant she wanted sex. This was a woman with a voracious appetite for pleasure and no hang-ups, a free spirit who knew how to enjoy life to the full with whoever she chose at any given moment.

Pocketing the phone as she walked round the corner, and still preoccupied with guilty thoughts of Fiona, Kate almost ran into DS Grant coming the other way. Atkins had sent him there to put pressure on the pathologist for cause of death. He'd luck out. Kate told him so. He didn't argue, just did an about turn and fell in step, overtaking her as she paused to glance at her watch.

Almost ten.

Grant strode ahead to open the double doors leading to the corridor and stood back to let her pass. Once through the door, Kate stopped to wait for him. He looked worn out. Unsurprising. He'd done the work of two all day, taking none of the credit. She knew the answer to her next question before she'd even asked it.

'Anyone still in the incident room when you left?'

'No,' he said. 'I was last out.'

'That's usually me.' Her smile hid her anger that Atkins was long gone. 'Listen, Colin, I know it's late, but it would be nice to grab a moment with you if you have the time. I didn't get the chance to thank you for your call earlier. To be perfectly honest, I'd like to pick your brains.'

'Pick away.'

'I'm hoping you can throw light on an issue that's been bugging me all day. Fancy a jar before heading home? I assume that's where you're going?'

'Home would be stretching it a bit.'

She didn't pry. 'You sure you I won't be keeping you?'

'I'm in the accommodation block at HQ.'

'Oh, that's grim.'

Grant laughed. 'It's not a place I'm particularly fond of. I'm flat hunting, or should I say my wife is, via the Internet. She's still in Essex. I hope she finds one soon. I'm no MasterChef. I'm eating out of cans and it's doing me no good.' He patted his midriff.

Kate ran her eyes over him. He looked too young to be in a serious relationship. 'How long have you been married?' she asked.

'Six months.'

'And before that?'

'I lived with my mum.' He pulled a face. 'At twenty-six, I should probably know better.'

Kate smiled. 'If my mum was alive, that's exactly where I'd be.'

'I'm sorry.' He'd seen the sadness in her eyes.

She quickly changed the subject. 'You like Italian food?'

'Love it.'

'Then come with me.'

Carluccio's, on Grey Street in the city centre, was one of her favourite places to eat. They were in time for last orders. Grant looked like he could do with a beer and perhaps a whisky chaser to go with it. He opted for a half, something Hank would never do if a pint were available. They chatted about his decision to move north, Grant telling her that his wife was from the area and had never settled in the south. Now he'd seen more of what the region had to offer, her nostalgia surprised him less than it had before.

After a while, the conversation moved to the case; more specifically to Atkins and his failure to interview the victim's parents, the very reason she'd waylaid him.

'Did he give you *any* clue as to why he delegated such an important job?' she asked. 'Not that I think you're incapable. Quite the opposite. It's just not ideal. Parents of murder victims deserve to have an SIO giving them the death message and holding their hands.'

Grant hesitated a beat, a forkful of pasta poised mid-air.

He was as wary of her as she was of him. Kate hoped he wasn't another Matthew Willis, a man who needed to sink a few pints before he'd open up. Not that she blamed the DS for being cagey; loose talk in their profession often had calamitous results.

She waited patiently, her eyes never leaving his. He reminded her of Hank as a young detective; a deep thinker, an officer with professional integrity. He obviously loved his job and took it very seriously. She could see that he was torn between loyalty to his immediate boss and doing the job as they both knew it should be done.

'Relax, Colin. I'm not trying to trip you up or cause you any undue anxiety. From where I'm standing, Atkins is handing you enough of that. I find it curious, that's all. Worrying too, if you want the truth.'

'He just said it would be best if *I* went,' Grant said finally.

'That's all?' Kate took in his nod, disappointed but not surprised. Atkins was a slippery customer. He wasn't daft. He'd say nothing to incriminate himself in what he knew was potentially a disciplinary offence. Another black mark against his character would finish him. 'I'm not trying to put words in your mouth, Colin. Would it be fair to say that you suspected he might know the family?'

'It crossed my mind.' He could see she wanted more. 'I can think of no other reason,' he added.

'Did you challenge him on it?'

'Yes, and he said he had other matters to attend to.'

'You weren't buying that?'

'Not entirely.' Grant stopped chewing. 'Every SIO is busy, but in my mind the boy's parents were top priority. Nothing should have been more important. His actions were reprehensible.'

'I agree.' Kate still felt his anxiety. She owed him an explanation. 'You'll have worked out that Atkins and I have history. Whatever you think you've witnessed between us, I give you my word that my line of questioning isn't a ploy to get even with him for something that happened in the past.'

'I did wonder.'

'Of course you did. Had I been you, I'd have drawn the same conclusion. I want you to know that my concern is purely professional. If it turns out that Atkins knew the victim and/or his family, it might jeopardize a conviction when the case comes to court.' Kate shoved her plate away, meal half-eaten, her appetite shot. 'Eat up,' she said. 'This conversation will go no further. I'm on leave the day after tomorrow. I'll sleep on it.' Fifteen minutes later, she paid the bill and dropped him back at the morgue.

19

By day, Otterburn Mill was a unique tourist attraction, a heritage centre housing antique mill equipment and spinning wheels preserved inside an original weavers' building, tenterhooks retained in the open air. Now a retail outlet, visitor centre and cafe, the former woollen mill sat on the edge of the Northumberland National Park, accessible by footpath from the village.

In the adjacent field, Beth Casey was sitting in the dark at a picnic bench, bleating sheep the only sound beyond that of cars passing along the main road a couple of hundred metres away. She often went there with Chris to get away from his mother, who was constantly on their case, refusing to allow them time alone, making them go downstairs and watch TV on the pretext of protecting Beth. From whom? she wondered. Her son? Herself? The woman gave them no peace.

Not like *her* mum.

Thinking about her made Beth feel instantly sad. It was unlikely she'd beat the cancer. They both knew that. It had been too far advanced when first diagnosed. The thought of losing her was intolerable. Having lost his father to the disease some years ago, Chris had been a rock throughout, someone she found she could rely on when things got tough. It was the glue that bound them together, as if he alone understood what she was going through. Beth doubted she'd ever come to terms with it.

She stiffened as a figure approached out of the darkness. It took a moment before she realized it was Chris. As he came closer, she noticed that his hands were pushed deep into his pockets, shoulders hunched against the evening chill. Closer still and she saw that he was breathless. He'd run all the way. Despite the cold night air, he had no coat. He'd probably sneaked out of the window rather than use the stairs, avoiding a confrontation with his mother, twenty questions on where he was going at this late hour.

Wouldn't be the first time.

Batting away irritating midges as they landed on moist skin, Chris straddled the bench, his mood matching the inky sky above their heads. He was angry. Beth could feel it rather than see it. For a moment, he stared into space, deep in his own miserable thoughts. Eventually, the tranquillity of their surroundings kicked in and he relaxed. He always did without his mother in his face, smothering him.

Couldn't the daft cow see that?

Taking hold of Beth's hand, he stroked her fingers, a touch so gentle it surprised her and brought tears to her eyes. Leaning in, she rested her head against his chest, a steady heartbeat pulsating through his thin shirt. He put an arm around her, the first physical comfort she'd received from anyone since hearing of Elliott's death.

When she spoke her voice was hardly audible. 'I can't believe I'm never going to see Elliott again.'

'Me either. I just shoved him, Beth.'

'I know.' She hugged him closer.

'He was fine when we left him.'

'Well, he's not any more.' Beth lifted her head. They both knew that 'fine' was overstating it. She pulled away. 'I'm not blaming you. I saw what went on . . .' She paused. 'I also saw Elliott hanging from Winter's Gibbet.'

'What? How?'

'There was a photograph on my dad's computer.'

'Shit! That must've been gross.' He stroked her hair.

'It was. You've got to speak to my dad, Chris.'

He let go of her hand. 'I told you, I can't!'

'Why not? You did nothing wrong. Everyone who was there knows what happened—'

'Yeah, like they'll stick up for me.'

'I will!'

'Well you would, wouldn't you?'

He had a point. And that's exactly what her old man would be saying. She tried hard to make Chris feel better. 'My dad might be an arse sometimes, but he knows I don't lie. It'll be ten times worse for you if you don't make the first move. His team are hunting for witnesses as we speak.'

Chris didn't react. Didn't give a stuff.

'They'll be looking for me too,' Beth said.

She wondered how far she dared push him. Couldn't imagine what it would be like when Chris and her father came face-to-face. She knew it had to happen, and it would sooner or later. She'd seen them both at their worst, slinging allegations around, testosterone-filled rage that hurt her feelings and kept her awake at night. The two of them in the same room wouldn't be pretty. And when her father learned that *she* had also been there, there would be hell to pay. He'd hit the roof.

Chris finally acquiesced. 'I'll speak to him.'

'Really?'

He nodded. 'Just don't complain when the shit hits the fan.'

'I won't.' Relief flooded through her. 'Thank you.'

He took in a deep breath. 'There's something I need to tell you first.'

His voice was drowned out by thumping music from a car radio at full volume. The vehicle it was coming from circled the empty car park twice. When it reached the far end, the driver did a handbrake turn and came the other way, the headlights like menacing eyes in the darkness. Grabbing her hand, Chris tightened his grip as the vehicle stopped at the gate leading to the field. They didn't need to see inside the car to know who it was or what his cronies were capable of.

The occupants got out, slamming doors that echoed against the mill buildings behind them. Phone torches were illuminated, bright lights moving in their direction like a police SWAT team. Beth stood up and took a step away, wanting to run. Chris got to his feet too, keeping hold of her, pulling her close.

'Oi! A word.' Liam Gardner's voice cut through the silence.

Chris didn't move. His eyes were on the approaching group, one figure a metre or two ahead of the rest. Gardner was backlit by torchlight, a hoody pulled up over his head. It made him seem even more intimidating than he did in the daylight. Fury erupted inside Beth as he came to a halt a few metres in front of them.

'Piss off,' Chris said, undaunted. 'Haven't you caused enough trouble?'

'Meaning what?'

'I think you know, or you wouldn't be here.'

'You saying Elliott was my fault?'

'I'm saying nowt.' Chris took a step forward, a protective left hand guiding Beth to a position behind him, out of immediate danger. 'Get in the car, Beth. It's time you went home. I'll handle this.'

Frozen in fear, she refused to leave.

'I'll be fine,' he said. 'Go! Go on.'

As Chris let go of her, Beth slid her hand inside her coat pocket, feeling for her phone, wishing she'd taken her father's advice and carried a personal attack alarm. He insisted that a loud noise might put an offender off if there was any chance of getting caught. She'd argued that they were sod-all use in the countryside. You could scream your head off and never be heard.

As she made a move towards her car, Gardner stepped into her path deliberately, barring her way. He was so close she could smell fags and alcohol on his breath. They had been this close before once. The memory made her recoil.

Chris squared up to him. 'You into bullying girls now? Leave her out of this.'

'She's staying put.'

'I said let her go. She's not the one you want.'

Gardner turned to his pals. 'He said she's not the one we want.'

They all laughed.

'She's the one I want,' one of them yelled.

'Put your dick away!' Gardner turned back to Chris. 'You wouldn't be setting me up now, would you?' Their foreheads were almost touching. Prize bulls locking horns. ''Cos someone is.'

The sound of police sirens ended the exchange.

'They're playing your song,' Chris said.

'Either of you dob me in to the law for fighting with Elli, you'll be joining him in the morgue, so keep it shut.' Message delivered, Gardner shoved Beth away, got in his vehicle and drove off at speed. She slid her arm around Chris. This wasn't finished yet.

20

Still determined to have another go at getting Matthew Willis to talk, Kate called Hank at the crack of dawn and asked him to head back to Elsdon in the hope of catching their witness before he left for work. She then set off for the station, arriving just in time to see Carmichael emerging from her car, a copy of *The Gallows Tree* in her hand.

While Lisa logged in to her PC, Kate made a strong pot of coffee, poured them both a cup then sat down in the incident room. On the way in, she'd been mulling over her conversation with Grant. It had been unfair to question him last night and she intended to apologize for it. Certain in her own mind that Atkins was failing to disclose knowledge of the Foster family, she required more than corroboration, she needed hard evidence to substantiate her claim. Without it, there was nothing she could do.

With so many ends to tie up before she went on leave, the Atkins issue continued to compete for space in her head among a long list of other jobs. The fact that Lisa and Hank had both picked up on the fact there was a history between Kate and the SIO had her questioning her motive in trying to get him removed from the case. Was she digging because of the bad blood between them or acting for the good of the investigation? Staring at her reflection in the blackened window, she asked herself why she cared when it clearly wasn't her problem. The sooner she could piss off on holiday, the better she'd like it.

Kate's team was hard at work when Atkins finally arrived at eight forty-five, quarter of an hour ahead of the scheduled briefing. When it began, he took the floor like a lead actor on stage, theatrically and full of self-importance, repeating every single scrap of intelligence she'd listed in the report she'd emailed him at midnight, almost word for word. To ensure that nothing got lost in translation, she'd sent a blind copy to every member of her team. Atkins' grandstanding therefore made him look like a total prick.

He'd be furious if he knew.

After fifteen minutes watching him strut up and down like a madman barking orders to a classroom of schoolchildren, Kate caught Carmichael's disinterested eye in a sea of bored faces. In spite of her own concerns over Atkins' ability to lead a murder investigation, Kate tried desperately not to show contempt for the man or undermine his position.

He wasn't making it easy.

She could tell from Carmichael's expression that she had something significant to say. She was nervous of the detective in charge, hesitant about interrupting: uncharacteristic behaviour for a police officer usually brimming with ideas and keen to contribute. Kate used her eyes to point in his direction, urging Carmichael to say her piece and put a stop to his gratuitous tirade, for her own sanity and the benefit of everyone present.

If anyone could, Lisa could.

'Boss?' Carmichael raised her hand. 'I have some important news to share.'

Atkins shot her down. 'I'll let you know when your views are required, DC . . . ?'

'Carmichael.'

'Well, Carmichael, I'll be the one to decide what is and is not important in this case. We'll have your input when I'm done and not before.'

'Yes, sir.'

Blinking away the embarrassment of a public reprimand, Lisa's eyes shifted to Kate, almost an accusation. Like the rest of the squad, Carmichael was dreading the next three weeks under Atkins' command. Guiltily, Kate thought of the suitcase lying on the spare bed at home, still empty, and the early start she'd promised Jo she would make in the morning. Already they had exchanged several texts. Jo had planned a million things to do while they were on vacation. Although desperate for a break, Kate hated the idea that she was leaving her motivated squad in the hands of a moron, someone capable of quashing team spirit, sending morale into a tailspin, splintering the solid team she'd spent years fostering.

Divide and conquer had always been his watchword.

'Now it's your turn.' Atkins was addressing the team collectively, scanning the room expectantly for detectives eager to raise outstanding issues or share intelligence he might be unaware of.

Kate waited for the explosion.

'Well,' he said. 'Is there anything further I should know?'

His jaw dropped as every single hand went up simultaneously, then went down again without anyone volunteering a response. The team were blanking him out, sending him a message that he wouldn't forget in a hurry. Colin Grant was almost beside himself.

'Carmichael?' Atkins' focus fell on Lisa. 'You had something to say?'

'No, sir.' She met his gaze. 'I don't think so.'

Faced with such defiance, the SIO was forced to climb down. He could argue until he was blue in the face with Kate, but without the support of her team he'd be helpless. It was impossible to conduct a murder enquiry on his own – and well he knew it.

Kate's eyes found the floor, a smile flitting across her lips.

Atkins had picked on Carmichael, believing her to be the path of least resistance – the officer he considered more biddable than the rest. He was a mile wrong. Kate raised her head, just as he realized he'd made a bad choice. In order to get the team back on board, Atkins backpedalled swiftly, offering a weak apology to Carmichael.

She made him wait before accepting it. 'The victim's brother Adam Foster is absent without leave,' she eventually said.

'Since when?'

'Since I raised my hand a moment ago.'

'I meant—'

'I know what you meant, sir.' Lisa's smile could melt steel. Under her spell, Atkins mellowed a touch. Satisfied that she had his undivided attention, Carmichael delivered her important news: 'I just got an email from his commanding officer. Adam has been missing four days.'

21

Proud of her team for standing up for themselves, Kate left the office to hook up with Hank in Elsdon. He was coming out of the Bird in the Bush as she drove round the corner at eleven o'clock. Pulling over, she wound the window down. 'Bit early to be drinking, isn't it, even by your standards?' Before he could answer, she closed the window and climbed out of the car.

'Get out of bed the wrong side?' He was grinning.

'Don't feel like I've been to bed, to be honest with you.'

'Well cheer up, you're on leave tomorrow. Are you all packed?'

'No, I'll do it later. I've *so* much to do, I shouldn't really be here.'

'If you'd have gone off on Friday like *normal* people, you wouldn't be—'

'Thanks for stating the obvious.' Kate was smiling. 'I had it in mind to make it easy on you. It seems I made the wrong choice. It won't happen again. I take it there's no news?'

'Of Willis? Nah.' Hank scratched his ear. 'I missed him by minutes.'

'Someone saw him this morning?'

'No. There's smoke coming out of his chimney though, so I know he was there earlier.'

'Unless he's in and not answering the door.'

'You want me to take another look?'

'No, leave it.' Kate swept hair away from her face, tucking it behind her ear. 'What else have you been up to?'

'A lot, considering I'm on light duties.'

'Light ale duties you mean.'

He made a face. 'I was thirsty!'

Kate pointed up the road. 'They serve tea in the village cafe.' She paused, considering. 'Don't suppose you've come across any army personnel on your travels?'

'Retired or serving?'

'Serving.'

'Thought you said this wouldn't involve the military.'

'That was yesterday. Adam Foster went AWOL from his base in Germany four days ago. Atkins is checking ports and airports. No results yet, as far as I know.' Kate glanced up at the smoking chimney on Willis's house.

Hank followed suit.

'What?' he said.

'I'm a miner's daughter, Hank. Chimneys don't smoke unless A, you just lit the fire, or B, you recently added coal. Unless Willis has a coal-fired range, he'd hardly stoke the fire and leave the house, so either he's hiding in there or someone else is. By his own admission he drinks with Adam Foster, a lad who can't go near his grandmother's home with the military police after him. Willis could be harbouring a fugitive. Maybe that's why he wasn't very forthcoming when we interviewed him. If it becomes necessary, I'll get permission to enter.'

'I could give the door a shove.'

'With that shoulder? Don't even think about it. No, Hank, we do this by the book. This is not my case. Atkins will have your warrant card if you bend the rules, no matter what plausible explanation you provide. I know for a fact he won't cover your ass. He'll drop you in it first chance he gets – and enjoy doing it. He's so keen to play the big man, let him deal with it.' She raised her hand to her forehead. 'I'm up to here with him.'

'If you're sure.' Hank's disappointment was short-lived, 'I do have *some* good news.'

'Oh?'

'When I couldn't find Willis, I knocked on a few doors. Met an old soldier who actually witnessed the punch-up. His name is Fred Downes. He claims he saw Elliott sitting with his back to the churchyard wall, minding his own business, as we thought. A car drew up. Some lads jumped out. Wrong 'uns, he called them. There were others there too. At least one lass who seemed to wander into the middle of the argument.'

'What time was this?'

'Just gone six . . . he thinks.'

Kate felt an adrenalin surge. It was the first confirmed sighting and only an hour or so before Elliott died. 'He can't have called it in or Lisa would've said so yesterday.'

'Atkins didn't share it with you last night after the briefing?'

'You're kidding. He wouldn't spit on me if I was on fire. Should he have?'

'Downes gave a statement to the house-to-house team. Maybe Atkins is angling to take all the glory.'

'That won't be hard. It's his case. Anyway,' she winked, 'he already tried that and it backfired with spectacular results.' Kate had a wry smile to herself, prompting Hank to ask what was so funny. 'I'll tell you about it later,' she said. 'C'mon, show me where I can find Mr Downes.'

As they started walking in the direction of Downes' house, Hank gave a mighty sneeze that immediately had him wincing in pain. She didn't pull him about it. Just kept on walking. Kept on worrying, like an anxious mother waiting for a teenager to come home. She'd lost a lot of sleep over allowing him to sign himself fit for duty.

'Did Downes tell you anything else?' she asked.

'Only that he'd seen enough. Heard enough. Apparently, there was more foul language than he'd witnessed on the parade ground in twenty years' military service. I gather he doesn't approve of bad language, in any circumstances, so watch your mouth.'

She punched his arm playfully. 'Like Willis, he left them to it?'

Hank was nodding. 'And went back inside to mind his own business. Says he turned on the TV to block out the noise. Didn't want to get involved. He's a bit upset. He knows Jane Gibson well. I gather they were an item once. He's eighty-four, so it could have been light years ago. They're still great friends. Poor bugger started to cry when he talked about her, feels guilty for not having done something to prevent Elliott getting hurt. I left it there. Told him you'd want to talk to him.'

'Did you ask him to wait in?'

'He's not going anywhere. He's not too good on his pins.

These days, the front door is about as far as he gets. He's vulnerable, Kate. Hardly surprising he's nervous of getting involved.' Hank observed her closely. 'He's also recently bereaved and very frail.' He pointed to a shabby front door. 'This is it.' He knocked loudly.

22

Fred Downes was as infirm as Hank had indicated. Stick thin, but clean-shaven, with shaky hands that were wrinkly and lined with raised blue veins. His hair was streaked with silver where it once had been dark. On the walls of his tiny sitting room he appeared in photographs as a fit young man, strong and proud in his Northumberland Fusiliers regimental uniform. Next to his military snaps were several of his late wife smiling for the camera – a lifetime of happy memories. Condolence cards were everywhere, hung on string like Christmas decorations. Sitting proudly on top of an archaic music system was a portrait of Her Majesty the Queen.

For reasons she couldn't altogether fathom, Kate found that touching.

Having shown the detectives into the house, Fred hobbled to his fireside chair, put down his shepherd's stick, and sat so close to the fire Kate half-expected to smell his clothes burning. He wore a thick grey V-neck jumper, bobbled and frayed at the sleeves, a grubby white shirt with a torn collar and regimental tie beneath. His trousers were several sizes too big, angular bones visible through thinning, shiny material, as if he'd recently lost half his bodyweight.

'Thank you for talking to Detective Sergeant Gormley

earlier and for agreeing to see me.' Kate bent over and shook his hand. In spite of the heat in the room, it was cold to the touch. 'I'm Detective Chief Inspector Kate Daniels, Murder Investigation Team. I understand you've given a statement to the house-to-house team already. I'd like to ask you one or two more questions if I may, then I'll be on my way.'

'Did I say something wrong?' The old man looked bewildered. 'I told the uniformed officers all I know. Did they send you?'

'No, sir, they didn't. I'm here in case you missed anything out.' Kate reassured him with a smile. 'I promise I'll be quick. And if you should receive a third visit from another detective, please don't concern yourself. I'm on leave as of this evening, so that would be perfectly normal. Nothing for you to worry about.'

He relaxed. 'You better sit down.'

Hank remained standing as Kate perched herself on the edge of the sofa, eyes scanning the room. It was clear that Fred Downes was someone for whom coping had become a struggle years ago. The cottage was in need of attention, the furniture scruffy and worn. There was clutter everywhere, the whole lot covered in a thick film of dust. Wherever her eyes landed was the same disordered mess.

The swirly carpet pattern alone was enough to bring on a migraine.

They spent a while talking about the fight across the green, his knowledge of her victim, his conviction that it was definitely Elliott Foster and not someone else he'd seen. As the discussion expanded to others in the group, Fred dropped his head, avoiding eye contact. When eventually he raised his eyes to meet hers, she could see how distressed he was.

'Mr Downes?' She waited. 'Do you have something more to add?'

'Elliott saw me in the doorway and waved.' Wiping a tear from his eye with a scruffy linen handkerchief, the old man recovered his composure. 'That was before the others arrived.' He paused. 'I can't get over it. I've known the lad all his life and his father before him. He was a good lad. Wouldn't hurt a fly. Used to run errands for me from time to time. Why on earth would anyone want to hurt him?'

Kate leaned forward in her seat, elbows on knees. She chose her words carefully. 'Mr Downes, if you could see Elliott, then it stands to reason you got a good look at the others. If you can't identify them by name, descriptions would help a lot. I'm inclined to think they might be local. Can you tell me who it was you saw?'

The old man didn't answer immediately. 'I'm a bit short of the lamp oil these days, pet.' His watery eyes met Kate's. 'I don't know who the others were, I'm sorry.'

'If you need more time—'

'No. I can't help you.'

Kate tried a gentle nudge: 'You saw well enough to know it was Elliott sitting by the churchyard wall.' It was a statement rather than a question. 'I need to identify the others. You want to help your friend Jane Gibson, don't you? I saw her yesterday. As you can imagine, she's completely devastated by the news. To be honest, I'm not sure she'll ever recover, especially if those responsible go unpunished.'

'I know.' Downes was struggling to get the words out. 'I

spoke to her on the telephone this morning. I still can't help you. The only reason I knew for sure it was Elliott is because I often saw him sitting there. He meets his pals there sometimes. As I said, he's a good lad, a quiet lad. Not like some his age. He minds his own business, know what I mean?'

Kate's eyes found the window. What was the old fella not saying? Had he perhaps seen Elliott's best friend, Richard Hedley? He'd still not surfaced and she wondered if he had been among the group. Maybe Fred was being cagey out of loyalty to another young man in the village. She didn't think he was deliberately lying. More likely, he was withholding the truth. She decided not to push him and to end the interview there.

'Thanks for your time,' she told him. 'We'll let ourselves out.'

As soon as they were in the hallway, out of earshot, she whispered, 'So, we're bullying our war veterans now?'

Hank turned, midway through opening the front door, as unhappy as she was at seeing a vulnerable old man suffer.

'He's scared, Hank.'

'You think that's why he's holding out on us?'

'Didn't he strike you as nervous?'

'Of you?' His expression was deadpan. 'Can't think why.'

About to dig him in the ribs, Kate remembered his injury and pulled back at the last minute. As the lock clicked shut behind them, Hank offered the opinion that their witness was just a tired old man who probably couldn't hack another police interrogation. Despite this, Kate couldn't shake off the feeling that Fred Downes was more intimidated than he was letting on.

23

Kate's office door stood ajar, allowing in the sound of the busy incident room beyond: ringing phones, the chatter of many conversations, laughter too. She was so used to it, she found it harder to work in silence than in noise these days. Continuing to observe her team, she leaned back in her chair, pushing away the sad excuse for a snack Hank had insisted on picking up en route from Elsdon.

The watch on her wrist seemed to be moving faster than it ever had before. It was almost one o'clock. For her, time on the Elliott Foster murder enquiry was running out. There were simply not enough hours in this particular day, yet her detective brain wasn't able to switch off or stop sifting the list of names in her head. Picking up her fountain pen, she began to scribble them down, categorizing them as she went:

Family members: Graeme Foster (dad), Gayle Foster (mum), Adam Foster (bro), Jane Gibson (grandmother), ? Gibson (uncle - suicide : why?)
Known associates: Richard Hedley (friend - missing)
Others: Tom Orde (finder), John Dodds (landowner)
Witnesses: Matthew Willis, Paul Dent, Fred Downes

So many names: all of interest to the investigation – and to her – but little or no evidence to class any of them as definite suspects. A harsh tone of voice drew her attention through the door. Atkins was on his feet, raking a hand through his hair, as frustrated as she was with lack of progress in the case. He was having a go at Hank . . . again.

Sick of playing referee, Kate got to her feet, compelled to deflect another unnecessary confrontation before it got out of hand. As she reached the threshold of the MIR, the two men were standing sideways on, eyeballing each other, neither paying her any attention.

'According to your boss, the pathologist needs more time.' Atkins spat the words out as Kate continue to observe him. 'All I want is a straight answer to a perfectly reasonable question. Bloody woman!'

'Kate or Su?' Hank was confused.

'Morrissey – she's a liability.'

'Not according to Stanton.'

'Yeah, what would *he* know?'

'With respect, he's been star witness for the prosecution in more enquiries than you've had hot dinners. Many a case would have collapsed without his input. Ask anyone—'

'He's right.' Kate arrived in the nick of time. Why she bothered to protect Hank from Atkins was something she didn't fully understand. Pound to a penny the two men would resume winding each other up the minute she turned her back and headed north. She locked eyes with Hank, urging him to back off and let Atkins' negativity wash over him.

'Any news on Tom Orde?' It was a question for both of them.

'He's in the clear,' Atkins said as Grant arrived by his side.

Kate threw the DS a smile and then focused her attention on the SIO. 'Can I ask why?'

He flicked his head towards Hank. 'He just heard from Lothian & Borders—'

'*He* means Police Scotland,' Hank said.

'Same difference,' Atkins bit back.

Hank checked his notes, a smirk of satisfaction on his face as he glanced at Kate. 'Orde was seen leaving Melrose on Sunday morning at six thirty-five a.m. His car was spotted exactly twenty minutes later on CCTV in Jedburgh. He must've been flying because he was clocked again in Otterburn at seven seventeen. Eight minutes after that, at twenty-five past seven, he was on the blower to Control saying he'd found Elliott's body at the gibbet.'

'Unless he wasn't driving the car?' Kate said.

Hank was about to say something when Atkins spoke over him. 'You have reason to believe otherwise?'

'I'm merely reflecting on the possibilities,' Kate said. 'If someone else was driving, it would provide him with a convenient alibi.'

'That was my impression initially,' Hank said.

'And now?' she asked.

'Orde stopped to buy petrol and fags in Jedburgh. We have a nice clear image of him doing so. There's no doubt. He was wearing exactly the same clothes he had on when first responders spoke to him later that morning. Take a bow, CCTV.'

Atkins appeared to accept that.

Kate was harder to convince. 'That still doesn't prove he's not our man. We don't know what Elliott was doing from the time he left his grandmother's home until the time of his death. Maybe Orde was the one who stopped to pick him up on the Alwinton Road where he left his bike.'

'Have you forgotten the altercation in Elsdon?' It was a sideswipe from Atkins.

'Not for a second,' Kate said. 'Su Morrissey found a subdural haematoma, the symptoms of which can include mental confusion. Badly injured, the victim would have been in a vulnerable state. What's stopping Orde picking him up on the pretext of offering to help him? Driving him somewhere, killing him, travelling north and then back down in the morning, covering his ass. Geographically, Melrose isn't that far. If he knew that garage was always open – chances are he did – he might have made it his business to smile for the camera.'

'Children!' Hank threw his hands in the air, interrupting the barney that was rapidly developing. 'Much as it pains me to put an end to this – especially when my DCI is winning hands down – I have more to say, if I can get a word in.'

He paused until he had their full attention.

Grant was gripped with the discussion, and so it seemed were the rest of the Murder Investigation Team. Their heads were down but they were earwigging the conversation all the same.

'Go on,' Kate said.

Hank continued. 'Orde's daughter got married at three o'clock on Saturday. The reception was held at a Melrose hotel where he stayed the night. We have photos of him doing the Military Two-Step and witnesses queuing up to testify he was there all evening, if you'd like them interviewed. The father of the bride booked a wake-up call at six a.m. and was seen leaving by the desk clerk. I'd say that's pretty conclusive, wouldn't you? A cast-iron alibi – unless he has an identical twin.'

'Good work!' Kate said. 'Reference him off.'

Hank looked at Atkins.

For once, he nodded his approval.

Kate glanced at him. 'No need to look so self-righteous, I never take things at face value, you should know that. Now we're sure, we can refocus. Is there any news of the Telford's coach Paul Dent talked about?'

'It does exist,' Grant said. 'It's a family firm operating out of Newcastleton. The bad news: they ran more than one coach to Alwinton Show. The good news: only one stopped off at the pub in Elsdon on the return journey. A list of passengers is on my desk, if you'd like—'

'I'll action them later.' Atkins stuffed an A4 sheet of paper in Hank's hand. 'This list takes priority. Chase it up and let me know what gives.'

With Kate peering over his shoulder, Hank studied the list. On it were the known associates of the dead boy, including some the SIO appeared to have conjured up from nowhere. The name Christopher Collins was underlined in red. Kate could see the list was a matter of concern to the receiver, Harry Graham, who'd also been handed a copy. He looked up from his desk, a mixture of anger and resentment on his face.

'Who the hell is Christopher Collins?' he demanded.

'First I've heard of him,' Kate said.

'Me too,' Hank echoed.

All eyes were on Atkins.

'Never mind who he is,' Atkins said. 'I want the scrote found.' Ignoring their collective concern, he turned his attention to Grant. 'Did you call his home?'

'Yes, sir. His mother doesn't know where he is. She claims not to have seen him since he went to bed last night. He was gone when she got up. Actually, she sounded worried. Says it's not like him to take off without popping his head in to let her know, even if he's working an early shift. They're very close, apparently.'

'And was he?' Kate asked.

'Ma'am?'

'Was Collins working an early shift?'

'Not according to his employer.'

'Is that so.' Atkins had a self-satisfied expression on his face as he barked another order. 'Maybe he has something to hide then. Gormley, get on to Area Command. Ask Wilkinson to deploy a team of uniforms to give us a hand picking him up. I'm sick of pissing about, asking nicely. Let's shake things up a bit. Maybe then we'll get some answers. The gentle touch doesn't appear to be working.' It was a swipe at Kate. The man clearly couldn't help himself.

Hank held up the list. 'Before or after I finish this?'

'Now!' Atkins raised his voice, addressing the whole

squad. 'The rest of you, get on with it. We can't afford to hang around. I want you to pull out all the stops on this one.'

Kate bit the inside of her cheek, trying to keep her temper in check. 'Before we do that, could you elaborate on what we know about Collins?'

'I know quite a lot,' Atkins said.

'And we'd like to hear it,' she replied.

'He has form and he's a process operative on a food production line.'

'He works in a slaughterhouse?' A chill ran down Kate's spine. She had visions of strong arms hauling sides of beef onto meat hooks in a refrigerated warehouse.

'As good as,' Atkins said. 'It's low-paid menial work: packing, basic cutting, labelling, shrink-wrapping, that kind of thing. Shift work. Unreliable too. I have it on good authority that he's not averse to the black economy: under-the-counter stuff HMRC never get wind of. He supplements his income by doing odd jobs. Always for cash, including farm work – occasionally using a quad bike – which means he'll also have access to rope.' He ended on that dramatic note. Smug didn't come close to capturing the expression on his face.

The team was stunned into silence, the words 'quad bike' and 'rope' together with 'slaughterhouse' compelling them to listen. Kate was as excited by the development as anyone in the room but deeply suspicious of information Atkins seemed to have plucked from the air. He appeared to be the only one privy to the new intelligence – a state of affairs adding weight to her theory that he had prior knowledge of the dead boy and possibly his friends.

'Hang on,' she said. 'Where did this information come from?'

'Later.' He waved a hand impatiently, dismissing her concerns. 'I'm due at the press office.'

'You're not going to make it public?' She was horrified.

Atkins was livid. 'I'll do as I see fit.'

'You can't! Please, we need to talk about this.'

'You have ten minutes,' he said. 'Then I'm out of here.'

She eyeballed him. 'What I have to say would be better said in private.'

'Here is fine.' He was banking on her discretion, point-blank refusing to leave the room, despite her warning shot. She wouldn't plead with him a second time. To hell with diplomacy: what was needed was a dose of brutal honesty.

'Don't say I didn't warn you,' she said. 'This is a chaotic way to run a murder enquiry. You need to authenticate that information. What do you expect Harry to do with it, reference-wise? A scrap of paper from an SIO just isn't good enough. He needs your source. Every member of the team needs to know where you came by the information, otherwise they're working blind. Things'll get missed. That's what the bloody guidelines are for.'

Atkins made no reply.

It was clear to everyone in the incident room that he had something to hide. Kate wasn't about to let things lie. She wanted a straight answer. Nothing less would do.

'Don't make things difficult for yourself,' she said. 'Tell us where the information came from.' Her mobile rang and he walked away. 'I'm not finished!' She flinched as his office door slammed shut. Hank opened his mouth to say something, then thought better of it and closed it again as she took the call.

'Daniels,' she snapped. 'What did I say about interruptions?'

The line was open but no one spoke. She glanced at the phone in her hand. It was her personal mobile, not her work one. She calmed down, counted to three before continuing.

'Hello?' She listened as the silence stretched between her and the caller on the other end. 'Who is this?'

Nothing.

Hank and the rest of the team were getting curious.

Rolling her eyes at them she spoke bluntly into the handset. 'This is DCI Daniels. Speak or the phone goes down.'

'Inspector, my name is Beth Casey?' It was a young female voice.

'Beth?' Kate was stunned to hear the name. 'Are you in trouble?'

'I'm outside. Can I see you? I know you're busy – I wouldn't ask, but it's dead important.'

Kate walked to the window, parted the vertical blind, scanning the car park below. A pathetic figure, with little on, shivered near the perimeter fence in the pouring rain. From her position the DCI couldn't see a face – and was unable to confirm identification. She was desperate to get out there and talk to the girl.

'Wait there,' she said. 'I'm coming down. Second thoughts, meet me in reception.'

The figure moved towards the station's main entrance and disappeared from view. Kate let go of the blind and hung up. Across the room, Hank's eyes were asking questions, imploring her to share what was going on. Dragging him into the corridor away from the others, she checked that they were alone before speaking, dropping her voice to a whisper, heightening his curiosity further.

'There's a girl downstairs. She wants to talk to me.'

'Girl?'

'Beth Casey.' She nodded towards Atkins' office door. 'Make my apologies. Tell Mr Angry I've been called away urgently. No details.' Raising her right forefinger, she pointed at him. 'And do *not* mention the name to anyone, understood?'

Hank nodded. 'Why?'

'Tell no one – I mean it.'

'Who is she?'

It was her turn to divulge a source. She glanced at the phone still in her hand, then at him. 'She's Atkins' daughter, and I happen to know that she lives in Elsdon.'

It was clear from the intrigue on his face that he was way ahead of her. 'You think she knows something?'

'I'm about to find out. Whatever you do, keep *him* away from the interview suite.'

'That won't be hard. Don't suppose he knows where it is.'

'This is no laughing matter, Hank.'

'I know, I'm sorry. How do you propose I keep him out of the way?'

'Pick a fight with him. It works every time.'

Hank grinned, rubbing his hands together as if this was the best offer he'd had all day. Kate watched him swagger into the incident room, then ran the other way.

24

Kate could feel the agitation through the door as it opened onto reception. Apart from the mascara running down the young woman's face, Beth Casey had hardly changed facially since the last time she'd seen her, over a decade ago. Now as then she was drenched and sobbing into a tissue. A sorrier-looking kid would be hard to find. There was an unmistakable flicker of recognition in her eyes as she looked up, a connection to a past incident they would both rather forget. One thing was clear: for the second time in her life, this woefully unhappy girl needed police intervention.

'Miss? Can I help you?' a civilian clerk called out from reception.

'I'll handle it,' Kate said, turning to Beth. 'You wanted to see me?'

The girl was nervous. 'Is there somewhere private?'

Kate glanced at the clerk. 'Is there an interview room free?'

'Number one needs a clean. I wouldn't go in there. Use four instead.'

'Can you arrange for some tea, please?' The woman nodded politely, although her expression said: *What am I – your skivvy?* Beth had risen to her feet, water dripping everywhere. Kate's eyes shifted to the desk clerk. 'Actually, cancel the tea, I have a better idea.'

Turning away, she punched a number into a security pad and led Beth along a corridor and up a flight of stairs to the women's rest room, somewhere she knew Atkins definitely wouldn't find them. There were a couple of easy chairs in there, washing facilities, dry towels and tea. It wasn't exactly homely, but there was a chance they might have a decent one-to-one conversation. It was better than a clinical, windowless interview room on the floor below, intimidating for those who'd not had the pleasure.

Grabbing a fresh towel, she handed it to Beth. 'Here, use this, before you catch pneumonia.'

While Beth dried her hair as best she could, Kate put on the kettle, dropped a teabag into a mug and waited for the water to boil, thankful that the girl was over seventeen. Had Beth been younger, she would have been legally obliged to find a parent or responsible adult – and that would have been a very different exchange.

When she turned back to the girl, Beth had slumped into a chair. She looked worn out – more sad, Kate guessed, than anxious. Handing her the mug of tea, Kate sat down across from her, offering a smile of encouragement. When Beth didn't return the greeting, the DCI chanced her arm. If Atkins knew the victim – and Kate believed he did – chances were his daughter did too.

'Have you come to talk about your friend, Elliott Foster?' she asked.

Beth immediately misted up. Her reaction was an answer in itself – the only one Kate needed to start a dialogue she hoped would bring her one step closer to finding a killer or killers and putting them away. Elliott's death was a tragedy for his friends and family; from what she'd seen, the entire community was in mourning for a popular young man.

'I'm very sorry for your loss,' Kate said. 'How are you holding up?' It was a daft question. The girl was obviously in bits. The DCI delved further, trying to gauge the strength of her relationship with the victim. 'Were you very close? Your dad never said—'

'Yeah, like he'd know.' The sentence was uttered with venom.

So they did know each other.

'He didn't even tell me who it was until I saw the report on TV. Can you believe that?' Beth's head went down and she began to cry.

Kate found herself defending Atkins – for his daughter's sake, not his. 'Don't be so hard on him, Beth. Maybe the name didn't register. In our job we come across a lot of people. To be fair, it's a long time since he lived up Alwinton way. Several years, isn't it? I'm sure he didn't do it on purpose. He probably has a lot on his mind.'

'Not me, obviously! And since when was *he* ever fair?'

'No, well,' Kate said. 'What can I do for you?'

There was a moment's hesitation before Beth calmed down, apologized for raising her voice and found her resolve.

'I was there,' she said.

A bomb exploded in Kate's head, shrapnel falling all around her. She wasn't sure if she'd misheard – if she was relieved or disappointed – but if Beth proved to be an eyewitness, serious repercussions would follow. Whatever else happened, Atkins could no longer take the role of SIO. And, if he didn't, with the department stretched to the limit, who the hell would?

Misreading Kate's concern, Beth began to panic.

'I was there,' she repeated, 'but not where he was found – I didn't mean that. I was in Elsdon in the early evening. That's what I meant.'

'You witnessed the fight?'

Beth nodded, tears streaming down her face.

This was difficult for both of them. From anyone else, this information would have been welcome. The fact that it had come from a colleague's kid made things extremely difficult for the DCI.

'Why didn't you come forward?'

'I wanted to . . . but I was scared.'

'Of who?'

The girl dropped her head in her hands and began to weep. Kate made the jump to Atkins in a flash. Beth raised her head, ashamed and humiliated by her irresponsibility. Her father was a policeman. She ought to have known better and didn't need Kate to tell her that.

The DCI took in her skinny frame. Beth's blonde, curly hair had frizzled in the rain. It hung damp and straggly around her face. Her tights were soaking wet, as were her skirt and shoes. She was positively shivering.

'Listen, we need to get you dry and then we'll talk properly.' Kate got to her feet. 'I have some spare kit in my car you can use. Wait here a moment and I'll get it.'

'I'm fine.' Beth pulled her coat around her, hanging on to

the familiar like a comfort blanket. 'Is he here, in the station?'

'Your father?' Kate gave a nod and sat down again. 'Don't worry, Beth. I'm sure we can sort this out. He's not going to like it, but I'll break it to him gently. Is that why you wanted to talk to me first, so I could deal with it on your behalf?'

She was nodding. 'I told Mum about Elliott this morning. It broke her heart. She adored him. We both did. When I told her I was there and that I hadn't come forward, she went ballistic. She gave me your number and told me to get in touch.'

'I'm surprised she still has it.'

'I'm not. She carries it in her purse wherever she goes. Mum said you'd given it to her in case she ever needed you. I didn't want to come. She said I had no choice.'

'She's right, Beth.'

'She said you'd know exactly what to do.'

Kate paused. 'You must realize that this is not something I can keep to myself – you being at the scene of the fight, I mean.'

'You can't tell my dad I was there. You can't!'

'He's the Senior Investigating Officer. If I don't tell him, someone else will.'

Beth stood up suddenly, her face set in a scowl. 'I'm going now.'

'Beth, please, sit down.' The girl glared at the DCI, as if by sticking up for him Kate was somehow betraying her. 'You're going to have to trust me, Beth. I'm all you've got. Think about it. You know I can't deal with this behind your father's back. Whether or not you or I like it, he's in charge of this case. Believe me, if there was a way round it, I'd take it. There isn't. You're an adult. If nothing else, he'll have taught you the difference between right and wrong.'

'He's a hypocrite!'

'Either way, you're going to have to front up and face the consequences. As soon as we round up the persons responsible for Elliott's death, your name will come up and then where will you be? You need to tell me exactly what you know. The sooner you do that, the sooner I can help you. I have to be honest, this is about as serious as it gets, for you and your dad.'

'I hate him!'

Her words were like a distant echo.

Kate was suddenly a young DS, standing in a street in torrential rain, a child's hand gripping hers, Detective Sergeant James Atkins' threats ringing in her ears, a terrified woman looking out through the window of the terraced house behind him. The image was so vivid, Kate could almost feel the weight of her sodden clothes, hear the squawk of her police radio asking if she required assistance.

She tried again. 'Are you a leader or a follower, Beth?'

Kate had asked herself the very same question all those years ago as Atkins tried to intimidate her, begging her to cover up his detestable behaviour. She didn't feel comfortable speaking to his daughter without his knowledge.

Still, this was no time to share that thought.

'I understand you not wanting to lose face in front of your dad or your friends, but if you cared for Elliott, you must see we need to catch whoever did this to him. These people are extremely dangerous. If they get away with it, they might do it again.'

'He'll kill me!' It came out in a whisper of confusion. Beth dropped her head in her hands and sucked in a breath. Kate felt for her. She was about to tell her that she was over-reacting, that her father loved her very much, even if he didn't always show it, when the girl began to cry. 'I can't . . . I . . . he's . . . so angry.'

'If it's any consolation,' Kate said. 'He's angry with me too.'

The uneasy expression on Beth's face lifted as she looked up.

For a split second, the DCI wondered if they were talking about her dad or someone else. She hesitated, not wanting to push her too far, too soon, for fear she'd lose her trust. Urging her to reconsider, Kate was relieved when Beth retook her seat, her childish outburst in check. Resigned to her fate, the girl began to speak freely. She was getting into her stride when the door flew open at the most inopportune moment, startling her.

Kate swung round to face the officer who'd wandered in. Resisting the urge to scream at her to get out, she said brightly, 'Jill, can you give us a minute, please?'

Realizing she'd walked in on something delicate, the officer apologized for the interruption. 'You want me to put an "Out of Order" sign on the door?' she asked.

'If you would.' Kate thanked her. 'By the way, anyone asks, you never saw me.'

Nodding her understanding, the officer backed away, leaving them to it.

Beth waited until the door closed behind her. 'My dad will hate that you're seeing me, won't he?'

Kate nodded. Honesty was being asked for. It was the least the girl deserved in return. 'We can't help that, though, can we? It's really him we should be talking to.'

'I can't talk to him about what I want for breakfast,' Beth said. 'What chance do I stand discussing something as terrible as this? Do you have kids, Inspector?'

'No. And you can call me Kate.'

'Want any?'

'No.' Kate thought twice about admitting that, but it was a truthful answer. She'd given up that option in pursuit of her career, creating a rift with her own father as a result. *Another one.* Why he wanted grandchildren when he couldn't stand the sight of his own daughter was one of life's mysteries. Some people were fickle. 'Why d'you ask?'

'Detectives make shit parents,' Beth said. 'Shit everything, in fact. No offence. It's because you're married to your jobs, Mum said.'

Kate couldn't argue with that. She'd made a mess of her own relationship for sure. 'How is your mum?' she asked, changing the subject. 'I've not seen her for ages.'

'She's dying.'

Kate was shocked at her bluntness.

'Cancer,' she said. 'Terminal.'

'Oh, Beth, I'm so sorry. I know how tough that is. I lost my mother to cancer too.'

'Yeah, it's pants. I don't want to talk about it. I'm sick of talking about it. It's the only conversation I've had for months. Everyone's so concerned about how *she* feels. They forget I have feelings too. Can we get this over with? I'll give a statement and then I'd like to go.'

'Of course, but if you ever need a chat, confidentially, the two of us, I'm a good listener. You have my number. Ring me, day or night.'

'Thank you.'

'You ready to start?'

Beth nodded.

Taking her phone from her pocket, Kate accessed the voice memos app and pressed record. She had a feeling they would be there a while.

25

Kate taped the interview so she could write it up later, reassuring Beth that she wasn't under arrest, and that any statement she gave was on a voluntary basis. She advised the girl to take it slow, starting with Elliott, her own attendance at Alwinton Show and what went on afterwards, giving as much detail as she could remember.

Beth nodded, bloodshot eyes on Kate. 'I've known Elliott my whole life. We always go to the show together. He was so excited about the wrestling this year. He was convinced he'd win and planned to treat his grandma with his winnings. It's her birthday soon. That's the kind of lad he was. Always thinking of others.'

'One of my officers suggested that someone might have relieved him of his cash, a mugging. Do you think that's possible?'

'No, I'm sure it wasn't that.'

'We didn't find his winnings on him.'

'I'd check with his grandma.'

'Thanks, I will,' Kate said. 'Go on.'

'A few of us arranged to meet up afterwards. Some went on ahead. I dropped a friend in Morpeth and then drove to Elsdon where I was meeting Chris—'

'Chris Collins?'

Beth couldn't hide her surprise even though she tried to. 'I told him you'd find out he was there. I begged him to come forward before you came looking.'

'Because he was a witness?'

Beth swallowed hard, her colour rising. 'Chris and Elliott were scrapping when I arrived, egged on by a crowd of others. I ran over and asked what was going on. Chris was all sweaty and out of breath. He said it was nothing. Just a bit of fun. It didn't look like it to me. I asked Elliott the same question. He told me to ask Gardner—'

'Gardner?'

'Liam Gardner.'

'Is he also a friend?'

'No! I hate him. So does— so did Elliott. I told them all they should know better and begged them to calm down. Gardner was winding them up, shouting at his cronies to rip Elliott's jeans off so they could see if he was still wearing tights underneath like a girl. That's the kind of wanker mentality he has.'

Kate leaned forward, nudging her gently. 'And what was Chris doing?'

'Nothing. He doesn't like Gardner any more than I do. There was another scuffle. Chris wasn't involved this time, just Gardner and his lot. They were laughing at Elliott. I shouted at them to stop. They wouldn't. Gardner told his mates to hold him down while he took a photo. When they did, he put the boot in several times . . .' Beth wiped a tear from her eye. 'He didn't hold back either. It was horrible.'

'I can imagine.' Kate paused, giving her time to compose herself. 'Did Gardner actually take a photo?'

'Yes.'

'Was Elliott conscious at this point?'

'Just about. He managed to stagger to his feet, but he looked weird, like he was dazed or something. He lunged at Chris. I don't think he was seeing straight. Chris yelled at him to get off. There was blood all over his shirt. Elliott hung on. He was incapable of standing up.'

'He was using Chris as a prop?'

Beth nodded. 'Chris pushed him away and he fell backwards onto the grass.' She blew hard into a fresh tissue, visibly distressed. 'He got up and Gardner shoved him down again. He hit his head on the wall. I heard a crack. It was horrible. There was loads of blood. Gardner and his mates ran off laughing, got in their cars and drove off.'

'And Collins?' Kate asked. 'What did he do?'

'He grabbed me by the hand and we ran too. I don't know why. I begged him to call an ambulance and stay with Elliott 'til it arrived, but there was an old man watching from across the village green. Chris said he knew Elliott and would call for help. He didn't want to get involved, so we legged it like the other cowards. I'm sorry . . .'

'Beth, this is really important. When you left, what was Elliott doing?'

'Sitting on the ground, dazed and covered in blood.'

'Conscious though, yes?'

'Yes.'

'Where did you go afterwards?'

'I dropped Chris at home in Otterburn. Drove to my

dad's and went straight to bed. I was exhausted and upset. I wanted to be on my own.'

Beth had a guilty expression on her face. She knew she should have hung around and made sure her friend received medical attention. Kate suspected she'd live with that on her conscience for the rest of her life.

Beth held her gaze. 'It would be best if Chris talks to you, wouldn't it?'

'Yes, it would. Do you know where he is? We're having difficulty locating him. He's not at home or at work.'

'You won't find him.' The statement was out of her mouth before she realized what it might sound like to a police officer.

Kate looked at her pointedly. 'I will if you tell me where he is.'

'He didn't do anything!'

'Then he has nothing to fear.' A gap opened up between them. It crossed Kate's mind that Beth might be scared of grassing up Collins, that there might be consequences if she did. 'He needs to hand himself in, Beth. Your father is organizing a search for him as we speak.'

'What? That's not necessary.'

'He seems to think it is. You said yourself we wouldn't find him. That sounds very much like he's gone into hiding. People don't do that if they're blameless.' Kate studied the girl as she protested her friend's innocence. Beth was torn in two, wanting to stick up for Collins and quaking at the thought of the manhunt her father had instigated. 'We're also trying to trace Richard Hedley. Was he at the show on Saturday?'

Beth shook her head. 'If he was, I never saw him.'

'And afterwards, at the scene of the fight?'

'No.'

'Are you sure? Elliott's grandma seemed to think that's was who he was meeting.'

'I wouldn't know.' Beth holding back.

'You've had no contact with Richard since the weekend?'

'No . . . I remember now: he couldn't make the show. I think he had stuff to do elsewhere.'

Convenient. 'Any idea what?'

'No, sorry.'

'Out of the area, or locally?'

Beth shrugged. She was hiding something.

'Might Chris know?' Kate asked.

'I doubt it.'

'They don't get on?'

'Don't put words in my mouth.' The girl's teeth began to chatter. She was shivering in her wet clothes. 'I'm sorry. I'm upset, that's all. I haven't got a clue where Richard is, but I can persuade Chris to come in of his own free will.'

'I can't let you do that,' Kate said.

'Why not?'

'He might lose his rag if he knows you've spoken to us.'

'He won't. We're good mates. He's not like that.'

'We'll go together then.'

'No. He's scared. We both are. Give me an hour and I'll bring him in to talk to you. I'm leaving anyway.' Beth stood up, suddenly full of bravado. 'What are you going to do, arrest me? I came here because my mum said I could trust you. She said you'd help me. Now I'm offering to help you. Trust is a two-way street. Are we on or not?'

Giving the matter some thought, Kate checked her watch. It was gone two thirty. The next briefing wasn't scheduled until five. Atkins was probably busy getting his notes together. And without Beth's help, Kate was certain she wasn't going to find Collins any time soon. 'Your dad could be in a meeting, I suppose.'

'Thank you.'

Beth didn't quite raise a smile but seemed satisfied, buoyed by the chance to bring Collins in voluntarily. Kate gave her two hours, telling her in no uncertain terms that if he didn't show, the matter would be out of her hands and firmly in DCI Atkins'.

26

Kate returned to the incident room with every intention of having it out with Atkins, but he was nowhere to be found. When he failed to materialize, she asked around and was told he'd nipped out for a late lunch – somewhere local, she guessed, as she'd checked his office and found his overcoat hanging on the door peg.

Pulling her mobile from her pocket, she called his number. It immediately switched to voicemail. She left a message: 'I have important news you need to hear,' she said. 'It's urgent. Call me.'

Hank caught her eye from across the room, a worried expression on his face. Holding an imaginary cup in the air, he waggled his hand from side to side, asking if she fancied a coffee. Nodding, she pointed at her office door, invited him to join her. He arrived moments later, two steaming mugs in his hand.

'How did it go with Beth?' He set the coffee down, loosened his tie and made himself comfortable. 'You look stressed to death. Am I to take it she has information about Elliott's murder?' Absolutely nothing got past him, let alone fazed him. For as long as she'd known him, Hank had always been a step ahead of the game, there for her whenever the going got tough. She was lucky to have such support.

'I want you to listen to this.' She pressed a button on her phone – the recording of her conversation with Beth – and set it to play on the desk between them. They listened to the audio clip together, then called Carmichael into the office. Taking her into their confidence, Kate gave her instructions to gather any information available on Christopher Collins and Liam Gardner.

'Who's Gardner?' Carmichael asked.

'One of a group of lads taunting Elliott Foster within hours of his death,' Kate said. 'We find him and I reckon we'll find the others, so act quickly. Lisa, please don't mention Beth Casey to anyone else until I've had a chance to speak to her father. Hopefully by then she'll have returned with Collins in tow and Atkins will be semi-grateful.'

Hank's eyes held a warning. 'Makes you think Collins will play ball?'

'Beth seemed fairly confident she could talk him into it. Claims he's done nothing to feel bad about.'

Carmichael wasn't persuaded. 'So why's he hiding?'

'I asked her the very same question,' Kate said. 'I have to hope that he'll cooperate. I'm not sure Beth is that confident. She said they're close, but there's something she's not telling me. What other choice did I have but to trust her? She wasn't going to volunteer the information. You should've seen her face when she found out her dad was after him. She was petrified.'

'He'll go apeshit when he finds out she was there,' Hank said. 'He'll like it even less that she confided in you and not him. Doesn't sound like they're in a caring, sharing relationship, does it? Put it this way, I wouldn't like to be in her shoes right now.' He grimaced. 'Or yours for that matter, boss.'

Kate shifted uncomfortably in her seat. 'I'll cross that bridge when I come to it.'

'Atkins is an oddball,' Carmichael said. 'He gives me the creeps.'

'Makes you say that?' The hair on Kate's head stood up like soldiers, a memory stirring deep within. She hid her anxiety well – at least she hoped she did.

'We were talking earlier,' Carmichael said. 'One minute he was giving me a shedload of stuff to do, the next he charged out of the building like it was on fire. No explanation. No long goodbye. To be honest, he looked like he'd seen a bloody ghost.'

A shiver ran down Kate's spine, an awful thought occurring. 'How long ago was this?'

Carmichael screwed up her face. 'Ten, fifteen minutes.'

'Where were you at the time?' Kate asked.

'In the guv'nor's office – does it matter?'

'Shit! Tell me he wasn't near the window—'

Lisa grinned at Hank. 'Watch her, she's psychic.'

'This is serious, Lisa.' Kate felt her stomach heave. 'I let Beth out of the rear door so Atkins wouldn't see her from his office. It never occurred to me he'd be using Naylor's. He must've seen her go. I don't even know where she was heading. She refused to say. Said she could handle it.' Kate put her hands on her head. 'What a monumental fuck-up.'

Hank and Lisa were nonplussed.

'Jesus!' Kate palmed her brow. 'I have to find her.'

'Boss, calm down,' Hank said. 'Assuming Atkins has the

nous to put two and two together and come up with four, what's he going to do? He'll be angry with her, of course. So would I in his position – I'd be giving our Ryan a talking to – but he'll get over it, eventually.'

'With all due respect, you're not Atkins.' Kate tried hard not to panic, to keep things in perspective. She knew stuff about the SIO that the others weren't aware of. No matter how hard she tried to put a positive spin on it, the fallout from her meeting with Beth Casey would dominate her last day in the office. The idea of leaving the lass in such difficult circumstances while she swanned off on holiday with Jo was inconceivable.

27

Beth turned off the main road into the Boe Rigg campsite. Chris's blue one-man tent was pitched on high ground within sight of the car park, the flap pinned open so he could see her coming. From this distance, it was impossible to gauge what mood he was in, although he did wave.

Always a good sign.

Parking on the gravelled area beneath the camping field, Beth got out of her car and locked it. She climbed the steep hill, past a kiddies' play area, arriving at his tent out of breath and anxious. He had a fire going and offered her a can of Coke from his haversack. She shook her head, telling him she didn't want one, and slumped down on the ground, thoroughly miserable and exhausted. Since her trip to the cop shop, she hadn't been home to change. Even her under-wear was still damp.

'You told your dad, didn't you?' Chris's tone was scathing. The hate in his eyes frightened her. 'You told him after I begged you not to. What's going on, Beth? You got someone better lined up, someone Daddy approves of? It would be a damned sight easier for all concerned if I disappeared per-manently, wouldn't it?'

'Don't be daft! Why would you say such a thing?'

He eyed her coldly. 'What did you tell him? I want to know.'

Beth reached out to touch him. Tried telling him how much he meant to her. He pulled away, said something spiteful. He was very angry. Understandably. She'd gone against his wishes. But then he hadn't listened to a word she'd said. She had to find a way of getting through to him. Her first real boyfriend, Chris was by no means perfect. He'd lose his temper one minute and show compassion the next, especially where her mum was concerned. Unfortunately, that part of him was currently nowhere to be seen.

'I asked you a question,' he yelled.

'I didn't tell him anything, Chris. I swear!' Under the intensity of his gaze, Beth was finding it hard not to avert her eyes. She decided to level with him and get her meeting with Kate Daniels out in the open. 'I've spoken to someone else, someone I trust who I know can help.'

'What? Who? Who have you fucking told?'

'Don't swear at me! You know I don't like it.'

'Pity for you.'

He threw an empty fag packet on the fire. They both watched it shrivel and burn. Chris's face was set in a scowl. When he looked at her, there was no understanding of what it was like to be the child of a copper, having to watch your Ps and Qs, never allowed to let the side down. Beth hated it.

'Where have you been? You said you'd be here hours ago. I've been waiting all day in the pissing rain.'

'Oh, it's all about you, isn't it?' Beth snapped. 'You're a selfish git sometimes. I went to see my mum. She had a bad night. Thanks for asking.'

'Don't lie to me—'

'I'm not! Where else would I be? I told you last night I was going. Not my problem if you weren't taking any notice. Anyway, I don't need your permission. I'm not your property.'

He clearly didn't believe she'd been to see her mum.

They had drawn the attention of a family in the next tent. Beth was lost in the memory of their last argument and steeling herself for more to come. On that occasion, he'd accused her of being unfaithful. He was an insecure loser sometimes, not the canny lad he made out when others were around. She was beginning to think that all men were the same.

He would never control her. No man would.

'I'm sorry,' he said, after what seemed like an age. 'I didn't mean to upset you—'

'Didn't you? That's what you said last time.'

Shamefaced, he pulled her close, rubbing her upper arm. This time, it was Beth who pulled away. She was angry, nowhere near ready to make friends. If he continued to behave like a prick, she couldn't see the relationship lasting. His mum and her dad were dead against it and, frankly, Beth didn't want to work that hard.

'I said I'm sorry!' He grabbed her hand. 'Beth, c'mon, I know I can be a twat sometimes, but only because I'm scared of losing you.' He smiled, the old Chris returning. Dropping his head on one side, he gave her big eyes, like a lovesick puppy begging for forgiveness.

'The police aren't the only ones you're scared of, are they?' she said.

'What? You reckon I can't handle Gardner,' he scoffed. 'Think again.'

'I know you stood up to him, but he'll be back. You know it and so do I. What did he mean when he said you were setting him up?'

'He's talking bollocks, like always. Trust me, I've met plenty of guys like him. You can't believe a word he says.'

'I do trust you, but it goes both ways. You have to learn to trust me too.'

'C'mon.' He pulled her closer. 'Don't let's argue. And don't let that wanker get to you either. You're safe with me.'

'Do you trust me? Because, sometimes, it doesn't feel like it.'

Chris put his hand on his heart, forcing her to smile. He reached towards her for a kiss, the light leaving his eyes as the focus of his attention switched to something he'd seen over her shoulder. The sudden change in attitude scared her. He pulled away. 'You lying cow! You said you hadn't talked to him.'

Beth recoiled. 'I haven't!'

'Oh no?'

Beth turned around, her eyes seizing on her father who was fast approaching up the steep incline from the car park, another detective a few metres ahead of him. Shoving her to the ground, Chris grabbed his stuff and ran.

28

Kate glanced nervously at her watch. It was almost five. She'd been searching every place she could think of: Atkins' home, Beth's mother's house, the hospital where Diane Casey was a patient, to no avail. Although she'd been there earlier, Beth was nowhere to be found. The couple of hours she'd asked for to bring Collins in had long since expired. She wasn't answering her mobile and Atkins hadn't re-appeared.

In desperation, Kate rang him again. As before, she got his message service. 'It's Daniels again. We need to talk. Please call me.'

'He's due to hold the briefing soon.' Hank said, as she put the phone down.

'*If* he turns up . . . He didn't last night. Doesn't seem to matter that he's the SIO.'

'Better get your stab-proof vest on, just in case.'

'Don't joke.' The phone rang in her hand.

'Is it him?'

Kate nodded, lifting the phone to her ear. 'Finally!' she said. 'Where the hell have you been? We need to talk urgently.'

'Never mind where I've been.' He sounded pissed off. 'Where are you?'

'In my office.'

'Stay put!' he barked.

'Before you go, I want you to know—'

The line was cut.

Kate's eyes found Hank's. 'The bastard hung up on me.'

Before he had a chance to reply, the door behind him burst open and Atkins appeared, as angry as Kate had ever seen him. Knowing what he was capable of, this made her uneasy. Seeing her wariness, Hank swivelled his seat round to face the door, anticipating trouble.

'Out!' Atkins barked. 'And close the door behind you.'

Hank glanced at Kate.

She nodded that he should leave.

He didn't hurry to get to his feet. Eventually he made the door. Behind Atkins' back, he mouthed: *I'll be right outside.* Kate didn't need telling that he planned to earwig the conversation, to be on hand if things turned nasty.

As the door clicked shut, Atkins stood there, eyeing her in a state of high agitation. She managed not to flinch as he made a sudden move towards her, lifted the landline from its cradle and dumped it on her desk, ensuring that they wouldn't be disturbed.

'I want Beth kept out of this,' he said.

'You know that's not possible. She's a material witness.'

'I don't give a shit. You will not associate my name or hers with shite. Beth has enough on her plate—'

'With respect, that doesn't change things.'

'She's my daughter!'

'Same goes. I assume you've had words.'

'Since when did my family become your business?'

Kate thought of a slick answer but kept it to herself. She tried to stay calm, hoping that if she did, he might. *He might.* She invited him to sit but he remained standing, towering over her.

'If you're worried that Beth's attendance at the scene will reflect on you personally,' Kate said, 'I can assure you it won't. We had a good long talk, Beth and I. If she's telling the truth – and I have no reason to suspect otherwise – her only involvement on Saturday night was as peacemaker. She's a sensible girl. She tried to stop the fight. She wasn't part of it. Even so, you're going to have to pull the plug on this one. You know the victim and at least one eyewitness. You're far too close to lead this investigation.'

'Stay out of this, Daniels. I'm warning you—'

'It would be so much better if it came from you. Naylor is a reasonable man, I don't think—'

'I don't give a fat rat's arse what you think!'

'I'm giving you the chance to come clean. If you don't, I'll do it for you.'

He glowered at her.

'For God's sake, man! Just once in your life, try listening to reason. Beth should have come forward, of course she should, but she witnessed a fight, not a murder. She claims the IP was injured and fully conscious when she left Elsdon on Saturday with Collins. She thought, wrongly as it turned out, that someone else was calling an ambulance. She didn't know Elliott had died until she saw it on *your* computer and later on TV.'

He seemed to take that in. He closed his eyes, pinching

the bridge of his nose, clearly under pressure. 'Silly bitch! She should have said something – to me.'

'Give her a break. She's young and scared. So she legged it. You're her dad and a policeman. You're not the easiest person to get along with. It's hardly surprising she finds you unapproachable, is it? And before you start yelling at me again, that wasn't a dig. If you don't engage with her, you'll lose her.'

Before he could reply, the mobile on Kate's desk beeped. She glanced at the phone. An incoming text from Jo:

I'm in the incident room. Last-minute admin if you can get away. I was thinking pre-holiday drink. X

Ignoring the message, Kate kept her concentration on Atkins, hoping to get through without him losing his temper again. Not a hope in hell, she thought, as he exploded. She half expected him to vault the desk and lamp her one. His angry outburst went on for several minutes . . .

'So, are we clear?' He pointed his finger rudely. 'This is not your concern. If you think for one minute I'm going to stand by and let my daughter be dragged down by the likes of Chris Collins, you're sadly mistaken.'

'She's used to it. I'm sure she'll survive.'

'You want me to beg? Is that it?'

'Did I say that?' Kate's mobile beeped again.

He barked at her to switch it off.

Jo again:

One more sleep!!! ☺

When a third text arrived, Atkins' yelling got louder. 'I asked you to switch that damned thing off.'

'No,' she said. 'You demanded that I switch it off. There's a difference. And therein lies your problem. You'd get a lot more cooperation if you weren't so bloody difficult to work with.' She picked up the device and read the text to make her point, then slung it on the desk. 'Collins handed himself in. I'll handle it.'

'Over my dead body.' He was almost smirking. 'This conversation isn't over, so don't go anywhere.' He left the room, slamming the door behind him, Hank appearing in his place a second later. Kate's last day had just got a whole lot worse.

29

The prisoner was waiting patiently in the interview room when Atkins arrived, DS Grant keeping him company. The SIO pulled out a chair and sat down directly opposite Collins. Switching on the tape recorder, he got straight down to business. 'The time is five o-five p.m. on Monday, 13 October 2014. We are in interview room one at Morpeth police station. I'm Detective Chief Inspector James Atkins, Northumbria Police. Also present is Detective Sergeant Colin Grant.' He eyeballed Collins. 'Please state your name.'

Collins sat there, chewing the skin around his fingernails. Didn't answer.

He was a handsome lad with deep-set eyes and a strong jawline. It was obvious he'd slept in his clothes. They were creased, wet and muddy in places, where he'd slithered around in the field at Boe Rigg campsite, DS Grant in hot pursuit. A fine runner he was too – like a whippet. The young detective had no chance keeping up and had finally lost him in the thick of a forest.

'I asked you to state your name,' Atkins snapped.

'What for?' Collins said, boldly. 'You know who I am.'

'I need a verbal response for the tape.' Atkins hated this kid with a passion, couldn't bear the thought of him anywhere near his daughter. 'Answer the question. I need your full name.'

'Christopher Collins. My friends call me Chris.'

Atkins nodded to Grant, his cue to administer the caution.

'You do not have to say anything . . .' Grant began.

'Hey!' Collins sat up straight, almost off his chair. 'What's with the caution? I handed myself in.'

'Your voluntary attendance is noted,' Atkins said. 'Surprising though it was, given that you ran away from us earlier. DS Grant, carry on.'

Grant started again. 'Mr Collins, you do not have to say anything, but it may harm your defence if you do not mention, when questioned, something which you later rely on in court. Anything you do say may be given in evidence. Do you understand?'

'I'm not stupid.'

'You have declined to have a solicitor present,' Atkins said. 'Is that correct?'

'Why would I need one? I've done nowt wrong.'

'That is yet to be determined.'

'Get on with it then. I haven't got all day.'

Atkins mocked him, leaving him in no doubt that he'd be the judge of that. He had every intention of keeping him in the station and away from his daughter for as long as humanly possible. He'd teach the toerag a lesson he'd never forget. 'You appreciate that you're here in view of a serious incident that occurred on the evening of Saturday, 11 October 2014?'

'I had nothing to do with that.'

'You deny being in Elsdon village on that date?'

'No, I was there. I meant the other thing, the stuff that was on TV.'

'You mean his murder.'

Collins gave a nod.

'I see. Well, I'll come to that in due course. For the moment, I'm more interested in what went on earlier that evening. A reliable source has indicated that you were involved in a fight in Elsdon village after the Alwinton show.'

'I didn't start it.'

'Did I accuse you?'

'No.' Collins sat on his hands, a ploy to keep them still, his boldness melting away. 'I'm just saying, I wasn't the instigator.'

'You were there though, weren't you, arguing with Elliott Foster?'

'Yes.'

'If you didn't start the fight, who did?'

'Not me, I swear. That was someone else. Ask Beth if you don't believe me.'

The reference to his daughter wasn't entirely unexpected. Even so, Atkins felt the blood drain from his face. Daniels was right. It was madness to think that Beth's name wouldn't come up in the course of the enquiry. The SIO could feel Grant's eyes boring into him, urging him to develop the interview based on Collins' response, specifically this Beth girl he'd never heard of until a moment ago.

Atkins took a moment to consider his options. A damage-limitation exercise was called for. Before he could react, there was a sharp knock at the door.

The handle turned and Hank entered the room like he meant business.

Immediately on his guard, Atkins wondered if he and Daniels had been watching the interview, such as it was, without his knowledge from another room. He spoke for the tape: 'Detective Sergeant Hank Gormley has entered the room.' Their eyes met. 'This had better be good.'

'It might not be good. It's certainly urgent. Detective Chief Superintendent Bright is in the building, sir. He wants to see you.'

'Now?'

'I'm afraid so.' Hank turned his attention to Collins, apologizing to the lad for the interruption, telling him he'd be taken to a holding cell until the interview could reconvene.

'You can't be serious,' Atkins said. 'I'm mid-interview.'

'Not any more.' Hank's expression was unreadable but there was no mistaking the derision in his voice.

Atkins curled his fist into a ball. Gormley was enjoying himself. As Daniels' second-in-command, his loyalty was to her. His job was to make her life easier. Atkins intended to do the opposite. As soon as she was out of his hair, he'd show Gormley the error of his ways and knock some respect into him. He'd be begging for mercy in no time.

'Please convey my apologies to the head of CID. Let him know that I'm conducting an important interview in connection with a major incident and that I'll be with him as soon as I'm done.'

Hank stood his ground. 'The Detective Chief Superintendent is well aware of that. He was quite clear that you should terminate the interview forthwith. He said to tell you that he's waiting in my guv'nor's office and is expecting you to join him right away.'

Atkins' jaw bunched. He was rising to his feet when Kate walked in. She leaned across the table, announcing her arrival for the tape and for Collins' benefit. Shooting her a hacky look, Atkins told Collins he'd be back and then barged past her out of the door, disappearing into the corridor beyond.

Detective Chief Superintendent Bright was waiting in Naylor's office. The most senior detective in the force struck a formidable figure behind a substantial desk that was facing the door. He didn't look up and Atkins didn't quite know where to put himself. He knew he was in trouble and waited for the dressing down.

'Sir, you wanted to see me?'

Now Bright looked up. 'Have you completely lost your senses, Atkins?'

'Guv?' Atkins stood firm, feet slightly apart, meeting his boss's eyes across the desk. Try as he might to keep his emotions in check, he was powerless to stop the heavy rise and fall of his chest due to the anxiety he was feeling. 'I was interviewing a suspect, sir. I asked DS Gormley to advise you of that. He seemed to think it couldn't wait.'

'It couldn't.' Bright sat back in his chair, arms folded, all powerful. 'In case it passed you by, you're conducting a high-profile murder investigation. You have the eyes and ears of the local and national press upon you and yet I have it on good authority that you have a conflict of interest that could jeopardize a conviction if not disclosed. I don't need to tell you what the CPS will think of that.'

'Guv, it's—'

'It's basis procedure. That's what it is. What the hell were you thinking?'

'Daniels had no right to go over my head.'

'*Daniels* has a rank. Use it!'

'My apologies, I meant DCI Daniels.'

'For your information, Kate Daniels is the best murder detective on this force, handpicked by me. You'd do well to remember that. She *had* to come to me. If she hadn't, I'd have had something to say about it.'

'I can explain—'

'I'm delighted to hear it. And while you're doing so, perhaps you'd like to enlighten me on another matter.'

'Sir?'

'Don't play the innocent with me. You began work two days earlier than instructed. Who gave you the authority?'

Atkins hesitated, suddenly wary.

'Well?'

'I was keen to make a good impression, guv. That's all.'

'So you took it upon yourself to cancel your leave?' Bright played the smiling assassin well. 'Why don't I believe you?'

'You should, guv. I've waited more years than most for the opportunity to run a murder investigation—'

'And we both know why, don't we?' Atkins felt the hairs on his neck stand up as Bright carried on. He was not a man to mess with or interrupt mid-flow. 'I was scraping the barrel bringing you in to replace DCI Daniels. You weren't required until *after* she went on leave. I signed the request myself, adding a handwritten note to that effect.'

'I'm sorry, I didn't see it.'

'You're a liar!'

'No, guv, I promise you. There was no ulterior motive. MIT is the department with more kudos than any other. I just wanted to get my feet under the desk and get to know the squad, I swear.'

'Bollocks. If I give an order, I expect it to be followed. You're back on normal duties.'

'Guv?'

'You heard me.'

'Will you hear me out?'

'I did.' Bright wasn't finished. 'Go near that case again and you'll be spending the rest of your days in Sunderland wearing stripes and a funny blue hat – which is where you are probably best suited. Is that clear enough for you?'

'Guv, that's unfair. It was never my intention to put the case in jeopardy—'

'So why did you?' Bright held up a hand to silence him before he could say another word. 'Don't waste your breath, Atkins. You are no longer part of the Murder Investigation Team. You're out. DCI Daniels is in. That's all I have to say on the matter. You can go.'

Atkins held his position. 'She's going on leave, guv.'

'*She* is going nowhere until I say so. You could learn a lot from her. Policing is and always has been her number one priority. She'll understand when I tell her I cancelled her leave. Know why? Because she's a professional, that's why. Unlike you.'

Bright closed the file in front of him and stuffed it in his briefcase, signalling the end of the conversation. Atkins didn't move. He didn't know what to do or say to make him change his mind. He couldn't bear to walk away with his career in tatters and let Daniels get one over on him. He had to persuade the guv'nor to let him continue . . .

But how?

Bright lifted his eyes but not his head, ending the impasse. 'I've made my decision. You can leave. You'd be wise to do so while you still have a job.'

Atkins almost choked. 'Guv, you can't do that!'

'OK, you're suspended. Now get out of my sight.'

Bright yelled so loudly Hank Gormley stuck his head around the door to see if the head of CID required assistance. Feeling stupid, Atkins turned on his heel and left the room. Daniels had gone too far this time. He'd make sure she paid for it.

30

Collins decided he wanted a solicitor after all. Kate put him in a holding cell to await his arrival, then headed off to conduct the evening briefing. Moving swiftly along the corridor, she almost collided with Atkins at the top of the stairwell. Blue in the face with rage, he attempted to bar her way. Sidestepping him, she walked on. She'd just made it to the incident room when his booming voice caught up with her, reaching every detective present.

'You conniving *dyke*!'

Meltdown.

Kate came to an abrupt halt with her back to him. It was like a missile detonation in the room: a big explosion, then nothing but white noise. Feeling a sudden rush of blood to her ears, she stood still, aware of a dozen pairs of eyes turning in her direction. She couldn't believe what she'd heard. Had Atkins really said that out loud, in front of her squad?

Oh God!

Jo was sitting at a desk in the centre of the room, her mouth stuck in the shape of the letter O. For a split second their eyes met, then Kate looked away. Hank was already on his feet, directly in front of her, having started the briefing on her behalf. For a moment, she thought he would march over to Atkins, smack him in the mouth and make him take it back. She was tempted to do the same thing, but what good would it do?

What had been said could never be unsaid.

Kate didn't know what to do. Atkins had persecuted her for years, but this was a new low, even for him. It surprised her only that he hadn't acted sooner to bring her down. No matter which way she handled the situation, he wasn't about to morph into a decent human being on her account, much less apologize. His eyes on her back weighed her down. He'd be expecting a reaction, proud of himself for getting one over on her, payback for stuff that happened years ago. His words pushed their way into her head. 'When I decide to come for you, Daniels, you won't know what hit you.'

Well, he wasn't wrong about that.

Outed to her team in the worst way possible felt like a gut-wrenching body blow. Kate had always known that her relationship with Jo was bound to catch up with her eventually. Atkins was big mates with a former ACC who'd left the force under a cloud, vowing to dish the dirt on her for doing her job and exposing him as the liar he was.

They deserved each other.

Up to this point that dirt hadn't reached her. Now it had, it was certain to stick. Slowly, Kate turned her focus on Atkins, everything and everyone else fading from view.

'It's rude to call someone conniving,' she said.

A chuckle began in one corner of the room and quickly spread to the other. Atkins wasn't fooled by her show of courage. It didn't put him off his stride for a second. He was laughing out loud, knowing she was in bits, dying little by little right before his eyes. And still he continued to taunt her . . .

'I notice you didn't deny it,' he said.

'Who I sleep with is *my* business.' Kate glared at the man who was singularly responsible for her current predicament. The reason she'd hidden her true self from her colleagues. She wouldn't put up with his bullshit ever again. Even so, he'd got to her – he knew it, and so did everyone in the incident room. He scanned the squad triumphantly, his eyes coming to rest on each and every one of her colleagues in turn.

'I'd say your boss has some explaining to do, wouldn't you? I can see how shocked you are to discover her *big* secret.' He laughed. 'Northumbria's finest fucks women. Who knew?'

'Shut your mouth!' Carmichael said. 'And for your information, we all knew. We're a gay-friendly lot, so take your homophobia and shove it up your arse. You're a disgrace to your rank. There's not a detective here who will work with you ever again.'

'Hear, hear,' DC Brown said.

'You need retraining, pal.'

The squad began to laugh out loud. Coming from Maxwell, the office misogynist, the comment was ace.

The only one not laughing was Hank. His fists were clenched into balls of pent-up aggression, an expression of unadulterated loathing on his face. He'd fell Atkins in a second if Kate didn't act to calm things down.

She knew what he was thinking. She half expected him to apologize on Atkins' behalf . . . on behalf of homophobes the world over. Touched by his support, and that of the rest of her team, she swallowed down the sob in her throat, damned if she'd show her emotions to an outcast like Atkins.

'Bright suspended me,' he said. 'Happy now?'

'Are *you*?' Kate said coolly. 'I did what I had to do.'

Unwilling to stand a public slanging match, Jo discreetly gathered up her papers and walked. Kate would have liked to walk too, but she stood her ground, eyeing her tormentor.

'You weren't prepared to withdraw of your own volition,' she said. 'You left me no choice but to have you removed. Think yourself lucky you'll be on full pay. He's threatening to cancel my leave. I rather fancied a few weeks off.'

'Hard luck. Going away with *her*, were you?' He pointed to the door Jo had just walked through.

'That's my business!' Kate said. 'Now get the hell out of my incident room.'

Of all the times she'd imagined sharing her private life with her team – and there had been many – this was the worst-case scenario. They had her back. That's the way they were. It felt like a betrayal not to have told them years ago. How could she have been so stupid?

How would she explain?

Atkins walked away, slamming the door behind him. You could have heard a pin drop in the silence that followed. Before anyone could speak, there was the sound of a scuffle and a clatter in the corridor beyond. No words were exchanged. Then the door opened and Bright came in, shaking his right fist, asking for ice.

Hank high-fived him and a cheer went up.

Bright dropped his voice as he approached Kate. 'Are you OK?'

'Yes, guv.' This was hard for her. Painful even.

He winked. 'He says another word out of place, I want to hear about it.'

'That's not necessary, guv.'

'It wasn't a request.'

'Understood.'

Kate felt her heart break just a little more. His unconditional support meant more to her than he would ever know. She turned away, keyed a number on her mobile and lifted the phone to her ear.

'Beth, your father's on his way home and he's not in a very good mood. If I were you, I'd make myself scarce.' Ending the call, she swung round to face the team – in control once more. 'Hmm,' she said. 'That went well.'

31

How she'd managed to struggle through the briefing was a mystery. Some progress had been made via a report from Forensics. The front tyre on Elliott's bike was badly punctured. It provided an innocent explanation for him leaving it unattended in a field. Other news was less positive. His brother Adam was still AWOL. No one had reported any missing rope and his best friend Hedley still hadn't surfaced. These issues had all come up in the course of the meeting and fought hard for space inside her head. They had no chance against the echo of Atkins' revelation. Kate couldn't remember the last time she'd *needed* a drink – she did now.

The Office public house was a Grade II listed early nineteenth-century former tollhouse beside the town's Telford Bridge. Ordering a Famous Grouse – no ice – Kate handed over cash to pay for it and made her way to a table near an open window, a welcome breeze providing respite from the clawing atmosphere of the incident room.

The slug of whisky had hardly settled in her stomach when the door opened and Hank walked in. Meeting his eyes over the top of the glass, she felt guilty, as if she'd run away in order to avoid the questions she could tell were on the tip of his tongue when she dismissed the squad. Like her, he'd seethed his way through the briefing, preoccupied, unable to concentrate properly on the task in hand. He was looking at her like she'd killed someone.

'What?' she said as he approached her table.

'Can I sit down?'

'Feel free.'

'Kate . . .' He stalled.

'Hey! Don't hold back. Spit it out. Everyone else has.'

He remained standing, his expression sympathetic. When he spoke his tone was soft, understanding, but all she heard was an accusation. 'I did tell you,' he said. 'But you wouldn't listen.'

'When I need your advice—'

'I know, you'll ask for it,' he said quietly. 'I came to see if I could help, not for a punch-up.'

'I don't need a shoulder to cry on, Hank.'

'So you're OK?'

'Do I look it?'

'Kate, don't do this to yourself. It was bound to come out eventually. Anyway, who gives a shit? I don't and neither does your crew. They're behind you, 100 per cent. You heard Carmichael. I could've kissed her in there. Maxwell too, come to think of it – on the lips.'

Kate laughed . . . then almost cried.

Placing her glass down on the table, she kept her focus on the floor. This was the very reason she'd come to the pub alone. She knew if he showed her any compassion, said anything nice or funny, she'd end up bawling and she wouldn't be able to stop. She couldn't cope with sympathy.

Disapproval was much easier to take. Why did he always have to be so bloody nice?

'You want a drink or are you just going to stand there?' She flicked her eyes towards the bar. 'The barman is watching us. He thinks we're having a lover's tiff. How absurd is that?'

Hank grinned. 'I won't tell if you don't.'

'Talk like that got me into this mess in the first place. Sit.'

A wide grin spread over Hank's face. He ordered a pint of John Smith's. It arrived before he'd taken his coat off and pulled up a chair. He took a third of it down in one long pull, wiping excess froth from his upper lip with the back of his hairy hand. He studied her as she sank her whisky, replacing the glass on the table.

She didn't speak.

He felt the need to. 'You're not brooding over Atkins, are you? The guy's a fucking moron.'

'Yes, an angry one with an axe to grind,' Kate said. 'In my experience, they're the worse kind. He's been biding his time, holding me responsible for stuff that happened years ago.'

'What stuff?'

'Never mind. Suffice to say it's a very long time to hold a grudge.'

'He doesn't deserve a second thought, much less your protection.' He was alluding to the fact that she'd kept her counsel on what had caused the rift. He chuckled. 'I cannot believe what he called you.'

'I've had worse.'

'I know,' he joked, 'though, not to your face. Way I see it, he may well have done you a big favour—'

'Mind telling me how?' Kate dropped her voice to a whisper. 'I want to be known for my ability as a detective, not defined by my sexual preference, Hank. Not thought of as odd, a dyke in need of a good shag to sort me out. I've told you before, I'd be scratching a living as a PC if I'd come out when I joined the force. I've seen good women passed over because they prefer the company of their own kind. We can take the jokes, the downright homophobia, we just can't fight it when it comes to promotion – and, believe me, it's even worse for men. Does that sound fair to you?'

'No it doesn't. But attitudes are changing—'

'Not quick enough.'

'So what is it you have on him?'

She knew the question was coming and lifted her empty glass. It wasn't unprecedented for her to have a second alcoholic drink while she was still on duty but it was rare. She didn't care. Hank switched his focus to the bar and made a hand gesture with two fingers, letting the barman know they both required a refill. The lad acknowledged the order with a nod of his head.

'He'll bring them over.' Hank told her. 'You were saying?'

'Er, no, I wasn't.'

'Look, what happened in the incident room stays in the incident room. I get that. But I deserve the build-up. I was traumatized in there. Think of it as therapy.'

Humour didn't work.

Kate checked her watch, a distraction tactic. 'It's gone seven. I'd better get going.'

'I'll find out eventually. C'mon, save me the trouble of digging.'

She looked up. She knew he wouldn't stop until she told him. 'This goes no further, understood?'

'Do you even need to ask?'

'I'm sorry.' Kate took a long deep breath. She didn't plan on telling him everything, just enough to stop him asking around. She wanted an end to the Atkins saga, once and for all. 'Years ago, I was in the sticks when a call came over the radio. Domestic disturbance. Screams heard. Child on the phone. It was an emergency. I was literally round the corner so I said I'd deal. Control gave me the heads-up that the address was the home of a copper, but not who. When I got there, a kid opened the door, a girl, six or seven years old. It was two o'clock in the morning.'

'Beth, I presume.'

Kate nodded. 'Pretty thing she was. I'll never forget the look in her eyes. She was terrified. There was yelling from the house. She hid behind me on the doorstep in her PJs. When she stopped sobbing, she told me her dad had pushed her mummy down the stairs and hurt her.'

'Like I said, the guy's a moron.'

Kate didn't argue.

'Did you question his missus?'

'For what good it did.' Kate paused. 'Diane Casey – or Atkins as she was then – couldn't look me in the eye. She admitted there had been a row. Agreed that it had become heated. She claimed to have been partly responsible. She'd had a drink, tripped and fallen. Her daughter heard the noise, got scared and dialled 999 without her knowledge, having mistaken the situation. You know the drill. When I asked if she was sure about that, Atkins went berserk. He grabbed Beth and shoved me out of the house, yelling at me not to put words in Diane's mouth. Ordered me to stay the hell out of their business.'

'Maybe she did fall.' Hank was playing devil's advocate.

'Yeah, and maybe I'll be chief one day. They were still yelling when I got there. You've seen what a bully he is. He's incapable of controlling his temper. Any female on the force will tell you that.' Kate stopped there. Disclosing more was not only unwise, it was fraught with danger – Hank would never let it lie.

He drained his pint as fresh drinks arrived. They thanked the barman and he moved away. The pub was getting busy.

Hank urged her to continue.

'Beth ran out of the house and took hold of me. She wouldn't let go. He screamed at her to get inside. Tried telling me it was all a false alarm, leaning on me to take no further action, warning me what would happen if I did. We were the same rank, but he was well in with the brass, threatening to shaft me good and proper.'

'Did you take further action?'

'I had to in case the lunatic killed her. I had good cause to think he might. I'd had dealings with him before. I logged it as I saw it: perceived domestic dispute, uncorroborated by his missus. He was spoken to and transferred to some obscure job in community relations. He didn't go any further in rank for a very long time. It took him years to recover.'

'And he blames you for it.'

'Exactly so. When I was promoted before him, he had a go at me. When I made DCI, it was the last straw. He couldn't handle it. He's taken a pop at me at every opportunity since, more times than I care to remember.'

Kate could see him filling in the blanks, realizing why their paths had never crossed operationally. He didn't know that she had something else on Atkins she could've used that night to verify her claim, ramming home the view that he was out of control. Evidence that Atkins was aware of. In the end, she didn't need it.

'I wish you'd said.'

'What, get my big brother on him? Yeah, that would work.' She smiled. 'I'm a grown-up, Hank. I can fight my own battles.'

'Did his wife hang around?'

'For a while, not long. A year later, I bumped into her in town. She was sporting a black eye, Christmas present. Atkins got drunk and lost it, unable to keep his hands to himself. Let's say we had a conversation. She was at her wits' end. Told me she was leaving him and begged me to help. She wasn't interested in rocking the boat, having him arrested and charged. She just wanted the hell out of there.'

'It must've been difficult for you, professionally.'

'It wasn't easy. Because I'd logged the domestic, Atkins' friends at HQ were forced to act. There were too many domestic violence incidents in our area without their own staff adding to it. Almost a hundred a day. Can you believe that?'

'Sounds like Diane wasn't helping herself either.'

'The daft cow was her own worst enemy. One minute she was screaming for assistance, the next telling me she loved him, warts 'n' all. I never knew where I was with her. She believed his bullshit about seeking help too. Every time he said he was sorry, she unpacked her bag and stuck around. It was Beth I felt for.'

'It can't have been a pleasant environment to grow up in.'

'No. She was young and vulnerable. I remember her fear the first time I saw her. It was there again yesterday, that same haunted look. I wouldn't care, but Diane told me she idolized her father as a kid.'

'You two have a lot in common.'

'And we both deserve better.'

Her words were heavy with regret.

'Did you intervene?' Hank asked. 'With Atkins, I mean.'

Kate nodded. 'I threatened to lock him up. Encouraged her to leave him and go into a refuge. She fled the house and her marriage in the middle of the night when he was on lates.'

'Taking Beth with her.' Hank gave her a sideways glance. 'And of course you had nothing to do with that.' He was being facetious.

'I did what I had to do.'

'No wonder he vents his anger on you though, is it?'

'She was a child in danger!'

'Yeah, but couldn't you find a friendly social worker to do it for you? Anonymous tip-offs not in your repertoire then?'

The dig hurt. 'That sounds a lot like I deserve the shit he's throwing my way.' *You have no idea.*

'I'm not saying that—'

'Aren't you? I acted for the sake of his kid, Hank. You'd have done the same in my shoes.'

211

'Probably. But there are ways and there are ways.'

'I know that now. Maybe I didn't think it through. Diane needed my help. I gave it willingly. I didn't have time to contemplate my navel. She was desperate.'

Kate's mobile beeped.

She took it from her pocket and checked the display. 'It's Bright,' she said. 'There goes my holiday.'

'Kate, you need your leave.'

'You can say that again. If you remember, it was *his* idea that I go in the first place.'

'Can't he find a replacement?'

'He wasn't confident. I need to call him.'

'Do it,' Hank said.

Kate made the call and then hung up, shaking her head. When she told him the outcome, he tried not to gloat. He'd never wanted her to go on leave. If it had been anyone but Jo she'd been going away with, he'd have begged her to stay.

'You made the right call,' he said.

'I didn't make the call. He did.'

'Well, you can hardly bugger off on holiday with this hanging over your head, can you?'

'Try telling Jo that.'

'She'll understand. You're going to have to meet this crisis head on, otherwise it'll look like you scurried away, rather than deal with it. That includes telling Jo.'

Kate glanced at her phone. That was one conversation she was dreading. Even worse than having the exchange was *not* having it. Either way, it would have to wait. She had something more important to do first.

32

Kate spat into the basin and raised her head. Now she'd freshened up, she didn't feel so bad. Dropping the tooth-paste tube and toothbrush into her wash bag, she glanced at her reflection in the mirror.

Same old Kate . . .

Labels didn't change people . . .

Ignorance and bigotry did.

So why did she feel so guilty for not telling her team?

The driving force behind her decision was her belief that she'd never fulfil her potential as a police officer if she came out. She had good reason for thinking so. Less cautious officers had faced a lot of opposition from above. Even their more liberal colleagues gave them a hard time over it. Those who'd tried being open had a tough job convincing people that they were like everyone else, that their sleeping arrangements made no difference to their investigative abil-ity. Kate had witnessed animosity many times. Sadly, Atkins wasn't a one-off.

Hank was already in the incident room when she arrived, an expression on his face that lifted her spirits. He had news, he told her. She couldn't wait to hear it.

'You were right about Adam Foster. I finally got a call from Matt Willis.'

'He's been hiding him?'

'No. But Adam's in the area, shacked up with a girlfriend and their kid. He made contact with Willis after reading about his brother in the *Evening Chronicle*. He's upset, naturally. Willis pointed him in our direction. Foster wants to talk to you in the morning. Then he plans to hand himself over to the military police.'

'What time?'

'Seven.'

Kate pulled a face. 'Here or in Elsdon?'

'Here. I could send him to yours if you prefer. I'll ask him to bring his bugle and play reveille through your bedroom window, make sure you don't sleep in.'

Laughing, she turned her head as a door slammed shut on the cell block. The custody sergeant was heading their way, boots squeaking as he moved along the corridor, keys jangling from his belt. Prisoners were shouting, banging on doors on either side of him, each with their own agenda.

'Hey, Sarge!' a male voice yelled. 'You been in touch with my lass yet?'

A female prisoner was begging a smoke from the custody sergeant as he passed her cell, offering a free blowjob in return. Another guest was making out he had pains in the chest and needed a doctor urgently. It was an excuse they had all heard a hundred times before, guaranteed to get you seen first. No copper wanted a stiff on their watch.

Remembering her own stint in the custody suite, Kate exchanged a wry smile with the sergeant, asking to be let in to Collins' cell. She followed the officer down the corridor, waited to one side as he unlocked the cell door and pulled it open.

Thanking him, she moved over the threshold. Her prisoner was lying on the bed. She gestured for him to stand.

'About time.' Collins swung his legs over the side of the bed. 'It's like a madhouse in here – and it stinks. Not that you care. The tea was like piss and I wouldn't feed *that* to the dog.' He was pointing at the untouched, curled-up cheese sandwich on a paper plate on the floor.

'I'm not interested in your opinion of our hospitality, Mr Collins. Have you had sufficient time to consult the duty solicitor?'

He nodded.

'Out you come then.'

They walked down the corridor to an interview room where the solicitor was waiting. Paul Bennett stood up as they entered. He was middle aged, wearing well, an experienced brief who wouldn't give her any hassle. She felt grateful for that after the day she'd put in. They shook hands and he returned to his seat. Placing Collins' police record on the table between them, Kate sat down opposite.

Hank switched on the recording device. 'I'm DS Hank Gormley.' He checked his watch. 'The time is eight fifteen p.m., the date Monday, 13 October 2014.'

Kate introduced herself for the benefit of the tape.

Collins' solicitor followed suit.

Hank repeated the caution and then Kate took over.

'Mr Collins, you understand that we are investigating a

very serious incident that took place at Winter's Gibbet at some time on Saturday night.'

'Yes.'

'Good. I've been informed that you had contact with the deceased, Elliott Foster, in the village of Elsdon that evening. I'd like you to tell me, in your own words, your recollection of events from the moment the two of you met. There's no rush, so take your time.'

Collins glanced at Bennett.

The brief nodded that he should comply.

Collins yawned. 'Sorry, I'm knackered. You get no kip in here.'

'Tell us why you were in Elsdon and how you came to be with Elliott,' Kate said.

'We met by chance,' Collins continued. 'I was waiting for someone who'd been to the show.'

'Someone?' Hank stopped making notes. 'We need specifics.'

'Beth Casey. I was waiting for Beth.'

'Go on.'

'She'd given a mate a lift and was running late. I was keeping an eye out for her car when I noticed Elliott being dropped off by his mum on the corner of the village green.'

Kate didn't react. That was news to her. Surely DS Grant had asked the woman when she'd last seen her son alive. Making a mental note to question him on it, she sought to clarify the details with Collins. He could have been mistaken.

'Are you absolutely sure it was his mum?'

He nodded. 'She waved at me as he got out of the car.'

'You've met before?'

Another nod.

'What time was this?'

Collins shrugged. 'Sixish.'

'Did you speak to Elliott?'

'I asked him how he'd got on in the wrestling. He told me he'd won. Said I should've gone along. It was a laugh.'

'Where were you exactly?'

'At home, watching TV.'

'I meant when you spoke to Elliott.'

'Outside the church.'

'At the scene of the fight or somewhere else?'

'Where the scrap took place.' Collins picked nervously at dry skin on his lower lip. He looked shattered and scruffy and worried enough to make her wonder why. Maybe he wasn't as innocent as Beth Casey had suggested earlier. Misreading her silence, he filled the gap.

'For the record, the fight wasn't my fault.'

'I'll come on to that,' she said. 'Why didn't you go to the show?'

Collins smirked. 'I'm too much of a city boy to join the Waltons.'

'I take it you're not into country pursuits.'

'Nah. My mum moved to Otterburn to work as a receptionist in a hotel. She needed the money. I had no choice but to come with her. She does funny shifts and couldn't get there in time on public transport. I couldn't let her come up here on her own, could I? Anyway, I didn't have enough cash on me to go to the pub with Elliott.'

Hank lifted his pen. 'Is that where he was off to?'

'That's what he said. I told him I was meeting Beth. I asked if he'd seen her.'

'And had he?' Kate asked.

'Not since midday,' Collins said. 'He said he'd been hanging out with mates before and after the wrestling.'

Kate knew that was true. She'd seen Elliott with a load of lads herself. 'Go on.'

'A car came round the corner. I knew it was trouble when I saw who it was.'

'Liam Gardner, I presume?'

Collins nodded uneasily.

'What happened next?'

'He jumped out of the car and started winding me up.'

'In what way?'

'He told me to watch my back. Said that Elliott had been putting the bite on my lass, or words to that effect. He was talking bollocks, as usual.'

'Your lass?'

'Beth . . . Casey.'

We're good mates.

Kate wondered why Beth hadn't told her that her relationship with Collins was more than a friendship. She could tell by looking at the lad that Atkins wouldn't approve. Probably the reason she'd kept it to herself – and who could blame her?

'What Gardner said has two connotations,' Kate said. 'What did you think he meant by that?'

'Eh?' Collins had lost the thread of the conversation.

'By "putting the bite on Beth" did he mean money or sex?'

'What do *you* think?'

'The DCI is asking you,' Hank said. 'She'd like an answer.'

Collins bristled, biting down so hard on his teeth it made his jaw rigid. It was clear he didn't like being told what to do. Eventually, he felt compelled to fill in the detail. 'He was suggesting Elliott was giving her one.'

'And was he?' Hank asked.

'She says not.'

'You don't sound too convinced, son.' Hank was trying to get him to open up and show his true personality. Collins wasn't stupid. Nor was he playing ball. Hank tried again. 'You've obviously talked to her about it. Are we to conclude that you thought there was some truth in it then?'

Collins sidestepped the question. 'Gardner is full of shit. He's always making things up.'

'Such as?' Kate asked.

'All sorts of stuff.'

'What things does he make up?'

'He claims he used to play in a band. He's a black belt at Judo. That he's—' He didn't finish the sentence.

'That he's what?' Kate wanted to know.

'A fucking celebrity. Shouldn't you be asking him?'

'We intend to,' Hank said.

Collins glared at him. ''Spose you'll tell him where the information came from too.'

'If it suits our purposes,' Hank said. 'On the other hand – apart from running from DS Grant earlier today – you appear to be cooperating. It might be possible to keep your helpful comments between the four of us for the time being.

Whatever you were about to add just now must've been important if you thought better of it.'

Collins made no reply.

'We get the picture,' Kate said, taking over. 'Would it be fair to say that Liam Gardner is a fantasist?'

'That's exactly what he is.'

'Sounds like you don't believe half the stuff he tells you.'

'No one does, even his arsewipe mates.'

'So you were fairly confident that Elliott Foster didn't have a thing for Beth?' Kate watched him carefully. He wasn't too sure about that one. She let him stew a while. 'OK, I can see you're not going to answer that one. How did Elliott react to the allegation?'

'He denied it. He's not daft.'

'He's not anything now, is he?'

Collins eyed the floor. 'He told me to take no notice. That they'd been mates forever, like I didn't know.' He seemed to drift away a moment, his expression darkening. 'She talks about him constantly. Elliott this, Elliott that. I told her they should get a room.'

'Did Elliott say anything else?'

'Nah. Just begged me to believe him. Said Gardner was only causing trouble, as usual.'

Kate sat forward, resting her elbows on the table, pressing on to the fight itself while she had the momentum. 'I don't want to put words into your mouth, but I've been in this job a long time and I have an imagination. I take it Gardner didn't like being called a liar. Is that when it all kicked off?'

'You could say that.'

'What did he do?'

'He started shoving Elliott.'

Kate looked down at the file on the table. 'I heard it was you who was doing the shoving?'

'What?' Collins' eyes flitted between the two detectives. 'Who told you that?'

The DCI let the allegation float in the air between them. This lad was nervous. Even so, his story matched Beth's.

So far.

'I did push him, but it wasn't me who started it, I swear.'

'Were you two fighting or not?' Hank asked.

Collins remained silent.

Kate raised an eyebrow to his brief.

'This is a serious matter,' Bennett said. 'Tell the DCI what happened. If what you told me is correct, Christopher, you have nothing to hide.'

Collins' focus switched to Kate. 'We were having words, that's all. Gardner was pissing himself, making out that Elliott was screwing my lass. When she arrived, she told us all to cut it out. She was upset. Who wouldn't be?'

'And did you cut it out?'

'Yeah man, we were cool.'

'Not the way Beth described it.'

'What? It was Gardner! He's a fucking psycho. He lashed out with his feet, split Elliott's lip wide open, I think he broke his nose. It was pouring with blood.' Collins was picking his face again, making it red. 'Elliott got up. He lurched towards me. He put blood on my kit and I shoved him off. Gardner smacked him again. Elliott went down like a bag of hammers. Gardner ran off with his lot, got in his car and drove off. I grabbed Beth and legged it too.'

Kate exchanged the briefest glance with Hank. The story about the blood covered the lad forensically. It was a plausible explanation should they find trace evidence on his clothing. Was he a clever liar, she wondered.

'Have you seen Gardner since?' Hank was asking.

'Once. He said if anyone talked to the law, they'd get the same.'

'He actually said that?'

'Yeah. That's why I didn't come forward when Beth asked me to.'

'That's not strictly true though, is it?' Kate studied him. Opening the file on the table in front of her, she made a meal of scanning the front page, taking her time, putting her prisoner under pressure. 'You have convictions for violence yourself, I see—'

'Look at the date,' Collins said. 'It was years ago.'

'Nevertheless, you've been inside. Twice. Does Beth know?'

'Depends if her old man's told her or not. He probably has, even though in the eyes of the law I'm rehabilitated. That'll be why she's not answering my calls. Can I go now? I need to get in touch with her, let her know I handed myself in. She begged me to. Not that it'll make any difference. Atkins will never let her see me again.'

'She's an adult. She can see who she wants,' Kate said. 'Be honest, Mr Collins. The reason you didn't come forward was because you wanted to hide your past from Beth, not because Gardner threatened you. Isn't that the case?'

Collins didn't answer.

Kate crossed her arms, leaned back in her seat, waiting. 'Question too hard for you?'

'He did threaten us,' Collins insisted. 'Like I said, he's mental.'

'Let's leave it there, shall we?' Kate stood up. 'You're free to go, but don't leave the area because I'll need to talk to you again.' The jury was out on Christopher Collins.

33

'There are a few things I'm not happy about,' Kate said to Hank as they made their way upstairs to the incident room. 'If he thought Beth was two-timing him, Collins has motive. He wasn't exactly seething but he *was* sulking.' She hesitated at the entrance to the incident room. 'Did you notice that jealous streak? He obviously doesn't trust Beth any further than he can throw her.'

'He didn't hide it well, did he?' Hank pushed open the door.

Kate stopped dead, checking her watch. It was gone nine and not one of her team had left for the evening. Their solidarity made her well up inside. She had to fight to keep her emotions under control. As their mentor, she couldn't afford to show weakness. It took Hank a second to recognize that she was struggling. He stepped up, taking the focus off her, something he'd done for years. He'd never know how grateful she was.

'Collins has been bailed,' he said. 'But he's still in the mix. What he told us in interview is fully supported by Beth Casey, unless they put their heads together and got their story straight before he came in. Somehow, I doubt it. They both claim that Liam Gardner was the instigator of the fight. I'm inclined to believe that he's the one we need to speak to.'

'I agree,' Kate said. 'Andy, Lisa, armed with everything we know about him, first thing in the morning go and bring him in. He's top priority until I say otherwise. Be careful. According to Collins, he's a nasty piece of work. Reckons he's into martial arts, so watch yourselves.'

Carmichael smiled at DC Andy Brown, pleased to be doing some real police work that didn't involve a computer keyboard.

'You seen his rap sheet, boss?' Maxwell said.

'No. He has form?'

'He does indeed. He's twenty-two years old, going on fifteen. Spent his short life in and out of care and prison. He has a string of convictions going back to his early teens, increasing in seriousness, including animal cruelty, inflicting unnecessary suffering. Dog fighting is his thing. Apparently, he'd bet on two flies climbing up a wall.' Maxwell's face went red as he realized he was sitting next to Robbo, who'd been fighting his own gambling addiction for a long time. He hadn't meant any offence and none was taken.

Kate moved on. 'Any suggestion Gardner uses any kind of weaponry?'

'A couple of vicious dogs,' Maxwell replied. 'Although I've been told he doesn't need any. He's built like a brick shithouse, according to Area Command.'

'Hank, I'm taking no chances. I'd like you to oversee the operation. Just be around when Lisa and Andy give Gardner an early wake-up call. Make sure we have enough troops to lock him up if he puts up a fight or makes a run for it. Get in touch with the Dog Section. He'll probably be on their radar. Tell them you need backup in case he sets his dogs on you.'

Hank made a frightened face.

Kate shivered.

The last time they had faced an angry dog, the animal had had to be destroyed. Not its fault. It had been bred and trained to attack. Under other circumstances, it might have led a long and happy life. Unwilling to indulge that thought, she turned her attention to the team. 'We've been led to believe that Elliott Foster's mother dropped him off in Elsdon on Saturday evening. How didn't I know that? Find Grant and get him in here—'

'I'm here, boss. Is there a problem?'

She hadn't noticed anyone entering the room, and turned to the voice.

Grant was on his feet. The door was still swinging shut behind him. 'Collins told us Elliott's mother saw him shortly before the fight, just hours before he died. You interviewed her. How come I had to hear that from a witness?'

Grant's reaction was immediate, his expression resolute. 'That's not my understanding. I specifically asked her when she last saw him. She told me it was three weeks ago. The statement is on your desk. I'm sorry, boss. I feel I've let you down.'

'People lie. Don't worry about it.'

'Told you I didn't like her.'

'Well, now you have a chance to redeem yourself. Give her a call. I want her in here first thing tomorrow. Don't tell her why and take no excuses. She has information we need urgently. Don't let her persuade you otherwise. Nothing she is doing is more important than talking to us. That's it. Go home, all of you, and get some rest. We've a busy day coming up.'

'I'm going to work on.' Carmichael was looking at Kate. 'I've got stuff to finish off, so if you need me, I'll be here.'

Andy's face dropped. It was obvious he had something else in mind.

Hank looked at his protégé. 'Lisa, don't stay too late. If we're on a dawn raid I need you at your best.'

Satisfied, Kate walked towards her office, leaving them packing away their stuff. As she reached for the door handle, she hesitated, and turned to face the squad. 'Guys, one more thing . . .' She waited for their attention. 'I don't intend to discuss it – we've got more important things to do – but thanks for your support today. By the way, my leave has been cancelled so you're stuck with me. Let's keep going. We need a result.'

Kate sat down at her desk to make a call. The number she dialled rang out for what seemed like ages. Glancing at her watch, she panicked, wondering if Jane Gibson had already gone to bed. Just as she was about to ring off, the old lady answered with a croaky voice that was hardly audible.

She didn't sound well.

'It's DCI Daniels, Jane. I didn't wake you, did I?'

'No, Inspector, don't concern yourself. I rarely sleep. Is there news?'

'I'm afraid not – and I'm so sorry to disturb you at such a late hour. Shan't keep you long.' Kate didn't want to involve her at all and failed to mention that her daughter had openly lied to Grant, concealing the fact that she'd seen Elliott on the night he died. It was unnecessary to add salt to a raw and gaping wound.

Kate felt the silence stretch out between them. She needed the answer to a question that only Jane could provide. If there were any other way of obtaining it, Kate would have taken it. There wasn't. 'Is now a convenient time?'

'My Alfie used to say there's no time like the present.'

Kate wondered if she was talking about her late husband or the son who'd committed suicide in the woods. They shared the same name. She didn't ask. 'My dad always said never put off till tomorrow what you can do today. Different words. Same sentiment.'

'What can I do for you?' Jane said.

Kate pictured her in a floral nightie, an audio book on the CD player, the opportunity to inhabit someone else's world for a time and leave behind another miserable chapter of her long life. 'We've been unable to find Elliott's winnings and I was wondering if he left them with you for safekeeping.'

'He did,' Jane said without a moment's hesitation. 'Apart from the ten pounds he took out with him.'

Not a robbery then – unless whoever attacked him expected it to be on his person.

'Do you want it back?' the boy's grandma asked.

'No, I just needed to know if the money was missing.' Kate was about to thank her and hang up when she had second thoughts. 'Jane, do you know Beth Casey?'

'Yes, dear.'

'I gather they were very close.'

'Inseparable.'

'Beth told me that Elliott intended treating you for your birthday. It was such a lovely gesture.' And a nice thought to leave her with.

Hoping that Jane Gibson would sleep easier tonight, Kate logged off from her computer, tidied away her papers and locked her desk drawer. Grabbing her jacket and briefcase, she was about to switch off her anglepoise lamp when Hank arrived, pulling on his overcoat. He shut the door, a sure sign he had something on his mind that couldn't wait until morning.

'You OK?' he asked.

'I thought you were long gone.' Kate zipped up her jacket. 'I'm fine. Why shouldn't I be?'

'You've had a heavy day, that's all.'

'Don't fuss, Hank.'

He made no move to leave.

'Did I forget something?' she asked. 'Did you?'

Hank glanced over his shoulder, then at her. 'I wasn't going to say anything.'

'I'm hearing a "but".'

He looked uncomfortable.

'Spit it out, Hank. I have a bed waiting and a few things to do before I get there.'

'You're trending on the force grapevine,' he blurted out. 'Not our lot, I hasten to add.' He wiped his face with his hand. 'I thought you should know that Atkins is making his mouth go to anyone stupid enough to listen to the gobshite.'

'And why is that of interest to me?'

For once, Hank was unsure of himself. 'Well, what do

you want me to say, should anyone ask? I don't want to put my foot in it.'

'What would you like to say?'

'That it's none of their business—'

'So there's your answer.' She quickly changed the subject. 'Everyone sure what they're doing tomorrow?'

'Geared up and ready to go. Are you sure you're OK?'

'I said so, didn't I?'

'What are you doing?'

'Now? In the morning?' Kate was confused. 'You fixed me up with Adam Foster. I'm up with the larks, remember?'

Hank glanced over his shoulder again. Kate followed his gaze. Apart from Carmichael diligently working away, the incident room was empty.

Kate's mobile went – a text arriving.

Tapping the 'messages' icon, she discovered a text from Fiona Fielding. She looked up without viewing what it said or showing any interest. 'What else is on your mind, Hank?'

He glanced at the phone in her hand, then at her.

Did nothing get past him?

'Well?' she said. 'I've got places to go, people to see, even if you haven't.'

'Have you told Jo you're not allowed out to play?'

She shook her head. 'Not yet.'

'Don't you think you should?'

'That's not a conversation for the phone.'

'It's not,' he said. 'Is that where you're going now?'

'What's with all the questions?' She walked round him and switched off the light, plunging them into semi-darkness.

'Are you?' he said as he followed her out.

Kate closed the door. 'It's not possible at the moment.'

'She's all packed!' He didn't try to hide his disapproval.

Hostility was not a trait Kate often saw in Hank. It hurt her to see him like that after they had been so close in Spain and since. The idea that he might find her uncaring gnawed at her. She ought to call Jo.

She would . . .

Later.

'I can't help that, can I?' she said. The words sounded lame. 'I have something else to do first.'

'Like what? Kate, you can't do this to her. Not again.'

She rounded on him. 'You tell her then!'

'Oh, that'll go down well,' he said. 'What could possibly be more important than—'

'Don't!' She withdrew her pointing finger and tried to calm down. 'Don't look at me that way or try or run my life.' She was almost yelling and resenting the implication that she was being unreasonable. 'My dad does that and I hate it. I don't take it from him and I sure as hell won't take it from you.'

'Well, if it's honesty hour, I'm not finished.' Hank came right back at her, coldly, like she'd let him down. Moreover, let herself down. 'Isn't it time you buried the hatchet with him?'

'Not a chance! The reason we're at loggerheads is not my doing. He drove *me* away and don't you ever forget it. You know why? I don't live up to his high expectations. He thinks I made all the wrong choices, professionally *and* personally. He's a homophobe, Hank. A man I used to love but no longer recognize. Today of all days, you should understand why I'm loath to make my peace with him. He's a monumental pain in the ass.'

His raised eyebrow said: *So are you sometimes.* 'Kate, I'm sorry. I spoke out of turn. I didn't mean to upset you.'

She hissed her response. 'You didn't even come close.'

Hank averted his eyes.

Kate let it go. It was too late in the day to get into an argument she knew she'd never win. Hank was right. She'd been selfish and unreasonable. Jo should have been her first priority. Kate owed her that much. But she knew Jo well enough to know what her response would have been to Atkins' shocking behaviour in the incident room. Once she calmed down, she'd have brushed it aside without giving it another thought. Maybe she was even glad. Kate no longer had any excuses to hide.

She pictured her at home: suitcases packed, music playing, chilling with a glass of red wine, feet up, researching where they might eat and what landmarks they might visit while in Scotland. She'd handle Atkins' outburst better then most, but Kate tried not to imagine how she might react to another broken promise. There was a limit to how many times you could disappoint someone. Kate had reached her quota – and some – months ago.

Hank was staring at her, reading her mind. 'What could possibly be more important than Jo?' He suddenly stopped talking as he realized what she was about to do. 'After what you told me earlier, you have got to be kidding me.'

She met his gaze defiantly.

'Are you mad?' he said.

Probably.

Kate turned away, her heart thumping in her chest. She'd not rest until she knew Beth Casey was safe. If that meant going through Atkins *and* pissing Jo off, then so be it.

34

There was a rap on the door. Beth threw up again, telling her father to go away, wishing she'd taken Kate Daniels' advice and given him a wide berth. Apart from tearing her to bits over her failure to confide in him – screaming at her because he'd been suspended – with Chris in custody he'd gone overboard, blaming them both for ending his precious career.

He'd enjoyed telling her that, with a criminal record, Chris would never get bail. 'If he goes down – and I'll do everything in my power to make that happen – it'll be years before you see him again.'

Those words were stuck in her head.

Beth couldn't shift them.

Flushing the toilet, she washed her face and opened the door quietly, hoping to avoid another confrontation. Her father was outside waiting for her. He'd been drinking heavily and that made her nervous. Ordinarily he didn't drink when she was in the house. Her mother said it was because he couldn't trust himself to stop before he fell over.

What she really meant was before he got violent.

'Get to bed,' he said.

'No! I'm leaving.'

'To go where?'

'Anywhere but here.'

'Sit down and act your age. This would never have happened if you'd come forward.'

'You said that already. I don't need to hear it again.' Beth made a move towards her room. Her father stepped sideways, blocking her way, arms folded across his chest. 'Get out of my way,' she said. 'I'm packing my stuff and going to Mum's.'

'No, you're not. You're staying where I can keep an eye on you. When you act like a grown-up, I'll treat you like one.' Seeing the hurt look on her face, he climbed down, though he stopped short of an apology. 'Some of the things I said were not nice. I didn't mean to call you names. You just made me so angry.'

'It doesn't take much.'

'Beth, sit down so we can talk. I don't think you fully understand what it is you've done, how serious it is to withhold evidence and waste police time when half the force are out looking for an offender who might well be a danger to others.'

'Waste *your* time, you mean. I don't care! I don't want to talk to you.'

'While you're under this roof, you'll do as I say.'

'You can't make me. I hate you!'

Kate parked at the rear of the building. A sign on the wall warned: *Residents' Parking Only*. She knew it was a bad idea to visit Atkins at home, but what choice did she have? Sober, she could handle him. Drunk, she wasn't so confident. Volatile men were unpredictable. He was bad-tempered within the confines of the station. At home, with no witnesses, there was no knowing what he might do to her.

Taking a deep breath, she pressed the buzzer next to Atkins' name.

No answer.

She was about to walk away when a man appeared at her shoulder, mid forties with a friendly smile. They entered together, separating on the ground floor. He turned out to be Atkins' neighbour.

Putting his key in the lock, he glanced back at her, cocking his head to one side, a smile beginning to form on his lips. 'You're knocking on the wrong door, love.'

Before Kate could think of a sarcastic retort, the door in front of her was yanked open. Atkins was unshaven, dressed casually in jeans and a pink sweater, his expression a mixture of surprise and contempt. His eyes were bloodshot and he reeked of booze.

'What do *you* want?'

Kate held his gaze, aware that the eyes and ears of his neighbour were upon them. Realizing they were under surveillance, Atkins told the 'arrogant shit' to sling his hook. He waited for the guy to disappear inside before turning to face her. There was not a flicker of regret or embarrassment from him. Away from the goldfish bowl of the MIR, with no audience to play to, she didn't expect him to carry on his assault on her personal life, but she couldn't count on it.

She returned his harsh stare. He might have influenced the way she'd be viewed by her team from now on. What he couldn't do was change who she was. Who she loved. She cleared her throat. 'I need to ask Beth a few more questions.'

'Use the phone.'

'Not my style,' Kate said. 'I prefer the personal touch.'

'Have you interviewed Collins yet?'

'I'm not prepared to discuss that out here.'

He opened the door and she stepped inside.

'Well?' he barked.

Stripped of his responsibility for the murder investigation, he had no authority and no entitlement to information.
She wasn't obliged to tell him sod-all. Still, she decided to
humour him so as not to alienate him altogether. 'Their
stories are practically identical. That's all I'm prepared to
say.'

'What are you implying?'

He was pushing his luck. 'I can see Beth here, or at the
station if you prefer.'

'It's late. You'll have to wait till morning.'

'You know how these things work, James. I'll see her
now.'

'What's the rush?'

'I need to know if the IP had a Twitter or Facebook
account. I can execute a search, but that'll take time I don't
have. Beth knew Elliott well. She might be able to help.' It
was a weak excuse, the only one Kate could think of. She
could see he wasn't buying it. He returned her gaze, ash falling from his cigarette onto his shoe.

Kate had encountered enough dodgy characters in her
time to know that he'd done something he wasn't proud of.
Instinctively she knew it had nothing to do with her. Her
gut feeling was that he'd bullied his daughter. And suddenly
she was standing in the pouring rain outside his marital

home. Then, like now, he was telling her to walk away and mind her own business; a stand-off in the street; a child's tearful cries and the vice-like grip of a tiny hand in hers.

'Where is she?'

'In her room sulking.'

'Is she OK?'

'What do you think? She knows we have her friend in custody. Where he belongs, in my opinion. I don't suppose she's too chuffed, but that's her problem. She shouldn't hang around with shite.'

'Chris Collins' involvement has yet to be determined. I gather he's been a support to her since Diane became ill. In his absence, she might need reassurance.'

'She needs a good hiding.' It was out of his mouth before he could stop himself.

'It didn't work with her mother,' Kate reminded him calmly. 'In my experience, it never does. Shouldn't you be picking on someone your own size?'

'Like you, you mean?'

'Give it your best shot.'

He was incensed. Wary too. 'I was a hothead then.'

Kate wanted to roll on the floor laughing. She held it in. He hadn't changed. The need to control – men, but mostly women under his command – was in his DNA. He didn't have the balls to try it on with anyone else. He hadn't learned from past mistakes, even though he'd lost a wife who, at one time, had been prepared to forgive and forget if only he'd accept help. He never would.

The idiot was his own worst enemy.

'Get the fuck out of my house,' he said.

'I need a moment with your daughter.'

'I don't give a damn what you need. I told you, she's in her room sulking.'

'Did you shout at her?' *Of course he did.*

Kate was kicking herself for not having come round earlier or sent Carmichael to check on Beth. Alarm bells were ringing. Was it only shouting? She'd seen what he'd done to Diane. Surely he'd not lift a hand to Beth? Kate stood her ground. She wasn't moving until she'd seen the girl. Neither would she give in to his strong-arm tactics or let him intimidate her into leaving. Still, for a fleeting moment she wished Hank were by her side. Wished even more that they hadn't fallen out.

'Please call Beth. I won't keep her long.'

'You have five minutes, then you're out of here.'

'That's all I need.' She pointed along the hallway. 'May I?'

He stepped aside, allowing her further into the apartment, her eyes drifting over an impressive open-plan lounge as she walked in. It was tastefully decorated, if a tad sterile for her taste. She noticed a tumbler of amber liquid on the arm of a chair. It was whisky, not beer. Unlucky. His ex-wife had told Kate that it made him unstable at best, violent at worst. The size of the glass was a dead giveaway.

Beth was nowhere to be seen.

Atkins had read her mind. 'She's probably on that phone of hers, telling all her mates what a sad fucking life she has.' He poured himself another drink, took a slug, and then walked to the door, yelling at the top of his voice. 'Beth, get out here.' When she didn't materialize, he turned to face Kate. 'Don't go away.'

She wasn't planning to.

Leaving her alone, he marched out, heading for Beth's room. Kate sat down, less nervous than before. If he was prepared to let her see the girl, she might have been worrying unnecessarily.

A shouting match took less time to heal than a slap.

She could hear him rapping on Beth's bedroom door. When there was no response, he started yelling. 'Beth, did you hear me? Daniels is here to see you.' The rapping turned to thumping. 'C'mon, stop your snivelling and get out here.'

Kate sighed. His parenting skills weren't woefully inadequate, they were non-existent. She wondered why some people ever had children. With a growing feeling of unease, she left her seat and walked into the hallway. Sensing her arrival, Atkins turned, training his bleary eyes on her. He opened the door and stepped inside. Seconds later he reappeared, taking another slug of whisky as he moved further along the hallway.

Slamming his fist on the bathroom door, he ordered Beth to open up. He turned the handle. It wouldn't budge. The door was locked from the inside. 'Beth? Unlock the damn door. Stop messing about. We haven't got all day.' He put his ear to it and listened, then shifted his gaze to Kate, fear penetrating the alcoholic haze.

She was already running down the hallway. 'Kick it in!' she said.

Turning sideways on, Atkins shoulder-charged the door, crashing through it so violently, he tripped over his daughter's body, saving himself by grabbing hold of the bath.

Whatever he said was incomprehensible. It came out like an animal wailing.

Beth was unconscious on the floor, a small amount of vomit visible on the left side of her mouth, an empty vodka bottle and a container of her mother's pills lying on the tiles beside her. Shoving him away, Kate got down on her hands and knees, cleared the girl's airway and felt for a pulse.

'She's alive but weak. Get her in the car!'

Kate scooped up the container and the tablets, Beth's bag too. There might be other drugs inside. Identification of everything she'd swallowed would be crucial when they reached the hospital. Kate wasn't waiting for an ambulance. By the time it arrived it would be too late. Atkins was frozen to the spot, wide eyes on his daughter. Kate screamed at him to move.

35

They crashed through the door to A & E. At Kate's request, a medical team was waiting to receive Beth into their care. The minute she was on a stretcher, they took over, rushing her into an examination room. The door swung shut, leaving Kate and Atkins standing in the corridor in silence. In her wildest dreams, she couldn't imagine what he was going through. She didn't see him as a religious man but he sure as hell would be offering a prayer to someone.

Kate checked her phone. There were no messages so she switched it off.

Dropping a two-pound coin into a drinks dispenser, she pressed for tea with sugar, watching as the weak liquid dribbled into a plastic cup. Atkins took it from her and slumped down heavily in a chair, eyes firmly focused on the door through which Beth had been taken. At this stage there was no way of knowing how bad her condition was or even if she'd survive. If she was lucky, medics would be pumping her stomach and bringing her round . . .

Whether she wanted it or not was another matter.

Fleetingly, Kate thought she'd been utterly selfish. How could she attempt suicide, knowing she'd be leaving behind a dying mother? Kate would give anything to have hers back for a few more moments, if for no other reason than to say a proper goodbye and tell her how precious she was. A chance to say all the things that had remained unsaid, one final opportunity to cuddle up in her arms, to feel the strength of her love.

Kate turned her head away before Atkins misinterpreted her sorrow. Although he'd played a part in his daughter's drama, Kate didn't want to spook him into thinking that she might not come through.

'Why did she do it?' He was talking to the side of her head.

Although she could see him in her peripheral vision, Kate kept her eyes front. She knew why but didn't say. She didn't trust herself to keep it civil. She didn't think he'd heard her telling Beth to hang on in there, even though she was unconscious as they raced to the hospital, blue light flashing. Apart from getting there, all Kate could think of was what he'd done to drive his daughter to suicide.

She turned her head to look at him. 'Has she tried anything like this before?'

'No!'

He was welling up, a man drowning in a misery of his own making. She wanted to be honest with him and tell him what a disgrace he was. Instead, and despite the fact that he didn't deserve reassurance, she found herself putting a hand on his shoulder, patting it gently. It was pity, not anger, she felt for him.

He made no attempt to shrug her off.

'She has everything to live for,' he sobbed.

Shame he hadn't thought of that before.

'Young people invariably do,' Kate said.

She wondered if Beth had heard her plea to come

through. People who'd come back from the brink of death had reported hearing those trying to communicate with them.

Kate willed it to be true.

'No, you don't understand,' Atkins said. 'Diane and I are going to give it another go.'

A tear fell from his cheek as he dropped his head in his hands. Kate couldn't believe it. She wondered if it was the drink talking. Surely if what he was telling her was accurate, Diane would have called him to explain Beth's predicament instead of giving the girl Kate's number.

It seemed highly unlikely that reconciliation was on the cards, but Kate played along, not wanting to antagonize a man who clearly still blamed her for the collapse of his marriage and for stalling his career the first time. Jo popped into her head briefly. They were hours away from their own reunion and still she hadn't come clean and told her that she couldn't keep her promise to go on holiday.

Kate resisted the temptation to take a peek at her watch, or walk away and make a call. She couldn't bring herself to give Jo the bad news over the phone. Besides, a private call was likely be misconstrued by Atkins. He was staring intently in her direction.

'Does Beth know?' she asked.

'No. Diane wants to wait until she's out of hospital. She's worried Beth might not be too keen. Doesn't think it would be good, coming from me.'

No wonder, Kate was thinking. He was rigid and controlling. Beth was a rebellious teenager. They weren't exactly a comfy fit.

'What's taking so long?' He glanced at the door to the emergency room, urging it to open.

In spite of all that had happened in the past twenty-four hours, Kate didn't have it in her heart to hate him. In the whole scheme of things, what had been said in anger in the incident room was unimportant. Beth was their sole focus.

'I'm sure she'll be fine,' Kate said, inwardly declaring a truce.

Atkins' hard eyes had softened.

Kate hoped he'd do right by Beth from now on. Her father must see that, with her mother so unwell, and Collins in the frame for a serious charge, he was her only support.

Fate had brought Kate and Beth together all those years ago. She'd been an unhappy little girl in distress. In helping her mother flee an abusive partner, Kate had hoped to avoid the scenario where *she* ended up on a dim hospital corridor, waiting to find out if she'd been too late to save a life. But it seemed there was no escaping the inevitable. Though it had taken them a while to get there, that's exactly where they had ended up.

Almost two hours later, in the early hours of the morning, Kate was struggling to stay awake when the door opposite opened and a female doctor entered the corridor, a solemn expression on her face. She looked utterly exhausted and, if Kate was any judge, uncomfortable too. She prepared herself for bad news as the doctor checked that there was no one around and made her way slowly towards them.

Feeling a presence, Atkins stood up.

'Any news?' he said. 'I'm James Atkins, Beth's father.'

No mention of his rank, Kate noted. *No wonder, the state he was in.* He was unsteady on his feet, invading the doctor's personal space, breathing second-hand whisky fumes all over her. She took a deliberate step backwards, shooting Kate a disparaging look. She obviously thought they were together, the irresponsible pair who'd neglected their beautiful daughter.

Kate showed ID to enlighten her and felt a change in the woman's attitude almost immediately. Bound by regulations, the medic switched her focus to Atkins, addressing her comments to him as next of kin, her tone of voice leaving him in no doubt that she was making judgements based on his condition.

She fixed him with a hard stare. 'It's too early to say. Beth's still in recovery.'

'What's taking so long? She'll pull through, won't she?'

'You're going to have to be patient, sir. Maybe you should return home and get some rest. Beth has ingested a cocktail of tablets. We're unable to accurately predict how many. What I can do is assure you that we're doing all we can for her and the baby.'

Kate saw the horrified expression on Atkins' face even before it was fully formed. It was clear he had no knowledge of any pregnancy. The news hit him like a body blow. He'd switched off and was pacing the corridor, his stress levels rising as the alcohol in his system began to wear off.

Kate covered for him. 'We appreciate your efforts, Doctor.'

Atkins swung round. 'Can I see her?' He was almost pleading.

'Not yet, she's still quite poorly.'

'I'm her father!'

'Yes, and the drugs she swallowed are strong, some with serious side effects in patients who don't require them. Beth will need constant monitoring, then close observation until we're satisfied that she and the baby are completely out of danger. We'll definitely be keeping her in.'

'Is she conscious?' he asked.

'She has been. She's sleeping now.'

The doctor excused herself and retreated.

Atkins resumed his pacing, up and down, up and down.

Kate wondered if Beth had told those caring for her that she didn't want to see him. She hurried off and caught up with the medic as she reached the emergency room. 'Doctor?'

The woman swung round.

'Would you keep us informed of progress, good or bad?' She was tempted to ask after the unborn child, but then decided not to. Unrelated to Beth, she was unlikely to get an answer and she didn't really want to know whether or not the baby had survived.

'Did you know?' demanded Atkins when she returned to his side.

'About the baby?' Kate said. 'No.'

'Jesus!' He put a hand to his forehead and shut his eyes. 'No wonder she was so upset about Elliott.'

'You think he's the father?'

'I know he is.'

'I knew they were good friends, but I didn't get the impression—'

247

'Open your bloody eyes, woman! They were inseparable. Jesus Christ! You don't think she's stupid enough to let that toerag Collins . . .' He looked away. 'How the hell didn't I see it coming?'

'You weren't to know.'

'No? She was throwing up yesterday and again tonight. I thought it was because I'd kept the news of Foster's death from her, because . . .' He stopped himself from finishing the sentence.

'Because?'

He dropped his head. 'Because she was upset.'

Kate sensed there was more to it than that. Whatever he was holding back, he was ashamed of it. She threw in a low-baller. She had to know. 'What were you really going to say?'

'Nothing.'

'You're lying.'

'I lost my temper, OK? She fell over—'

'She what?'

He tried to hide the guilt but his emotions got the better of him – he was almost in tears. He'd helped Beth on her way. This time Kate didn't offer any sympathy. She'd tried so hard to support him and be reasonable, disregarding his attack on her, but there was a limit to her patience and she'd reached it. Unable to look at him for a second longer, she walked away.

36

Of all the despicable things Atkins had done in his lifetime, pushing his daughter around was probably the worst. Kate marched down the corridor, her face set in a scowl, saddened and outraged. He'd lived up to his reputation as the Angry Man. Angry with himself because of the way he'd treated Diane, angry with her because she'd intervened. He could drown in despair for all she cared. The tosser deserved to rot in hell. Poor Beth: pregnant to a dead boy and out on a limb with no one decent to hold her hand.

It didn't get much worse.

New theories began to form in Kate's head as she thundered down the corridor. If Elliott was the father of Atkins' unborn grandchild, assuming Collins knew about the pregnancy, it went some way to explaining his jealousy. It changed things considerably. Even before the argument with her father, Beth had been under a lot of stress – a contributing factor to her suicide attempt perhaps. The overriding thought in Kate's mind was the motive it gave Collins.

'Kate? KATE? Wait up!'

A female voice and the sound of footsteps rushing up behind her sucked Kate back into the hospital corridor. She turned, her eyes locking onto to the approaching figure, heart sinking as she recognized the familiar profile. Jo walked quickly towards her, pale and distressed and, if Kate was reading her right, getting ready to deliver a mouthful.

She groaned inwardly.

Thanks a bunch, Hank.

Whatever her plans were after she left the incident room, several hours ago, she hadn't followed through or told Jo that her leave had been cancelled. She simply hadn't had the time. It looked like her brilliant DS had gone and done it for her. Her own words echoed in her head:

You tell her then!

Kate hadn't expected him to take her literally. No matter how well intentioned, he shouldn't have interfered. It was her place to break the news, no one else's. When would he learn to stay the hell out of her private life? She didn't need his input and it had done more harm than good this time.

No wonder Jo looked so pissed off.

'Where on earth have you been for the past three hours?' Jo came to an abrupt halt, hands on hips, a gesture of frustration. 'I've been searching all over for you. There must be a dozen messages on your bloody phone.'

Kate ran a hand through her hair, apologizing. Taking her mobile from her pocket, she switched it on. She could only surmise that Jo had been in touch with Control, heard about Beth Casey's overdose and come to remonstrate with her. Glancing at her mobile, Kate wondered how long she'd been waiting. There were seven voice messages and a number of texts, two from Fiona Fielding. She was in the area and keen to have some fun. After the day she'd had, Kate was more than tempted. Sex, with anyone, would be a welcome release.

'Jo, I'm sorry,' she repeated. 'If you let me, I can explain – but not now. I'm wasted. I've been up since six and I've had enough drama today to last a lifetime.'

'Oh, it's all about you, isn't it? Feeling guilty, is that it?'

'Hank had no business contacting you.'

'Well, someone had to. You didn't think I should know?'

'Of course—'

They stopped talking as a porter rounded the corner with a sickly patient on a trolley. Acknowledging the two of them, he pressed the up arrow. The lift pinged its arrival almost immediately and he disappeared inside.

Jo turned back to Kate, apologizing for her outburst. 'Let's not fight. I was frantic when I couldn't raise you. I . . . I thought you'd had an accident.' She stepped forward, put her arms around Kate and held on tight, making her feel worse than she did already.

Kate felt her body go limp. She was dead on her feet. 'I'm sorry too.'

'Don't be,' Jo released her. 'I shouldn't have yelled at you like that. You were going the wrong way as it happens. He's on ICU, next floor up.'

He's on ICU, next floor up.

Kate was at a loss. It took a moment to make sense of it, a moment longer to realize that they had been talking entirely at cross-purposes. Finally, she made the jump, her stomach taking a dive. She'd known Hank wasn't 100 per cent fit when he returned to duty, but she'd never figured him for a hospital case.

'How bad is it?' Her words were hardly audible.

'He's asleep. The consultant wants to talk to you—'

'She's here, at this hour?' Kate checked her watch. It was almost two a.m.

'She was a few minutes ago. If not, she'll be in first thing tomorrow.'

'Are we talking serious?'

Jo was nodding. Behind her tired eyes there was fear. No wonder she was drained and upset. Hank meant the world to her. 'C'mon, I'll take you.'

Kate refused to move. 'What's the prognosis?'

'Believe me, it'll be better coming from his physician.' Jo grabbed her upper arm, propelling her down the corridor. 'Don't worry, Kate. He'll be fine. He's in good hands.'

They took the stairs two at a time, exiting the stairwell on the floor above. Kate's thoughts were all over the place as they entered an identical corridor, turning right towards a set of closed double doors. They were practically running.

'Did he fall, collapse?' Kate heard a tremor in her voice as she noticed they were heading for Critical Care, the unit for high-dependency patients requiring intensive nursing. She couldn't get her head around why Hank was at this particular hospital. He hadn't left the station until late. With an early start on his agenda, she'd assumed he was going straight home. The dawn raid on Gardner's house was going down in a matter of hours. Lisa and Andy would have to be told. Kate couldn't think about that now. Her mind was in turmoil. 'What I meant was, it's a bit far from home for him, isn't it?'

'I gather he was visiting a friend when it happened.' They had reached the ward.

Kate hesitated. 'Tell me the deal before I go in.'

'I won't lie to you.' Jo opened the door. 'It's bad. He's had a massive heart attack. They lost him for a while.'

No!

Kate's hands flew to her mouth. It was all she could do to suppress a scream. This could not be happening again. She remembered the race to Santa Lucia Hospital in Cartagena. Being helped from a car by a Spanish police officer and thrust inside, hoping, no, praying that he was fit enough to survive the shooting. She never dreamt he'd suffer a cata-strophic setback following discharge.

'This is my fault.' *I should never have let him return to work.*

'Don't do this, Kate. It really isn't helpful.' Jo was leading her by the arm, dragging her almost. She pointed to a door on their right. 'He's in there. I gather he stabilized. He needs surgery though, so be prepared. You want me to come in or wait outside?'

Kate took hold of her hand and felt the pressure as Jo squeezed it gently. They entered together but Kate stopped dead in her tracks as soon as they got inside. The lights were dimmed, a heart monitor blinking away beside his bed, numbers lit by coloured LEDs increasing and decreasing to reflect changes in vitals: blood pressure, pulse rhythm, res-piratory rate.

It wasn't Hank in the bed. It was her father.

'Oh God!' Kate felt like she'd received a kick in the gut. A combination of regret and relief battled for space in her heart, a guilty heart that was beating much faster than it should. Her voice broke into a hoarse whisper. 'I thought you were talking about Hank.'

'What?' Jo's eyebrows pinched together in confusion. 'I thought you knew. I thought that's why you'd come.'

Kate shook her head. 'I've been here for hours.'

'What? Why?'

'Long story, tell you later.' She studied the ventilator tube in her father's mouth, the intravenous drip fed through a cannula in his hand, wires everywhere, all of it intensely distressing. 'He looks dreadful.'

Jo put a forefinger to her lips, indicating that Ed Daniels might well be sedated but that didn't mean he couldn't hear.

Kate's thoughts fleetingly turned elsewhere:

Hang on, Beth . . .

Couple of minutes . . .

You're going to be fine.

With a lump in her throat, she pulled a chair towards the bed and sat down quietly, taking hold of her father's hand. It was cold to the touch. Kate realized then that she'd not touched him physically in years. Even when her mother died, he'd pushed her away.

His loss.

'Dad, it's Kate . . .' Her voice broke. A hot, salty tear fell from her eye. She wiped it away, swallowing her grief. They used to be so close. *What the hell happened*? 'I'm here,' she said through a sob. Her heart was breaking. 'You're going to be fine, Dad. You're being well cared for. We'll have you out of here in no time.'

37

They left an hour later, having spoken to a cardiologist. Tests had revealed that two of Ed Daniels' coronary arteries were blocked. A serious condition if left untreated. They needed to open up the vessels carrying blood to his heart and check for any permanent damage. A bypass was on the cards as soon as it could be arranged, to reduce the threat of another attack that could well be fatal.

Afterwards, Kate walked Jo to her car and climbed in beside her, a chance to talk. As exhausted as she was, Kate couldn't leave without telling her what had gone on in the past few hours. She deserved an explanation.

'I have something to tell you,' she said.

'Whatever it is, it can wait. You need sleep.'

'No, I need to tell you now.' Kate took a deep breath. 'Bright suspended Atkins from duty. He's off the case. To cut a very long story short, he went home and got legless. He had a go at his daughter.'

'Physically?'

'I think so.' Kate dropped her head, then glanced at Jo, her voice breaking once again. 'We found her unconscious on the bathroom floor having taken a cocktail of cancer drugs. That's why I'm here.'

'Is she OK?'

'I really don't know.'

'What a moron he is.'

'Tell me about it. You saw for yourself what a vicious temper he has – unless of course there's real humpy, then you don't see him for dust.'

'I've heard rumours,' Jo said. 'Nothing substantiated, mind.'

'They're true. He's a coward. I know it for a fact, unless he has a whisky in his hand, then he's a fucking prize-fighter, especially if you're female. There's a lot of bad blood between us.'

'So I gather.'

'I'd fill you in, only—'

'I can wait. You've had a bad day. What he said in the incident room, his assault on Beth, your old man's heart attack and your concern for Hank – these are all more important than Atkins. You need to get them in perspective. Be kind to yourself. Don't let him drag you down.'

Jo was mistaken.

When one thing went wrong, Kate got upset. When ten things did, she tended to laugh it off. Her grandmother's disapproval forced its way into her head . . .

'That smile will get you into deep trouble one day, young lady.' It was a telling-off for reacting inappropriately to sad news: the sudden deaths of two family friends on the same day. It was the solemn expression on everyone's faces that started her off. Her parents looked so funny she just couldn't keep it in. They were appalled when she began to giggle. It was a nervous reaction, of course, a defence mechanism, a physical and emotional release to something bad. Even now Kate had the overwhelming urge to grin.

There had been many laughs in her career, many in the face of adversity. Others brought on by hysterical happenings that stayed with her for years afterwards. One particular set of colleagues sprang to mind.

'Did I miss something funny?' Jo asked.

The grin had almost progressed to a laugh. 'I was thinking about a shift I was once attached to. They were known as the wildebeesties.'

'Dare I ask why?'

'Wildebeest follow the herd.' Lifting her arms, Kate spread her hands and placed them behind her head like antlers, thumbs in her ears, making Jo laugh. 'If a call came over the radio, didn't matter what it was, the whole shift turned up.'

'Sounds hilarious.'

'It was. I happened upon a burglary once, a drunk trying to break into a chemist's shop. I'd just locked him up when several panda cars screeched to a halt. Every one of my colleagues jumped out, with the exception of Atkins. I thought it was because I was new to the squad and single-crewed, that they were watching out for me, until I realized they never went anywhere by themselves.'

It felt good to walk down Memory Lane.

'They were as good as gold,' Kate added. 'What they lacked in experience they made up for in enthusiasm. The point is, they looked out for one another, rather like my current team.' The smile disappeared. 'Atkins wasn't worthy. He didn't deserve them. He was a drain on morale, a bully with no balls, even then. That's serious shit if you happen to be working alongside him. The job relies on trust. You've got to be able to count on colleagues to come to your aid.'

'I can imagine.'

'He should've been suspended years ago. A shout went up once: *Officer requires assistance.* I grabbed my keys and sped out of the station like a shot. He was sitting in a side street having a smoke; no attempt to get involved or even start the car. Another time I found him hiding in a lay-by.'

'Isn't that a dereliction of duty?'

Kate nodded. 'He's always been a liability, especially where I was concerned. Bright made sure we never worked the same nick after that. There were other reasons I won't go into.' Checking her watch, she changed the subject. 'I better get going.' She glanced up at the windows of her father's ward. 'Do you think I should go back in and see if he's awake?'

'No, I think you should go home and get some rest.' Jo put her key in the ignition. 'I'll drive you?'

'No, my car is . . .' Kate scanned the car park, her memory deserting her. 'Actually, I don't know where my car is. The day I've had, I wouldn't be surprised if it's been towed away. I parked it at the entrance to A & E. I should go and check. It had a POLICE sticker on, so it should be OK.'

'You want me to wait around, in case?'

'No, you go. If it's not there, I'll get a lift in a panda. I need to reschedule a meeting with Adam Foster that Hank arranged for seven. In the meantime, I need to lie down before I fall down.' Kate leaned in, cradled Jo's face in her hands and kissed her gently. 'I can't leave tomorrow but I'll make it up to you. You go on ahead and I'll come as soon as I can get away.'

'No,' Jo said. 'Family takes priority.'

Kate dropped her head, guiltily. 'Even without this latest drama, I couldn't have gone. Bright cancelled my leave.' *There, she'd said it.*

'When?'

'After he suspended Atkins.'

Jo looked crestfallen. 'And you didn't think to call me?'

'I was busy, I'm sorry.' Kate waited for the backlash.

'I understand,' Jo said quietly. She was trying and failing to hide her disappointment. 'Now is not the time to have a dig at you. With your old man up there,' she flicked her eyes towards the hospital. 'You couldn't take leave now even if you wanted to.'

'I do . . . want to.'

'I know. But I also know that you'd fret about the case if you went. I wanted to go too, of course I did, but what I wanted more than anything was for you to benefit from a break and not wander around aimlessly stressing about what's going on here, ringing Hank for updates, wishing you were at work.'

'I wouldn't have—'

'Yes, you would.' Jo managed to smile through bitter disappointment.

Kate glanced up at the first-floor windows. 'Well, I'll have to drop the case now. Bright can't possibly refuse me compassionate leave—'

'He'll try.'

'Tough. He'll have to find cover. I'm good but I can't be in two places at once.'

'Your old man wouldn't look after you,' Jo said pointedly.

Kate could see that it hurt her to say it. 'Yeah, well he's got no one else, has he?'

'He's got me.' Jo's eyes reflected determination, a hint of mischief too. 'I've already booked the time off. It's no skin off my nose to look in on him during and after his operation until your case is resolved. In fact I've been waiting for an opportunity to tell him what a brilliant daughter he has, if only he'd care to open his eyes and take a closer look.'

'I don't deserve you.' Pecking her on the cheek, Kate got out of the car and walked away without a backward glance. She didn't want Jo to see how choked she was.

38

Six a.m. Pitch dark. The streets were quiet. No one about as tactical support, dog section and CID vehicles moved silently into their positions across Ashington and the Redesdale area of west Northumberland. The plan was to hit the properties simultaneously, a coordinated strike. It was DC Lisa Carmichael's operation. On her mark, the target's known associates would be woken from their beds, placed under arrest and transported to the nearest nick.

Hank winked at Carmichael.

As her mentor, his role was to oversee the operation, to act in an advisory capacity only. She'd overheard Kate Daniels instructing him not to take over, not to get involved unless it was absolutely necessary to do so, and she knew why. Hank hadn't argued with their boss. He'd agreed to remain with the outside team, covering front and rear of the target's house to prevent escape. Given what they knew of Liam Gardner, no one expected him to raise his hands and go quietly.

Good luck to him if he upset Hank.

Carmichael gave a silent nod to the TSG leader sitting on the opposite side of the vehicle. Speaking softly into his radio, he instructed all units under his command to make their move, simultaneously warning his own team that the dog handler would go in first.

They piled out of their vehicles, moving silently and swiftly to Gardner's house, the spreaders taking the front door out at the first attempt.

'POLICE! Police!'

A dog, trained to attack – moving so fast it was hard to tell the breed – leapt along the hallway, crazed eyes illuminated by torchlight. The dog handler held up an Armadillo electronic shield as protection against attack, an effective deterrent for rapid-entry situations. Sensitive to the electric current and the sound of it passing between terminals, the dog backed off, cowering from the officer, snarling and barking – an American pit bull.

Carmichael relaxed.

So far, so good.

She'd spoken too soon.

The dog ran at them again, this time coming into contact with the shield and triggering a 40,000-volt shock, more than the standard Taser gun used on humans. The animal yelped and fell away stunned, landing heavily on the bare floorboards. Before it had a chance to recover, the handler used a snaffle pole to get a loop around its neck and remove it from the house.

A dangerous breed exhibiting such aggression – Carmichael knew it would later be destroyed. With no time to indulge that sad thought, she crossed the threshold. As two officers peeled off to check the living room, she followed several pairs of police-issue boots up the stairs, DC Andy Brown bringing up the rear.

Carmichael flicked a light switch. 'Police! Stay where you are!'

Alerted by the dog, Gardner had already begun a run for freedom, leaving his skinny, waiflike girlfriend alone in bed. He'd pulled on some tracksuit bottoms and was halfway out the rear window, trying to access the roof of the bay window on the floor below. Two TSG officers managed to grab him and haul him back inside.

'You're going nowhere, mate,' yelled one officer, placing him in a stranglehold. 'Stop struggling!'

Gardner's efforts to escape proved futile. The more he thrashed around, the more pressure was put on his Adam's apple. The fool was almost choking, face turning red, eyes bulging and full of hatred, as ferocious as the dog they had encountered in the hallway.

'Get your pig hands off me!' He lashed out with bare feet at those trying to search for weapons, making contact with his target. 'Get the fuck off!'

'Oi! Cut it out.' Carmichael was getting impatient. 'Hands on your head and he'll let you go. Don't make this more difficult than it already is, Gardner. You're coming with us.'

'I'm going nowhere, bitch.' He stuck a middle finger in the air. When he badmouthed her a second time, the guy restraining him increased his grip, cutting off his air supply.

'He's choking, you bastard!' The girlfriend threw a jumper over her head, pulled it down over sizeable breast implants and reached for her phone. 'Get a good look?' she said to Carmichael, her eyes shifting to Gardner. He was still being restrained. 'Hey! You can't do that. I'm calling his brief. He's done nowt wrong.'

Carmichael ducked – not fast enough – as Gardner ejected saliva with all the skill of a marksman. 'He has now,' she said, wiping spit from her face and hair. 'Resisting arrest will get him eighteen months. Assaulting a police officer will get him more. Do yourself a favour, pet. Find yourself a new boyfriend.'

Carmichael wouldn't allow either of them to see her disgust, although she certainly felt it. She couldn't wait to reach the station and jump in the shower. Smiling at her prey, she spoke the words she'd dreamt of saying her whole career:

'Liam Gardner, I'm arresting you on suspicion of murder.'

39

Kate opened one eye, startled by the noise that was dragging her from sleep. Her clothes lay on the floor where she'd dropped them last night. Unusual for her to be untidy but she was wasted when she got in. It took a split second for her memory to kick in, a second longer to realize that her mobile phone was ringing.

The hospital.

Rolling over on one side, she hauled herself into a sitting position, panicking over whether her father had survived the night while she slept soundly in her bed. The room was chilly. Goosebumps covered her skin. Pulling the duvet around her, she snatched up her mobile, braced for bad news.

'Hello?' Her voice was thick with sleep.

'Morning, boss.' It was Andy Brown.

Kate's relief was momentary. He wouldn't have called her if it hadn't been important. Unless . . . her eyes shifted to the digital clock on her bedside table: eight twenty-one. *Shit!* She flew out of bed, dragged open a drawer looking for underwear, snagging a pair of red lacy knickers on a splinter as she yanked them out.

'Shit! Shit!'

'You OK?'

Kate's eyes came to rest on a dusty suitcase she'd lugged out of the loft. It lay empty on the bedroom floor waiting to be filled. The sight of it made her both angry and sad. 'OK might be pushing it, Andy. But you'll be pleased to know I'm human like everyone else.'

'Boss?'

'I overslept. You probably worked that out all by yourself.'

'Hank suspected as much—'

'Since when did you become his errand boy?' There was a long silence on the other end. Kate quickly back-pedalled. 'Sorry, forget I said that. I didn't mean to bite your head off. Did he reschedule the briefing?'

'For eleven o'clock.'

'Thanks. Tell him I appreciate it.'

She meant it – and didn't need to ask why Hank hadn't called himself. With no knowledge of what had gone down since he saw her, her devoted DS was most likely still brooding, angry with her for repeating past mistakes, putting her job before her private life. They had fought over the issue often. He'd get over it – eventually – and so would she. They respected each other too much to keep an argument going for long. Candour was good for the soul.

'How did the raid go down?' she asked.

'Just as Lisa planned it.' Andy was eager to praise her as always. 'Gardner and his cronies are under lock and key, awaiting your company.'

'Good. Anything else?'

'Grant said to tell you that Gayle Foster would rather not come to us. She's asked that you see her at her place of work.'

'Fine. Arrange it. Listen, I've got to go. I'm supposed to be seeing Adam Foster an hour and a half ago. Is *he* at the station?'

'He was when I got in.'

'Trust a squaddie to be on time.' Kate grabbed some grey strides and a stripy shirt from her wardrobe and threw them on the bed. She practically ran to the shower, the phone still in her hand. Leaning in, she turned on the tap to let the water warm up, the list of things she had to do making her head spin. 'Do me a favour,' she said. 'Get a message to him. Make an excuse and give him my profound apologies. Tell him to wait. I'll be there within the hour.'

Sometimes things don't go according to plan. Even before she'd woken up, it was set to be one of those days. Kate was almost halfway to the station when her mobile rang loudly in the car, Andy Brown's number appearing on screen. Turning the volume down, she knew what he was going to say before she took the call. 'Don't tell me, Adam Foster got bored.' It was a statement, not a question.

''Fraid so.'

'Damn!' Kate pulled hard on the steering wheel, guiding her Q5 off the road and into a lay-by. 'He's legged it?'

'Not exactly. Front desk said he got a call from his lass. He had to rush off. Said to tell you he'd be at her house when you have time to see him.'

'Did he leave an address?'

Andy confirmed that he had.

'The poor guy's recently bereaved. Like it or not, I'm going to have to follow through and grovel. I only hope he accepts my apology.' As Andy reeled off the postcode, she reprogrammed her satnav. 'Tell Hank to handle the briefing if I'm not back.'

She rang off.

Engaging first gear, she was about to pull out of the lay-by and into heavy traffic when a text message came in from Jo. It was brief and to the point:

Didn't call earlier in case I woke you. I've been at the hospital since early doors. Your dad had a comfortable night.

Kate keyed a reply:

Is he awake?

Yes, but not up to visitors according to nursing staff.

Won't rush in then.

No point.

What are you not telling me?

He thinks it's YOU waiting to see him.

Figures. You do know it's an offence to impersonate a police officer?

☺ Did you sleep?

Like a log. Need to go. I'm flat out. Tell him I'll be in later.

Let you know if there are any developments. x

Owe you one.

I will collect. x

Ending the exchange, Kate put her foot down and sped away.

By the time she arrived at the given address, military police were slamming the door of their van with Adam Foster inside. A crowd had gathered. A pregnant girl Kate assumed to be his girlfriend was in hysterics, sobbing into a handkerchief on the pavement outside a rundown terraced house, begging the redcaps to let him go. One of four males standing with her was having a verbal go at them.

Screeching to a halt, blocking the van in, Kate jumped out of the car and marched round the back, curbing a growing desire to rip heads off with her bare hands.

This could not be happening.

'Guys?' She held up ID. 'I'm DCI Kate Daniels, Northumbria Police. Can I have a minute please? I need to speak urgently with your prisoner.'

The two soldiers stood to attention when spoken to. Ignoring the abuse he was getting from the dickhead on the pavement, the most senior of the two, a sergeant, allowed his eyes to dart sideways, an explanation of sorts for what he was about to impart . . .

'Sorry, ma'am. No can do. We're under orders to transport Corporal Foster back to base to face disciplinary action for being absent without leave.'

Kate stood her ground. 'I'm fully aware of that.'

'I'm not authorized to deviate from our intended route, ma'am.'

'I'm not asking you to make a detour. Just give me a moment with him in the back of the van before you take him away.'

'I can't allow that while he's in our custody and without legal representation. I'm sure you understand.'

Kate bit her lip, taking a deep breath. After her row with Hank, a public slanging match with a jobsworth was not what she needed. She was about to try again when more swearing ensued from over her shoulder. Turning on her heels, she sauntered across the road until she was facing the mouthy civilian.

'Shut it!' she said. 'One more word from you and you're nicked.'

He laughed. 'You wanna call for backup, pet?'

'Are you saying I need it?'

'Fuck off, you daft cow.'

He turned his head to smirk at his mates, playing the big man. Before he had chance to turn back, the DCI had removed her snips from her trouser pocket, snapping them on his wrist in one deft motion, twisting them sharply, disabling him. He cried out in pain as she kept the pressure on, securing the other end to Victorian railings that bordered the small front garden.

'Now will you shut the fuck up?' Silence prevailed as she returned to the van.

'Nicely done, ma'am,' the MP said.

'I don't want your admiration, Sergeant. Foster's brother was murdered. I must speak with him. It would've been nice if he'd been able to stick around to support a grieving grandmother. I appreciate that isn't possible, but cut me some slack here. Going AWOL for a couple of days is hardly a capital offence—'

'That's a matter for my CO, ma'am.'

Kate asked him to be reasonable.

A pair of ice-blue eyes stared back at her. He wasn't going to budge. 'We'll be keeping him in a holding cell. He's going nowhere. You can interview him there.'

'Thank you so much for the cooperation,' Kate said. 'I'm sure your commanding officer will be very proud of you.'

She looked on as they locked the van, climbed in and drove off. She cautioned her own whingeing prisoner and called Control to have him taken away. There was no way he was getting in her motor. This day couldn't end soon enough.

40

'Mr Gardner, will you tell us where you were between five p.m. on Saturday the eleventh of October and eight a.m. on Sunday twelfth?' Gardner had already been cautioned and given the opportunity to consult with a solicitor. Charles Moffatt, the legal man he'd chosen, had a sickly complexion. He was completely bald with dark circles under his eyes. He checked his watch, as if he had somewhere else he'd rather be. Trying to move the interview along, he advised his client to answer.

Gardner yawned, exposing surprisingly good teeth. A scar ran through his left eyebrow, giving him a sinister appearance. A war wound. Kate wondered if the flesh had been stitched by an amateur, causing the skin to pucker slightly above his eye. Apart from that, he wasn't unpleasant to look at. Bruce Willis fans might even find him attractive.

'What was the question again?' he asked.

'Five o'clock Saturday to eight o'clock Sunday,' Hank repeated. 'Where were you?'

'Hmm . . . I have no idea. Can't remember, can I?'

'Oh, come on.' Kate held his gaze for a moment. 'You can do better than that, surely, young lad like you. It was only a

couple of days ago. I know exactly what I was doing, everything I had to eat, every call I made. Why don't you give it
more thought.'

'Nah, don't think so. I'd like to help you out, pet, really I
would, but I was pissed most of Saturday. That's what week-
ends are for. Least they are in my book. You should try it
some time. It's called letting your hair down.'

'You're not helping, Mr Gardner.'

'The name's Liam.' Gardner smirked, enjoying himself. 'I
had a skinful yesterday 'n' all, come to think of it. And now
I've got a hangover. Why d'you think I was so incensed
when your lot dragged me out of bed in the middle of the
night, terrifying my lass and upsetting my dog?'

'Shame about the dog.' Hank's expression was deadpan.
'You have our condolences . . . For the tape, Mr Gardner
just raised his middle finger.'

'For the tape, the cops are smiling,' Gardner said.

'Maybe I can help jog your memory,' Kate interrupted.
She didn't want to rile this kid. Not yet, anyway. That would
get them nowhere fast. Three days into the enquiry and she
wanted to make it count. She sat forward, elbows on the
table, hands clasped in front of her. 'Let's start from the
beginning, shall we, Liam? When you woke up on Saturday
morning, what time was it and what did you have for breakfast?'

Gardner made no reply.

'Too hard a question?' Kate moved on. 'So where did you
go after breakfast? I'm assuming you were sober when you
woke up.'

'Met up with some lads, didn't I? Went to the show like everyone else.'

'You mean Alwinton Show?'

'That's the one.'

'That's better. And you were there until what time?'

'Couldn't say.'

'You were in Elsdon village later that day though, weren't you?'

'Told you, I was pissed.' When the DCI said no more, Gardner felt obliged to add something. 'How do I know where I went? I reckon I was at the show until three or four o'clock. After that was a bit of a blur to be honest. I'd been necking booze all afternoon. It sometimes has that effect.'

'I'm sure that's true. It seems rather convenient, if you don't mind me saying so.'

'I'm not lying.'

Gardner's legal representative sighed. He seemed bored with his job and, on this shitty day, Kate understood exactly where he was coming from. She was sick and tired of dealing with the likes of Gardner. Her investigative skills and vast experience meant zip when interviewing suspects like him. He'd sit there for weeks and give her nothing she could use against him in a court of law.

His brief was getting impatient. 'My client has answered your question, Inspector. He told you he's unable to recall. He told me the same thing during our consultation. Can we get on with it, please?'

'With pleasure.' Kate switched her focus back to the accused. 'I have two witness statements claiming that you were in Elsdon having a heated discussion on Saturday evening with someone who was found dead on Sunday morning. If you weren't there, I have a dilemma. It's your word against someone else's; someone who, for the record, wasn't inebriated on Saturday. If you refuse to cooperate, I'm afraid this is going to be a very long process for you and for us.'

'Who's dead like?' Gardner was pleading ignorance.

'I think you know. It would be hard not to. It's all folks round here are talking about. You being such a friendly soul, I'd have thought someone might have filled you in.'

Another yawn. 'I've not been out much.'

'Nor seen the TV, listened to the radio?'

'Xbox. That's my thing.'

'I'll take your word for it.' Kate paused. Time to put him under some pressure, gauge a reaction. 'The dead boy is Elliott Foster. If I'm not mistaken, you know him.'

'No! You're kidding me.' His eyes opened wide in fake surprise. 'Don't suppose there's any chance of a bacon butty? Only I missed my bait and my stomach thinks my throat's been cut.'

'You'll be fed in due course.' Kate flicked open the file in front of her, taking a moment to study it, then raised her eyes to her prisoner. 'For someone who claims not to have heard the news, you don't seem too upset by it.'

'I am. Elli was cool.'

Elli? 'You saw him at the show, didn't you?'

Gardner kept his lip securely buttoned.

'Stop stalling and answer the question,' Hank said.

'Liam?' Kate was wondering if the shortening of Elliott to Elli was a term of endearment or a cruel nickname. 'Did you see him at the show or not? It's a simple enough question.'

'Yeah.' The arrogant shit was smiling. 'Course I saw him. He was in good fettle too. I shook his hand, gave him a pat on the back for winning his bout at the wrestling, didn't I?'

'Literally or metaphorically?' Kate asked.

Gardner eyeballed his brief.

Whether for clarification or playing for time, Kate wasn't sure.

Moffatt was losing patience. He knew where Kate was heading and had the good grace to look embarrassed on behalf of the despicable loser he was representing. 'She means did you actually touch him or was the pat on the back a verbal one.'

Gardner shifted his gaze from Hank to Kate. 'I gave him a big old bear hug. Ask anyone. I remember now. Must've been before I got pissed. After that I couldn't tell you. I made it home somehow. Woke up on the sofa, freezing my balls off with the TV on and a mouth like a sewer. My usual state on a Sunday morning.'

Very attractive.

Kate wanted to wipe the smug expression off his face. Gardner was an idiot, but not altogether stupid. If he persisted in this vein it made life difficult for her. He was clever enough to avoid the suspicion of a 'no comment' interview, blaming drunkenness for his memory loss. He'd already admitted knowing the victim, touching hands, putting his DNA all over him, all of which he knew she'd find on Elliott's body or clothing.

Time to turn up the heat.

'So, just to be clear, you shook Elliott's hand and gave him a hug.'

Gardner rolled his eyes. 'Said so, didn't I?'

'Is that the extent of your contact?'

'Eh?'

'Was there any other transferring of bodily fluids between you, either then or later?'

His eyes found Moffatt again. 'What *is* she on about?'

'I'm trying to establish if you bled or spat on him. I understand you're good at that.'

'That bitch had taken my dog!'

'I'm not keen on people gobbing on my DCs,' Kate said calmly. She could see he was riled. 'Your cuddle with Elliott Foster didn't go any further than you're letting on, did it, Liam? When I examine his clothes, for example, your semen won't be on them?'

His hackles were up and it showed. 'What the fuck—'

'No need to get abusive, Liam.' There was no emotion in the DCI's voice. It was flat calm and businesslike. 'I'm just trying to establish how far this contact went. If you were jealous of his success you might have fought with him. If you were close, it could have gone the other way. See what I'm getting at?'

'Jealous? Of him! Do me a favour.'

'Does it upset you that I might think that?'

'I don't give a fuck what you think.'

'No, I don't suppose you do.'

Moffatt cleared his throat, an attempt to get Gardner's

attention. It worked and he shook his head, warning him not to lose his rag. If this were a game, Kate was winning.

'So you weren't bitter then?' she said.

Gardner dropped his voice. 'Quite the opposite.'

'Sounds like you were proud of him.'

'Yeah, really proud.'

'If I'm "really proud" of someone, I might celebrate in style. How about you and Elliott? I don't know either of you, do I? Were you more than good friends?'

'I didn't say we were *good* friends.'

'You didn't kiss him then?'

'You think I'm bent?' He turned to face his lawyer. 'Is she allowed to call me a faggot?'

'I don't think I did.' Kate knew she'd be in trouble for this line of questioning. *Needs must.* With a murder to solve she thought she could justify it to Naylor if push came to shove. 'You seem, how can I put it, offended by my suggestion—'

'Damn right! I never kicked him, punched him. And *for the record* I never fucked him either.'

'You fucked him over though, didn't you, Liam?'

Gardner checked himself, took a long, deep breath.

'We have corroborative evidence that puts you at the scene of a fight. We have witnesses who claim that at six thirty or thereabouts on Saturday you, along with a number of others, male and female, were in the area of St Andrew's Church in Elsdon fighting with Elliott Foster who, as I already said, was subsequently found dead. You are still under caution. Why don't you tell us what happened?'

'You can shove the caution up your arse.' Gardner glared

at Moffatt. 'They've got the wrong guy. Chris Collins is the one they need to speak to. I'm not saying another word.'

'As you wish.' Kate pulled up her sleeve to check her watch. 'I take it there's no love lost between you and Collins.'

Gardner shrugged. 'I can take him or leave him.'

'Really? That's interesting. He claims you're a bit of a fantasist. Any idea what he meant by that?'

Gardner blushed but didn't speak.

'Very well.' Kate left him to cogitate that one. There was a story there somewhere. If his reaction was anything to go by, she might even use it against him if she could discover what it was. 'You'll remain in custody for the time being. Interview terminated at ten fourteen.' Exchanging a look with Hank, she nodded towards the door. 'Please show our guest back to his cell.'

'It's like a madhouse in the custody suite,' Hank grumbled when they met in her office afterwards. He threw himself down in a chair, loosened his tie and undid the top button of his shirt. 'I could hardly hear myself think in there. What a bloody waste of space Gardner is. Told you we should've left him to Maxwell. They could have bored each other to death.'

Kate laughed. 'It wasn't all garbage.'

'You think so? He didn't give us anything useful, did he?'

Kate tugged her earlobe. 'Depends if you were listening or not.'

Hank grinned. 'You saw me dropping off?'

It was nice to see him smile. 'He's adamant he didn't screw the victim, kick him or punch him. I have every faith in Su Morrissey to prove beyond any doubt that he did two of those things. By the way, talking of pathologists, have you heard how Maddie Stanton is doing? Last I heard she was still in hospital, milking it for all it's worth and running rings around her dad.'

'Girls and their fathers, eh?'

Kate went quiet.

Hank misread her and apologized.

She didn't correct him. Even from his sickbed her father was able to piss her off. She thought about telling Hank about her old man's heart attack but decided against. He'd only fuss over it and end up telling Naylor, who, in turn, would insist that she stand down. She didn't want that. In her absence, Jo could handle her dad with both hands tied behind her back. No need to go all Swiss Family Robinson because he'd taken a wobbler he'd most likely brought on himself. Besides, their missed vacation would be all for nothing if she didn't stick with the Elliott Foster case.

She changed the subject. 'Tell me, Hank. When I was winding Gardner up about bodily contact with Elliott, was his a natural blokey reaction, do you think? It seemed over the top to me.'

He shrugged. 'Why do you ask?'

'Did you notice he called Elliott "Elli"? He only said it the once, but I got the impression he wished he hadn't.'

'A nickname, surely?'

'Or a piss-take he's so familiar with he let his guard down.'

'You think Elliott might be gay?'

The thought unnerved Kate. She didn't even want to

consider how she might feel if his death had anything what-soever to do with his sexuality. Hank was staring at her, expecting an answer. He knew her well enough to know that she was churning inside. Seething would be a more apt description. All her cases mattered but, suddenly, this one felt very personal.

Poor Elliott.

Hank was done waiting. 'That's why you were baiting him?'

Kate nodded. 'I'm not proud of it.'

'You might even get a complaint out of it.'

'C'est la vie. I wanted a reaction—'

'And you got one.'

'I have a horrible feeling I can hardly bear to acknowl-edge,' Kate said. 'You think this could be a hate crime?'

'Because Elliott was homosexual? Aren't you jumping the gun? Your theory makes no sense if he fathered Beth's baby.'

'You think gay men can't father children?'

'Did I say that?'

'No. But *I* didn't say he was the baby's father. Beth didn't either. Atkins did.'

'Collins?'

She nodded.

'Blimey! When the Angry Man gets wind of this, he'll blow a gasket. If I had a crystal ball, I'd see a paternity test coming right up.'

'Not a word to the team until we're sure,' Kate said.

41

Kate gave her condolences but felt little warmth for the victim's mother. At Gayle Foster's request, they met at her place of work, a swish solicitor's office off Oldgate in Morpeth where she worked as an administration manager. Understandably nervous of being questioned about her son's death – especially as she hadn't told the truth about the last time she'd seen him alive – she'd asked the DCI to take a walk.

Grabbing a coffee to go, they walked past the clock tower, turning right into Newmarket, headed for the towpath that ran alongside the river Wansbeck.

Gayle cleared her throat. 'You must think me callous for being at work when my son is lying in a hospital mortuary,' she said.

Kate glanced at her. 'I don't judge people.'

I'm here talking to you with my father on his deathbed.

'Don't worry, Inspector. You're not the only one to think so. My secretary has been in tears all morning. She can't look me in the eye. She went to school with Elliott and can't understand why I turned up this morning. She's substituted practicality for lack of feeling. She's heartbroken and I obviously don't fit the stereotype of a grieving mother. Whatever you might think of me, I loved my son.'

They crossed Elliott footbridge into Carlisle Park. The coincidence of the name wasn't lost on the DCI. She wondered if there was a connection there somewhere, but didn't voice it. There wasn't a breath of wind. The river flowing beneath the bridge was dead calm. Seagulls were ducking and diving over the surface of the water. It was peaceful, unlike the simmering atmosphere between the two women.

As they walked on, Gayle's eyes strayed to the children's play area. Kate wondered if she was remembering happier times. Guilt-ridden for not attending her own family trauma, Kate's thoughts turned again to her father lying in hospital, hooked up to a myriad of heart monitors and breathing apparatus, her ex-lover offering to babysit until it was convenient for *her* to make an appearance.

'One thing I've learned in the years I've been doing this job is that people are individuals,' she said. 'We all cope with things differently, grief included. For what it's worth, I'd probably have kept on working too under the same circumstances.'

'You're either very nice or trying to make me feel better.'

'I'm a pragmatist too,' Kate said. 'I find it helps to focus on something specific.'

'Forgive me, Inspector. You don't seem the type to play social worker. Many have tried and failed where I'm concerned. With me you get what you see. Like it or lump it. However, I appreciate your efforts.'

Their eyes met.

'I meant it,' Kate said.

'That's very kind of you.' Gayle paused. 'So, now we've

established that I'm not too fragile to answer your questions, can we get to the point? I have a meeting soon and I'm pushed for time.'

'Suits me.' Aware of her own abrupt manner on occasions, Kate wondering if Gayle was the unfriendly woman she'd been painted or, like her, a busy professional with an important job to do. She checked her watch. It was ten forty-two. 'I have a briefing to conduct myself in less than twenty minutes. I've been straight with you. Now it's your turn. Why didn't you tell DS Grant that you'd seen your son early on Saturday evening?'

'He didn't ask.'

'Mrs Foster—'

'OK, he did.' The woman sighed. 'Please, call me Gayle. I've not been a Mrs, Foster or any other kind, for a very long time.' She seemed to float away to some place else for a while. Kate sensed regret but didn't pry or draw attention to it. Then Gayle was back on the towpath weaving her way around a pool of muddy water from last night's rain.

'I apologize,' she said. 'It was stupid to mislead. I didn't think it through. I kept quiet for egotistical reasons. I didn't want Graeme knowing that I was in Elsdon that evening. I was meeting one of his mates.'

Kate stopped walking. 'Gayle, I'm investigating your son's death!'

The woman turned, a shameful expression on her face. 'It's complicated. I don't expect your understanding. I couldn't see what difference telling you would make, after the event, when it would cause me a lot of hassle I could well do without.'

They both knew how weak that sounded.

Grant was a good judge of character: this woman *was* cold. Kate, on the other hand was, if not boiling, then ready to explode. 'How could you not?' she asked. 'You work in a law firm.'

'As an administrator, not a lawyer.'

'You're a material witness to your son's murder and you're bothered about what your ex-husband thinks of your current squeeze?'

She didn't answer.

Kate held her temper. There was no point showing her frustration or making an issue of it. She'd sought clarification and Gayle had delivered. Job done. Still, it niggled at her. It wasn't the resources she was bothered about. It was the time wasted piecing together a sequence of events that had more holes than a championship golf course. Had she known then what she knew now, MIT might have been closer to the person or persons responsible for Elliott's death than they presently were.

Sensing the end of her patience, Gayle apologized again for not being honest. Binning her empty coffee beaker in a nearby rubbish can, she gestured to a bench facing the river. They both sat down, staring at the reflections of the overhanging trees. Ducks and swans made a beeline for them, hoping for crumbs.

'We know that Elliott left your mother's house on his bike because she saw him leave,' Kate said. 'We have a witness who saw you drop him off in Elsdon not long afterwards. I need to fill in the detail.'

'I can help there,' Gayle said, her face finally showing

some emotion. 'The daft sod was walking on the wrong side of the road heading for the village. I stopped to pick him up so he wouldn't get run over.' When she glanced at Kate there were tears in her eyes. 'You know what that road is like. There's room for two cars, no more. He had dark clothing on. I nearly ran him down myself.'

'What explanation did he give for being there?'

'He'd had a puncture.'

'We know about that. What I meant was, did say who he was meeting?'

'No.'

'You didn't ask?'

'He didn't even tell me he'd won a prize at the show. Though it pains me to say it, not all offspring are on speaking terms with their parents, Inspector.'

Wasn't that the truth.

Kate regretted all the wasted years. Not having a father around was difficult at first, but she'd got used to it. So used to it, she hardly gave him a second thought these days. The shock of seeing him in the Coronary Care Unit following resuscitation brought her to her senses. On the way home she'd formed a plan to put aside their differences. To try, however hard a task it might be, to accommodate his point of view. As soon as this case was solved, she'd be on it, something she knew the woman walking by her side could never do.

For her it was too late.

'Elliott and I . . .' Gayle turned to look at Kate, tormented by past mistakes. 'Well, let's just say things were difficult between us. He was a little boy when he went to live with my mother. We saw each other occasionally, of course. It would be hard not to, living in such close proximity. There wasn't the mother–son bond you might expect. If I'd known that he'd be in more danger in the village than on that road I'd have left him to take his chances with the heavy traffic. Maybe if I'd kept on driving he'd still be alive.'

42

Back at the incident room, Kate was met with laughter she couldn't share. Gayle Foster was still very much on her mind. She might not be Mother Teresa – she'd lied to police – but she'd *torture* herself for the rest of her life for delivering her son to his killers. That's the way she saw it. Nothing Kate had been able to say on the walk back to her office had changed her mind.

The DCI couldn't help but feel sorry for her.

Across the room, Hank was sharing a joke with Carmichael, one or two detectives looking on. 'So the barman pours a cocktail, shakes it up and puts it on the counter. The ACC looks at it and says . . .' He forced a Glaswegian accent: '"What the hell's that?" The barman is thrown. "It's what you asked for," he says. "A piña colada." The ACC looks at him and yells: "I said a pint o' lager!"'

A roar of laughter went up.

'Haven't you got work to do, Hank?' Naylor said as he wandered in, catching Kate's glum expression before she could hide it. The group dispersed. 'Kate, can we have a word?'

'Sure. In your office?'

'No, I'm on my way out. Here's fine.' He led her to the window away from the others. 'Take a seat.'

She sat down, crossing one long leg over the other. 'How can I help you, guv?'

Naylor did a rapid head check of the room. Team members were taking their places for the briefing. 'Can you give me a quick update on the state of play? I'm due at HQ and Bright is bound to ask.'

Nothing was more certain.

The head of CID had left messages for Kate too. He wanted the case wrapped up, was expecting progress now she'd taken over. But Kate wasn't fooled. Naylor was stalling. He had something else to say and this was the preamble.

She played along. 'There's not a lot to tell. Gayle Foster has put her hands up to deceiving us. It would appear that Gardner is the ringleader of those involved in the fight. His mates are scum. There's no way his crew are going to betray him. Without exception, they say it was Collins did the kicking. We can talk to them until Christmas but we'd be wasting our time.'

Naylor considered this for a moment. 'If Collins did the kicking, wouldn't Beth have said so? She wouldn't cover for someone who killed the father of her child—'

'Elliott may not be the father,' Kate said. 'I had the same discussion with Hank earlier. I think Atkins may have got hold of the wrong end of the stick. There's only one way to be absolutely sure and that's to ask her.'

'Question is, will she answer?'

'I think so. She trusts me.'

'You think Collins is the father?'

'They're close. I tried telling Atkins . . .' She let the sentence float away.

'He'll be furious.'

'When is he anything else?' Kate stopped herself saying what was really on her mind. 'If Collins *is* the father it puts an entirely different complexion on things. Beth might lie for him.'

'Are you bringing him in for further questioning?' Naylor took in her nod. 'OK, check it out and keep me posted.' He was studying her closely. 'If you don't mind me saying so, you're not looking your best. Is there something upsetting you, other than yesterday's nonsense? If there is, I'd like to help.'

'No,' she lied. 'But thanks. I've been up half the night, that's all.'

'I heard. How's Beth?'

'Comfortable. It's the baby the medics are concerned about. I don't know what possessed her.'

'Me either,' he said. 'At her age I was having the time of my life. How's Atkins taking it?'

'Who cares?' Her response was callous and out of her mouth before she knew it. Her adversary deserved little consideration and even less sympathy. Kate wondered if he'd informed Diane of their daughter's suicide attempt, or kept her in the dark.

'Kate, you need to relax. He's not worth it.'

'Move on, is that what you're saying?' She gave him a disparaging look.

Naylor took off his jacket and sat down, studying her closely. 'I'm not his greatest fan either—'

'Could've fooled me,' she snapped.

'You doubt my loyalty?'

'No, of course not.' She apologized. Like his predecessor, Naylor was a great guv'nor to work for, an even better friend. 'I just can't understand your concern for Atkins. He brought about his own family crisis. No one else is to blame.'

'How so?'

Kate said nothing.

'I'm aware that his current predicament might be viewed as just deserts,' Naylor said cautiously. 'Payback for outing you to the team – but you wouldn't wish his situation on your worst enemy, would you?'

'No, guv.'

He stood up, ready to leave. 'Please give him my regards when you see him.'

'Yeah, like I'm relishing the thought of *that* encounter.'

'I'm sure you'll cope. You always do.'

Under his steely gaze, Kate looked away.

Through the window, fluffy clouds sailed by on a stiff breeze, stripping a horse chestnut tree of its leaves. She stood up too. Opening the window, she took a deep breath. What she wouldn't give to throw on her running kit and hit the tarmac through Jesmond Dene, where there was a spectacular display of autumn colours to enjoy. She'd run and run until she was too exhausted to carry on. Then she'd run some more, pushing herself to the limit, until she felt re-energized – the reverse of what she was feeling now.

Naylor still hadn't moved. 'Are you feeling guilty for dropping him in it with Bright?'

'Not one iota.' She turned to face him.

'So you're stewing over what he called you?'

'No, guv.'

Kate didn't want it known how deeply upset she was by Atkins' homophobic rant. So much so, she'd avoided the subject when she saw Jo last night. In the whole scheme of things, it was low on her priority list. There were more important considerations on the table. Life and death for two people whose lives had touched hers – her father's and Beth's – three, if you counted her unborn child.

Naylor wasn't fooled. 'You sure about that?'

Kate crossed her arms. 'Perfectly.'

He didn't dwell on her reluctance to expand on it. Like everyone else, he was probably wondering why she'd not come out sooner. And what the hell was he finding so amusing, she wondered. He was very nearly grinning.

'Do you remember the night at training school when I asked to be let into your room to save my arse?'

She smiled at the memory. 'How could I forget?'

He was in trouble, on a final warning, and highly inebriated at the time. He'd returned to base in the small hours to find all the doors of the accommodation block locked. Undeterred, and in spite of a long drop that would certainly have killed him had he slipped and fallen, he'd scaled the ledge in order to knock on her window. There was no other way in. Had he missed roll call, he'd have been sent packing. It would have been curtains on his career before it had even begun.

'What made you think of that?' she asked.

He was unable to keep a straight face.

'What?' she said, eyebrows knitting together.

'Hmm . . . how can I put this?' He was teasing her.

She waited.

'I'd done it before, only you had company.'

'You what?' Kate felt her cheeks burning. Leaning in, she dropped her voice to a whisper. 'You knew all this time and didn't say?'

'You were keeping it under wraps. Thought I should too. You were having fun with women. So was I!'

Throwing her head back, Kate laughed, a real belly laugh she couldn't control. It felt good and her embarrassment melted away.

Naylor grinned. 'You looked like you were having a lot of fun.'

'It was my experimental phase, guv. I swung both ways back then.'

'No law against it,' he said.

She thanked him.

'For what?' he asked.

'Everything. Your friendship means the world to me.'

Now it was his turn to feel embarrassed. He checked his watch. 'I must go. We will return to the subject of Atkins at some point. His suspension hasn't yet been made official. Bright is gunning for him, for what he said to you, rather than his failure to disclose prior knowledge of Elliott Foster, but we have to come to a decision on his future.'

'His future?' Kate felt sick. 'I would have thought that was obvious.'

'Not to me.'

'You want *me* to decide what action is justified? If you don't mind me saying so, that's hardly my responsibility.' She didn't hide her contempt for what he'd said. 'I take no pleasure in seeing any officer suspended, Ron. You know that as well as anyone. But he sure as hell doesn't deserve to be reinstated, if that's what you're suggesting.'

'I agree, and he won't be, not to MIT.'

'Hallelujah,' she mumbled under her breath. 'So what's the catch?'

'No catch.'

'Why don't I believe you?' she said.

Naylor paused as a detective walked by and waited for him to move off before speaking. 'Ask yourself what will happen if Atkins loses his job. Who will support Beth and her kid when her mother dies? Think on it.'

'With all due respect, that's not my problem. From what I've observed, there's no love lost between them. Beth probably wouldn't want his help anyway.'

'He's her father!'

'And they don't get on. The world is full of warring families who never see each other. Why should those two be any different?'

Naylor was perplexed. 'I've lost you.'

'I've lost me too, guv. Don't worry about it.'

He cocked his head on one side, thrown by the sarcastic edge to her voice and the fury in her eyes. 'Kate, I know you've had a rough couple of days. Even so, you're never this temperamental. Are you sure there's nothing else I need to know?'

'Don't you know enough?' *He didn't know the half of it.* Violence bred violence. If Kate thought she'd get away with it, she'd deck Atkins herself. Not for what he'd done to her. For what he'd done to Beth and Diane. She couldn't bear to think that he would be offered another chance to keep his job and carry on as if nothing had happened.

'You're going to have to help me out here, Kate. I'm not a mind-reader.'

'It's nothing.'

He knew she wasn't telling the truth. He also had a point. Who *would* take care of Beth and her baby when her mother was gone, assuming the foetus survived a hefty drug over-dose? From past dealings with Diane Casey, Kate knew that there was no extended family to step in or help out when times were tough. When the inevitable happened, Beth would be a vulnerable young mother, living alone, unable to work. At the very least, she'd require financial assistance. As far as Kate was concerned, she'd be better off on the social.

She could swing for emotional support.

'Hello?' Naylor was still waiting for a response.

Over his shoulder Kate caught Hank's eye. He could see that they weren't arranging a night out on the tiles and was showing concern. He'd quiz her later. Her eyes shifted back to Naylor. 'So, you're hoping this might be Atkins' wake-up call?'

'Anything wrong with that?'

'And you're prepared to sweep his behaviour under the carpet?'

'That's not what I said.'

'That's what you're implying—'

'No, it's not. And don't put words into my mouth.'

'I'm not,' Kate said.

'Maybe we should take this into my office.'

'I'm fine here.' Kate wanted the conversation to end. 'I thought you had to be somewhere.'

'Everyone deserves a second chance, Kate. Even arseholes like Atkins.'

'Guv, someone else used those exact words to me over a decade ago when he assaulted his wife. These days he's graduated to bullying his daughter, bullying me. How many chances does he get? He crossed the line.'

43

Making her apologies for a delayed start, Kate called for attention and took her position at the front of the room. She found Grant in a sea of faces. 'Colin, I'll start with you. Gayle Foster misled you and has expressed regret. Her mobile has been examined and I now have unequivocal proof that Elliott called her from his own mobile and not the village telephone box. That means his device is still in circulation.'

Carmichael raised her hand.

'What is it, Lisa?'

'Before he rang his mother, Elliott used the phone several times on Saturday afternoon.'

'You know this how? It's my understanding that he had no contract.'

'You raised an action to check out Morpeth supermarkets.'

'And?'

'There aren't that many. Andy spotted him on CCTV behind Sanderson Arcade. There's a Morrisons on Dark Lane, nearby. Their security cameras caught him topping up his credit, a tenner's worth on Wednesday. I got the number by comparing till receipts with the time on the footage.'

'Who did he call and when?' Kate asked.

'That's where it gets interesting. He tried the same number five times unsuccessfully. It's registered to his friend, Richard Hedley. The calls were made between two and four o'clock. Only the last one was answered and it lasted less than half a minute. I tried Hedley several times. The phone appears to be switched off. They're with the same service provider: EE. My contact claims that Hedley has missed calls – two on Sunday, three yesterday and one this morning – all from a mobile that *is* on a contract.'

'Beth Casey?' It was pure guesswork. A nod from Carmichael confirmed it was accurate. Kate knew that Beth hadn't been entirely honest.

'Sounds like she was frantic,' Grant said.

'Yeah, but what about?' Hank was talking to the room. 'Was she warning him to keep his head down or letting him know what had happened to his mate? None of Gardner's gang mentioned him, did they?'

There was a collective shake of heads.

'Which means she was probably telling the truth about not seeing him,' Kate said. 'Lisa, place all of the actions with regard to the village box in for referral and get on to your contact at EE. Ask them to flag up Elliott's number and also Richard Hedley's. I expect a call if either phone is used again.'

'This Hedley doesn't want to talk to us,' Maxwell said.

'I reckon he's legged it,' Robbo said. The DS looked shattered. His poorly child had kept him up half the night. He glanced at Carmichael. 'Any sign of Hedley's car?'

'No. I rang his neighbours again. They've not seen it or him for days.'

'Did you complete a background check?' Hank asked.

Carmichael nodded. 'He has no form and he's a second-year student at Newcastle College. According to his tutors, he's a quiet lad. He got excellent grades at school, good enough to get him into university had he stayed on for A-levels. I gather he wanted to study locally for personal reasons.'

'That fits with what I picked up from villagers in Elsdon,' Kate said. 'He doesn't mix much. Never has, apparently. Not since he moved in. When was he last in college?'

'Friday.'

'The tenth?'

Lisa nodded.

'I want the registration number of his vehicle ASAP.'

'I have it,' Lisa said. 'Hank asked me about it last night.'

Kate's eyes were on Hank. He raised a hand in apology for the lack of communication, something they were normally good at. She put it down to his preoccupation with Atkins generally, which had worsened after his outrageous attack on her yesterday. She made nothing of it. With so much going on, they were all feeling jaded.

'Have you put a trace out for the vehicle?' Kate asked.

Hank nodded.

'No joy so far,' Lisa said.

Kate smiled. 'You two are on a roll.'

'But if he's legged it we might be too late.' Maxwell was a master in the art of stating the obvious. 'You want an all ports warning out?' It was a good idea. It meant the focus would be on Hedley, rather than his car. The action was entirely justified, given that he was the person Jane Gibson swore her grandson was going to meet on the night he died.

'Do it,' Kate said. 'What have we done to find Elliott's mobile?'

Robson had his hand up, drawing her attention.

Kate indicated that he should take the floor.

He stood up to make himself visible. 'Fingertip search at both crime scenes revealed nothing. There are no reports of any "lost" mobiles being handed in to any police station locally. I don't even know if they record stuff like that any more.' For clarification, he eyed the uniformed sergeant he was sitting next to.

Scotty had been seconded to MIT to assist with the investigation due to his local knowledge, a shrewd move that was paying off. He'd been able to offer advice to officers conducting interviews with Liam Gardner's cronies who, he informed them, had been the bane of his life for years. 'They *should* log all lost property,' he said defensively.

'That's not the same thing as it actually happening though, is it?' Hank said. 'The service is going tits up and no one gives a stuff.'

'So we keep looking,' Kate said. 'Where's Andy?'

'Here, boss.' Brown's strawberry-blond hair poked out from behind Carmichael. They were never more than a few metres from one another. They had joined the team on the same day, were great friends as well as colleagues. Few of the other detectives associated outside of work, barring special occasions. These two enjoyed going out together, a platonic relationship founded on similar interests and taste in music.

'Did anyone manage to speak with Adam Foster's commanding officer while I was with Gardner?' Kate asked.

'I certainly passed on your message,' Brown said.

'And what was the outcome?'

'He said his officers had acted appropriately, then hung up on me and went over my head.'

'He called Naylor?' Kate frowned. 'He never mentioned it.'

'Worse,' Brown said. 'He called Bright.'

'Oh, let me guess,' Kate said: 'he's since backed down and we can interview Adam Foster at our earliest convenience. In fact he'll throw in afternoon tea for good measure.'

'That's pretty much how it went.'

Hank chuckled. 'I'd love to have been party to *that* conversation.'

Kate continued, still with Andy Brown. 'Did you speak to Dodds about the tyre tracks found at the scene?'

'They don't belong to him. He's not been near the perimeter of his land for months. His son has. Given the close proximity to the gibbet, which naturally draws a lot of tourists, that area is checked on a regular basis in case anyone has thrown litter over the fence that might harm their livestock.'

'Gut feeling?'

'They're as good as gold. And mortified that someone has been murdered on their doorstep.'

'The farm vehicles have all been checked?'

Brown nodded. 'None of the tyres match.'

'Missing rope?'

'Still no joy. To be honest, I can't see how a farmer would

301

know if any was missing. Most yards and barns have piles of the stuff shoved in untidy heaps all over the place. It would be hard to tell one length of rope from another. The saying "how long is a piece of string?" really fits the bill in this line of enquiry.'

Maxwell held a finger in the air. 'Do you want me to increase the search radius to include other farms?'

Kate thought about this for a moment. 'Have we exhausted every possibility in the boundaries I gave you?'

'Not quite.'

'Then don't. We need to keep this tight.'

'I agree,' Hank said. 'If we're done with the rope, I'd like to return to the army for a second. Military personnel at Otterburn have been extremely cooperative. They're happy for us to talk to any of their men. However, the guy I spoke to was quick to point out that they were on special ops on Salisbury Plain at the weekend.'

'All of them?' Kate asked.

'So that's where they were off to.' Scotty was thinking out loud. 'My missus saw them leave in convoy last week,' he went on to explain. 'She said it was like we'd declared war.'

Kate ignored him in favour of Hank. 'No squaddies left behind? No one sick?'

He shook his head. 'No guys like Neil in *their* unit.'

Maxwell was taking the dig in good spirits, rather than protesting his innocence. He'd been known as Sicknote since taking up his post. Arriving at MIT under a cloud, he'd taken too many days off, leaving a depleted squad, putting a strain on those who were left to pick up the slack.

Consequently, Hank wasn't his greatest fan – hence the snide remark.

While detectives carried on the banter, taking the piss out of Maxwell, Kate asked Hank to arrange for those guarding Otterburn camp to be questioned. She needn't have bothered. He was already on it. She drifted to the murder wall to study some stills of the victim, specifically the injuries he'd sustained to his face.

'Liam Gardner.' She turned back to face the team. 'For those who've not yet had the pleasure, he's a nasty piece of work. Ask Lisa. I understand she got more of him this morning than she bargained for.'

'No matter how hard I scrub, I still feel contaminated,' Carmichael said.

'It was a clean operation otherwise?' Kate immediately apologized for the unfortunate choice of words. Every day the police risked transference of diseases like HIV and hepatitis via saliva and other bodily fluids. Lisa had accepted a shot of antibiotics as a precautionary measure but Kate wouldn't rest until she was given the all clear. 'What I meant was, are Gardner's crew all present and accounted for?'

Lisa nodded. 'The cell block is heaving, but they're all here.'

'Great work,' Kate acknowledged publicly. 'We appear to be deadlocked: Beth and Collins saying one thing, Gardner and his mates saying the exact opposite. The *only* thing they agree on is that the victim was punched and kicked—'

'Not quite,' Hank said. 'Although Gardner's mates aren't actually admitting having done anything themselves, other than being present when the fight took place, they know they're in a lot of trouble. They all state that Elliott Foster was alive when they left the scene and swear that they all stayed together that evening and through the night, Gardner included.'

'Well they would, wouldn't they?' Maxwell said. 'They're covering his ass.'

Kate took over. 'Did anyone ask where they spent the night?'

Brown was first to respond. 'My punter said it was Gardner's house.'

'Mine too,' Robbo said.

Gardner's voice filled Kate's head: *Woke up on the sofa, freezing my balls off with the TV on and a mouth like a sewer . . . my usual state on a Sunday morning.* 'Well, if that's true, why didn't he mention it to me in interview?' She was talking to Hank. 'He had no way of knowing we had them all in. I assume you kept them away from each other?'

Interviewing officers were nodding. 'At different stations,' someone said. 'But they had plenty of time to work out their story immediately after the body was found.'

Kate looked at Hank. 'So why wasn't Gardner hitting us with an alibi his mates were primed to corroborate?'

'Because it stinks, that's why,' Hank said. 'He knew fine well we wouldn't buy it.'

'No other weapons used apart from hands and feet?' It was Maxwell who'd asked, the only team member not involved in interviewing those brought in for questioning.

Carmichael confirmed it: no baseball bats, no sticks or knives, none that anyone had mentioned so far. On Kate's say-so, Lisa sprang to her feet to hand out blown-up images of the stills the DCI had been studying so intently on the murder wall.

Kate waited for her to retake her seat. 'Take a good look at these marks on the victim's face. Initially I thought they might have been made by a knuckleduster, even though we don't see them used so often these days. On further examination, Su Morrissey – that's our new pathologist, for those who don't know – has suggested that they're more likely to have come from metal boot eyelets. In light of the argument over who did the kicking, I'm having Collins brought in again. Both his and Liam Gardner's footwear preferences and purchases are now top priority. I've spoken to Gardner. He claims he doesn't possess any boots.'

'We only found trainers at his gaff,' Brown said.

'Then search it again.' All eyes were trained on Scotty. 'He's lying through his teeth. He wears cargo pants and desert boots all the time. Thinks he's a bloody paratrooper.'

Kate scanned the appreciative faces of her team. The murder investigation had wound up a notch.

44

It had been the mother of all briefings. Kate left the incident room and finally sat down in her office for a few moments of peace and quiet. She called Jo but her phone went straight to voicemail. She called Collins' mother, asking for permission to search her house, telling her why it was important. She was in luck. The woman gave her consent without a fuss.

Hank stuck his head round the door as she hung up.

Kate put the phone on a desk littered with papers and Post-it notes, an untidy mess organized into piles: Urgent, Not So, Rubbish. The latter would hit the bin as soon as she had time to sift through it.

'Don't get comfy,' she said. 'Collins' mother reckons he has nothing to hide. I need you to organize a search for boots at their place. Get her signature on a PACE search form while you're at it. The Police and Criminal Evidence Act isn't all bad.'

'What are you going to do?'

'I'm going to get some air.'

Without telling anyone where she was going, she left the building, drove straight to the hospital and made her way to ICU. Visiting time wasn't due to take place for another hour, so she asked to see whoever was in charge. Seconds later, a woman in uniform walked towards her, a friendly smile on her face.

'I understand you want to see me,' she said. 'How can I help?'

She was taller than Kate, around six two with green eyes and blonde hair tucked neatly into a bun at the nape of her neck. Calm and unruffled, she was younger than Kate expected for someone with such an important job. Then again, *she* held the record for being the youngest detective in history ever to make DCI in her force area. If you wanted to reach the top in an organization as big as Northumbria Police, you had to start early.

'I'm Kate, Ed Daniels' daughter.' She stuck out a hand. 'How's he doing?'

'Oh. He's not here. We transferred him to the Coronary Care Unit this morning.'

On the ground floor, Kate rushed into the ward and collared another nurse. Introducing herself, she enquired after her father, keen to chat with him, buoyed by the rapid transfer from ICU. It was positive news. He'd died and come back to her. He was strong.

A survivor.

'He's getting there,' the staff nurse told her. 'But I have to warn you, he's not out of the woods yet. He's a lucky man. Had there been any delay in getting him here, he might never have made it. He's been monitored closely overnight and the duty cardiologist will see him again later.'

'I understand.'

'Don't worry. He's in the best of hands.'

'Thanks.' They stood aside as a patient was wheeled onto the ward, far too young to be having heart problems. Kate turned her attention back to the nurse. 'I know I'm too early for visiting but I happen to be in the middle of a murder investigation.' She showed ID. Proof that she wasn't trying to pull a fast one. 'Is it possible to see my father for a few minutes? I won't stay long. I wouldn't ask, but we've not spoken since he came in. I was here last night, only he was unconscious, asleep anyway. It would help a great deal if I could call in whenever I can slip away. It's impossible to meet set visiting times.'

'As long as you realize he needs lots of rest.'

'Of course.'

The nurse nodded. 'We can be flexible up to a point. He's in a private room so your visits won't disturb other patients. Most of them are very poorly.'

'A private room?' Kate repeated. 'He asked for that?'

'Your sister wouldn't have it any other way. In fact, she insisted. The problem is, we sent him for tests. He might be a while. If you like, I could ring down and see how long. If he's already been seen, although I doubt that, he may be waiting for a porter to bring him back.'

'No, it's fine.'

Kate glanced over her shoulder, wondering if Jo was still around. It was so like her to take charge and not mention it, to do right by Ed, even though she fell woefully short of his expectations. Perfect partner material she was not. She didn't fit the profile in any way. Kate wished her father would just get over it. She felt unworthy of Jo. They should be on the east coast of Scotland by now. Getting to know each other all over again. A new beginning. That had been the plan.

'If you're looking for your sister, she just left,' the nurse said.

'Oh,' Kate played along. 'I tried calling. She's not answering.'

'She said she'd be a couple of hours. She was here at dawn, so I imagine she's gone home for a rest. I told her your father's tests would take time. There was no point hanging around. Without being unkind, she looks like she could do with a break. She's very considerate, your sister.'

'Yes, she is . . .'

Unlike me.

Kate considered telling her that Jo was no relation, but had neither the time nor the inclination to get into it. She glanced at her watch. It was almost one o'clock. She couldn't afford to hang around. 'I'll try and get in later. When my father returns to the ward, will you tell him I've been in, please?'

'Yes, of course.'

Taking a business card from her pocket, Kate handed it over. 'Call me if there's anything you're concerned about, or if he asks for me.'

He probably won't.

Thanking her, Kate walked away. The chances of her old man asking to see her were zilch. He'd know how concerned she'd be for his well-being. No doubt he'd be waiting for her to make the first move. He was a stubborn git sometimes.

*

Visiting times were different on Beth's ward. Kate was making her way upstairs to see her when her mobile rang. Pulling it from her pocket, she saw that it was Hank and sat down halfway up with a view through the window over the busy car park. People were flooding in to visit sick relatives.

She hated hospitals.

Kate lifted the phone to her ear. 'Tell me you found matching boots?'

'We found boots at Collins' place. Several pairs. Whether they match Elliott's injuries or not is open to question. Su Morrissey will be in touch.'

'What do you want then?'

'Hey! We may be divorced. Doesn't mean I don't miss you.'

Kate laughed.

In Spain, while hunting a fugitive, they had gone undercover, pretending they were married. It was an easy deception to pull off, given their propensity for falling out. An image of him arriving on their hotel balcony wearing a ridiculous Hawaiian shirt, a pair of knee-length pink shorts, Jesus sandals and socks jumped into her head.

Hilarious.

The socks were so he couldn't feel the sand between his toes, a phobia she didn't know about. She liked nothing better. The memory of that case had stuck with her, cementing their relationship in a way no other had. They had grown closer, the difference in rank fading away to nothing. Professionally, they had always been great together. The experiences they shared in those short few weeks had altered the dynamic forever.

The door from the stairwell above opened and swung shut.

A middle-aged woman with a head wound and a black eye appeared. Already reeking of nicotine, she was fumbling with a fag packet as she walked down the stairs, keen to get outside for another hit. Shuffling to one side, so as not to block her access and prevent a swift escape, Kate smiled at her. She could do with a cigarette herself.

'Don't suppose you've found a lighter?' the woman asked.

'No, sorry.'

The patient practically ran down the stairs to the floor below. The door to the grounds creaked as she pulled it open and did the same as she let it go.

Hank had overheard. 'You still in the station?'

'Hospital.'

'Is that a good idea?'

He'd be furious if he knew why she was really there. 'It's an idea,' she said. 'Whether it's a good one or not depends on the outcome.'

'How's Beth?'

'I've not seen her yet.' *I've not seen anyone yet.* 'She was admitted to the assessment unit as an emergency measure. Had she not been pregnant, she'd most probably have been treated and shown the door. This morning a decision was taken to transfer her to maternity for monitoring. I assume to remind her that she's carrying a child and has a lot to live for.'

'The baby survived?'

'So far.'

'Can I give you a piece of advice?'

'You're going to anyway.' Kate knew what was coming.

'Don't get involved.' It was a good call, if a little predictable.

'I'm already involved, Hank. I was there, remember.'

'Then be sure you ask Atkins before you visit. Don't make yourself a target for him to shoot at.'

'Yeah, yeah.' Hank was right. No point aggravating the Angry Man. If she were to interview Beth without his permission he'd only make an issue of it – another reason to have a go at her. He lived less than five miles away. It wasn't as if she'd have to go out of her way to consult with him. 'You win,' she said. 'I'll swing by his house and ask nicely if it'll make you feel better. Can I go now?'

'Want me to meet you there?'

'No, Hank, I need you at the station in case there are any developments. I promise I'll leave if he starts. Is Collins in custody yet?'

'Yes.'

'Good. Keep the pressure on him and Gardner's mob. See if you can't get his mates to drop themselves in it. I don't believe they hung out with him on Saturday night. I suspect we already have our offender in the cells – we just have to prove which one – but if you're scratching for stuff to do after that, contact the military police. Adam Foster needs to be alibied – and I feel bad that we haven't yet given our condolences.' Kate hung up and headed for her car.

45

The DCI drove out of the hospital, turning left and on through Ashington, an area proud of its mining heritage, as demonstrated by the eye-catching brass sculpture of a pitman to be found en route to the market town of Morpeth. Atkins' home was only a short drive through open countryside, around five miles away. With any luck, he'd be so hung over he'd give permission for her to talk to Beth. It would save him the trouble of doing it himself. A difficult task for him . . .

He wasn't exactly socially skilled.

Ten minutes later, she arrived at Atkins' apartment block.

At the entrance, she rang hard on the buzzer next to his name. Either he wasn't in or he'd seen her arrive and wasn't answering. Leaving the premises, she walked to the municipal library where she'd left her Audi, popping the doors open as she walked to the car. She was about to get in when two men caught her eye.

Without waiting for the lights to change, they pelted across the road.

Kate watched them head along Bridge Street for a few metres and into Shambles, a pub and restaurant.

Maybe . . .

Pressing her key fob again, Kate relocked her car. Following the men, she entered the pub. They were already ordering.

Three other customers were standing with their backs to the bar, their eyes glued to a flat-screen TV showing Sky Sports on the opposite wall. Next to them, Atkins too was on his feet, turned the other way, staring into an empty pint glass, a newspaper spread out in front of him. His posture told her that he was incapable of reading the print. She made her way over to him and leaned on the counter. The popular free house was always busy.

Sensing her gaze, he looked up. 'What do you want?'

His voice was like gravel. It reminded her of Hank's on occasions when he'd been to the match and had been yelling too much. If you were a frustrated Newcastle supporter you did a lot of that. Atkins was dressed in the same kit he'd worn yesterday. She imagined he'd been drinking all night and hadn't been to bed.

'Thought I might find you here,' she said. 'Have you got a moment?'

'Shove off.' He tapped the glass. 'Put another in there, Terry.'

The landlord didn't look happy to serve him. Kate thought he might refuse. Then he acquiesced, as if arguing with Atkins was more bother than it was worth. She knew the feeling. Picking up a fresh glass, the man held it under the Moretti beer tap and took hold of the lever, ready to pull a pint.

'Second thoughts,' Atkins said. 'Make it a Grouse, a double.'

Taking his hand away, the landlord picked up a stainless steel measure and threw Kate a half-smile. 'You too? You look like you could do with one.'

'She doesn't,' Atkins said. 'I'm choosy who I drink with.'

Embarrassed, the landlord apologized with his eyes.

Kate sent a silent message in return: *He's a dick. Don't worry about it.* Somehow, she didn't think the landlord needed telling. He'd probably had dealings with Atkins before. Turning his back on them, the guy lifted his measure to the whisky optic. He pushed twice, asking Atkins if he wanted anything to go with it.

What he meant was to dilute it.

Atkins told him, no.

'You want ice?'

A morose shake of the head was all the reply he got.

'Can we sit down?' Kate glanced into a room at the rear of the pub. It was fairly quiet, save for a family of four who were eating. 'There are things we need to discuss.'

'I'm stopping here.' Atkins sunk his whisky in one mouthful without taking unfriendly, bloodshot eyes off the man behind the bar. Pushing the glass towards him, he asked for another. Hell bent on getting shitfaced. Kate knew there wasn't a damned thing she could to do to stop him, but she had to try.

The shake of her head was barely visible, a gesture to the landlord to hold the order.

Atkins glared at him. 'Terry? Fill it up!'

'Take it easy,' Kate hissed.

'What for?'

'There are bairns in the back room,' she said.

He yawned widely, giving her a view of his wisdom teeth.

In his mouth they were just teeth.

'OK, drink yourself stupid then. That's going to do Beth a lot of good. How is she – if I'm allowed to ask?'

'She's conscious. That's something, I suppose.'

'You've been in this morning?'

'What do you take me for?'

'So why are you here?'

'I'm fucking celebrating! She's made it crystal clear she doesn't want me around.'

You reap what you sow, mate.

Kate held that thought. He was supposed to be the grown-up, the responsible parent, not the petulant child. 'I meant medically. How is she medically?'

'Sore from having her stomach pumped. What do you expect? Why the hell do you care?'

Kate did care – and well he knew it. Fleetingly, she considered her own medical emergency; whether or not her father would make a full recovery or experience another coronary before surgery. An ever-present threat, she supposed. She wondered about the tests he was undergoing, if the prognosis had altered in light of the results. Atkins was mumbling about the very thing in her head: organ damage.

'They didn't find any, did they?'

'Fortunately not.'

'And the baby?'

He didn't answer.

'You didn't ask?' she said.

'I will, soon as she gets home.'

'Unbelievable!' Whether to serve another customer, out of discretion, or to take himself out of the firing line, the barman moved away. Kate kept her voice to a whisper. She moved in close, right in his face. 'Your only daughter tries to take her own life and you bury your head in alcohol and don't ask whether her unborn child has suffered any permanent damage? How could you be so bloody insensitive?'

'Don't lecture me. It's a family matter.'

'That's right, it is. You're going to be its fucking granddad!'

'That's nowt to do with you.'

'Oh, and where have I heard that before?' She looked away. At various points in the bar, old rifles were displayed on the walls, secured by heavy brass brackets. Shame they were only for show. Right now, Kate could use one. She eyeballed the angry man. 'You want to lose Beth altogether? Keep it up. You might get your wish. Does Diane know? Because if she doesn't, she sure as hell should.'

'Stay out of my business.'

'She has a right to know.'

'I said—'

'Fine!' Kate moved away.

'Where you going?' Atkins stuck a hand out, grabbing her arm until it started to hurt. He was smiling at her. 'Don't be like that, Kate. I thought we might kiss and make up. I know you're on the other bus, but maybe I could show you what you've been missing all these years.'

Shrugging him off, Kate slid along the counter. She held up ID to the barman. 'You serve him any more alcohol today and I'll have your licence. Understood?' The landlord nodded, relieved to have an excuse to refuse him and get him off his premises.

'Sling your hook!' Atkins yelled. 'And make sure you nail

that bastard Collins! You can tell him from me, if he goes near my daughter again I'll swing for him.'

An unfortunate choice of words.

The venomous way in which they were delivered made Kate's blood run cold. He was drunk – undoubtedly – but not enough to forget that threats to kill could land him in trouble. A twinge of suspicion began to form in her head, burrowing deep inside her investigative brain. She held his gaze, her thoughts all over the place. She'd assumed his eagerness to sign on early and get his foot in the door of MIT was motivated by spite, designed to get back at her. Could there possibly be another reason? Was he out to pin a murder on Collins, a lad he despised openly and fingered for the crime early on? He'd yet to explain how that came about. Or was she the one stretching it – projecting her hatred back at him? Dismissing the theory as too far-fetched, she blew out her cheeks as she walked away. Tiredness did strange things to people.

46

Turning into the hospital grounds, Kate parked in almost the same location she'd left less than two hours ago. Angered by her encounter with Atkins, she'd grabbed a sandwich in Morpeth and found a peaceful spot, halfway to Ashington, so she could eat it in peace, surrounded by open country-side – guaranteed to take her blood pressure down.

Hank would be jealous.

Kate finished her lunch. Relaxing into the headrest a moment, she shut her eyes, mulling over her suppositions in the pub and discussion with Naylor earlier. His concerns for Beth's future financial security were valid – of course they were but what of her physical security? Had he thought about that? Deep down Kate knew that someone needed to put a stop to Atkins' violent conduct once and for all. If she didn't report him, who would? If Hank ever found out that he'd manhandled her there would be hell to pay.

Getting out of the car, Kate strode purposefully towards the main entrance of the hospital. She'd almost reached it when her mobile rang. She lifted it to her ear. 'Hank, I'm trying to be in three places at once and I'm running late in two of them. Is it important?'

'You sound out of breath.'

'As I said, I'm in a hurry.'

'To see Beth?'

'How the hell—'

'Atkins just gave me a mouthful over the phone – most of it incomprehensible – I gather you guys had words. It didn't sound like he'd given you the lickings of a dog. You OK?' He didn't wait for an answer. He'd have come to the conclusion that if she was talking, she was still breathing. 'Hold on a sec . . .' He paused to talk to someone in the office.

Kate could hear Andy Brown's steady voice in the background.

Moments later, Hank returned. 'So,' he said. 'I'm guessing you're doing what you always do?'

'What's that then?'

'Making your life difficult when there's no need. You didn't ask his permission to see Beth, did you?'

Intuitive.

'You know me, Hank. Never ask a question you don't want the answer to.' She stepped through automatic doors, pulling up sharp behind an elderly couple. They had come to a sudden stop in front of her, eyes raised to scan the information boards. 'What did Atkins want?'

'I've no bloody idea – I wasn't listening. Your name came up though and the air turned blue.'

'Figures.' Mounting the stairs, she detected a faint whiff of nicotine. She felt sorry for those forced to freeze their bits off outside, even though a smoking ban was eminently sensible. 'What did Andy want?'

'There's nothing wrong with your ears then?'

'Cut the sarcasm, Hank. Enlighten me.'

'Our boy, Chris Collins, hasn't been totally honest with us.'

'In what way?' She pushed open a door at the top of the stairwell.

'In relation to his previous.'

'What do you mean? We know he has convictions.'

'But did we know how nasty they were?'

'So hurry up and tell me.'

'Both offences were against young women. The affray on his record happened outside a pub late one night. Others involved said Collins was laying into a girl big style. They got stuck in and someone called the law. The judge took the view that they were as guilty as each other and they all went down, including the girl. She had form herself apparently: violent conduct, public order, breach of the peace and so on.'

'And the grievous bodily harm case?'

'Was against his then girlfriend. He glassed her with a bottle.'

'Nice.'

'Not nice, she lost an eye. So whatever you think of Atkins' bullying tactics vis-à-vis you, his determination to separate Collins from his daughter is entirely justified.'

'Takes one to know one.' Kate's theory was back. It stung like a prod from a branding iron.

'There's more. Andy has done a thorough background check on Collins. We knew he was a city boy. He said as much in interview. All the stuff he was spouting about supporting his mum was bollocks. It appears they weren't always so close.'

'Go on.' Kate stopped walking, the better to pay attention. 'What else did Andy say?'

'Collins spent years in care as a kid. According to reports prepared for the County Court, his mother took him in again when he was sixteen. She threw him out six months later when he got into trouble. When he left Deerbolt YOI after his last sentence she refused to have him back.'

'Where did he go?'

'His uncle offered to care for him. It didn't last. When their relationship deteriorated he too threw him out. Young Christopher has a whole other persona we didn't know about. He's not as nice as Beth would have us believe. Maybe she's not either.'

'I'll bear it in mind,' Kate said. 'Thanks for letting me know.'

Having found the maternity unit, Kate took a moment in the corridor to get her head in gear. There was so much information about her case whirring round in there she was beginning to feel drained. She walked on to the ward like she owned the place. Bright had taught her that the more confident you were, the less people challenged your reason for being there.

It worked every time.

She found Beth in the first bay of a small six-bed ward. She was awake, pale and unhappy, staring at the ceiling, deep in thought. It was heartbreaking that a girl her age should've encountered so much stress in her life. Sensing a presence, Beth turned her head and began to cry when she saw Kate standing there.

Drawing the curtain around the bed for some privacy, the DCI pulled up a chair and sat down. 'If anyone asks, I'm your favourite aunt.'

Beth managed a weak smile – she had no words.

The upbeat expression slid off her face almost immediately, replaced by a much darker one, a toss-up between shame and embarrassment. A bit of both, Kate guessed. Lifting a jug of water from the bedside cabinet, the DCI poured some out, inviting Beth to take a sip. She complied without argument, recovering her composure.

'I'm sorry I let you down.' She was fiddling nervously with the edge of the sheet. 'I don't know what got into me.'

Kate rested a hand on hers. 'Don't apologize to me, Beth. It's your father who should be doing that. He should also be right here by your side, your mum too. I assume she's unaware of what's happened. If she was, she'd move heaven and earth to support you.'

'Is that why you're here – because he's not – because she can't be?'

'Something like that.' Kate wondered if Jo was having the very same conversation with her father. Who was she kidding? *If* didn't come into it. Assuming Ed Daniels had agreed to see her, he'd be making his mouth go for sure. If Kate knew anything about Jo, he'd be getting it thrown right back at him.

She wouldn't take his bullshit.

'I thought you might like some company,' she said. 'And I need to talk to you.'

'Does *he* know you're here?'

'Not yet.' Kate made out that it wouldn't be an issue. She'd deal with Atkins when the time came. 'I'll tell him later. Does he know you've been transferred?'

'Probably not. Is he angry with me?'

'More sad than angry, I'd say.'

'So why isn't he here then?'

Because he's drunk and incapable, Kate thought, and too stupid to admit he might be at fault. It is his fault – *all* his fault. 'He doesn't think you want to see him.'

'Yeah, and why's that?'

'You told the nurse to turn him away.'

'That's true. He didn't stick around long though, did he? I would have, given the same set of circumstances. My mum would. I bet you would too.'

'People react to stress differently . . .' In spite of Atkins' loathsome behaviour, Kate found herself defending him again in order to lessen his daughter's pain, to dispel the sentiment that she was unloved and in the way. Kate knew exactly how that felt. 'He has been here . . . all night,' she said. 'He probably needs a kip. He'll be in later, I'm sure. How are you feeling?'

'Crap.'

Kate had to ask. 'And the baby's still OK?'

Beth's eyes filled up as she gave a nod.

'That's great news. You must be very relieved. I should warn you that your father knows—'

'Well, there was no hiding it once they put me in here, was there?'

'No, I suppose not.'

'Is Chris in custody?'

So he was the father.

'For the time being,' Kate said. 'We need to question him further.'

Hank's wise words jumped into her head: *Maybe she's not either.*

Beth presented as a lovely girl, but even lovely girls – especially mixed-up ones – got into trouble occasionally and lied to get themselves out of it. This time her tears wouldn't wash. Kate maintained a professional distance. Beth Casey might have suffered more than one underserved misfortune in her past but she was a witness to a very serious crime.

'What did you want to talk about?' she asked.

'I need to be sure you've been totally honest with me.'

'I have.' She sounded innocent enough. 'Why would I lie?'

'To cover for Chris, maybe.'

'No, everything I told you is true. Is he going to be charged?'

'Not at the moment, no.' Kate was still wondering if the tears were real. Or had she developed an ability to turn them on and off at will to manipulate a situation or gain sympathy? 'Were you aware of his criminal history?'

She flinched. 'What history?'

'I didn't think so.' If Beth was acting she was RADA material.

She sat up, searching Kate's face. 'What's he supposed to have done?'

'I can't tell you that. You'll have to ask him when you see him.'

'You're lying!' She snatched her hand away. 'My dad told you to come round here and say that to put me off him, didn't he?'

'C'mon, Beth. Friends don't lie to each other—'

'Why should I listen to you?'

'Because I'm trying to help you, like I helped your mum.' Kate had to tread carefully. She couldn't afford to alienate the girl completely. She'd clam up and visiting rights would cease – as they had for her father. 'I can tell you that Chris was in trouble before he moved up this way. He claims that he hid at Boe Rigg campsite to keep out of Gardner's way.'

'He did.'

'That wasn't the only reason though, was it? He kept out of our way to hide his past from you. That's why he ran from your dad.' Kate paused, giving Beth time to reflect. 'You can see how it looks, can't you? Chris has demonstrated a propensity to lie. That calls into question his account of what happened on Saturday.'

'I don't care how it looks. I told you the truth and I'm sure he did too.'

'Are you? Really?' Kate wasn't as convinced. Her eyes shifted to the mobile phone lying on the bedcover. 'You never told me you'd been calling Richard Hedley constantly since Sunday, did you?'

'You didn't ask.'

'No, I didn't.' Kate's tone was harder than before. 'I'm investigating your friend's murder. Did it not occur to you to mention it?'

Beth held her gaze defiantly.

Kate watched her flesh turn colour. A mottled patch of

pink crept up her neck and settled in her cheeks. Nerves did that sometimes. She'd been found out.

'Beth, you're not going to like what I'm about to say, but I'm going to say it anyway.' Kate gave it straight. 'I'm not a parent. If I was I know that nothing would be more important than protecting my child from harm. You should take some time while you're in here to think long and hard about your relationship with Collins. I'd hate you to make the same mistake your mother made.'

'You can't compare Chris with my dad!'

'Listen, Beth, I've been a detective long enough to know that abused women, damaged women, seek out a certain type of man. They may not do it consciously but it does happen.'

'No. Chris isn't like that. He might fly off the handle occasionally, but he wouldn't do that to Elliott. He wouldn't.'

'Your dad thinks Elliott is the father of your child.'

Beth couldn't hide her shock.

'He's not, is he?'

'No! That's ridiculous.' Beth was losing it. Her hand flew to her mouth, stemming a sob. Big tears were falling from her eyes. 'We were soulmates since being kids . . . just mates.'

'Chris is the father?'

Beth nodded.

Finally Kate was making headway. 'Do you know where Richard Hedley's parents live? I need to trace him urgently.'

'Brighton,' she said. 'I don't have an address.'

'Phone number?'

'No, sorry.'

Kate stood up, leaned over and gave Beth a hug, patting her gently on the back. Beth clung on tightly as tears turned to sobs. 'C'mon, Beth. You need to stay calm and get some rest for the baby's sake. We don't want your blood pressure going through the roof, do we? We can talk again when you're feeling better. You must be exhausted. Get some kip.'

Lying back against her pillows, Beth shut her eyes, her hand relaxing its grip on Kate's, her anxiety fading away.

'That's better,' Kate straightened the bedcover. It felt starched and uncomfortable. 'I'll be in later.' Taking hold of the privacy curtain, she drew it open, then turned. 'One last thing, Beth.' The girl opened her eyes. 'You called Richard because you were worried about him, didn't you?' Kate took in her nod. 'Because he and Elliott were partners?' Beth didn't give an answer and Kate didn't need one. Tears were flowing again.

47

Kate checked her watch. *Damn it*. She'd been with Beth for almost forty-five minutes and there was less than fifteen minutes left of visiting time on the Coronary Care Unit. Jo was sitting on a chair outside the ward, tapping a message into her mobile phone, probably concerning her lateness.

Kate's mobile signalled an incoming text. **Where are you?**

Before Jo had managed to put the phone in her bag, Kate leaned in close, too close for those who might be watching. 'I'm here.' She sat down sideways, facing Jo. 'Sorry I'm late – and thank you.'

'For what?' Jo asked.

'Everything. Being here. Being you. Arranging a private room. You didn't have to do that.' Tucking hair behind her ear, Kate took in Jo's dishevelled appearance. Unusual. She wouldn't visit the dump unless she'd brushed her hair. Perhaps she hadn't been home and had rested in the car. She was getting more like Kate every day. 'Have you had *any* sleep? You look shagged out.'

'You don't look so hot either. But unlike you, I have manners, so I wasn't going to mention it.' Jo widened her eyes seductively. 'On second thoughts, maybe you do look hot.'

'Stop it.'

Jo grinned. 'For the record, I care less about what you

look like than I do that you're finally here. How's the case going?'

'Slowly.' Kate head-pointed over Jo's shoulder to the ward entrance. 'How is he?'

'He's doing OK; baby steps, but he's making progress and coming the terms with what's happened. It's shaken him up a bit.'

'But not enough to knock any sense into him.' It was a statement from Kate, not a question. She could tell Jo was being cagey, leaving out the unpalatable stuff.

'I can handle a pain in the arse,' she said. 'I'm used to it.'

Kate ignored the attempt at humour. 'You shouldn't have to. If he's giving you grief—'

'He's not.' Jo was quick to defend him. 'He doesn't get it, Kate. He doesn't get us.'

Her expression was playful, not depressed. She'd obviously talked to Ed Daniels at length about the barrier that existed between him and Kate. *Good for her.* Kate didn't have the time in her life to hold his hand while he got his head round it. Jo was different. Having worked in many prisons, she was used to making the most of a captive audience with no escape route. The stupid bugger would have to listen, like it or not.

Jo's mouth was moving again, her words drowning out Kate's thoughts, becoming clearer and louder in her head . . . 'Of course, he's avoiding the subject. He's not about to acknowledge that we have *any* kind of connection, let alone a sexual one. But now is perhaps not the most appropriate time to tackle him. I don't think his ticker is up to a deep and meaningful on that subject.'

Kate wasn't laughing.

'You'd think he'd done it on purpose,' Jo said.

Kate rolled her yes. 'Timing is everything. He's probably been planning to scupper our trip to Scotland for months. I wouldn't put it past him.'

'Give him a break, Kate. He's from a different generation. It must be hard for him to accept that you'll never have kids, that you prefer to spend your life without a man to fend for you . . .'

Kate didn't hear the rest of the excuses. In spite of her wish to improve her relationship with her father, all she could think of was his profound disapproval; an unwillingness on his part to accept her for who she was. There was no harder thing to cope with than indifference. As far as he was concerned, she was invisible. Unworthy of the bond they once shared. He'd shut Jo out for years. He'd be civil to her, but he'd never accept her as part of his life – let alone his daughter's.

Kate sighed.

Had her mother lived, things would have been different.

'Kate? What's wrong?'

The voice sounded muffled in her ears. Kate tried to listen, but her thoughts were louder. Angrier. She'd tried everything in her power to persuade her father to acknowledge that she was as precious as any daughter: cosying up to him, arguing her case, occasionally even writing to him. As close as she was to Jo, Kate had never told her about the letters. The replies had been so hurtful she hadn't been able to share them.

'He's a dinosaur,' she said.

'He's *your* dinosaur.' Jo placed a cold, slender hand on Kate's cheek and stroked it gently. 'Don't go there now. He's not well. We'll have this conversation some other time. If he's still not willing to admit that he's in the wrong, then pity for him. Go on in, he's waiting for you.'

Through the glass panel in the main entrance, Kate could see nurses running around after patients. He'd be nice to them – no doubt about it – and yet he couldn't be civil to the one person who was always there for him. Why did she even care? He didn't. She tried to stem her anger. Her father was blind if he couldn't see what Jo meant to her.

As she stood in the corridor, two separate trains of thought merged like the storylines of a book or film. Suddenly she couldn't differentiate between her own situation and that of Elliott Foster. If she found out that his death was connected to his homosexuality it would open up a wound she'd been hiding for years. A bleeding open wound she'd been trying and failing to live with. The reason she'd thrown away all that was good in her life.

'I'm sorry, I've got to go.' Kate kissed Jo and walked away.

'Kate? Kate!'

The DCI kept walking.

48

The noise in her head increased as Kate sat in her Audi, arms resting on the steering wheel. Poor Elliott. She wondered if he'd shared his sexuality with his parents, as she had tried to do. The only living relative who knew of her secret was hanging on to life in a hospital bed. He'd rejected her, at pains to point out that she'd had 'normal' relationships. Used in this context, the word *normal* was like a stick to beat her with. Her thoughts swung wildly. She was tempted to run – start the car and drive as far away as possible – but she had to face her father at some point.

In the end, she did neither.

To go back inside and pretend she had any kind of meaningful relationship with him felt like a betrayal of all gay people. The lid on Pandora's box was lifting. Kate pressed it down tightly. This was no time to let her demons out. Frozen to the seat, the memory of her first altercation with Atkins wormed its way into her thoughts. She was a uniform PC at the time, with aspirations to become a detective . . .

It had been an average night, an unremarkable shift at a busy station: a couple of burglaries, an assault on a prostitute, an arson with intent that got out of hand, a warehouse going up as wind fanned the flames. She'd been out sweeping surrounding premises, making sure that they had been properly evacuated, the only woman on her shift.

A couple of hours later, she'd received a call to return to the station. She was a mess when she arrived, her uniform sweater singed from getting too close to the flames, white shirt blackened by dense smoke and smeared with blood from a casualty hit by flying glass. Her then sergeant, James Atkins, told her to get cleaned up. She'd gone upstairs to take a shower and grab a change of clothes and had just stripped off her shirt when he appeared in the doorway of the women's locker room.

'Thought you might like some company,' he said casually.

'Sarge, you scared the hell out of me.' She thought he was messing around, trying to put the wind up her, except that wasn't his style. He was the bully in charge of her shift, the one with all the clout and none of the charisma. No sense of humour.

She pointed at the open door. 'Do you mind?'

'I do, as it happens.' He pushed the door shut.

The lock clicking home sounded loud in Kate's head.

'I heard the rumours,' he said. 'Came to see if they were true.'

She held his gaze. 'What rumours would they be?'

'They call you Ice Maiden.' He grinned. 'It's strictly business with you. You're friendly enough, but that's where it ends. Boyfriends are out, that's the word in the bait room anyway. I'm inclined to believe it. It's not like you even look interested—'

'In you? I'm not.'

'*Watch your back with Atkins.*' *Kate remembered the warning from PC David Reynolds the day she arrived at the station. When she'd asked what he meant, he repeated what he'd said and left it at that. Never in a million years did she think he was referring to their sergeant's sexual appetite for rookie female officers.*

'*Aw,*' *Atkins mocked.* '*Don't be like that.*'

She wasn't scared of him, but his fixed stare made her nervous.

He took a condom from his pocket and held it in the air. '*No one needs to know. Shift'll be tied up for a while yet.*'

'*They'll be stood down soon—*'

'*And who's going to do that then? I'm the boss. They'll stay put until I say so. Even if they return to base, they're hardly going to come in here, are they?*'

'*Sod off.*'

He made no attempt to leave. He was there by design, not by accident, the shout for her to return to the station a deliberate ploy to get her kit off while the rest of her shift were following his orders, dealing with a major incident elsewhere.

Clever.

Kate didn't know what to do. She was nineteen years old.

She felt sullied, thinking about the wretched experience. Even though she was safe in her car, her recollection of that night made the flesh beneath her clothing crawl, anguish tug at her heart. No amount of time or hot water would ever wash away the sickening episode. The memory was as much a part of her as her arms and legs.

Rain began to spot the windscreen.

Kate raised her head. The hospital car park was half-empty. Umbrellas were up as people rushed to find transport.

Visiting time was over . . .

Jo would be furious . . .

Get a grip.

If Jo had known the real reason Kate couldn't face her father, she'd be more than angry. She'd been the victim of a similar attack from someone she ought to have been able to trust – Alan Stephens: the man she was once married to. He was a serial philanderer, not unlike Atkins. Jo had baggage of her own to carry.

From the moment Jo confided in her, Kate had vowed that heaping more misery on her was never going to happen – she'd kept the darkness of her own abuse buried deep within where it couldn't be seen. *That was the theory anyway.* In truth, Atkins' actions – that night and since – had not only scarred her, they had shaped the way she'd conducted the rest of her life, much of it in secret. Now he was in her face again. She couldn't bear it.

Kate had felt every step he took towards her as a body blow. He oozed ill intent and seemed confident that she wouldn't resist whatever he had in mind to do. He was wrong. Something snapped in her head and she retaliated – a push in the chest, no more – enough to make her point and let him know that she wasn't about to go along with his plans. He seemed to find her resistance amusing. The longer the pushing and shoving went on, the stronger her feeling that she wasn't the first woman to suffer at his hands.

Kate dropped the Audi's window, took a gulp of fresh air and switched off the engine. Had it not been for her mother's unconditional love and understanding, she would have gone under, or left the force. She'd felt stuck in a rut, believing that she'd never make it to the top in her chosen career. They had talked about it before she died. Her mum had worried about her isolation, urged her to seek help. Counselling from a professional with whom she could discuss the 'dilemma' they both knew was ruining her private life. At the time, Kate hadn't listened. Afraid of being stigmatized, she'd gone against her mother's advice.

She wasn't the one with the problem.

Kate had seen other officers marginalized by vindictive, ambitious colleagues. She'd witnessed their exclusion from the elite club that is the upper echelons of the police service in a world dominated by men. She didn't want her sexuality to open up her career to negative scrutiny. She wanted to be revered for her professionalism, not put down by gender stereotyping. Why should she tell all? Her private life was simply that – no one's business but her own.

Her phone vibrated on the dash, startling her. The third call in as many minutes. She wasn't ready to take it. Not for Jo, Hank, or anyone. She needed time to get her shit together. She was bigger and better than guys like Atkins. Always had been. That didn't mean it didn't hurt.

He laughed as she stepped away from him. Kate stood her ground, her senses heightened by the need to protect herself: she could smell the spicy aroma of Paco Rabanne; hear the sound of old floorboards creaking beneath his feet; taste the bitterness of bile in her mouth. As he came within striking distance, her self-defence training – still fresh in the memory – kicked in. In one rapid upward movement, she straightened her arm, hitting him in the face, the heel of her hand striking the underside of his nose, incapacitating him. It was so swift a jab, and so unexpected, he was unable to duck in time.

'You fucking dyke!' Eyes watering, he slammed her against metal lockers, knocking shampoo bottles and other personal items on top of her. 'Shame you feel that way.' He wiped snot and blood away on his sleeve. 'You're finished, Daniels. Get ready for the shit jobs, because that's all your kind are good for. It's all you'll ever get from now on. I'd rather jerk myself off than have sex with half a woman.'

She flinched, taken aback by his hatred.

'Step away,' she warned.

When he stayed put, she kneed him in the groin.

The door to the next room slammed shut.

The cleaner's cupboard.

Kate's eyes flew to the party wall.

Atkins placed a hand over her mouth, his voice barely audible. 'You'll keep quiet if you know what's good for you. One word of this gets out and you can forget ever making the CID. They don't take bent bitches like you.' It was his only leverage. He knew how much she wanted it. She grabbed her shirt and started to put it on.

The phone vibrated again. Kate stared at it for a long time, the memory slipping away from her. It would return. No doubt about it. The warbling stopped. She picked up the phone as a voicemail arrived, lifting it to her ear.

'Where the hell are you?' Hank sounded frantic. He was not in the station as far as she could tell. There was no chatter of radios, phones ringing. No conversation or office banter going on.

Worrying.

She pressed redial.

'Finally!' he said.

Through the windscreen, Jo came into view, walking quickly to her car. She didn't look happy. No bloody wonder. She was babysitting a man who'd much rather she would get the hell out of Kate's life. No place would ever be far enough away.

'Kate? The signal is weak. You still there?'

'Sorry I missed your calls, Hank. I'm at the hospital.'

'Oh yeah? I rang maternity. They have no record of you being there.'

'That's because I slipped in unannounced.' Kate watched Jo get into her car, drive out of the car park and disappear. She wanted to follow, to explain, but her attention slid back to Hank. He was asking if she was on the level. Clearly, he knew she was hiding something. 'I told you where I am. Don't question me, please.'

'What's wrong? You're upset, I can tell.'

'Oh, so now you're a mind-reader?' She wiped a tear from her cheek.

'My mistake; sorry for asking.'

'No, I'm the one who's sorry. I have a headache, that's all. Has there been a development?'

'Hedley's been located.'

At last: some good news.

'Stick him in a cell. I'm on my way in.'

'That would be difficult. He's dead. A rambler found him hanging in Harbottle Forest an hour ago. No suspicious circumstances this time. There's a note addressed to Beth. I'm at the scene waiting for the pathologist. The finder is with me. We'll wait for you.'

'It's almost dusk, Hank.'

'Tell me about it. I'm in the deep dark wood. The only thing I'm missing is a Gruffalo.'

'Get an incident van, arc lights and photographers—'

'Already taken care of.'

The DCI started the car.

'Kate, did you get that? Damn this bloody phone! Kate, you still there?' She'd hung up and was driving away.

49

Harbottle Forest was part of Northumberland National Park, a vast area. No one with any sense would venture into it without reference to an up-to-date Ordnance Survey map. Kate didn't have one to hand so, as night fell, she rang Hank for information. When he didn't answer, she called Control requesting explicit directions and GPS coordinates for the discovery site. It was almost seven fifteen by the time she arrived.

Turning left off the main road, she followed a dirt track for as far as she could go, stopping her Audi in a small clearing, a visitor's parking area, alongside other police vehicles. The forest was silent as she got out of the car, an eerie silence broken only by the odd hoot from an owl or rustle of vegetation as wildlife came out of hiding in the hunt for food.

Tucked away under the trees, to the south of the car park, there were two other civilian vehicles: a rusty Ford Focus and a VW Polo, neither with a local registration plate. Wondering if one of them might be Hedley's, Kate walked towards the Focus. There was a small dog bed inside, the window slightly ajar, the remains of a picnic and a map lying on the front passenger seat. Kate moved to the Polo. Nothing visible. The car was locked and secure.

She rang the incident room to crosscheck the Polo's vehicle registration with the PNC. It was Hedley's. Thanking Lisa for the confirmation, Kate hung up. With a police-issue torch for company, she set off on foot. She didn't need to check her bearings. Around half a mile ahead, a light cut through the darkness, guiding her. Sheltered by oak and birch, the forest floor was largely dry, moss-covered, like a natural carpet. Nevertheless, it was difficult terrain, with many hazards in her way: fallen trees, rabbit holes and rutted ground.

Breathless and wrung out when she arrived, she was dreading the next few hours. Hank seemed pleased to see her. The blinding white light of arc lamps against the pitch-black forest gave the appearance of a sci-fi movie shoot. Kate half-expected to hear a director shout: 'ACTION!' In reality, *she* was the one giving the orders, the person authorized to give advice to Hank and Home Office pathologist Tim Stanton, who was standing by in full forensic kit waiting to get to work.

'Nice to see you, Tim.' Kate managed a smile. 'How's Maddie?'

'At home, being cared for by her mum,' he said. 'None the worse for her experience of a night in hospital.'

'That's great news.'

'But not a priority conversation.'

'I'm sorry?'

'Small talk isn't your thing.'

Kate assumed he was anxious to get on and get home. Ordinarily a suspicious death of this nature wouldn't fall within the remit of the Murder Investigation Team. A straightforward suicide wouldn't involve her. Stanton had been kept waiting because of Richard Hedley's close association with her victim.

'Just pulling your leg,' he said. 'It's always a pleasure to see you, Kate. I hear you've had a tough couple of days.'

'You could say that.' Kate wondered what he meant. Who he'd been talking to. She was going to say she'd had worse, but that would have been a lie. With Atkins on her case, things were about as bad as they could get.

Checking that the photographers were finished, for the second time this week she gave permission for the body to be cut down and laid on plastic sheeting. She stepped away as Stanton knelt beside the corpse, opening up the medical case he'd brought with him, the initials TWS engraved on its side. Watching him get to work, she knew he'd take his time. He'd share his views on cause of death when he was ready and not before. Meticulous in his approach to his work, she had every confidence in him as a colleague.

Waiting for his verdict was par for the course in her job.

Kate sighed, another suspicious death of a young person on her patch filling her with despair, chipping away at the shell she hid behind in order to stay sane. The first time she'd viewed a dead body, Bright had been by her side. He'd told her it would get easier. It never had. But that was not something you shared it if you wanted to get on and move up.

She shivered.

It was getting chilly.

Pulling her coat collar up for warmth, Kate glanced to her left as Hank arrived by her side. Looking every bit as exhausted as she felt, he handed her Hedley's suicide note, already in an evidence bag. The note was written in fountain pen, the message short and to the point, his handwriting shaky, a watery splodge on the last line of the note she suspected might be tears.

Beth
    By the time you read this I'll be dead. When I heard about Elliott I thought he'd killed himself because of me. We fought before the show, a stupid argument, not even worth mentioning. He called me later, full of himself for winning his bout. I refused to meet him and put the phone down. I know now that he was murdered but I feel responsible. He was my world – I can't live without him. I'm sorry.
    Rich

A combination of grief and fury swamped the DCI. Beth Casey would be devastated by this news.

'What do you reckon?' Hank asked.

'To the note?' Kate shrugged. 'Very sad, a bloody waste – I could go on. Are we even sure it's him?'

'Pretty sure.' Hank held up a second evidence bag containing the lad's college ID. 'You believe what he wrote in the letter?'

'Sounds plausible. We know from his phone records that Elliott rang him several times on Saturday. When he did get through, the conversation was short. Why? You think he was involved with his boyfriend's death and couldn't live with the guilt?'

'The thought crossed my mind.'

'Mine too, but not for long. If Hedley were about to hang himself, don't you think he'd have told the truth? I know I would. Look at the size of him. He must be what, ten, eleven stone. Hardly built to haul a dead weight onto an ancient gallows tree, is he?' Kate's eyes travelled the length of Hedley's body. 'Isn't he a bit slight to be a wrestler?'

'It's all in the legs, Kate. The longer they are, the more advantage you have. When they lock hands behind each other's backs it's hard to unbalance an opponent who's much taller than you, let alone dump them on their arse. C'mon, I know where there's a flask of mediocre coffee, if you'd like some.' Hank knew that standing around doing nothing was something she found difficult.

Kate appreciated his thoughtfulness. 'I'm craving gin, not coffee made hours ago. Give Carmichael a ring, would you? I need a handwriting comparison to confirm Hedley actually wrote this.' She held up the note. 'Beth told me his parents live in Brighton. Lisa can get the ball rolling while we're out. Tell her I want them traced and spoken to by Sussex Police ASAP.'

Stanton pulled car keys from Hedley's pocket, along with a fountain pen, possibly the one he'd used to write the note. Kate's eyes once again fell on the victim. She'd attended enough hangings to know that he'd been there a while. There was a groove on his throat where the ligature had dug into his skin. No other injuries as there had been in the case of Elliott Foster. Except . . . She leaned in closer, examining a minute amount of blood on Hedley's lower lip.

'Has he bitten his tongue?' she asked.

Tim Stanton raised his head. 'Correct.'

Kate scanned the scene.

A rotten log lay on its side not far from the overhanging branch of the tree. Hedley had placed the noose around his neck, kicking it far enough away to do the business. Once it was gone, even if the poor bugger changed his mind at the last minute he was done for, a thought too awful to contemplate.

With nothing to do but wait, Kate considered the suicide in light of what she already knew. Two connected hangings – days apart. Young men she now knew to be lovers. Their lives destroyed, directly or indirectly, by the actions of one or more offenders who so far had eluded the law. The depressing thought spurred Kate into action. She'd obtain proof. Find the person or persons responsible. She owed it to Elliott and to Richard.

50

It was late, almost nine thirty, when they got back to the incident room. On Hank's say-so, team members had already packed up and gone home, put on notice to report at seven a.m. sharp. There was only one update on the murder wall: *Adam Foster – interview report in my in-tray*. DS Robson's initials were scribbled next to it. Because Hank had been called away to the gruesome discovery in Harbottle Forest, rather than cancel or reschedule, Robson had taken the initiative and stepped in to interview Elliott's brother and written it up. Kate was lucky to have two DSs she could rely on.

The report was comprehensive. She speed-read the document, along with an attached note informing her that an even fuller statement had been passed to admin to be typed up first thing in the morning. Robson had called it how he saw it: the soldier was in the clear and that was good enough for her.

Hank arrived at her elbow. 'What you reading?'

'Robbo's report on Adam Foster.' Rolling her eyes, she gave a shake of the head. 'Unbelievable! The army omitted to tell us that he was no longer operational when he went AWOL. He's an Afghanistan amputee with aspirations to return to active duty or else work in a support role behind enemy lines. After a period of recuperation, they sent him to Germany to see how that might work out for both sides.'

'He's office based?'

She tapped the report. 'It's all in here. He has a few, shall we say, ongoing problems: one arm, a gammy leg, psychological issues . . . a heavy dose of survivor guilt, according to those treating him. No wonder that mouthy civilian I told you about gave the military police and me such a hard time when he was lifted. Make sure he gets a caution. In fact, write him off as NFA.' Kate sighed. 'Adam posed no threat to the army. He's a mess. Confidentially, the military are considering his discharge as we speak.'

'So why go missing?'

'He got wind of the fact that they were going to bounce him.'

'He jumped before he was pushed?'

Kate nodded.

'I'd probably have done the same in his shoes,' Hank said. Kate's anger grew as she read on. 'What a despicable way to treat a veteran who laid his life on the line for Queen and country. He must be gutted and wondering what it was all for. Robbo reckons he's on the edge of a breakdown. His brother's murder might just push him over.'

'I'm pretty close to the edge myself.' Hank yawned, rubbing at the stubble on his chin. He had an impressive five o'clock shadow and dark circles under his eyes.

'Bizarrely, this report makes our job a lot easier. Adam is out of the frame – he couldn't have killed his brother without a great deal of help. If Stanton references Hedley off as a sure-fire suicide, our list of suspects gets smaller.'

'The way I like it,' Hank said.

Her eyes shifted to the A4 sheet in his hand. 'What's that?'

'A précis of a coroner's report on Jane Gibson's son.'

'Verdict?'

'Straightforward suicide following a prolonged and well-documented period of mental illness according to medical records gathered at the time.' Hank yawned again. Apologized. 'He'd been sectioned twice and treated at St Mary's numerous times.'

'I thought the old asylum had closed down.'

'It did,' Hank confirmed. 'This was late eighties, early nineties, following unsuccessful attempts by Gibson to do away with himself. Not a happy family, were they?'

'No.' Kate went quiet, guilt over her father rearing its ugly head again, tormenting her as it had done all evening. There had been no calls from Jo. No update on his condition since Kate had bolted from the hospital without seeing him.

In her mind, she ticked off several other distressing family dramas: Elliott's parents had washed their hands of him, his grandmother, Jane Gibson, taking over their role as guardian; Beth had chosen to end it because of *her* father's despicable behaviour; Richard Hedley had left Brighton to make a life in Northumberland. Had he run away too?

When would she stop doing the same?

For years Kate had tried to pull the veil away, to be seen for the person she was and not the unattached free spirit she pretended to be. Atkins was the reason she hadn't managed to achieve it. He'd found her Achilles' heel and she hated him for it. It was the one area of her life in which she was weak – *the single most important area.* She hated herself for lacking the moral fibre to stand up and be counted as a lesbian. Every time she had tried – and there had been many – she bottled it, building an opaque shell around her so that no one could see in or observe her too closely, her skills as a copper, and later as a detective, soaking up the majority of their interest.

'Go home to your family, Hank.'

He stood his ground, his eyes on her. He felt her sadness, even though he knew nothing of the reason behind it. He probably assumed it was because she'd missed her leave, or because they had fallen out over it. Her attention wandered again. An explanation wasn't the only thing she owed Hank.

There was so much more to it than that . . .

There were times when her approach to her work was unconventional. She wasn't afraid to fly solo, beneath the radar of professional standards. When her questionable tactics landed her in trouble, as they invariably did, he stood by her, offering unconditional friendship and support, took her arsey comments on the chin, covering for her when she bent the rules. He deserved her thanks and her honesty.

In the morning she'd tell him the truth – *the whole truth and nothing but the truth* – about Atkins, her father's coronary, all of it, assuming they could steal an hour together. Now was no time to broach the subject. It was far too late for such a momentous heart-to-heart. He'd not sleep with it on his mind and he'd bend her ear for not confiding in him sooner.

Tomorrow . . .

'Get your coat,' she said. 'I need you out of my hair, tucked up in bed where you belong.' She raised a hand to the objection before he managed to voice it. 'I'll be leaving myself shortly, I promise. I've got a few bits and pieces to finish up and then I'm out of here too.'

'If something is bothering you, I'm happy to stick around and talk it through.'

'I'm fine, Hank. I'm going to make myself a brew and call Jo.' That seemed to do the trick. 'I'll be working in my office though, so turn off the lights on your way out, please.' She stared at the fluorescent tubing above her head. 'That flickering bulb is doing my head in.' As soon as he was gone, Kate went straight to her office and shut the door. With only a desk lamp for company, she reached for the phone and dialled Jo's number.

51

Jo picked up before the ringing tone hit Kate's ear, as if she'd been waiting for the opportunity to have it out with her for having run off, rather than face her father. Kate took a deep breath. She deserved whatever was coming her way. In semi-darkness, she felt the temperature plummet before a word had been exchanged between them.

She didn't need to see Jo's face to know that she was pissed off.

No one with any common sense would attempt to justify a wrong if they were out of order. The only thing Kate could do was to offer a heartfelt apology. With no influence over what reception it might get, she mentally crossed her fingers, hoping it would suffice.

'I'm sorry,' she said. 'What happened earlier was unforgiveable.' She echoed what she had told Jo in the hospital: 'If you'll let me, I can explain—'

'Do you mean earlier this afternoon earlier, or tonight's visiting time earlier?' Jo spat out her disapproval with much venom. 'You have so many apologies to make, I can hardly keep up.'

'I fully intended coming to see him tonight, I—'

'So why didn't you?'

An icy silence followed for a beat or two. There was a

limit to Jo's patience. However tolerant a person she was –
and she was, *very* – it was clear that she'd had as much as
she could take of Kate's nonsense. Pushed too far, she was
bound to retaliate.

Kate closed her eyes, the darkness transporting her back
to Harbottle, to that spongy forest floor she'd been tempted
to lie down on and fall asleep. It would be several hours
before she could do that. 'There was another suspicious
death,' she said finally. 'Elliott Foster's boyfriend hung himself – my attendance wasn't optional.'

'I'll tell your old man that you'll be there if he ever makes
it to the morgue, shall I?' Jo said. 'No doubt he'll find it very
reassuring.'

Kate pressed her lips together, resisting the urge to laugh
out loud. Her ex sounded more like Hank every day. Kate
was under no illusions. The words were humorous but not
remotely funny. Jo was hurt. More than hurt: she was distressed, disappointed, angry – arguably so – and poised to
have a go. It wouldn't be an exaggeration to say that she was
on the verge of losing her temper big-style.

She certainly wasn't finished . . .

'Let's not pretend that you are any more interested in
your father than he is in you, shall we? I'm fed up with both
of you. If you want my honest opinion, you deserve each
other.'

Kate didn't argue.

It wasn't always so.

There was a time when she and her father were inseparable, when every moment they spent together was precious and fun. From an early age, she'd realized he was a

petrol-head. She'd accompany him to Croft Aerodrome or Oliver's Mount in Scarborough to watch the motorcycling, just the two of them. He'd taught her how to ride on a strip of private land where it mattered not that she was under age. He'd introduced her to Hartside Pass, a location she loved, her destination of choice since she'd grown up and joined the force, the place she escaped to whenever she needed to think through a heavy case. She rode on his pillion, just ten years old the first time they went there, already an adrenalin junkie.

As a little girl, she adored him.

As she got older, nothing she did pleased him. He hated the clothes she wore as a teenager, the career she chose and, later, the company she kept – especially that. She wasn't feminine enough, nor considerate like other girls. She was selfish and single-minded, putting her career above all else.

Why can't you be more like Tracey?

Tracey was a girl who lived nearby, a Barbie doll with nowt between her ears and even less to say. Did he *really* want her to turn into pink mush, continually pregnant with no life of her own? Kate had a brain. She wanted to make a difference, not babies.

She felt suddenly weary. 'It's complicated, Jo—'

'When was it any other?' Jo fell silent. Kate thought she was going to calm down. She couldn't have been more wrong. She was just getting started. 'I'm sick of lame excuses that don't stack up. It might come as a surprise but you are not the only DCI in the force. The Northeast won't descend into anarchy if you're not at work. My suitcase is packed. I thought you were up for it this time—'

'I am, was—'

'I thought you could . . .' Jo choked on her words. 'I thought you *would* put us, me, at the top of your agenda just the once.' An ominous gap opened up in the conversation. It had Kate wondering if Jo was in tears at the other end. She wasn't. 'I was kidding myself, Kate. The holiday was a pipe-dream. I know you'll never change. I'm sorry, I can't do this any more. I think we're done.'

It felt like a body blow. Winding Kate. Wounding her. In the pit of her stomach something died instantly. This was a defining moment, the fatal car crash she'd seen coming but was powerless to prevent. Her life was about to change in the worst way possible.

She pleaded. 'Jo, please don't do this. I need you—'

'As nursemaid to your old man?'

'No! I didn't ask you to sit with him. You offered.'

Bad choice of words . . .

When the phone went down Kate let out a scream of rage. She'd blown it this time. Seconds later, it rang. She snatched it off the desk, lifted it to her ear.

'I'm sorry,' she said. 'Please, please forgive me?'

'Why? What have you done?' It was the pathologist, Su Morrissey.

Covering the speaker, Kate shut her eyes, bit down hard, trying to batten down her emotions. With Jo's words echo-ing in her head, refusing to leave, she was incapable of speech . . .

I think we're done . . .

I think we're done.

Taking in a breath, Kate let it out again, removing her

hand from the speaker. Her voice was flat calm. 'My apologies, Su. I thought you were someone else.'

'Clearly . . . Well, you're forgiven.'

'I doubt it.' *She knew it.*

'I meant by me.'

'I gathered that.'

'Tough day?'

'I've had worse.'

'Not many, I bet. Anything I can do to help?'

'No, I'm fine.'

'Good, because I'm about to heap more bad news on you – the eyelets on Chris Collins' boots don't match the injuries on Elliott's face.' Hanging up, Kate looked at the phone. When one door closes, another slams in your face.

52

Next morning, Kate woke early, Scotty's words popping into her head the minute she opened her eyes. *He's lying through his teeth. He wears cargo pants and desert boots all the time. Thinks he's a bloody paratrooper.* She showered quickly, got dressed and texted Jo before she left the house. Having received nothing back, she called her landline and mobile on the way in to work.

No answer.

Bypassing the MIR, with no time to indulge her personal crisis, Kate went straight to the exhibits room and signed for all five of the mobile phones seized from her prisoners at the time of their arrest. She took them to her office, put on a brew and sat down to examine them. Two hours later, she'd uploaded all the evidence she needed to put the frighteners on Gardner and his mates. She was ready to face the team.

'I've got twenty photographs of Gardner, in different locations, on different days,' she said. 'There's not a pair of trainers to be seen, so round of applause for Scotty please.' She clapped her hands together silently, smiling at the blushing officer. 'In every picture, Gardner is wearing big boots. I've just come from the cells. He still denies owning any. Claims he used to. They wore out and he threw them away months ago. I want his house searched again, inside and out: sheds, garden, coalbunker, refuse bins – the lot.'

'Does he have a lock-up?' Hank was looking at Scotty.

The officer shrugged. 'Not to my knowledge, I'll ask around.'

'Do it now please,' Kate said. As he stood up and left the incident room, she delivered the bad news. 'Unfortunately, I don't yet have any proof of what Gardner was wearing on the day of Alwinton Show. None of our prisoners' phones were helpful in that respect.'

A groan filled the room.

Kate raised her hand to silence the team. 'It's not all bad. Beth's claim that he photographed Elliott during the fight that took place afterwards is now proven. There are two photographs on his device showing Elliott alive and being held against his will. We can extrapolate the exact timing of the fight from those images.'

Maxwell was trying to get her attention.

'You have something important to add, Neil?' He sometimes interrupted just to crack a joke and the DCI wasn't having that.

'The images your journalist friend sent over aren't much use,' he said. 'I caught Elliott on one or two – and the back of you and Jo, if I'm not mistaken – but there's not a single one of Gardner or his mates. I reckon they spent most of the day getting bladdered in the Rose and Thistle, just as he said. Area sent a PSO to find out.'

'Don't they have any real coppers?' Hank was being sarcastic.

Kate was still with Maxwell. 'Try Alan Tailford again. He's a "real" copper – at least he was before he retired. Helen said he had a new camera. Tell him I want sight of all the photographs he took. Although we haven't yet nailed Gardner at the show, he freely admits to being there. Maybe we'll get lucky.'

'I think we already did,' Carmichael said. 'The images you shared with me this morning are gold dust.'

Grant hadn't yet seen them. 'They place his cronies at the scene?'

'Of the fight, yes. All four of them,' Kate said. 'Faced with such hard evidence, I'm betting they'll drop Gardner in it faster than Usain Bolt can run a hundred metres.'

'He'll say he didn't take them,' Robson offered.

'He will, but they're on his device and Beth Casey saw him take them. Who do you think a court will believe? And how else would she know of their existence? The chain of evidence is getting longer.'

'Will she testify?' Brown asked.

'Damn right: she doesn't like Gardner any more than we do and Elliott was her best friend.'

'Are the images available to view?' Grant asked.

'Soon,' Kate said. 'They're being examined, documented and copied as we speak. They'll be displayed on the murder wall later this morning. I'm going to find those bloody boots if it kills me. Hank, come with me. I want to search his home myself. The rest of you, keep up the good work. We're on the home straight. I can feel it.'

'Gardner's place has been boarded up, boss.' Robbo again.

'You forget,' she grinned, 'I have Hank the tank. Only

joking. We'll stop by the cells and get Gardner's permission to search. If he won't give it, we'll tap the uniform inspector and get a PACE authority instead.'

In the end, it wasn't necessary. Gardner gave permission willingly, arrogantly even. That didn't bode well. It made Kate think he'd got rid of any incriminating evidence or that she'd have to look very hard to find it. If he had killed Elliott Foster, it begged the question why he hadn't deleted the photographic evidence too.

Was he really that stupid?

Kate and Hank left the station immediately, taking the short drive to Ashington. They rang ahead, asking council officials who'd made the house secure to meet them at the property and let them in. A painstaking search proved fruitless. They scoured every inch of the house: cupboards, the loft space, even under loose floorboards where Gardner normally kept his stash or hid his ill-gotten gains and other items he didn't want the police to find.

Ashington was a coalmining area that hadn't changed in years. It was still possible to have an open fire in the town. In the living room, Kate got down on her hands and knees to examine the grate. It had been swept clean. Given the state of the rest of the shit-pit, that caused her to wonder why.

She stood up, brushing soot from gloved fingers.

The sight of dirt on her hands produced a sudden flashback: a BBQ in the rear yard of Jo's Victorian terrace, her face smeared with charcoal dust after an abortive attempt to get it going. When they realized that the bag of briquettes was damp and wouldn't catch fire even if they poured a gallon of lighter fuel over it, they binned the idea and went to the pub.

Happy times.

'Something I missed?' Hank had seen the rueful expression on her face.

'Not sure.'

'Want to swap jobs?' Hank had been dragging out the contents of an old blanket chest that doubled as a coffee table in the centre of the room. He grimaced at the stuff he'd removed: items they might've expected to find beside Gardner's bed, not in his living room. In among a pile of horse-racing magazines, there was hardcore porn, condoms and intimate lubricant. Worst of all, a vibrator in a smeared plastic bag and what looked suspiciously like used toilet roll.

'Gross,' Kate said.

'Thank God for these.' Hank pulled at the edge of the nitrile glove on his left hand, and let go, allowing the material to snap back into shape. It paid to be careful in their job. 'Check out the sofa,' he said. 'He probably wanted to keep an eye on the telly while he was—'

She raised her hand. '*Too* much information, Hank.'

He chuckled.

Kate didn't. She'd already seen the state of the furniture and didn't want to speculate on what had taken place on the sofa and with whom. She glanced through the kitchen to the rear door. One of the panes of glass was boarded up and there were massive bolts top and bottom. Her eyes were focused on the key in the lock, a novelty poker chip key ring

361

hanging from it. She could feel the heat of Hank's stare even though she was looking the other way.

'I've seen that look before,' he said. 'What have you found?'

Kate switched her attention to the soot on her gloves, then him. 'Nothing yet.'

'I'll rephrase. What do you think you've found?'

'I'm not entirely sure – have you checked the yard?'

'No.'

Kate stepped into the tiny kitchenette he'd already searched. Cupboard doors were hanging open. There wasn't much in them: hardly any food, a few beer glasses she assumed had been nicked on account of the brewers' labels etched on the side. Hank had been thorough, carrying out a meticulous search of every space big enough to hide a pair of boots. 'Did you try the salad tray in the fridge, the freezer compartment?'

'You need to ask?'

'Just checking.'

'Why? You peckish? There's a couple of beers and half a Chinese takeaway in there, if you fancy a snack.'

'Think I'll pass.' She threw him a grin. 'Feel free to help yourself though.'

The soles of her shoes stuck to plastic lino as she approached the rear of the kitchen. She drew back the bolts on the door to the outside yard and turned a key.

'Won't be long.'

She stepped out into a filthy yard, overflowing with empty wine bottles, beer crates and other paraphernalia, the remnants of a half-decent summer. In one corner of the rectangular space was a makeshift BBQ made from an old oil drum cut in half. If there was one thing she knew about offenders, they liked burgers and beer, at the same time if they could manage it. She peered into the drum, her hopes dying. Like the fire grate inside, it had also been swept clean . . . *almost.*

Kate went back into the kitchen. 'You got your penknife on you, Hank?' He handed one over and she walked outside. Scraping ash from the very edges of the drum, taking as much care as an archaeologist might, she found what she was looking for. 'Bingo!' she whispered under her breath.

53

Midday. Armed with photographs of Gardner's yard, the BBQ drum and a close-up of her find – one tiny eyelet, burnt but otherwise intact – the Murder Investigation Team had cause for celebration. And it didn't stop there. While Kate and Hank were searching Gardner's house, luck had finally dealt them a good hand. Amid hundreds of images Alan Tailford had taken at the show were a few of Gardner in the beer garden of the Rose and Thistle wearing a pair of heavy-duty boots. At last, Kate was in a position to expose his lies.

'There's no arguing with hard evidence,' DS Robson said.

Brown was nodding. 'You'd think shite would learn that if they lie to police, they have to be good at it. Not many are.'

Morale was lifting, every detective thrilled to be one step closer to cracking the case. The MIR was filled with excited chatter: *We have him bang to rights . . . well and truly sewn up . . . there's still a way to go.* This final remark came from Carmichael. It rang true for Kate. To some extent, it had been all too easy to pick out Gardner as the culprit. She still had no evidence to link him with the gibbet and was unable to say with any certainty that he was responsible for the death of Elliott Foster. Grievous bodily harm, yes. But did he actually string him up?

Kate called out to Maxwell.

The sound of his name made him sit up and take notice.

'Get a blown-up image of the boots Gardner was wearing,' Kate said. 'Then source two identical pairs for me, please. I want you to set one pair on fire to replicate what happens to them. If I'm not wrong, the similarity will be startling. Keep the others and do it now.' She shifted her gaze to Carmichael. 'Lisa, get on to Gardner's brief. Whatever else he's dealing with, tell him I need him down here ASAP. I have to pop out for a short while. Text me as soon as he arrives. If he can't make it, tell him he'll have to send an associate. I want this case wrapped up.'

'Need me along?' asked Hank.

'No, you take over. I have a personal matter to take care of.'

The team appeared somewhat relieved. Hank too. More than that, he seemed pleased. Kate couldn't fathom why. Then she realized that they had misread her, believing that she was going to see Jo. This was no time to make up the truth.

'My father had a coronary,' she explained. 'He's in hospital.'

Hank's mouth fell open. 'When did this happen?'

'Late Monday night.'

'It's Wednesday!'

'I'm well aware of the day of the week, Hank. Don't worry about him, or me. He's getting the best of care. Fortunately, he's in Wansbeck so I won't be long. I want you primed and ready to go when I get back.'

As she walked away, Hank yelled after her: 'Give him my best.'

Ed Daniels was awake when she arrived, propped up against a stack of pillows in bed. There was evidence that he'd been reading – a few newspapers scattered across the service tray that spanned his bed, a half-finished crossword puzzle – next to them, the remains of a cup of weak tea. A good sign that he was making progress.

He was extremely pale, his eyes vacant.

On the bedside cabinet, there was an untouched bowl of fresh fruit and a Get Well card, a hospital scene depicting a man in bed, a male doctor standing by his side, a stethoscope around his neck. The caption read: '*Give it to me straight, doc, how long will my car have to spend in the hospital car park?*' It was a MATT card – Jo's favourite – the product of award-winning cartoonist Matthew Pritchett MBE, who, if Kate remembered correctly, had studied at the School of Art in London and now worked for the *Telegraph*.

If she'd sent one too, would her father crack a smile?

He didn't do that, or say hello.

He didn't do or say anything.

Unable to summon up an appropriate emotion, Kate walked to the bottom of his bed and unhooked his medical chart – something she knew was guaranteed to annoy him. There was nothing written there that caused her undue concern. Without making any comment, she put it back, eyes firmly on her father.

'You're too early for visiting,' he said.

'Some people make allowances. They appreciate the

demands of my job.' She approached his bedside, leaned over and kissed his forehead gently. She could've sworn that he, if not recoiled, then tensed somewhat. She wondered why on earth she'd bothered leaving a major incident if nothing good was to come out of her visit.

Must try harder.

Prepared to meet him halfway, she made up her mind to keep it civil. To give him the opportunity, should he wish to take it, to heal the open wound that was the current state of their relationship before it was too late. Whatever he thought of her choice of profession and lifestyle, he was her father, 'her dinosaur', as Jo had put it.

She tried for a smile that didn't come off.

This was so difficult.

They had hardly spoken since he'd assisted her with a complex child murder case she'd been struggling with. She'd linked a set of plastic pearls from her victims to an Ashington miners' welfare celebration around the time of the Coronation of Queen Elizabeth II. He was a boy then, living in the town, set to become a miner himself. Despite their estranged relationship, he'd been a great help, revealing a family secret in the process – the death of his twin when they were four years old. Up to that point, Kate knew nothing of Mary. Her death had been a tragedy – an undetected hit-and-run – another black mark against the police, and her. Another secret . . .

Maybe, as people, they weren't so different.

'How are you feeling?' she asked. 'If that's not a daft question.'

'Hasn't your girlfriend said?' It was a definite dig.

Why was he always so bloody judgemental? 'I've been here too, Dad. Just not when you were awake.'

'So I gather.' He began smoothing his bedcovers. 'She said she'd be in this morning.'

'*She* has a name.'

'Jo, I meant. I was expecting her.'

'Ask yourself why she *didn't* come.' It was out of Kate's mouth before she could stop herself. The guilt was there, as plain as day. He couldn't hide it. She dropped the acid tone. 'I want you to know it was her and not me who organized and paid for your private room. Be sure to thank her next time you see her.'

'I will. She's been very kind.'

'She *is* very kind.' Kate allowed the comment to sit with him a moment. She could feel the frost from ten feet away. She backed off, changing the subject. It wouldn't do to antagonize him in his condition. 'Being in Wansbeck must feel like coming home for you.' She was referring to his mining heritage.

He didn't answer.

On second thoughts, bringing it up wasn't her best idea. Set against her passion to serve as a police officer, it was partly responsible for splitting them apart. There were other reasons too, a complete disregard for her circumstances being one. Was there anything they could talk about that wouldn't instantly lead to a dead end?

She sat down.

The least he could do was acknowledge that it was difficult for her to be there. She'd spent many hours sitting by her mother's deathbed, on behalf of both of them, waiting for her to die. Arranged the funeral. Given the eulogy. Actually turned up. He was too weak to face it. Hoping she'd never have to go through the experience again invoked a tremendous amount of sympathy for Beth Casey. Kate would do anything to take her pain away. They had much in common.

Thinking about Beth brought to mind Atkins' recent attack. The quandary over his future weighed heavily on her mind, as did the heart-to-heart she was determined to have with Hank. It was time to stop hiding. Time to reveal her true self.

'Hank sends his regards,' she said.

'How is he?'

At last, some interest.

No matter what her father thought of her, he got on brilliantly with Hank and was profoundly distressed to learn that he'd been shot and wounded in Spain. She'd called her father from Cartagena to warn him before the news hit the media, to let him know she was safe in case he read anything more into it. He was grateful for that.

A first.

'He's not 100 per cent but he's getting there. I'll tell him you were asking after him. Between the two of you, you'll be the death of me.' It was her way of letting him know that he meant something to her. Then he went and spoiled it by asking her to leave.

54

By the time Kate reached the office, Maxwell had sourced the boots. Without going into Newcastle, fifteen miles away, there were only so many places to buy footwear. He'd worked fast. These days he was so much more motivated, able to demonstrate his potential when he put his mind to it – a team player, almost.

She commended his effort.

'It's time to talk interview strategy,' she said, placing one pair of boots into an A3-sized brown envelope. 'I have a plan. Hank will lead the interview. I'll direct operations. Ordinarily, we'd ask you to stay away. No interruptions. Not this time. I want to drip-feed the fact that we are moving forward as the interview progresses. Otherwise, Gardner will see the whites of our eyes and think he can sit there all day and tell us nothing. I want him under pressure. I want to drill it into him that we're not two daft coppers interviewing him, but a team of clever detectives squirrelling away in the background. It's what's going on behind the scenes that'll scare him the most.'

'I'm hurt.' Hank feigned a dagger to the heart. 'You never call me clever.'

'I will . . . when you deserve it.' Kate laughed.

So did everyone else.

She switched her attention to Carmichael. 'Give Hank five minutes' head start, Lisa. Then deliver Tailford's photographs and leave the room. On my cue – I'll text you – bring these in next.' Kate handed her the new boots. 'Wait for another cue and return with the remains of the burnt pair. This irrefutable evidence will rebut Gardner's lies. Faced with the truth, he'll have nowhere to go. When he runs out of excuses, maybe he'll cough.'

Having decided on a strategy – there were no dissenting voices – Hank began the interview at exactly three p.m., Kate acting as backup. Reminding Gardner that he was still under caution, they got straight down to business. It was time to turn up the heat.

'During your last interview, DCI Daniels advised you that we have witness statements. One of them alleges that you were involved in a fight with Elliott Foster prior to his death. Although you admit to seeing him at the show, you couldn't recall seeing him afterwards due to the amount of alcohol you'd consumed that day. Is that correct?'

'What can I say? I was in a haze, mate.'

'Really? That's interesting, because a witness has since claimed that you took photos of your mates holding Elliott down. Do you have anything to say about that?'

'She's mistaken.'

'She?' Kate raised her eyes, not her head, eyeing Gardner's brief over the top of her reading specs, a smile developing. She could've sworn Moffatt rolled his eyes. Scribbling a note on her pad, she spoke without looking at the prisoner. 'I don't recall DS Gormley saying that either of our witnesses was female.'

'Didn't he?' Gardner shrugged, unconcerned. 'I thought he did, sorry.'

Now Kate looked up.

'I must need my ears syringed,' Gardner said. 'They're full of wax and my hearing's not too good.' The arrogant shit had an answer for everything.

'Let's move on, shall we?' Hank said. 'You told us yesterday that you don't own any boots, Liam. What if I told you that, on the day of the show, a man was taking photographs that'll prove you're lying. It's unfortunate for you that the man in question also happens to be a well-respected ex-copper who knows you well.'

'So where are they – these pictures?'

'We're having them blown up as we speak.'

'Yeah, right.' Gardner smirked.

There was a tap on the door. Perfect timing. Carmichael appeared. Announcing her arrival for the tape, Kate stood up and approached her. Handing over some A4 stills, Lisa left the room as planned. The DCI turned slowly, eyes on Gardner as she retook her seat. After sharing the photographs with Hank, she placed them face up on the table and slid them towards their suspect.

'If I'm not mistaken,' she said. 'That's you in the centre, is it not?'

Gardner eyed the stills but kept quiet.

'Clever how he managed to catch the show flags behind your head,' Hank added. 'You look like you don't have a care in the world. It'll be a while before you get another day out in the fresh air.'

Gardner gave him a dirty look. 'I said I was there.'

'Can I draw your attention to your footwear then?' Hank tapped the images. 'These must be the boots you forgot you were wearing.'

Gardner wiped a film of sweat from his upper lip and gave no reply.

'We got lucky this time,' Hank said. 'Both of our witnesses were very observant. They claim that *you* instigated the fight, *you* asked your mates to hold Elliott down and *you* took photographs of them doing it.'

'Not me.'

'Well, guess what DCI Daniels found on your mobile phone this morning.' Hank opened the file in front of him and slid another image across the table. It showed his associates restraining their murder victim on the ground, struggling to keep him still, the graveyard of St Andrew's Church visible in the background. 'This image seems to corroborate the fact that our witnesses are telling the truth, doesn't it?'

Gardner shrugged. 'I know them but they're nowt to do with me.'

'Hmm . . .' Hank exchanged a silent message with Kate.

She took over. 'If your mates are holding him down, who do you think is doing the kicking?' She paused, adding weight to the comment. When Gardner didn't answer, she feigned boredom and checked her mobile. Disinterested. She texted Carmichael and put the phone in her pocket. 'No idea? You're an intelligent guy, Liam. Maybe you could take a punt at who might've been using your device. You can't have lost it. It was in your possession at the time of your arrest.'

'You're the detective. You work it out.'

Kate stopped talking – Hank's prompt to resume.

'There's a lot of fingers pointing in your direction,' he said. 'I wonder how long before your mates start blabbing. I hope they're good mates because, believe me when I say one of them is going to rat on you. It's not going to be a hard sell, is it? They're as keen to go home as you are. You don't actually think they'll take the blame for you with a murder charge on the table, do you?'

Another knock at the door . . .

A second delivery from Carmichael . . .

Hank waited for her to leave again before removing the boots from their packaging. Placing them on the table, he lined them up with the photograph Gardner had just been shown. 'Would you agree that these boots are exactly the same as the ones you're wearing in this photograph?'

'It's difficult to say.'

'I can assure you they are. We confirmed it with the manufacturer. You're a bit of a trendsetter. Did you know that? They're the very latest technology. Only came on sale three weeks ago.'

Kate was smiling, texting again.

The final knock on the door produced the ash and eyelets from the boots she'd asked Maxwell to destroy by fire. Gardner knew what the ashes were. Moffatt was undecided. Carmichael gave them both a flash of teeth as she left the room, closing the door quietly behind her.

Hank thumbed in Kate's direction. 'My boss here is smart, Liam. She had a brilliant idea to buy two pairs of boots and burn one to replicate what you did at home.'

Moffatt looked confused.

Gardner didn't.

'Don't you think that's clever?' Hank pressed. 'I'd never have thought of it myself. That's why she's a DCI and I'm a modest DS. Anyway, I digress. Let me tell you the good bit. The eyelets of those boots, when burnt, match the one we found in your BBQ when we searched your property earlier today.'

Gardner's shoulders dropped.

Kate sensed defeat.

'So,' Hank said. 'I put it to you that following your fight with Elliott Foster, you attempted to get rid of your boots because you were concerned that they would implicate you in a very serious offence. If you're going to destroy evidence, you should be more careful. If you sweep a BBQ, make sure you get right into the joins or you might miss something.'

Gardner knew he was done for, as did Moffatt. The solicitor hadn't said a word the whole interview and there was nothing he could say now. Covering his mouth with his hand, he whispered to his client.

'Listen,' Gardner said. 'I can see I'm in the shit. I knew Elliott had died. I didn't kill him. I admit I gave him a good kicking and that's why I burnt my boots. I swear I didn't stamp on him or nothin'. I connected with his face but I had nowt to do with the gibbet.'

55

Kate typed a text message and pressed send:

> The case won't be long. We're not far away. I have an admission. There's still time. We still have the booking and you're off for ages. I'll be able to disappear for a week before I have to sign off on the file.

The answer was short and to the point:

> Use the Crail cottage by all means. I've made alternative arrangements. I've been to see your dad again too. Wanted to let you know he's fine. I know you're busy.

> Please reconsider . . .

> I've made my decision.

> I love you.

Kate stared at the screen hoping for more. There was no response.

Beyond her office door, a cheer went up in the incident room. Kate put her mobile on the desk. Seconds later Hank walked in, the din of a riotous MIT celebration leaking in as he opened the door. He stood facing her, a look of triumph in every facial feature. The tension of the past few days had vanished completely.

'News from the morgue,' he said. 'The metal eyelet in Gardner's BBQ matches the circular marks on Elliott's face perfectly.' He held up his hand for a high-five. Kate obliged, trying to engage with his enthusiasm. The good news could never wipe away the bad. In his excitement, he hadn't noticed that her head was down. 'We got him, the bastard!' he said. 'And this time he's going to stay got.'

It had been a long time coming. Finally, they were within touching distance of solving the case. It made the text exchange with Jo so much harder to take, their break-up so unnecessary. Behind a calm façade, Kate was inconsolable.

'What are you going to charge him with?' Hank asked. For once, he hadn't picked up on what was going on under the surface. 'We have sufficient evidence for a Section 18.'

Wounding with intent didn't cut it for either of them.

'Depends on Su,' Kate said. 'She asked me to give her an hour. She's conferring with Stanton. I need that post-mortem report before I take it to Naylor.'

'We let Gardner stew?'

'That's the plan.'

There was no need to explain her reasoning. Hank was very well aware that she had enough on Gardner to substantiate a charge. If the clock ran out and she wanted to keep him beyond his detention time, she could go to court and explain that she was investigating a fast-moving murder enquiry involving multiple offenders.

Technically, as soon as she had sufficient evidence to charge, she should do so, but that would mean she couldn't interview him again in relation to the matter. The fact that she was waiting on post-mortem results was justification to delay. No sensible magistrate would refuse a request for further time to interview suspects. She wanted to charge Gardner and his mates with murder. They were all there. In the eyes of the law they were equally guilty.

Kate and Hank had moved from her office to the station bait room, grabbing refreshments during a lull in proceedings. Carmichael was on food duty. She'd nipped along to Marks and Spencer with a list, bringing a chicken salad for Kate, a hoisin duck wrap for Hank, sparkling water for both. Kate had a wry smile to herself. Hank was much more careful about what he put in his mouth since his wife had taken him back, and he'd lost weight. Sadly, he still ate too fast and talked with his mouth full.

'How's your dad?' he asked.

'He sends his regards.'

He stopped chewing. 'That's not what I asked.'

'He's a pain in the arse. Is that any better?'

Hank grinned. 'He's not going to croak then?'

'Not unless I put my hands round his throat and squeeze very hard,' she said. 'Believe me, I was tempted.'

'Perfect. I love a status quo. Change unsettles me.'

Kate laughed.

'Have you seen Jo lately?'

She nodded, tried to act normal.

'And?' He looked at her. He wasn't stupid. This time her

poker face hadn't worked. He'd cottoned on immediately that the question was unwelcome. 'What the hell happened this time?' He could tell something fairly major had gone on. 'Kate? Kate, talk to me . . .'

She sucked in a breath. 'She's ended it, Hank.'

'What?' His mouth fell open. Whatever he was expecting, it wasn't that. He seemed genuinely floored by it. 'Why?'

'I'm a crap lesbian.'

He laughed out loud but underneath she could see how upset he was.

Kate didn't hear him disagree. *I think we're done . . .*

Now was as good a time as any to level with him. To explain, once and for all, why she'd not come clean – not come out. She'd come very close to doing so in Spain, pulling out at the last minute, her bottle gone. Hank let her talk, dipping in occasionally to cheer her up and raise her spirits. He was the most significant male in her life, the only person she'd trusted enough to open up to.

There was so much he didn't know about her.

'Your brush with death forced me to re-evaluate,' she said. 'It scared the hell out of me, if you want the truth. I took a long hard look at what's important. I can't change the past. I figured I could do something about the future. My leave period was to have been a jumping-off point for that. Atkins' arrival put the dampers on it. His intolerance is a bloody big reminder of what I stand to lose.'

He waited as she took a moment.

'I wasn't entirely honest with you after you sussed out my relationship with Jo—'

'You don't say.' He threw her a brotherly smile. 'And there

was me thinking you were throwing your life away because you wanted to go places. I always suspected there was more to it than blind ambition.'

Kate drifted away to another time, daring to revisit that dark and painful memory she'd kept battened down under lock and key for most of her adult life. Atkins had a lot to answer for. He'd exerted such influence over her. What pained her most was that she'd let him do it. She hated herself for it.

Hank's voice pulled her back into the room.

'Is Atkins the reason you were never open?' he asked.

'I didn't mean to be deceitful.'

'So why were you?'

'It's a long story.'

'I'm a good listener.'

'He tried it on when I was nineteen, a fresh-faced rookie with hopes of becoming something more. I knocked him back. We fought. Physically.'

'He hit you?'

'A push, a shove – nothing more – he came off worse.'

For a man who'd heard it all before, Hank was shocked. That didn't happen often. Sensitive to her hesitation, he didn't push for more detail, but bided his time, appreciating how hard it was for her to share her innermost secrets. There was anger too, the majority of it earmarked for Atkins . . . and some, she suspected, winging its way to her.

'Why didn't you tell me?' he asked.

'I didn't want to talk about it.'

'Jo knows though, yeah?'

Kate shook her head.

'Why not? It would've explained so much. Didn't you tell anyone?'

'What? And give him the satisfaction of shafting me? No thanks. He led me to believe that there was no room in the job for people like me, no hiding place either.' Her voice died to a whisper. 'I was so traumatized by what happened, I kept my distance from female colleagues for a time. Can you believe that? I was worried that he'd turn against them too, tar them with same brush.'

'Guilt by association.'

A nod. 'I've spent my career looking over my shoulder ever since, keeping my private life to myself to avoid becoming the butt of jokes for those cruel enough to know better and weak enough to say nowt if they came across bullying in the workplace. There's a lot of it about. More than you think. Any expectations I had of rising through the ranks had been knocked out of me   '

'C'mon. Your detection rate alone would've got you there.'

'You believe in a meritocracy?' Kate gave him hard eyes. 'You know as well as I do, it doesn't work like that, especially with guys like Atkins dishing the dirt. The only reason he kept his mouth shut was because I threatened to expose him, via a third party, for what went on in that locker room.'

'Which you let him get away with—'

'No, yes, not exactly.' Kate shut her eyes, the memory pushing its way back into her head. 'I was young and green. To be honest, I wasn't going to tell a soul about it, but someone clocking on for the next shift came in and found me in tears, picking my kit up off the floor, stuff that had fallen off the lockers when he was pushing me around . . .'

She was suddenly back in that locker room.

'It'll be your word against mine.' Atkins was in her face, his forearm across her neck, his knee between her legs. 'Who do you think they'll believe, eh? So keep it shut.'

As soon as he'd gone, Kate rushed next door to ask the cleaner if she'd heard any of the altercation through the wall.

She shook her head. 'No, sorry, love.'

Returning to the locker room to tidy up and compose herself, Kate jumped as the door behind her swung open. Fearing another round of abuse from Atkins, she scrambled to her feet. A female sergeant from the next shift was standing in the doorway in a tracksuit, a bag slung over her shoulder, a badminton racket sticking out the top. She'd come in early to take a shower before the daily parade.

Kate panicked as the older officer surveyed the scene, personal toiletries scattered across the floor. Kate was unable to think on her feet or come up with a reasonable explanation for them being there. There was an accusation in the sergeant's voice as she spoke.

'What's going on here then?'

Kate blushed. 'Nothing, Sarge.'

She wasn't buying that. 'Well, something clearly is.'

She was matronly to look at, reminding Kate of her mum: a kindly face, a wise one, piercing blue eyes. Brown hair, cut short. With twenty-five years' service in and nearing retirement, she had a reputation for fairness when dealing with offenders and staff alike, and was someone Kate admired.

Frightened by the consequences of grassing on Atkins, Kate wanted to avoid a fuss. Only when the sergeant promised not to make an official complaint did she find the courage to blow the whistle on him . . .

'I have no proof, Sarge. No witnesses.'

'You have me.'

'You didn't see what happened though. It's my word against his. He told me he has friends in high places. I'm just starting out. Please,' she begged. 'I'll resign if you take it any further.'

'Kate, think! What if he does it to someone with less backbone than you?'

Little did Kate know those words would return to haunt her.

Seeing her predicament, the sergeant laid a comforting hand on her shoulder and took charge. 'OK, have it your own way. It's your fight, not mine. This is what we do. You write up the incident. I'll have words with him. He won't like it, but that's tough. It'll stay with me, to be used only if it happens again and I need to prove evidence of system.'

Kate didn't understand.

'Repetition,' the sergeant explained. 'Then the gloves are off. Agreed?'

Kate nodded. They later signed, timed and dated the notes and said no more about it.

'That wasn't the end of it,' Kate said. 'Atkins began a vendetta, making life impossible for me. My shift got suspicious. They questioned me. I never said a word. My best ally on the shift was David Reynolds.' Hank knew him well. He was a good man, an excellent colleague. 'He pressed me on it, took me to one side, asked what was going on. I lied. The words were out of my mouth before I had time to breathe. What else could I say? Atkins had threatened to reveal what he called my "dirty little secret" if I said a word. I had no inkling that it wouldn't be the only head-to-head we were destined to have.'

'The domestic at his house?'

Kate nodded. 'You know the rest.'

Hank put a hand on hers. 'I'm sorry,' he said.

Kate wasn't: *she'd finally been straight with him.*

'The old sergeant I told you about is dead now,' she said. 'Atkins probably thinks he's home and hosed, that he's got away with it. I can think of no other reason why he went for me in the incident room. What he doesn't know is, my fairy godmother gave the notes to me when she retired. I could have used them on the night I was called out to his home, but Diane begged me not to report him. I'm going to use them now, though. He has to be stopped.'

56

Kate couldn't remember resting her head in the crook of her arm and shutting her eyes. She must've dropped off in seconds and would have remained asleep, had it not been for footfall on the other side of her office door echoing from the empty incident room beyond. It seemed vague and far away. Try as she might to lift her head from the desk, she couldn't. Her eyelids felt like lead, the need for sleep dragging her down to a warm safe place where murder couldn't reach her and relationships were simple. It was the tap-tapping on her office door that startled her, a familiar voice jolting her awake.

'Good evening!' it said.

The voice was female. Loud and boisterous. It had come from someone who had no business sounding so energetic after the shift she'd put in. Kate raised her head, blinking her eyes open, picking sweaty strands of hair from her forehead.

Pathologist Su Morrissey was standing on the other side of her desk, slightly ill at ease, a manila folder in her hand. She looked for all the world as if she was on her way to work, not on the way home. Kate, on the other hand, found that five minutes' shut-eye had done little to refresh her or improve on her mood.

'I have a raging headache,' she said, apologizing for having nodded off. 'I've been getting a lot of them lately.'

'Well, don't let them go on too long before you see a physician.'

'Thanks for the advice. A bit of stress, that's all.'

'Ah, the *silent* killer.' Su raised one eyebrow. 'That's tricky for someone like me. Give me stab wounds, blunt-force trauma, matted blood anytime. I was on my way home and took a short detour to drop this off. One post-mortem report, as requested – signed off by Tim. Sorry it's late.'

The report hit Kate's desk with a solid thump.

'Thanks for the hand-delivery,' she said. 'I might have been here when the cleaner arrived in the morning had you not called in.' She nodded towards the report. 'Does it contain anything I don't already know?'

'See for yourself.' Su pointed at the chair. 'Can I sit? I'm not as tired as you, but I've been on my feet all day and they're killing me.'

'Be my guest. You want coffee?'

'At this hour?' The pathologist's eyes found the wall clock. 'You detectives never learn. I'll pass, thanks. Never drink the stuff after midday. Don't let me stop you though.'

'Water?'

She shook her head.

Kate grabbed a bottle from her bottom drawer. Taking the top off, she tipped the liquid into her mouth, wiping a dribble from her chin with her fingertips.

Su Morrissey was shaking her head like a disapproving head teacher. 'You need educating, DCI Daniels. You should never leave water in your desk or carry it in the car.'

'Why?'

'It warms up and cools down. Plastic water bottles are made from polyethylene terephthalate,' she said. 'When heated, they release harmful chemicals.' She listed them. 'Not good for you.'

'OK, I promise.' Kate took another sip.

Picking up the post-mortem report, she read the contents carefully, stifling another yawn. She felt unpleasantly warm as she read on. Then she looked up, meeting the surgeon's eyes across the desk. 'Let me get this straight, the blow that killed Elliott isn't the one to the back of his head?'

'Correct. Take a look at the appendix: SM18.'

Kate scanned the attached photographs until she found the one Su Morrissey was referring to. She stared at it for a long while, unable to make out exactly what part of the anatomy she was looking at.

'What is that?' she grimaced. 'Or do I not want to know?'

'That,' Su said, 'is the inside of the victim's head. The impact of the kick was severe. The nasal bone is completely shattered. Of itself, it's a devastating injury. If it had travelled up through the skull and into the brain, it would certainly have killed him.'

'It didn't?'

The pathologist gave an unequivocal shake of the head.

Kate sat back in her chair, elbows on the armrest, hands clasped loosely in her lap. 'That makes sense to me,' she said. 'Witnesses swear that Elliott got up after he was kicked. Is that possible with the injuries he sustained?'

'Yes,' Morrissey said. 'He wouldn't have stayed on his feet for long, mind. That kick would have hurt and caused internal bleeding. Ditto the injury to the back of his head, probably the result of hitting the churchyard wall. There's evidence of sandstone in the wound.'

There was more. Kate sensed it. Her intuition was spot on.

Su raised an eyebrow. 'Ah, I see you want the even more important news.'

'And I can see you're dying to tell me.'

'You're not going to like it.'

'I already don't.' Kate braced herself.

'Elliott wasn't kicked to death,' the pathologist said. 'He died of asphyxiation. He was alive when strung up.'

57

There was a negative reaction to the post-mortem findings within the Murder Investigation Team. The atmosphere in the incident room was grim. No one had yet uttered the words 'back to square one', but they would. Knowing she'd have her work cut out lifting morale, Kate called for order.

'Can I have everyone's attention please?' She paused momentarily, waiting for the team to settle down. 'You'll all have seen from the murder wall that I've bailed Collins and charged Gardner and his mates with Section 18 Wounding. They will remain in the cells until they appear in the remand court first thing tomorrow morning. The CPS will oppose bail and, with any luck, the five accused will be remanded in custody to await trial. A Crown Court listing could be months away, so they'll all be seeing Santa in Durham jail.'

'Even so,' Maxwell muttered under his breath, 'feels like the tossers got away with it.'

'Prove their guilt then, Neil. Then we can all go home.' Kate scanned the room, a dozen pairs of disillusioned eyes focused on her. 'Look, I can see you're all disappointed, but you can't let your heads go down. We may only be in a position to prove Section 18 at the moment but it's a dead-cert conviction carrying a hefty sentence and we have a cast-iron case. In the meantime, we have serious work to do. Some-one is guilty of murder and we *will* find them.'

The chatter that followed was more like an open argu-ment, a free-for-all with no holds barred. Kate let them gripe and share ideas. After the euphoria of thinking they had cracked the case, they deserved time to reflect and let off steam. As always, they would have a moan and then give it their all.

She'd accept nothing less.

'If not Gardner, then who?' Maxwell was asking.

Grant was shaking his head. 'It's him, it has to be—'

'Or one of the others,' Brown suggested.

'No,' Robson chipped in. 'Gardner would have dropped them in it from a great height if that were the case. If it's not him, my money's on Collins. He's a meat processor with serious convictions for violent conduct. I don't like the sound of that, do you? Atkins said he works on a farm. That means he has access to rope. Problem is—'

'Problem is, Sarge, we're pissing in the wind trying to find any missing rope and Collins denies any casual labour,' Brown reminded him. 'Despite extensive enquiries, no one has verified where he works or even *if* he works outside of his proper job. Atkins said he did, but I for one am not pre-pared to take *his* word on anything.'

'Who would?' Carmichael threw Kate a smile.

'The fact that we can't yet confirm it means nowt,' Hank argued. 'Collins is cheap labour. It'll be under the counter. Cash in hand. Rates of pay that fall woefully below the minimum wage. No farmer is going to admit to employing him on that basis, even if it's true. It's exploitation.'

'Happens all the time,' Grant said to no one in particular. 'And if he works on a farm, he has access to rope *and* machinery.'

'Even so,' Maxwell interrupted. 'If Elliott was alive when he was hung, Collins would be hard pressed to handle him on his own. I imagine it would be difficult to put a rope around the lad's neck and hoist him up there while he was kicking and screaming.'

'He was badly injured in the fight, Neil,' Carmichael jumped in. 'If not comatose, then not far off. Have you even read the post-mortem report? If not, you should. His injuries were severe. That suggests to me that the poor sod wouldn't be in any fit condition to either kick or scream. The fact that he was breathing doesn't mean he could put up any kind of fight. I wouldn't rule out Gardner's lot yet.'

'OK, you've had your say, now wrap it up.' Hank had to raise his voice to be heard over theirs, exchanging an optimistic smile with Kate. The team was back in the saddle . . . almost. There was no room for infighting. 'As you've just demonstrated, our case is far from over. So, ladies and gents, you're going to have to suck it up and move on.'

'He's right,' Kate said. 'I know you all want to level a murder charge, but we have no proof. Not a shred of evidence as to who is responsible for murder. Not one of Gardner's mates so much as hinted at his guilt. That doesn't mean he's innocent. You know as well as I do that when faced with life imprisonment, friendships collapse and people start talking.'

'I agree,' Hank said. 'If they even suspected he did it, they would have turned on him, no doubt about it.'

'So,' Kate said. 'We're not ruling anyone out. Keep Gardner in your minds, by all means, but keep going. We regroup, perform a thorough review of where we're at and carry on.'

A groan reverberated around the room. There was a lot of eye contact between team members. The case hadn't exactly ended in failure, but they were nowhere near resolving it. They were baying for justice, for Elliott Foster and his grandmother, Jane Gibson. Yesterday was market day in Morpeth. Even in her darkest hour, the old lady had baked a cake and had it delivered to the station by a kindly neighbour, along with a thank you card for all their hard work.

They felt unworthy.

Kate knew the feeling.

'The important thing to consider here is why the gibbet was used,' she said. 'The area around Elsdon is rugged and desolate in places. There are literally hundreds of square miles where Elliott's body might have lain undiscovered for years had the killer chosen to dump or bury it. He didn't. There *must* be a reason.'

The noise level died down as the team chewed on it.

'We know the fight happened,' Kate said. 'That's already in the bag and there'll be no dispute when the case gets to court. I want you all to think laterally. Consider things that you may have discounted. Everything is in the mix until I say otherwise. I'd like a volunteer to concentrate on the relationship between Gardner and Collins.' Carmichael's hand shot up. 'Thanks, Lisa. I don't like what's going on between those two. I'd like to know if they have ever been locked up together. The rest of you have a job to do. I know, it's a bummer, but you should think yourself lucky. Hank and I will have to analyse every action to see where we go next. If we all dig deep, we *will* find answers. We always do.' Catching Hank's eye, she gestured towards the door, indicating that he should follow, then stood up and left the room.

58

Kate hadn't even made it to her desk when the phone rang: *Atkins*. She very nearly didn't pick up, but since she'd left the hospital after that awful meeting with her father, Beth Casey had remained on her radar.

Desperate for an update, Kate lifted the receiver. 'Daniels.'

Nothing.

Kate could feel his hesitation down the line and wondered if he was drunk again. 'C'mon, I haven't got all day – is there something I can do for you?'

'Beth's coming home,' he said. 'I thought you'd want to know.'

'And that concerns me how exactly? I thought I was the hard bitch who didn't care.' Kate waited for the ulterior motive.

'I thought you might like to pop in on your way home.'

She was irked by the man's cheek. 'For . . . ?'

'Hold on.' The phone went down on a hard surface and the line fell silent. Kate scanned her desk, her eyes coming to rest on an old-fashioned message spike Jo had bought her one Christmas. It was full, almost to the top, with scrappy notes she hadn't got round to dealing with yet, the desk itself piled high with paperwork awaiting her signature:

overtime forms, a budget report she'd hurriedly dictated before going home last night, Maxwell's yearly evaluation that had lain there for weeks.

She glanced out of the window, wishing she were in Crail with Jo. It was a beautiful day: clear blue sky, bright sunshine, not a breath of wind. Hank popped his head round the door. She beckoned him in.

He sat down, taking the weight off his feet.

Atkins' voice hit her ear again. 'Are you coming or not?' There was no apology for keeping her waiting, no explanation either.

'You've got a neck. You treat me like shit and expect me to help you out?'

'OK, don't—'

'I didn't say I wouldn't.'

Hank ran a critical eye over her. Realizing who she was talking to, he shook his head, his mouth turned down at the edges. The call was not one he'd ever sanction after hearing of the history that existed between them. When he opened his mouth to speak, she put a forefinger to her lips to silence him.

Now he was sulking.

'What time would suit?' Kate ignored the rolling eyes that seemed to send a silent message: *You're your own worst enemy sometimes.* That was very true, but Kate wasn't the important one here: Beth was.

'Whenever you can get here.'

There was no gratitude from the Angry Man. No thanks offered. The selfish git's attitude was as hostile as it had ever been. He expected her to do his bidding like she was still a rookie cop and he her sergeant. It must've been killing him to think that he could no longer boss her.

She looked at her watch. It would take a while to go through the actions with Hank. Their priority would over-shadow all else, including Atkins. It had to. 'I'll be a couple of hours, maybe three,' she said. 'Do yourself a favour. When Beth gets home: she talks, you listen.'

'What's that supposed to mean?'

'I'm sure you'll work it out.' She hung up.

Atkins put down the phone. He'd spent the last twenty-four hours in a drunken stupor and had a raging hangover. He simply couldn't cope with the idea of facing his daughter alone. She seemed to get on with Daniels. He understood why. As a young copper she'd come charging into Beth's life like some friggin' guardian angel, spouting feminist shit that turned Diane and his kid against him.

Bitch.

If anyone else had been available to help, he'd have left Daniels out of it. There wasn't. He'd burned his bridges with almost every female he'd come across in recent years, including his mother, who wouldn't talk to him any more. He only hoped the dyke wouldn't contaminate Beth.

When told that she was being discharged from the hospi-tal, he'd taken a breathalyser kit from his car to test himself – and then decided not to bother. Who was he kidding? He didn't need the results to confirm that he was well over the legal limit to drive. Unable to risk picking her up, he'd sent a taxi – too bad if she was expecting him in person. Mired in the trouble he was in at work, assuming he still had a job, he wasn't about to jeopardize it by losing his licence over a stupid kid with less sense than she was born with.

Bright would finish him for sure.

Beth arrived two hours later. She was wobbly coming in, extremely pale and sickly. Hospital staff had warned that it would take a few days before the drugs properly cleared her system, a few more before she felt completely well.

'Can I get you anything?' he asked.

She shook her head and slumped down on the sofa, avoiding eye contact. This was awkward. Heavy going. With Daniels' words ringing in his ears, Atkins took a deep breath. He'd been so angry lately, he'd almost forgotten how to be nice.

'You want some tea?' he asked.

'No, I'm fine.'

'Look, Beth, since your mum and I split up, it hasn't been easy for any of us. It's time to put the past behind us. I want you to know that you don't have to do anything you don't want to. If you decide to keep the baby, that's all well and good—'

'Of course I'm keeping it.' She looked horrified at the suggestion that she might consider the alternative. 'I'm not having an abortion, if that's what you're thinking, so don't even go there!'

'If that's your decision.'

'It is.'

'Are you sure?' *He had to try.*

When the inevitable happened and her mother was gone, he wasn't looking after Foster's sprog. There were reasons that it was never going to happen – reasons he'd held onto for years . . .

None he cared to share with Beth.

'You've got your whole life ahead of you,' he said. 'Looking after kids ain't easy—'

'Yeah, like you'd know.'

He poured himself a drink, two fingers of neat whisky. She'd been there less than ten minutes and already they were at each other's throats. This was never going to work.

He saw the drink off and tried again. 'Look, I admit I've made mistakes—'

'Mistakes? Is that what you call them?'

'It was a long time ago, Beth.'

'Yeah, my whole life,' she bit back. 'Thanks for nothing.'

'Beth, I don't want to fight with you. There's been enough of that around here lately.' He took in her scowl. She wasn't swallowing the deception. The stupid bitch was savvy, like her mother – more than he'd given her credit for. He wondered what rubbish Daniels had been feeding her this time.

'You think on it,' he said. 'I'll support whatever choice you make. I want to forget the arguments. We owe it to ourselves, to your mum, to be a family again.'

She glanced sideways at him. 'That sounds so weird, coming from you.'

It did.

Which was why she'd never go to term. Not if he had anything to do with it. If the mad cow insisted on going through with the pregnancy, she was on her own. As soon as she was well enough, he'd find her a flat and send her packing.

He'd help out financially, of course – he wasn't a monster – but his days of caring for rug rats were over.

She'd made her bed . . .

Beth was staring at him. 'Did you mean what you said before?'

She was so gullible. 'Of course.'

'Why should I believe you? You've been saying it for years to Mum. I heard you. You never followed through, not once, even when she begged you. Even when you found out she wasn't well. I don't know why she even talks to you.'

'People change, Beth.'

'Not you.'

'I won't if you don't give me a chance. Think about it. We could move away . . . not far, to Newcastle maybe. It would be perfect, a completely fresh start.'

'What?' She glared at him. 'No! I have a home with Mum. I don't want to move.'

'It would be for the best. That way people wouldn't know—'

'That I'm pregnant?' She looked like she wanted to smash his face in. 'You're despicable! I hate you.'

'I'm trying to help you!' Atkins slopped more whisky into his glass and put the bottle back without replacing the top. This was not going well. 'Meet me halfway. You're going to be a mum. Think of the baby and not yourself. With Elliott gone, you're going to need my support.'

'I need nothing from you.'

'Well, I'm all you've got. You're going to have to take it or leave it.'

'I'll leave it then,' Beth said defiantly. 'He's not the father—'

'Excuse me?' Atkins' stomach dropped.

'Elliott. He's not the father.'

The glass flew across the room, smashing against the wall.

59

There was a hierarchy of actions in any murder enquiry. In the early stages of a case, investigators dealt with only those of the highest priority. The rest had to wait. Having exhausted all actions concerning Gardner, Kate and Hank turned their attention to those specifically related to Collins.

'You wanna go first?' Hank asked.

'OK.' Kate ticked the points off on her fingers. 'Collins had motive, possibly the means and opportunity. Beth was upset after the fight and wanted to be alone. At her own admission, she dropped him at home in Otterburn. But his mother was working that night – I checked with her employer which means he has no one to vouch for him after that.'

It was hot in her office. Hank got up and opened the window. 'Atkins didn't disclose his source?' he asked.

She shook her head. 'I'll ask him about it when I see him later.'

'Good luck with that. I'm coming too.'

'There's no need—'

'There's every need.'

Kate didn't argue. His mind was made up and hers was still on the lad with form she'd bailed that morning. She was running out of time and had no evidence to detain him any longer. 'We're five days in without a lead,' she said. 'We have to consider the possibility that the intelligence on Collins conjured up by Atkins may be true. The lad is strong. He works in a meat processing plant hauling animal carcasses all day long. He may or may not work on a farm and have access to rope or machinery – a quad bike – and he admits to being involved in the fight.'

Accessing the HOLMES database, Kate began to type, calling up all actions associated with the lad. As she scrolled through digital pages, originators' names appeared, listed in chronological order in the centre of her computer screen. Atkins was at the top, Jo a close second. Intrigued, Kate clicked on her name.

'Come and look at this,' she said.

Hank stood up, dragging his seat round to her side of the desk, his eyes seizing on the information in front of him. On day one of the enquiry, Jo had asked for information on Collins. It had them both wondering why.

Kate looked at him. 'Did you know she'd instigated an enquiry into him?'

He was shaking his head. 'I didn't know she'd even looked at the case.'

'Me either.'

Kate glanced at her phone, a text from Jo entering her head: *I'm in the incident room. Last-minute admin if you can get away. I was thinking pre-holiday drink.* 'Although technically on leave, she was here on Monday . . .' Kate paused as an earlier memory clicked into place: *This Atkins guy who's giving you grief? Why don't I know about him? I thought I knew all your secrets.* 'If I'm not wrong, she was here on Sunday too,' Kate said. 'She spoke to Lisa. Get her in here.'

Hank picked up the phone and called Carmichael's extension. 'Can you join us for a second, Lisa . . . the boss's office, soon as you can . . . Yeah, won't keep you long.'

Seconds later, she arrived.

'Shut the door and take a seat,' he said.

His protégé was immediately on her guard.

Kate had never seen her so worried. 'I gather you and Jo had words about the case when she popped in on Sunday. She and I had a brief conversation afterwards about the Angry Man.'

Carmichael blushed like a kid who'd been caught telling tales. Kate tried to reassure her. 'Don't worry, Lisa. Do you know if Jo looked at the case papers when she was here?'

'Not to my knowledge, why?'

'So you can't throw any light on why she might have wanted more detailed information on Collins?'

Carmichael shook her head. 'Have I done something wrong, boss?'

'No,' Kate said. 'I find it curious, that's all.'

'She did glance through what was on my desk on Monday,' Carmichael remembered. 'We hardly spoke though. I was on the phone. She said something about Collins' name ringing a bell.'

Kate was curious. 'She never told me.'

'Maybe it slipped her mind.'

'Nothing slips her mind.'

Carmichael's eyes shifted to Hank. He was her supervisor, the one she wanted to impress. Her evaluation was due soon.

She'd passed her sergeant's exam and was hoping to progress a rank in the next round of promotions. She transferred her focus to Kate. 'As I said, I was otherwise engaged. Jo was waiting to see you. She said something about a client at the Regional Psychology Service with the same name. I think she said she'd look into it if she had time before you went on leave.'

Except she didn't have time . . .

She was busy caring for my dad.

'Did she say anything else?' Kate asked. 'It could be important.'

Carmichael thought for a moment. 'I might be totally wrong, so don't quote me on it. I think she said something about Collins' state of mind at the time his offences were committed. That if it was the same lad, he might even have been the subject of profiling by one of her colleagues.'

Hank narrowed his eyes and spoke in a fake Belgian accent. 'Then we have the work serious to do, Miss Lemon.'

Carmichael looked at Kate.

She grinned. 'He's channelling his inner Poirot.'

Lisa laughed. 'I'm sorry I can't be clearer. The person I was talking to on the phone was giving me earache at the time. I was only half-listening to Jo, and she'd gone by the time I hung up.'

Kate was about to dismiss her when Carmichael spoke again . . .

'The address—'

Hank raised his head. 'What about it?'

'It was different,' she said. 'She checked out his address

and I got the impression it was another lad altogether. It's a common enough name. I thought nothing of it after that.'

'That's it then,' Hank said.

'That's what then?' Carmichael was confused.

'For reasons unknown to us, she requested further enquiries into Collins' background,' Kate explained. 'Do you know if she checked his date of birth against this other guy?'

'I'm sorry, no.'

'That's probably why she wanted to flag him up then.'

'So why didn't she follow through?' Carmichael said. 'You know what she's like. If he had form for violence—'

'He only beats up females,' Kate interrupted. 'She probably ruled him out as a candidate for Elliott's murder. It's not really his style.'

Carmichael looked relieved. 'He was low priority at the time. Jo's request was too.'

'No need to justify it.' Kate reassured her. 'Everything is fine, Lisa. Those sergeant's stripes will look good on you. You can go now.' As her office door closed, Kate grinned at Hank. 'Remind you of anyone?' she said.

60

Kate hated loose ends. Her concern over Collins remained on her mind throughout the journey to Atkins' place. She tried contacting Jo en route. The call went straight to voicemail. When finally she arrived, Kate tried again with the same result. She left a message, put her phone away and got out of the car.

'No joy?' Hank asked.

She shook her head, slamming the car door with more force than she'd normally use. Hank followed suit, the passenger door thudding closed. They crossed the road, heading for the apartment block, his attempt at making her feel better sounding hollow.

'It was probably a coincidence,' he said. 'Lisa hinted that she was in two minds.'

Kate raised a sceptical eyebrow. He didn't believe in coincidence any more than she did. Jo had originated the action on Collins for a reason. Until Kate discovered exactly what it was, she wouldn't rest. What's more, he knew it. That didn't stop him trying to convince her.

'Probably a different lad,' he said.

Kate glanced at him. 'That's as bad as a definite maybe. Let's stick with facts and certainties, shall we? I'll call her

406

again later and see what she has to say.' They had reached the entrance.

'Waste of time,' Hank said. 'When has Jo ever raised a query and left it unresolved?'

Kate tried the buzzer to Atkins' flat. 'She might have been distracted.'

'Doing what? You said yourself she doesn't forget things.'

'She doesn't.' Kate didn't turn her head to look at him. 'But she was on starter's orders because we were going away—'

'Even so, she's too much of a pro not to follow through.'

'Whatever.' Kate hadn't the energy to argue over it.

'Maybe you're right,' Hank said. 'Maybe you should try her again?'

'Stop interfering.'

He put a hand to his chest pleading innocence.

Kate narrowed her eyes as if to say: *it won't wash*. 'I know what it is you're trying to do, Hank, but don't waste your energy. She's still angry with me. I can feel it. She probably thinks I'm going cap in hand, begging for forgiveness she doesn't want to hear, let alone give. Anyway, she'd be wrong. Dead wrong. Life is too short. I'm moving on. Say hello to the new Kate Daniels.'

A young woman approached, ending their conversation. She buzzed another flat, gaining entry immediately. She was about to close the door on them when Hank got hold of it, flashing ID. The girl glanced at it and walked in ahead of them.

They all heard yelling immediately, a slanging match, as audible from without as within Atkins' apartment. The young woman who'd let them in lingered, disturbed by the commotion but giving the impression that it wasn't the first time. 'Sounds nasty,' she said. 'Noise pollution bods would have a field day. Hope you've got your body armour with you.'

'There's nothing to see here,' Kate said.

'Just being friendly.' The girl moved away.

Kate exchanged a look with Hank. Whatever was going down inside wasn't good. The door to Atkins' place was locked. Kate rang the bell. When no one answered, she kneeled down, lifted the brass flap of the letter box and peered in. The hallway was empty, the door to the living room open. She couldn't get a visual on Atkins or Beth.

Sound was another matter.

The din was appalling.

Atkins was out of control, yelling like a madman: 'The same Chris Collins languishing in police cells as we speak? You have got to be joking, Beth! Well, I'm telling you now, you can forget having *his* bastard. The kid is a moron—'

'Takes one to know one. I *will* have his baby and you'll never see it—'

Kate called out to them.

No response whatsoever.

She rapped on the door with her fist and rang the bell again, keeping her finger on the buzzer. Neither one came to answer. This was not going well. Taking her mobile from her pocket, she called Atkins. On her knees once more, she opened the letter-box flap again and heard his mobile ring out in the apartment.

The ringing stopped as he declined the call . . .

He was winding up to something . . .

They needed to get in there.

'For Christ's sake!' he said. 'Collins has convictions for violence against women.'

'You're lying! If he had you would have told me—'

'I'm a policeman, Beth. At least I was – I'm not so sure now – I'm not allowed to tell you.'

Beth hesitated.

Outside, Kate knew why. She'd warned her about Collins. Maybe Beth was beginning to accept the truth.

'Beth, please don't cry.'

'Tell me the truth.'

'OK, fine! He's a thug who glassed his lass with a bottle. She lost an eye. I'm trying to protect you—'

'I don't believe you! He'd never do that.' Beth was sobbing. 'You're the one who's the bully—'

'And you're a slag, like your mother!'

Outside the apartment, Kate glanced at Hank. 'So much for reconciliation.'

'The man is delusional,' Hank said.

Kate continued listening . . .

'I'm ringing Mum,' Beth said.

'Like hell you are,' Atkins raised his voice even further. 'Put down that phone. Give it to me!'

Kate heard a scuffle, something falling to the floor.

'Atkins! It's Daniels! Open the door!' And still the argument raged inside with no sign of abating. The idiot had asked Kate there. What the hell was he playing at? She counted to ten and then stood up, eyes on Hank. 'He's had long enough. Kick it in.'

As the door burst open, Beth ran out of the living room and down the hallway towards them, like a rerun of the time she'd called the police on her parents all those years ago. She reached the front door ahead of her father.

Hank stepped in between them, shielding her.

'Back off!' he said. 'Gimme a reason to deck you and believe me, I'll take it.' Hank was right in Atkins' face, daring him to take a step closer, in danger of sticking the nut on him.

'Beth, are you OK?' Kate could see she wasn't. She was in a state, reliving a terrible nightmare. She was shaking violently, mascara running down a blotchy face, eyes red and desperately unhappy. History was repeating itself. Kate too was back in the pouring rain, holding the hand of a child she'd never seen before. 'Go to your room and stay there please, Beth. I need a word with your father.'

'You stay put,' Atkins barked at his daughter. 'I'm not finished with you.'

'And I'm not finished with you,' Hank said. 'Now piss off and calm down.'

'Hank, go with Beth.'

Gormley hesitated.

Kate's eyes held a warning not to undermine her authority by defying her in front of Atkins. Seeing her determination to handle him alone, Hank yielded and led Beth along the hallway to her room. Once the door was closed, Atkins launched a ferocious verbal attack, keeping his voice low so he wouldn't be overheard.

'Get out of my house and take my daughter with you! She

can rot in hell as far as I'm concerned. I'm not playing happy families with Collins' kid. Not now. Not ever.'

'You're a disgrace. Unfit to be her father.'

As Atkins lifted a hand to slap her, Kate deflected his arm, delivering the same blow she'd used as a nineteen-year-old rookie under his command. It sent him reeling backwards and on to the floor. 'You missed it once . . .' She stepped over him. 'You should've learned to duck.'

61

It was a pleasure removing Beth from her father's fury. She packed, or rather stuffed her possessions into a bag and gave permission for Hank to take her car so that he could pick up supplies on the way. Basic provisions to tide her over for a day or two.

Kate drove Beth to Alwinton in her Audi.

Diane Casey's house was small but homely. Kate lit the fire, allowing Beth time to gather her thoughts, have a bath and get into her pyjamas before Hank arrived. Seeing her ready for bed reminded the DCI of the first time they had met, and after that on the maternity ward at Wansbeck Hospital.

A theory took shape in her head, one that hadn't occurred to her before, one that possibly should have. Beth was not only an eyewitness to a fight. She was central to the murder investigation: close to Elliott, friends with Chris and she knew Gardner, if not by name then by reputation. What's more, her father had failed to divulge a conflict of interest or disclose how or why he'd dished the dirt on Collins. Why?

There was a missing link here . . .

Kate needed to find it.

She sifted permutations, trying to work out if her case

was more to do with Beth or Atkins. Her mind flitted between the two, making connections, discounting them. Father and daughter were both keeping secrets. There must be a reason why. Watching Beth pad across the floor, Kate wondered if she should hold her counsel or tackle the girl while she had the chance and they were alone. Kate worried that Hank would arrive at an inopportune moment, just as Beth was getting in the flow or giving up her secrets, assuming Kate could persuade her to open up.

Pulling out her mobile, the DCI texted Hank, telling him to stay away until she heard from her. As she put her phone away, Beth stopped poking the fire and sat down on the sofa, curling her legs beneath her, happy to be back on home soil.

'Thank you for bringing me home,' she said.

'You're welcome. Can I get you anything?'

Beth shook her head.

It was time to seize the moment.

'When I visited you in hospital, you were holding out on me,' Kate said. 'That's fine. I take it you had your reasons. People do that when they're frightened, but I'd like you to be honest with me now. You have my word I'll do the same. I desperately need your help.'

'What do you want to know?'

Kate sat forward, elbows on her knees. 'Beth, I'd do anything not to have to say this, but I'm beginning to think that you are the key to Elliott's murder. Is there something you're not telling me?'

Beth's gaze fell to the floor, her face draining of colour.

Kate waited patiently for confirmation. She could see

how tired the girl was. Her eyes were shut tight now, the heat of the fire combined with the stress of the past few hours getting to her. It was vital to keep her engaged in conversation, not allow her to retreat inside herself. Whatever she was hiding was killing her.

Gently . . .

Don't scare her . . .

She wants to tell you . . .

Give her a chance . . .

Kate could see cogs turning, decisions being made. Another gentle nudge was required. 'I'm not daft, Beth. I can see you know more than you're letting on. Tell me what it is. I might be able to help. We can help each other. I can't solve this case if I don't know what it's about, can I? Without your cooperation I'm stuck.'

Blinking her eyes open, Beth apologized for drifting off. Not in a sleep sense, she admitted. She was wondering how she'd got herself into such a bloody awful mess and was considering her future as a mother with no parents to turn to.

'It looks grim,' she said.

'You're a survivor, Beth. You'll be fine.'

Kate deliberated on how long it had been since Beth had eaten, since the baby had eaten, if that's how it worked. How should *she* know? That part of womanhood had passed her by. She imagined the umbilical cord connecting mother and child like the tube drip-feeding her father in hospital. The last she heard, he wasn't eating.

Beth's confession snapped her out of her daydream. 'It's true,' she said. 'I didn't tell you everything. I couldn't bring myself to.'

'Can we talk about it now?'

Having taken a huge stride forward, Beth was almost on the edge of backing off. After what seemed like forever, she took a deep breath and stopped avoiding eye contact. 'A couple of months ago, I was attacked walking home in the dark. I didn't see who it was because Elliott intervened. He'd spotted someone following me. He screamed at me to run and I did. I was terrified. He got a good kicking for his trouble.'

'Did you report it?' Kate knew that she hadn't. Carmichael had checked the PNC for incidents in the area involving anyone currently listed on HOLMES database for this enquiry. Still, she allowed Beth to confirm her inaction.

'No,' she said. 'I wish I had.'

'Does your father know you were assaulted?'

Beth gave a nervous laugh. 'You saw him earlier. Imagine his reaction if I had told him. Anyway, it was my own fault—'

'Who told you that?'

'I was using the cut Mum warned me never to use.'

'The cut?'

Beth gave Kate the details. 'It's a bridle path she doesn't think is safe. Now I know it's not.'

Kate wanted to tell her that she could walk wherever she pleased. That she shouldn't have to curtail her behaviour in any way for fear of ambush by men. But the sad fact was, like millions of women around the world, she was forced to compromise her freedom and make changes for her own protection.

'Did you tell anyone else?'

'Not then, no. I made Elliott swear not to tell anyone either.'

'And did he?'

A single tear ran down her face and neck. Beth left it there, a tiny river of salt water. Kate knew she'd gone off track. She was in that cut, a dark and scary place where, if Kate were reading her right, something dreadful had taken place. Beth wanted to talk to someone prepared to listen.

'If Elliott hadn't been there . . .' She choked on her words. 'If he hadn't come along when he did, there's no telling what might have happened. He could've killed me. I wish he had.'

'Don't be selfish,' Kate snapped at her. There were times when only the truth would do. This was one of them. 'Your mother and your child deserve better.' Beth hung her head in shame but Kate wasn't letting her off that easily. "This is not a dress rehearsal, Beth. You have one life. I want you to promise me you won't try anything stupid like that again. If not, I'm ringing social services to protect your baby.'

'I won't do it again, I'm sorry.'

Kate gave her a moment and then moved on. 'Did Elliott say who attacked you?' Seeing the way she shied away from that one, Kate decided to return to it later. 'When I asked you just now if you'd told anyone else, you said "not then". So who did you tell subsequently?'

'I told Chris.'

'When exactly?'

'A couple of weeks ago.'

'And what was his reaction?'

'He didn't believe me at first.'

'Why not?'

'He's a prat sometimes. Not very trusting.' There was no sign of upset from Beth. She was done crying over it. Despite an attempt at taking the easy way out, Kate could now see that she was a stronger personality than she at first appeared. After the events of recent months, it would be surprising if the girl had any tears left to shed. 'I don't understand Chris half the time. I don't understand men.' Her attention evaporated before Kate's eyes.

'Beth?'

She appeared utterly confused, as if time had inexplicably jumped ahead and she couldn't comprehend how Kate got to be sitting next to her, holding her hand. The DCI considered contacting her mum and then discounted the idea. Realistically, what could the woman do? It would distress both of them. On the other hand, if *she* were Beth's mum, she'd want to know.

'Can I get your mum on the phone so you can talk?'

'No, don't . . . she mustn't know. Kate, she's so fragile. It would break her heart. I'm fine . . . please, carry on.'

'We can do this tomorrow.'

'To be honest, it's a relief to get it out.'

'Are you sure?'

'If I don't, it'll drive me mad.'

Kate had no choice but to ask Beth a question she knew would distress her greatly. 'How far did the assault go?'

'His intentions were obvious. He wasn't asking either, he was . . .'

She stopped, dark thoughts taking away her ability to complete the sentence. Kate couldn't lead her. She gave her a moment and, in doing so, gave herself one. This case was about bullying, an abuse of power that mirrored her own ugly experience as a teenage cop.

'He was going to rape me,' Beth said finally.

'You will get over this, I promise you.'

Kate could feel herself misting up and hoped it didn't show.

Their eyes locked. In that moment, they exchanged an understanding, a bond of solidarity forming between them. This perceptive teenager knew she wasn't the only one to experience the darker side of men. To a greater or lesser extent, she knew that Kate had been there too.

Kate looked away, masking her eyes.

In her case, if Beth even suspected that the attacking low-life was her father, it would finish her. The DCI backtracked, pushing away memories of her own physical and psychological abuse. 'So, no one else knew about the attack apart from Elliott and Chris?'

'Only Gardner.'

'It was Gardner who attacked you?'

Beth nodded soberly, her lips forming into a thin hard line.

The motive hit Kate like a brick. In her head she was in the interview room, taking in his features, the recent scar running through his eyebrow – *his war wound* – the amateur stitching job that had heeled into a raised straggly line above his right eye. No wonder he hadn't gone to a hospital to get it seen to.

Had Elliott hit him with something?

Had Gardner taken revenge?

'Beth, one on one, who'd come out on top in a fight – Elliott or Gardner?'

'Elliott every time.'

'He was small by comparison,' Kate said.

'But quick on his feet,' Beth jumped to her friend's defence. 'I wish you'd met him. He was an amazing wrestler. He could put a much heavier guy down easily. Why d'you ask?'

'They're very different builds, that's all.' Kate didn't disclose that she'd seen Elliott before and after his death for fear it would open up raw wounds. 'Did he mention using a weapon on Gardner?'

The expression on Beth's face was a dead giveaway. 'A fence post,' she said. 'He was terrified afterwards in case he'd hurt him seriously.' Her voice dropped to a whisper. 'He won't be terrified now though, will he?'

'Do you know if he kept his promise not to tell?'

'He did, until—' She stopped abruptly.

Kate gave her a nudge. 'Until?'

'Doesn't matter.'

'I think it does.'

'There's no more.'

'Beth, c'mon. Elliott didn't deserve to die. He didn't deserve any of it. One thing he does deserve is justice.' Kate was finally getting through . . .

'After the assault, Elliott and I grew closer than ever. My father got hold of the wrong end of the stick. He thought we were too close. He had some ridiculous idea that we were seeing each other. Elliott denied it, but my dad didn't believe him.'

'So Elliott told him about the assault.'

Beth nodded, the flames of the fire reflected in eyes that were ready to spill more tears. 'He questioned me. I denied it. I didn't want to talk about it. He warned Elliott off. Called him a liar. Told him not to come near me again. There's some shit going on between our two dads that neither of us understood. I think it has something to do with my mum.'

'Did you ask her about it?'

'How could I?'

Kate left it there. She had an offender in custody who'd fought, not once, but twice with her murder victim. From where she was standing, revenge seemed as good a motive as any. In addition, Elliott Foster was the only material witness to the assault on Beth. Potentially, that might add attempted rape to Gardners' charge sheet – an offence that carried a hefty sentence on its own – longer still if the sitting judge ordered it to run consecutively. Kate and Beth would sleep easy tonight.

62

It was dark when Kate turned into Holly Avenue. Home at last. As she pulled up outside her house, she noticed someone leaning against a lamp post a few metres further along the street. This was no stranger. It was Fiona Fielding, head bowed as she laughed into her phone, a wicked expression on her face as she toyed with the person on the other end.

Watching her was a joy.

Kate felt a tug of jealousy. She couldn't stop herself speculating over the identity of the person Fiona was flirting with. Unaware of Kate – or that she was under surveillance – the artist continued to chat. She was practically shivering, shoulders hunched against the cold. No wonder. Her outfit was fit for spring, not autumn: a three-quarter-length heavy linen jacket, slim-ankle jeans and Italian slide mules.

Calling the office, Kate requested forensic examination of the bridle path where Beth claimed she'd been attacked, giving specific instructions to retrieve any fence posts found in or near the scene. As she hung up, Fiona did likewise, glancing in her direction, flashing a wide smile through the windscreen as their eyes met.

Out of the car now, Kate ran an appreciative eye over her unexpected visitor as she approached. 'Well,' she said. 'My shitty day just got a whole lot better.' Giving Fiona a hug, a peck on both cheeks, Kate held on to her hands as she stepped away.

'You look amazing,' Fiona said.

'And you're a God-awful liar.' Kate had almost forgotten that husky voice, the shape of her mouth as she talked, the ability to carry off a designer ensemble as if it was something she'd picked up on a market stall. Her laugh was infectious.

It felt good to be around her.

Fiona held up her mobile. 'Thought I'd drop by, seeing that you don't answer my texts or return my calls. I'm a penniless painter and you're using up my battery for no apparent reason.'

Kate laughed.

Fiona was a lot of things. Penniless wasn't one of them. Her work sold across the globe. A successful businesswoman, she was answerable to no one. Suddenly Kate felt awkward – embarrassed at the state she was in after scrapping with Atkins . . .

He was done for now.

'Hello? Are you in?'

Fiona's hand waved in front of Kate's face, pulling her from her daydream. The DCI tripped over herself to explain her preoccupation and uncharacteristic shabbiness. 'An unfortunate clash with a misogynist,' she said. 'He'll get his just deserts as soon as I get to the office.'

'Outstanding! Can I buy a ticket?'

Kate grinned, tugging at her clothing. 'This not how I'd have chosen to look when renewing our acquaintance—'

'Is that what we're doing?' There was an intense quality to Fiona's gaze.

'I don't know. What are we doing?' Kate combed a hand through unkempt hair. 'I'm sorry if I seem out of it. It's been a helluva day—'

'Still apologizing, I see.'

'I am, aren't I?' Kate blushed, reminded of the day this woman blew into her life. An expert witness, on more than one case as it turned out. She was a friend now – sometimes more. 'You coming in?'

'That was the plan. Tell me to shove off if it's inconvenient.'

Kate looked around. 'I don't see a queue.'

'I brought you something.' Fiona pointed at a large flat parcel wrapped in brown paper propped against Kate's front door. 'I hope you like it.'

'Wow! I love surprises.' From its shape, Kate guessed it was a painting and hoped it was one of Fiona's. 'How was Milan?' For the past month, Fiona had been exhibiting her work at the Padiglione D'Arte Contemporanea, and before that in Mexico City.

'Great,' she said. 'I earned enough to buy you dinner.'

'I got your postcards.'

Fiona had been sending them for a couple of years, sometimes two or three a week. They were a way into Kate's head while she was abroad, insurance against losing touch.

Fiona was nothing if not relentless.

'*You* need company,' she said.

'Who told you that?' Kate was on her guard. An emotion she couldn't quite nail flashed across Fiona's face: guilt, shame, something else?

'No one!' the artist said. 'Don't be so touchy. Are we on for a bite to eat or not?'

Kate hesitated for a split second.

Putting her hands together, Fiona put on her best begging face. 'You should know, I never take no for an answer.'

'Was I turning you down?'

'Weren't you?'

'No,' Kate said. 'I missed you.'

Fiona grinned. 'Nice to know I haven't lost my touch.'

'I'll let you know later,' Kate was teasing, tormenting her. 'I warn you, I'm dog-tired. If we go out, you'll have to work extra hard to keep me awake. After the day I've had, I need good conversation and more gin than is good for me. Where do you want to eat? Did you have somewhere special in mind?'

'You choose.' Fiona was normally a decisive woman.

Not today . . . Kate detected a hint of uncertainty. 'Is there something you're not telling me?' It was the same question she'd asked Beth earlier. The world, it seemed, was full of people keeping secrets.

'Nothing gets past you, does it, DCI Daniels?'

'Not a lot.'

The good mood vanished, replaced by a much darker emotion. Fiona knew she'd been rumbled and didn't try to cover it up.

'When I arrived,' she said. 'Jo was here.'

'What did she want?' Kate asked.

'Promise you won't shoot the messenger?'

'Promise.'

'She said she'd come to return this.' Withdrawing a key

from her pocket, Fiona handed it over. 'She was about to push it though your door. She saw me drive up and asked me to pass it on.' She watched Kate carefully, trying to judge her reaction.

There was none.

'I wasn't going to tell you in case you sent me packing,' Fiona said. 'She is too, by the way.'

Kate was thrown. 'She is what?'

'Packing. I gather she's booked on the four o'clock Heathrow to JFK tomorrow afternoon. There's time to catch her if you hurry. She'll probably take the midday flight out of Newcastle tomorrow, the one I take. It's fine if you need to go. We can do dinner some other time.'

'No . . . we'll do it now.'

Kate made a mental note to call Jo about her raised action before she left the country. She needed to know for certain if Collins was the same offender she'd told Carmichael about.

Fiona misread her silence 'Go after her,' she said.

'Unnecessary.' Kate knew when she was beaten. Jo could so easily have dropped the key through the letterbox. In giving it to Fiona she was repeating the message: *I can't do this any more. I think we're done.* Kate would always love her, but timing had never been kind to them. They would stay friends, of course. Close colleagues, definitely. Beyond that there was nothing more to be said. Jo was complicated. The reverse of the woman Kate was looking at.

She fumbled the key in the lock.

Fiona guessed that she might be wavering. 'Kate, promise

me you won't do anything you'll live to regret on my account.'

Kate turned to face her.

'I'm serious,' Fiona said. 'Has something happened between you two?'

Kate hesitated, decided to level with her. 'She's given me the brush-off. We were supposed to go on holiday together. The day came and went. We didn't make it, mainly though not exclusively because work got in the way . . . again.'

'Bummer. Are you sure you wouldn't rather give me a rain check? We've been here before, remember?'

'How could I forget?' Their eyes met and Kate's indecision melted away. 'Jo decided to cut and run. I'm a free agent, Fiona. And I'm hungry.' She let the sexual innuendo fill the space between them, picked up the package and pushed open the door.

63

Kate showered quickly, allowing the water to wash away all thoughts of Jo, another round of indifference from her father, Beth's suicide threat and the hideous argument with Atkins. If there had been any doubt in her mind how to handle him, it had now gone. He couldn't blame anyone but himself for his predicament – any more than she could hers.

Forcing the day's drama from her mind, she stepped from the shower, slipped into a robe and towel-dried her hair. As she threw her head back, she caught Fiona's blurred reflection in the steamed-up mirror. She'd arrived in the room without a stitch on, music wafting in with her, Alex Parks: 'Maybe That's What It Takes'.

Kate's desire to explore every inch of her guest arrived instantaneously.

Flushed with the need for sex, Fiona moved in, not a hint of self-consciousness or hesitation as she untied the belt of Kate's robe and watched it fall open, eyes travelling the length of Kate's body, still damp in places from the shower, damper still where it couldn't be seen. 'I'm raven-ous,' she said. 'How about you?'

'I see no need to go out.' Kate grinned. 'You're beginning to resemble my favourite takeaway.'

'Get stuck in.' Fiona slid her arms inside the robe, hands

drifting down Kate's spine to the cheeks of her ass, her right leg parting Kate's. She hesitated then, her smile dissolving. 'You are *sure* about this?'

As Kate leaned in, Fiona held a hand against her breast.

'Kate, I mean it. There's still time to say no.'

They kissed, their bodies coming together, skin on skin.

Set alight by Fiona's touch, Kate lost herself in the evocative lyrics of Parks' haunting voice, her pulse keeping time with the rhythm of the music. Driven by lust, she felt an urgent need to get this enigmatic woman into bed. They were in for an incredible night. Good sex. No strings or complications. There would be other women in Fiona's life. That was fine. It made her all the more attractive – and Kate thrived on the mystery.

Fiona had got under her skin from the moment she set eyes on her. Since the last time they had slept together, Kate had thought of her often. On each occasion it had produced a desire to see her one more time. Right now, that urge was as strong as it had ever been.

When was the last time she'd had any fun?

Kate kissed her again. No guilt. No wish to hold back, her tongue searching for its mate. Teasing Fiona. Tempting her. She smelt divine. Tasted good. She'd taste better later.

'What would you like to eat?' Kate whispered.

Fiona chuckled. 'I was thinking spicy.'

Taking her hand, Kate led her from the shower room.

64

Kate rolled over as the landline rang. Turning on her side, she hooked a leg over Fiona's, ran a hand over her warm, flat stomach. Propped up on her elbow, Kate ignored the phone and leaned in for a kiss, not wanting the night to end.

Fiona responded in kind. 'Am I always going to have to share you with the boys in blue?'

'That's the deal,' Kate said.

'I'll take it.' Fiona smiled as the ringing stopped, pushed Kate onto her back and climbed on top. 'Now, where were we?'

'We were asleep.'

'Such an overrated pastime.'

'I agree.' Another kiss. Kate lifted a finger. 'Wait for it: one, two—'

On cue, her mobile rang.

Cursing and laughing at the same time, Fiona lay down again, pouting her lips in a sulk, cheeks flushed with having been under the duvet for the past half-hour, wiped out and dead to the world. Kate scooped up her mobile and turned on the light.

'Daniels.'

'Excuse the late call, Inspector.' It was the custody sergeant. 'One of your prisoners is refusing to settle. He wants to see you before he goes to court in the morning. I'm shipping him out at eight o'clock.'

'That's almost six hours from now,' Fiona said.

'I appreciate the time, ma'am.' He'd overheard, assumed that it was Kate who'd made the comment.

Supressing a giggle, Kate placed a pillow over Fiona's face to silence her and turned her attention to the phone. 'I can't see him,' she said. 'He's already been charged.'

She pointed at Fiona as she wriggled free, warning her to behave. The artist sat up, kissing Kate's neck, biting her free ear. Across the room, Kate caught a glimpse of herself in the portrait Fiona had painted, an amazing likeness inspired by, not copied from, photographs she'd taken at her apartment in the middle of a night not dissimilar to this one.

'He's waiving his right not to be re-interviewed,' the custody sergeant said.

'Which prisoner is it?'

'Pearce. He has something to say you'll want to hear, ma'am.'

Kate was suddenly interested. Beth had told her that Pearce was the weak link, the youngest of Gardner's mates, the kid least involved in the assault on Elliott, the only one who'd looked away when Gardner was kicking the shit out of the lad on the ground. He'd even tried, if not to intervene, then to persuade the others to leave the scene.

'Did Pearce give you a clue?'

'He did. You need to get over here.'

Telling him she was on her way, Kate swung her legs over the bed and called a taxi. She showered and dressed quickly and shut the door quietly behind her so as not to wake Fiona. From the rear of the cab, Kate called the custody sergeant asking for details of Pearce's solicitor. Armed with her notes, she dialled the number and waited.

The voice that greeted her was thick with sleep and incomprehensible, little more than a groan.

'Mr Carrick?'

'Who is this?'

'I'm Detective Chief Inspector Kate Daniels. SIO: Major Incident Team. Your client Robert Pearce is in custody awaiting a remand appearance tomorrow morning for Section 18.'

'You're not going to tell me he's topped himself, are you?' Carrick yawned.

'No, sir.' Given the time of night, it wasn't too far-fetched. 'He's asked to see me urgently and wishes to waive his right not to talk to me again in relation to the matter. I'm told he's agitated, desperate to share something that can't wait 'til morning. He's happy to do so with or without you present. However, he's facing a serious charge. I'd rather you were there.'

Carrick groaned. 'Inspector, it's two a.m.'

Kate thought of Fiona asleep in bed, having succumbed to exhaustion. She was out of it when Kate left, a tangled mess of hair against a white pillow, as attractive asleep as when awake.

'I'm well aware of that, Mr Carrick.'

'Is this really necessary?'

'My custody sergeant seems to think so. Pearce is insisting on being heard. I gather the information he wants to pass on is crucial to our case. That rather suggests his testimony may be to your advantage too, something a judge will take into consideration when the case comes to trial.'

'You've sold it to me, Inspector. I live locally. I'll be there shortly.'

65

Kate could hardly believe her luck. The evidence against Gardner was undeniable, but she'd been trained to be sceptical. If something seemed too good to be true, it usually was. She stared at Robert Pearce, wondering if the prisoner was taking her for a ride. Had one of the others in the adjoining cells put him up to it, she wondered? Somehow, she didn't think so. He was snivelling, feeling sorry for himself. His disturbed emotional state seemed genuine, not put on for her benefit alone.

'So let me get this straight,' Kate said. 'You seriously expect me to believe that Liam Gardner brags that he's the descendant of a hangman?'

'He does!'

'That's quite a claim.'

Carrick hid another yawn behind his hand. 'One my client wouldn't be making unless it was true—'

'It is true,' Pearce said. 'Ask the others.'

'Forgive me for doubting you.' Kate wasn't ruling it out altogether. Collins had already fingered Gardner for being a fantasist. Maybe there was some truth in it after all. 'I'm wondering why you didn't tell us this before, given that you were questioned about a hanging.'

'Why d'ya think?'

'I'm not a mind reader, Robert.'

'Liam can be weird, really weird. I'm scared of him.'

Kate locked eyes with him. 'You're not from around here, are you?'

'What's that got to do with anything?'

'How long have you known him?'

'Couple of years.'

'I can see you're not keen.' Kate allowed the comment to fill the space between them. 'So why hang out with him? No pun intended.'

'Eh?' The lad blushed. 'Oh, I get you. Very funny.'

'Do you see me laughing?' Kate gave him hard eyes. 'Answer the question.'

'I dunno, he's good crack sometimes.'

'Is he?' Kate said. 'Where did you meet?'

'Quad Squad.'

The DCI exchanged a look with Carrick.

The brief shook his head. He had no clue.

'It's a quad-biking safari,' Pearce said.

Kate didn't react. 'Whereabouts?'

'Otterburn. We'd both been given vouchers as Christmas presents. It was awesome. Y'know, riding through rugged terrain, up streams and through puddles and stuff, getting plastered with mud—'

'I know what a safari is, Robert.' This was way too easy. Too convenient. Kate didn't like this kid any more than she liked Gardner. He was playing games. Even so, she'd raise an action to establish if any quad bikes had been stolen from the safari business. 'Do either of you own a bike?'

'Kiddin' aren't ya?' he scoffed. 'You know how much those things cost?'

She had to ask.

She threw in a lowballer to gauge his reaction. 'Have you ever met my colleague, DCI James Atkins?'

Carrick looked up from his note-taking. 'Is that relevant, Inspector?'

'I'm not sure. How about you, Robert? Is it relevant?'

Pearce didn't know where to put himself. He hadn't anticipated the change in direction. He looked away, a shrug of the shoulders, a shake of the head.

Kate wasn't fooled. She made a mental note to research in what context they might have come across one another. She couldn't work out what was going on there but she didn't like it. 'Maybe it's not Gardner you're scared of,' she said. 'Even if it is, I wouldn't worry. He's going away for a very long time.'

'Yeah,' Pearce said. 'And because of you I'm going with him. I already told the DS who interviewed me that I had nowt to do with the fight. Gardner thinks I'll grass him up. How long do you think it'll take him to have me done in?' He dropped his head. 'I need protection.'

'If you're so scared of him, why *are* you grassing him up, feeding me this cock-and-bull story about him coming from a long line of hangmen? Did he put you up to it to wind us up? Or did someone else?'

'What? No!'

'You're having a laugh, aren't you, Robert? You got everyone out of bed under false pretences—'

'I swear it's the truth!'

'So why didn't you tell us earlier?'

'Telling ya now, aren't I? I've done nowt wrong. I shouldn't be charged for just being there. I'm not guilty.'

'With respect, that's what they'll all say tomorrow at court.'

'Yeah, well I'm telling the truth. I should get credit for that.'

'You may well do, but I hope you haven't been watching too much TV, Robert. This is not America. There's no plea-bargaining here.'

Kate rushed upstairs to her office and switched on the light. In her tiredness she couldn't remember where she'd put the book Carmichael had given her. She searched frantically, lifting papers, opening drawers, all the time visualizing the volume in her mind: black cover, white script.

Come on, think!

She hated working in a space that was unfamiliar. Morpeth was a gentle town. There wasn't much crime at all, let alone murder. Major investigations that had taken place in this part of the county had been run from Ashington or Bedlington, stations with designated incident rooms. Kate was beginning to think that she'd taken the book home in her briefcase when her eyes happened upon it on the small shelf near the door.

Fetching it to her desk, she turned to the index. The Gs were listed on page 155. She ran her index finger down the page. Nearly halfway down she stopped on the name: **Gardner, William**. A page number was written next to it.

Quickly, she selected page 58 and began to read . . .

The text concerned the trial of William Winter and his accomplices, Jane and Eleanor Clarke, three violent tinkers and members of a group known as the Faw Gang. Found guilty of burglary and of murdering Margaret Crozier, in keeping with eighteenth-century law, they were sentenced to be hung, their bodies to be dissected and anatomized by surgeons.

Kate read on, discovering that the following day, the sitting judge (Baron Thompson) cancelled the arrangement in relation to Winter, ordering instead that he be gibbeted at a place near the scene of his crime, to be hung in chains on some conspicuous part of Whiskershiels Common at a distance of one hundred metres from the Turnpike Road, near Elsdon.

Kate shivered as she read the last paragraph, an entry taken from the Public Record Office. It referred to another execution to be carried out on the county gallows outside the Westgate in Newcastle, a man called William Gardner, a convicted sheep rustler whose sentence was reprieved after he agreed to be the executioner of William Winter and the Clarke sisters. For taking that office, his death sentence was substituted for transportation to New South Wales for seven years.

66

On less than three hours' sleep, Kate wasn't feeling her best as she entered the briefing at precisely eight a.m. On the way in, she'd thought long and hard about her meeting with Pearce. On the surface, the information he'd supplied was a breakthrough, a eureka moment for her to savour and the team to celebrate. It seemed to seal the fate of Liam Gardner.

She wasn't sold on it.

Gardner was shite. There was no disputing that – but was he guilty of killing Elliott Foster? If not, it would be a terrible injustice to finger him for the crime, no matter how much circumstantial evidence she had in her possession.

If not him, then who?

Whoever it was, they were still out there and Kate couldn't live with that. 'Can I have some hush, everyone?' She was standing in front of the murder wall, facing the assembled squad. 'I want to tell you a story.'

Hank raised his voice above the din. 'You heard the boss. Are you sitting comfortably?'

The noise level died . . .

'I'm going to share a compelling narrative and I want you to listen carefully.' Kate waited for absolute silence. The team were restless, inattentive. Not like them. Some were finishing the remains of their breakfast, drinking coffee, glancing at mobile phones. She needed a way in. 'It's a matter of fact that there have been shady characters or criminals, call them what you will, with the family name of Gardner going back in history. I'm sure the same could be said of Daniels, Gormley and *definitely* Robson, a good old Reivers' name. We all know what *they* were like.'

She grinned at Robbo.

He took it in good spirit and the team were finally onside.

'OK, so we've had our laugh. I'll start again now that you're all listening, shall I? This time I want your undivided attention. I have serious points to make. As you know, Liam Gardner and his mates are at court. The man himself has been a wrong 'un since he was eleven years old. He has a long criminal record, including periods in custody for a variety of offences that have escalated in seriousness in the last five years. He's known to every criminal justice agency and social services office you can name in a fifty-mile radius of here – for all the wrong reasons. More recently, he committed an offence that you'll not find listed in any public or police record.'

'It wasn't reported?' Carmichael asked, and then apologized for interrupting.

'Round of applause for Lisa,' Kate said. 'Last night, Beth Casey alleged that Gardner attacked and attempted to rape her. Fortunately, someone saw it happen and intervened. That someone was Elliott Foster.'

'There's your motive then,' Maxwell said.

Kate was nodding. 'Beth told me that Elliott fought Gardner off while she made a run for it. Although she didn't see it happen, she claims that Elliott hit him with a fence post in order to make good his own escape, something the poor bastard will never be able to corroborate one way or the other. It's my opinion that the girl is too traumatized to have made it up. Are we clear so far?'

Heads were nodding.

'I have good reason to believe her.' Kate said. 'For those who haven't seen Gardner in the flesh, there is a scar on his forehead that has been poorly stitched – unprofessionally, in my opinion. Let's put it this way: I don't think you'll find any trace of him having been treated in hospital for the injury. Now we all know why.'

'What happened to the fence post?' Brown asked.

'Good question,' Kate said. 'And the answer is, I don't know. Forensics are on it. If we're lucky enough to find it, I'm very much hoping it'll be possible to extract forensic evidence from it. It was a deep cut. Any DNA will be used to support an attempted rape charge.'

'Is Beth happy with that?' Carmichael again.

'Unless she changes her mind,' Kate replied. 'Given what happened to Elliott, I don't think she will. And now for the even more exciting news.'

Kate noticed Hank's brow crease. He didn't know there was more to come and knew nothing of what she was about to say. She simply hadn't had the time to confer with him before the meeting.

'Robert Pearce, one of Gardner's so-called mates, got me out of bed in the small hours. He claims they both took part in a cross-country safari on quad bikes earlier this year on land adjacent to the Otterburn army ranges. And if that isn't enough – I saved the best 'til last – Pearce claims that

Gardner brags that he is the descendant of a man named William Gardner.'

'Never heard of him,' Maxwell said.

'Who is he?' one of the civilians asked.

'He's the man who executed William Winter in 1792 on behalf of the Crown.' It was Lisa Carmichael who'd made the connection. 'Jesus! Boss, I never thought—'

'You weren't to know.' Kate could see that one or two weren't so quick off the mark. 'For those of you who are still asleep, let me fill you in. Winter had a gibbet named after him, one that remains to the present day as a monument to murder.'

The team were attentive as she delivered the news of this bizarre, self-fulfilling prophesy. Kate saw attitudes changing, but not everyone was excited. There was more than one sceptic in the room. It was all too perfect. Too pat. She waited for someone to verbalize what the others were thinking.

The team remained silent.

They needed a nudge.

'None of what I've said necessarily proves that Gardner killed Elliott. Pearce insists that the tale has been passed down through the generations, cemented in history, perpetuating a myth until it reached our numpty who bought it hook, line and sinker.' Kate scanned the room. 'What worries me is, if Pearce knew this, then who else did?'

'C'mon!' Robson was shaking his head. 'You might fantasize over your dodgy forefather, but you'd hardly go out and hang someone, would you? It would be a bit obvious.'

'My point exactly,' Kate said. 'So who else is prepared to accept the possibility that someone is deliberately pointing us in Gardner's direction?' She asked for a show of hands. The team was split, more hands up than down. 'That's what I thought. Looks like we have work to do. Neil, get your coat on. You're outward bound this morning. Get over to Quad Squad. I want to know if Liam Gardner and Robert Pearce were booked on the same quad-biking course in February last year. Be sure to ask them if they've had any bikes stolen. Feed anything suspicious to me.'

She looked for DC Brown.

'Andy, liaise with crime scene investigators. See how they're getting on with their search of the bridle path. I want a report every hour until they find that fence post. When, or should I say *if* they manage to locate it, I want you to contact Matt at the forensic science lab. Ask him to fast-track it for me. Remind him he owes me a favour.'

'I seem to think he already paid you back,' Andy said.

'Well, ask nicely, it always works for me.' Kate pointed at Carmichael. 'Lisa: in-depth interview with Gardner's parents, quick as you can. Let's see if there is any truth in the bullshit Pearce gave us last night.'

'His mum is dead,' Carmichael said. 'Massive cardiac arrest six months ago.' She pulled up abruptly, eyes on Kate. 'Boss, I'm sorry. That was insensitive. How is your dad?'

'He's doing fine,' Kate lied.

'Do *you* think Pearce is playing games?' Carmichael asked.

'I think it's a load of bollocks but we need to check it out. Hank, go with Lisa please. Gardner's old man might not be too happy with the police. Like his son, he's a nasty piece of work. That's it. There'll be another briefing later.'

67

Kate settled in her office for a couple of hours, a never-ending list of administrative duties to perform. She had a million calls to return while the team carried out her instructions. Liam Gardner occupied the majority of conscious thought as she went about her business. Without doubt he was guilty of wounding Elliott Foster and attempting to rape Beth Casey, whether or not a case against him for the latter could be proved in a court of law. As regards a murder charge, Kate had the distinct impression he was being set up somewhere along the line.

At ten to ten, her mobile rang: DC Brown.

She scooped it up off the desk. 'Andy, tell me Forensics found the fence post.'

'They found two, as it happens. Either one could fit the bill. Both are en route to the lab as we speak. Too early to say if we'll find the evidence we're looking for. Anyway, that's not all. Your journalist friend Gillian Garvey is sniffing around. Trying to get in via the back door. She wants the lowdown on Gardner and his mates.'

'I hope you sent her packing.'

'I did, but not before she told me that they were all remanded in custody for three weeks. She had one of her minions covering the case. Anything happening at base?'

'There is some truth in the rumour Pearce was spouting. Hank and Lisa say that Gardner senior is almost as flaky as his son. He's adamant that they are related to William Gardner, executioner.'

'Daft sods.'

'I reckon it's a fabrication used by the family as a scare tactic. I guess it worked to reinforce the hype. Their associates are wary of them for sure. Shows how bright they are. Only someone with the brain of an amoeba would believe it.'

Brown chuckled.

A 'call waiting' alert drew Kate's attention. 'Gotta go, Andy. Someone else is trying to get through.' She thanked him and hung up, glancing at the handset. Whoever was calling, the screen showed: *Number unknown.*

Pressing to receive, she lifted the device to her ear. 'Hello.'

'Ms Daniels, my name is Claudia de Jong. I'm calling from the Freeman Hospital. Your father has been transferred to us from Wansbeck as an emergency admission. His condition deteriorated in the past hour or so. He's scheduled for surgery at noon.'

Kate felt her scalp tighten, a quickening pulse. The room began to swim, walls closing in, reducing in size until her only focus was the glass panel in her office door. Beyond it, detectives went about their business – seemingly in slow motion – unaware of the drama taking place elsewhere, mostly in her head. She wanted to bolt in there and scream at them to stop.

My father is ill . . .

He might die . . .

He can't die.

Imagination in overdrive, Kate saw green scrubs, mask-covered faces, surgical loupes, head torches and bloody gloves. Her father's chest clamped open, electrodes attached to an electrocardiograph machine, a respirator tube in his mouth, a bleeping monitor nearby, a team of surgeons and nurses huddled over his beating heart to perform a bypass. She shook violently, unable to control the stress she was under.

Breathe!

Focus!

'Ms Daniels?'

'Yes, I'm still here.'

Kate cleared the frog from her throat and stood up.

Opening her window, she took in a huge gulp of air and then sat down again. In a matter of seconds, the room had returned to normal. The dutiful daughter morphed into unflappable professional investigator.

She checked her watch: 10.05. 'Noon is a bit short notice, isn't it?'

The woman's hesitation filled in the blanks.

'I get it.' Kate was ever the pragmatist. 'Someone on your list was unable to make it?' She meant dead.

'Yes, sadly.'

'I'm sorry to hear that.'

'Your father is a priority for us. We can't afford to wait. I gather you're in the middle of a major investigation, however, the surgeon would like to see you beforehand, if that's possible, so he can explain the procedure and answer any questions you may have. Is that doable for you?'

'Yes, what time?'

'The sooner the better.'

'On my way.' Kate put down the phone and blew out her cheeks, her stomach heaving once more. It was time to build bridges before it was too late.

She was taken into a small office where the cardiologist briefed to perform her father's operation was waiting. The surgeon was an Asian man, slim-built, not much older than her. He had a kind face and the most penetrating eyes she'd ever seen.

They were trained on her.

'Take a seat, Ms Daniels.' He waited for her to sit. 'My name is Mr Rai. Your father tells me that you are his next of kin, his only kin in fact.'

'Yes, that's correct.'

'I wanted to introduce myself before I carry out the procedure.'

What he meant was: *I'd rather meet you now in case he doesn't make it.*

'I understand,' she said.

'I'm sure I don't need to tell you that there are risks associated with any major heart surgery. The operation itself can last anything between six and eight, sometimes even ten hours, so you need to prepare for that.' The statement was delivered with Buddha-like calm.

Kate knew all this, of course; he was underlining it for her, as he was duty bound to do. She could feel her own heart pumping faster as he elaborated on the procedure. She was in awe of this man, of all men and women skilled enough to open up a patient's chest and perform surgery on their most vital organ outside of their brains.

The cardiologist's voice faded out as her stress levels rose again. She was in meltdown, suffering an out-of-body experience, as if she were floating on the ceiling, looking down on herself from above. She was scared. Small. Terrified of what came next.

'On the plus side,' the surgeon said, 'the operation is one with a high success rate. However, your father's condition is unstable, so the risks of survival are difficult to assess.'

Her father was awake but drowsy, having been prepped with drugs to sedate him. He didn't look scared – a little apprehensive, perhaps – and incredibly relieved to see her as she approached his bedside doing her very best to hide anxiety and show certainty.

'How are you, Dad?'

'Not too bad.' The squeeze of her hand was weak, like a child's, and cold to the touch.

The smile on her father's face looked forced. Kate recognized that look. She'd seen it a hundred times before. It was the smile on the lips of every victim's family she'd ever known if she happened upon them after the event, either by accident or design, no matter how long had elapsed since their loved ones had suffered a violent death, crippling assault or rape. Weeks, months or years later, it was there . . . *The polite smile . . . The embarrassed smile . . . The haunted smile* . . . It appeared every time she asked the same stupid question she'd asked her old man.

She bent over and kissed his clammy forehead, drew up a

chair and sat down. 'You look great,' she lied. 'It'll all be over soon and you can go home.' Except it wouldn't be soon. Six to ten hours in a life-and-death situation was a bloody long time. What if Rai got tired halfway through? Kate knew only too well what happened to a person's concentration after such a prolonged period of time. It would surely wane.

'Who told you I was here?' her father asked.

'The admissions secretary rang to let me know you'd been transferred and why.' She tried to keep her voice level. It sounded shaky to her. She hoped he hadn't noticed. 'I understand they've been putting you through your paces since you arrived.'

He nodded. 'ECG, chest X-ray, blood tests, a proper bath.'

'I bet that was heaven.'

'It was – but also exhausting.'

How could a bath be exhausting? He'd always been so strong. He was breathing heavily. Maybe she should seek out the anaesthetist to inform him of that in case no one had clocked it. It might have been missed. The ward was busy. Staff rushed off their feet. Her father was new. They might think it was normal. It wasn't.

She must tell them.

'I'm told you're in pretty good shape for your age,' Kate said. 'You'll be back on your bike in no time. Maybe we could ride out together to Hartside Pass . . . it's been a while.'

'You still go up there?'

'I do,' Kate said.

There was a faint twinkle in his eye. Enough to show her he remembered the good times. It brought a lump to her throat the size of Texas.

'I'd like that.' His attention strayed to an earlier visitor. 'Did Jo ever tell you she doesn't like you riding? She blamed me. Said I should never have taught you. I like her, Kate . . . a lot.'

Too fucking late.

Kate's heart was breaking.

She allowed her eyes to drift to another bed while she regained her composure. A male patient had arrived from a stint in intensive care. He looked ghostly white, his wife even more so. Kate had seen healthier-looking corpses. The man looked so ill, she wondered if he was ready for a general ward.

She didn't tell her father that she and Jo had split up. That it would never have worked. That it wasn't all her fault. It was his too. That Jo found his overt condemnation as hurtful and incomprehensible as she did but was too polite to say. That he was part of a much bigger problem. That he was as guilty as Atkins, the reason Kate had screwed up her life and denied herself openness.

'Is she here?' he asked.

Kate shook her head, unable to answer.

'We're ready for you, Mr Daniels.'

The voice had come from over Kate's left shoulder.

No! She began to panic. *I need more time . . .*

I haven't mentioned that he's in good hands, or told him that his surgeon looks like a winner, not a quitter. That HE is MY dad. That he'll survive the operation, if only to take that motorcycle ride. That I have regrets; that his approval matters; that we've wasted so much time; that if it was in my power to turn the clock back, I would . . . or that I love him.

I need time . . .

Kate felt excluded as porters took over. Not in a physical sense. They were kind enough to allow her to accompany them on the long journey along the corridor to the operating suite, all the time holding his hand. 'You're going to be fine, Dad. I'll be in later.' She kissed him goodbye and somehow managed to keep a smile on her face until the operating theatre doors crashed shut. In the corridor she wept.

68

Half an hour into her father's surgery and all Kate could think of was the *No Admittance* sign on the theatre doors and whether she'd ever see him again. His life was in the hands of Mr Rai and his team. No matter how many times she told herself that they were highly skilled and dedicated professionals with a great success rate – that the Freeman Hospital was one of the best heart units in the world – her father's unstable condition dragged her down.

'Cuppa tea, boss?' Carmichael lowered the tray she was carrying.

Kate chose the mug with the stronger-looking brew.

'Lemon drizzle?' Lisa asked. She was famous for supplying the team with the delicious cake, made from a secret family recipe handed down through the generations.

'Not for me, Lisa.' Ordinarily Kate would have jumped at the chance. She felt sick and couldn't face it.

'I'll have yours.' Grabbing two slices, Hank put one in his mouth, devouring it in seconds. 'Mm . . . this is great!' He pointed at the second slice lying in the palm of his shovel-sized hand and looked at Kate. 'Sure you don't want it?'

She smiled. 'You'd only sulk if I said yes.'

They all looked round as the door to the incident room

opened. Atkins appeared in the doorway, drawing the attention of everyone there. It had completely slipped Kate's mind that he was coming in. *My office. Tomorrow. If you don't arrive I'll come and find you.* That had been her parting shot when she had left his apartment to drive Beth home. Hank had left by then. It seemed like months ago.

So much had happened since.

Sensing trouble, Hank handed his cake to Lisa and approached Atkins. Kate let him handle it. She didn't have the energy, much less the inclination to deal with the Angry Man herself. Another altercation with him would be unwise in her current mood.

'What do you want?' Hank said. 'You're not supposed to be in here.'

Atkins stood his ground. 'Your boss is expecting me.'

'I don't think so.' Hank glanced at Kate.

She shook her head.

'Something came up,' Hank said. 'She's busy. You'll have to come back.'

'Are you serious?' Atkins threw Kate a hard stare. 'I just paid for a taxi. You see me now or I walk.'

'It's fine, Hank.' Kate walked across the room towards them. Atkins didn't acknowledge her. His eyes had strayed to a place they didn't belong: the murder wall.

He swung round to face her. 'You bailed Collins?'

'Not that it's any business of yours.'

'Can I ask why?'

'Are you deaf?' Hank said. 'The boss just said—'

'Hank, I'll deal with this.' Kate appreciated his attempt to protect her but ordered him to butt out. She turned to face

Atkins. 'There was no evidence to hold Collins. I can't keep him in because you don't like the look of him. I charged Gardner and his mates with Section 18. I'd have told you last night if you'd been reasonable. Slept it off, have you?'

He made no comment.

'If what Beth told me is true, Gardner may be charged with a damned sight more than that.'

Not a flicker.

Kate studied him.

He looked dreadful.

She noticed that he was dressed in the same clothes he'd had on when she last saw him. He hadn't shaved and was sweating profusely. Whether from the heat of the room or the mess he was in was anyone's guess. He hadn't spoken or reacted since she'd alluded to the attempted rape. It made her wonder if he was devious enough to have manipulated a terrible situation to meet his own ends. His money had been on Collins from the outset.

Was that in order to throw her?

Kate's mind was working overtime. Atkins had tried unsuccessfully to drive a wedge between Beth and Elliott because they were too close for his liking. Elliott had given him a valid reason for their deep attachment – coming to her aid after the assault by Gardner – something she later denied to her father. The rest came to Kate in Beth's voice: *He warned Elliott off, told him not to come near me again.*

The sentence stuck in Kate's mind.

'Follow me,' she said.

'Here's fine,' he said. 'Spit it out and I'll be on my way.'

'My office or there's the door.' Kate never took her eyes off him. She didn't like the way her latest theory was shaping up. 'The things I want to say to you can't be said publicly.'

'Want me along?' Hank said.

Kate shook her head. 'Not this time.'

He stood aside.

Atkins moved gingerly towards her office.

As she followed him out, the DCI speculated further on his role in her case. She couldn't make up her mind who he was trying to shaft: Collins or Gardner. At his own admission, he hated Beth associating with Collins and wanted Elliott out of the way. Had he seen the fight and taken advantage, finished off what Gardner started and killed the boy? Or had he seen Gardner do it, then thrown Collins into the mix to get rid of all three? Many an affray had ended in tragedy for all concerned.

Although when challenged Beth had denied the assault to her father, he was aware of the allegation. If he knew that, what else did he know? Or maybe *who else* was the better question.

He knew the snitch: Pearce.

Logically, it followed that he might also know of Gardner's alleged colourful family history and willingness – whether or not it was true – to believe that he was the descendant of an executioner. If Atkins knew Gardner wasn't guilty, where better to dispose of Elliott's body than on Winter's Gibbet to frame him for the death?

Was that what this case was about – vigilante retribution?

Atkins had always been in the hang 'em and flog 'em brigade.

Kate hoped she was wrong, for Beth's sake.

Shutting the door so they wouldn't be interrupted, she invited him to sit and walked round her desk to do likewise.

'I'm fine standing,' he said. 'Get it over with. I haven't got all day.'

'I have some questions for you.'

She pointed to the chair and waited.

Taking her cue, Atkins sat down, his arm hanging over the backrest, his right foot resting on his left knee. He oozed arrogance.

'Last night, Beth told me that Liam Gardner assaulted her and that you knew.'

'She denied it. She tell you that too?'

'She told me a lot of things. I'd like to hear them from you.'

He appeared to give it some consideration. In the end, he said nothing. How could he? He'd dug himself a hole and didn't know how he was going to climb out of it. His behaviour during the investigation was indefensible.

They both knew it.

Kate gave him a helping hand. 'You went to see Elliott to warn him off Beth. Why was that?'

'I didn't want him near her.'

'Why not? By all accounts he was a lovely lad—'

'Was he? I had my reasons.'

'Did something happen between Diane and his old man?'

'What? No!'

'Beth seemed to think there was weird stuff going on between you and Elliott's father.' The sentence had hardly left her lips when she made the jump. A missing piece of the story fell neatly into place. *If stuff doesn't make sense, try the flipside.* That was Bright's mantra. 'Ah, now I get it. It wasn't Diane that was the root of the problem, was it? It was *you.* Of course it was. You had an affair with Elliott's mother, didn't you?'

Kate didn't expect him to admit it, although, from where she was standing, there was too much information on the table to deny it, the majority of it coming from his estranged daughter.

He decided to come clean. 'Yes, Gayle and I had a fling.'

'When was this?'

'Diane was pregnant at the time. What's a man to do?' His grin brought with it echoes of the past. It made her cringe. 'Oh *please*,' he said, 'save the disapproving looks for someone who actually gives a shit. I was reckless. I've been paying for it ever since. I don't expect you to believe that I loved my wife. I messed up. What more can I say?'

'You weren't the only ones to suffer.'

'Hell no, the perfect couple suffered too. Why should they be any different? Graeme and I were good friends before that. We got into a fight over it and his kid, Adam, ended up with his grandma.'

Jane Gibson looked after two boys.

Atkins actually had a tear in his eye. Kate was joining dots. Reading him. And he could see she was making connections to a secret of his own. 'This was before Elliott was born?'

He swallowed hard. 'There was talk that he was mine.'

Kate tried not to react. 'Did Gayle arrange a paternity test?'

'She did.'

'And?'

Atkins ignored the mobile ringing in his pocket. 'I refused the results.'

'To read them or accept them?'

'The former. She threw a fit and tore them up.'

'She didn't tell you later?'

'Have you met her?'

Kate nodded.

'Then what do you think?'

The bravado had gone. He dropped his head a moment, then looked up, meeting her eyes across the desk. He was a torn soul, tormented by his past. Fleetingly, she felt sorry for him. If Elliott *was* his son, it made sense of the close bond between the lad and Beth. It also explained why Atkins gave Grant the job of informing the family. He didn't want to face Gayle.

'You should've told me,' Kate said.

'What, cry on your shoulder? I don't think so.'

'Would that have been so bad?'

He didn't answer.

'The kids had no idea?'

He shook his head. 'I didn't tell Beth and I know for a fact that Gayle wouldn't have confided in Elliott. Like everyone else, she hates my guts. After all this time, she'd die rather than reveal the truth to me. The stubborn bitch will take it to her grave.'

'You could have apologized.'

'I did. I begged and pleaded with her for years afterwards. She said I'd had my chance and blew it. I'm not proud of the affair. When I saw how close Beth was to Elliott, I had to put a stop to it.'

'You were under the impression he was after her.' It wasn't a question.

Atkins nodded. His mobile rang again. He took it from his pocket and switched it off.

'Elliott told you he was in a relationship with someone else.'

'Yes, and I didn't believe him.'

'You should have. He was gay.'

'Yeah, pull the other one.'

'What? You think no son of yours could be gay?'

He didn't try to hide his disgust, nor she the irony.

'Elliott was no threat to Beth,' Kate said. 'In fact you owed him for saving her from a serious sexual assault. The way she tells it, he'd gone to her rescue in the nick of time. Do you expect me to believe you couldn't see her distress afterwards?'

'I didn't.'

'No wonder she lied to cover it up rather than discuss it with you.' Kate paused. 'When did you finally realize that Elliott was telling the truth? Was it before or after she'd confided in Collins?' Kate could see the sad and downtrodden Atkins give way to the Angry Man. She didn't want to accuse him of killing Elliott outright, given what he'd just told her. Still, she wondered if he might have, for no other reason than to get even with Gayle. And then there was the assault by Gardner on Beth.

Two birds. One stone.

'Tell me,' she said. 'When did you twig the gibbet connection?'

'The what?'

'What better way to get retribution than to set up the thug who tried to rape your daughter – and for a murder you knew he didn't commit.'

'Don't be ridiculous!' He knew where she was heading and didn't repeat his denial. 'That scum has escaped the law too many times, I agree – but I didn't set him up. What do you take me for?'

'It's not looking good.'

'You don't seriously think I'm stupid enough?'

'I don't know what to believe any more. I think you should consider legal representation though.'

'Go to hell!'

'So tell me what you know.'

He hesitated.

'For fuck's sake! Talk to me. Where were you on the evening of the Alwinton Show?'

His hesitation was damning.

'You were in Elsdon, weren't you?'

He chewed the inside of his cheek before coming clean. 'I took Beth's key and went to Diane's place to have a poke around. I wanted to make sure she hadn't moved anyone in. I didn't see the fight, I swear, but I knew Beth was in the village. I saw her car parked a short distance from the church.'

Kate's phone rang. She glanced at the clock on the wall: 12:45.

It was far too early for the hospital . . . unless . . .

'I have to take this,' she said. 'Can you wait outside?'

He didn't move.

'Fine, stay where you are then.' She took a deep breath and pressed to receive, adrenalin flooding through her body. 'Hello.'

'Control here, Inspector. We've had a report of a possible abduction in Elsdon village. The eyewitness claims a girl was manhandled from her house, bundled into a motor and driven away at speed in the direction of Otterburn. Her name is Beth Casey. She's the daughter of DCI Atkins, ma'am. I can't raise him.'

Kate looked across her desk at Atkins and kept her voice calm. 'Do you have any more details, Control?' His reply was lost in the noise inside her head. She asked him to repeat it.

69

The operator's words faded away as Kate put down the phone. She was looking at Atkins, hearing his daughter's voice. *He'll kill me!* When Beth blurted out those three words, the expression on her face had been uneasy. Kate remembered her mumbling to herself when she'd come to the station for help. She recalled her own confusion over whether or not the girl had been referencing her dad.

Was she talking about Collins?

His was the next voice to enter Kate's head, vociferous and full of malice, reminding her that Atkins wasn't the only one of the opinion that Beth and Elliott were too close for comfort. Kate had specifically asked him what Elliott's reaction had been to Gardner's windup that the two were intimate. *He denied it. He's not daft,* came the reply. Maybe in Collins' head, it lacked sincerity.

The announcement chime was followed by a cultured female voice coming over the public address system in Heathrow's Terminal 5: 'This is an urgent call for passenger Josephine Soulsby travelling on transatlantic flight BA0113 to New York. Please contact the nearest information desk.'

Jo had only just cleared security. She'd arrived early in order to shop and eat. She listened intently as the message

461

was repeated, until she was sure it was her name she'd heard. She tuned the rest of it out, her stomach in knots. Outside of her two sons, Tom and James, only one person knew she was there: Fiona Fielding. It stood to reason that she'd since passed the information to someone they both knew. Knowing she was about to leave the country, Jo could think of only one scenario that would prompt Kate Daniels to try and get in touch.

Her father.

Glancing up at the departures board, Jo saw that her flight was on schedule, due to leave in a little under three hours. She couldn't deny she needed some downtime but she couldn't leave now. Kate would be putting up a good front. That was her way. Underneath that hard exterior she'd be destroyed. Inconsolable. Riddled with guilt for not having made her peace with Ed.

What a shame.

Reaching down, Jo lifted her phone from her bag and switched it on. Kate had called several times and not been able to get through. Earlier texts had gone ignored. Feeling guilty, Jo called her mobile. The ringing tone had hardly begun when she came on the line.

Her tone of voice was flat and depressed. 'Thanks for returning my call. I'm sorry to disturb you.'

'Kate, I'm so sorry. I'll take the next flight home.'

'I don't expect you to do that. I'd rather you didn't.'

'What does that mean? I don't understand.'

In that split second, Kate realized that Jo had jumped the gun. 'It's not my dad,' she said. 'He's fine – at least, I think he is, he's still in surgery. Please don't worry about him or me. This is work-related.'

'Well that's a relief.'

'Not really. Beth Casey is missing.' Kate sounded hassled and shocked. 'Abducted from her mother's home. Collins, we think.'

'I thought he was in custody.'

'I bailed him this morning. You put a query on HOLMES, requesting more information on him. Lisa said you thought you knew him, at least knew of him.'

'It may not be the same guy.'

'And if it is, he's got a screw loose, right?'

'Let me make some calls,' Jo said. 'I'll get back to you.'

Jo dialled another number, had a brief discussion with her office and hung up as her name was once again transmitted over the airport's public address system. Checking in at the nearest information desk, she confirmed who she was and cancelled any further summons.

Thanking the desk clerk for her assistance, Jo found an empty table in a cafe. She took out her MacBook, fired it up and opened up the mail program. The confidential email she was waiting for dropped into her inbox seconds later.

Kate felt the weight of an impending disaster as soon as she answered the phone. Over the years she'd worked in major incident teams, she'd developed a sixth sense. She knew what Jo was going to say even before she started talking.

Kate spoke first. 'You're going to tell me he's mentally ill, aren't you?'

'Yes.' Jo gave it straight. No messing. No attempt to soften the blow. 'He was a client at the clinic. Not one of mine. I've read his file and spoken to his caseworker. He was referred following a stint in prison. I'm sending you the file. This is highly irregular, so keep it to yourself.'

'Understood – and thank you.'

Kate's eyes seized on her computer screen as the email arrived.

There were literally dozens of documents: social services, probation and parole reports as well as half a dozen psychiatric assessments from various medical facilities.

'Jesus,' she said. 'It's a big file. It's going to take forever to digest this lot. Can you précis it for me?'

'I'll try,' Jo said. A tall, well-dressed businessman approached from nowhere, asking if he could join her. She glared at him as he drew up a chair without waiting for an answer. Then told him, in no uncertain terms to get lost.

'What?' Kate was confused.

'Not you, hold on.' Jo didn't bother to cover the speaker as she glowered at the drip sitting opposite. 'Do you mind?' she said. 'I know it probably comes as a surprise to you but I prefer my own company.' Embarrassed by her offhand attitude, the man picked up his briefcase and scurried off. 'Sorry,' Jo was back on the phone. 'It's pick-up central in this place. If you're sitting alone, you must be desperate. I had to be blunt.'

'Forget him. This is more important.'

'Sorry.'

'Don't apologize. Just get on with it.'

'Collins is delusional, obsessively jealous, morbidly so. There's a report in the file from his social worker, Andrea someone, Oxford Social Services. Can you see it?'

'Andrea Corrigan?'

'Yeah, that's her.'

'Got it.'

'It's very detailed and will tell you all you need to know without going round the houses,' Jo said. 'Andrea cooperated fully in the investigation into his behaviour post-sentence. She made it her business to. I have to tell you she had big concerns. It'll be no surprise to her when she learns what's going on in Northumberland.'

Kate accessed the report. 'Is he on licence to anyone?'

'No. He refused to acknowledge his condition initially. Wouldn't accept that he was in the wrong. Eventually, he began to play ball. Agreed to a brain scan. Took medication. Responded to treatment. His fixation diminished. Despite what you might think, it is possible to treat and work with patients with this pathological condition. So long as they cooperate, they pose no threat to the wider community.'

Kate didn't doubt it. But in her line of work, she'd seen the worst-case scenarios become a reality far too often. Treatment programmes had gone horribly wrong, some ending in death at the hands of someone with a personality disorder where paranoia was present. She couldn't accept that Collins was anything other than a manipulative freak who deserved all that was coming to him.

'And if he's not taking his medication?' she asked.

The pause that followed was an answer in itself.

'That's why we got involved.' Jo said. 'I'm so sorry for not alerting you sooner.'

'It's not your fault.'

'It feels like it is.'

'According to Control, Collins has already lost it. He wasn't pulling his punches when he got hold of Beth. We're searching for them. It says here that he deteriorated quickly before his last serious assault on a girlfriend. That worries me.'

'It should,' Jo said. 'His victim was terrified to leave the house. He used to follow her, everywhere, even to the toilet. If she so much as smiled at another boy, he'd accuse her of having a full-blown affair. If the phone rang, he'd pick up an extension and listen to her calls. He read her mail, banned her from using a computer, drove her to and from work, examined her underwear. Can you imagine?'

'I'm reading it now.'

Kate's eyes flew over the text.

The information contained in those digital pages made her blood run cold, her stress levels rise to an all-time high. There was reference to impaired mental capacity, antipsychotic drugs she couldn't pronounce, as well as a statement from his victim that her fidelity was intact. According to the report, Collins was having none of it.

'Blimey!' she said. 'We all experience jealousy from time to time but this is *way* beyond the norm. He sounds like a bloody madman. I detected jealousy when I was with him, but nothing like this.'

'He has Othello Syndrome—'

'Oh, terrific! All I need is a diagnosis that will let him off the hook.'

'It's a recognized condition, Kate.'

'Is it?' Kate snapped. 'I'm sorry to sound cynical, but it goes against the grain to treat him like a patient and not the violent perpetrator his is. Give guys like him a label and they think they're home and dry. It also hands him a convenient defence in a court of law. I've been dealing with guys like him all my working life. I don't give a stuff about his various manifestations. As far as I'm concerned, he's a bully out of control. There's a lot of it about. Treatment didn't do him much good, did it?'

'Some you win.'

'Tell that to the Angry Man. He's another headcase—'

'He knows about the abduction?'

'He was with me when I found out. He went for me—'

'What? Did he hurt you?'

'No, but guess who he's blaming. It might not be my signature on the bail form but I was the one who authorized the release of the boyfriend from hell.'

'I can only imagine how angry he is.'

'I don't think you can. You know what? If he'd kept his cool, I'd have taken him with me to find her. He's a bloody liability. The guv'nor was so incensed when he kicked off this time. In spite of the horrendous stress Atkins is under, Naylor frogmarched him to the custody suite and locked him up.'

'He's in the cells?'

'A padded cell is what he needs.'

'With his daughter's life in danger?'

'Is that a euphemism for "next time I see her she'll be lying on a mortuary slab"?'

'I never said that.'

'You didn't criticize me either. It just sounded like you did.'

'It seems a bit callous, that's all.'

'I'm aware that the situation is less than ideal. Atkins may be a victim on this occasion, but he doesn't deserve your sympathy. He should've engaged his brain before he went berserk. Who knows, time in the cells might knock some sense into him. I need to find Beth – preferably alive – and I don't need his hateful rage in the car while I do it.'

'Don't give up, Kate.'

'Not while I'm still breathing.' She paused. 'Othello sufferers injure and kill spouses they consider unfaithful, right?'

'Or make their lives hell.'

'How dangerous are they in relation to those they perceive to be their partner's lover?'

'I can't answer that.'

'Give it your best shot. I need your help.'

'I don't want to rattle you.'

'Then don't.'

'Collins is dangerous—'

'That much I know.'

'His convictions were all against women. That's why I didn't think he was responsible for the hanging. I'm sorry, I should've checked into it more thoroughly. Going on leave is no excuse.'

'No, it isn't.' Kate didn't forgive her. 'He wasn't only a risk to Beth, was he?'

'What are you asking?'

'Given the right trigger, might he have killed Elliott?'

'It's impossible to tell. I've read of cases where patients have killed a partner and then committed suicide. There'll be other permutations.'

'Last question: any idea where he might take her?'

'That's even more difficult. If he murdered Elliott and abducted Beth, he's out of control. He might take her to the gibbet just to rub it in.'

It was a sobering thought.

Kate said she had to run and told Jo to enjoy New York.

70

With every available police vehicle keeping observations for Beth's car, Kate sat in her Audi waiting for news, Hank by her side. As time ticked by they hardly spoke. Words seemed inadequate. They were too tired and too wired to properly convey how they were feeling. Collins had been in their custody. Now he was God knows where, doing God knows what to Beth Casey. The situation was as depressing as it was grim.

The heels of Beth's hands hurt. They were scuffed and bleeding where Collins had thrown her out of her mother's house so violently she'd fallen heavily onto the thin strip of tarmac outside her front door. She'd never been so terrified. Not even when Gardner attacked her in the cut that night. At least then, there was a possible escape route.

Ten minutes ago, Collins had forced his way into her home, high on drugs and swigging vodka, screaming obscenities, eyes filled with rage. As he dragged her through the front door by her hair, she'd pleaded with him to go back inside and talk.

She was wasting her breath.

'Get in the car!' he'd yelled.

When she didn't move, he'd opened the door. Shoving her

in the back seat, he got in and started the car. He'd been in a bad way when they first met, she knew that, but he was much worse now. He'd promised he wasn't using any more. Had sworn he was clean. Stupidly, she'd believed him. Now she could see he was switched wrong, a hothead knocking booze back like there was no tomorrow.

Beth wished she'd heeded Kate Daniels' advice – and, to a lesser extent, her father's. She didn't want to believe that Collins was a thug who'd glassed his ex, but it was probably true. She wondered what it must've been like to face him at his worst, knowing deep down that she was about to do the same. Kate and her father had been right to dissuade her from having anything to do with him.

Even his mother had tried . . .

If only *she* had listened.

Having witnessed her abduction, one of her neighbours had come flying out of his house. Despite his age, around sixty, he'd sprinted towards them in order to intervene. Not quickly enough. Before he'd managed to reach them, Collins slammed his foot down, heading straight for him, forcing the man to dive onto the village green to avoid being knocked over. Through the back window, Beth had watched him get smaller. She'd never forget the look of shock on his face.

Kate glanced out of the window at the gibbet where police tape flapped in the breeze, sealing off the ghoulish monument to its many visitors. It was deathly quiet, a beautiful afternoon, though she hardy noticed the sunshine. In her head, there was an early morning mist, Elliott's body suspended on a length of mildewed rope she doubted she'd ever find the provenance of. For days, the lad had been lying in the morgue, cold and alone, just as she'd found him last Sunday morning. She hadn't yet managed to lay him in a warm place and cover him up.

With Hank's help she would.

The priority now was finding Beth. Neither detective, nor any other in the Murder Investigation Team or the wider force, could bear the thought of anything bad happening to her. Atkins might not be their favourite copper – and was hated by some – but they didn't need reminding that his daughter was an extended member of the police family. The responsibility to find and protect her was overwhelming.

A phone rang.

Kate used the hands-free to answer.

'It's me. Any news?' Jo would never forgive herself if anything happened to Beth.

Kate wouldn't either. 'Not yet.'

'You OK?'

'I've been better.'

'Is Hank with you?'

'He is.'

Kate glanced again at the gibbet, wondering if Beth would survive at the hands of a madman. Collins was on the edge, unpredictable and dangerous. There was no telling what such a disturbed individual might be capable of. Kate had two lives to save, not one. That unborn baby was a person too. 'Have a nice break, Jo. I've gotta go.'

'That was a bit abrupt,' Hank said as Kate hung up.

He was still trying to play happy families. He was every bit as shattered as she was over Jo's decision to take off without her. Except Kate had come to terms with it better than he had. She intended to concentrate on her own life from now on. As the cliché so aptly put it: there was no point trying to flog a dead horse.

'I need to keep this phone free,' she said.

He thought twice about pushing her on it and changed the subject. 'How long are we going to wait?' he asked.

'As long as it takes.'

He turned in his seat to face her. 'He's not going to show, Kate. Not here. He's going to make a run for it and get as far away as he can get. He'll make for major routes, north or south.'

Kate didn't entirely disagree with Hank's assessment. 'I don't care if we have to stay all night. We're not leaving. Collins may be incapable of rational thought. Jo thinks he might come here to torment Beth. That's good enough for me. We're going to sit it out until we have more information, a sighting at least. Whatever happens, I don't want to find a pregnant teenager hanging here in two days' time.' It was a sobering thought and he let it go.

71

Collins was out of breath, bent double with his hands on his knees after hauling Beth out of her car and into his. She was like all the crazy bitches he'd ever known. More trouble than they were worth. Prepared to fuck around but not take the consequences. He spat on the ground, got in and sped away. He wasn't finished with her yet.

'Chris, stop! Think of the baby.'

'I'm not the one just overdosed.' He threw a black look over his shoulder, paying no attention to the road ahead. 'You think I care about *his* bastard?'

'It's not Elliott's,' Beth cried. 'I told you.'

'You're a liar!'

'No, it's yours. You've got to listen to me—'

'Like I listened to him, you mean? He begged me not to do it. Wept like a girl.' Collins turned his head away, chuckling to himself. 'Even said he was a poof, the lying git. Except I wasn't born yesterday—'

'He was telling the truth,' Beth sobbed.

Collins shot round a bend, fighting to keep his focus on the rear-view mirror. Beth's eyes flew to the nearside wing mirror, no doubt looking for her father, that head-fuck Daniels, or any other copper. Beth was hysterical. Too bad: this was all her fault. Sick of her whingeing, he switched on the radio and turned the volume as high as it would go to block out her hysterics. Rap music. He loved a bit of rap.

'Control to Seven-Eight-Two-Four: Target vehicle found in a disused barn. Eyewitness claims to have seen it drive in. One male. One female. Arguing. The girl was screaming to be let out. Minutes later, they left in a light-blue Ford. No registration number given.'

'That's received.' Kate glanced at Hank. It wasn't ideal, but it was a step in the right direction, confirmation that Beth was alive at least. 'Control, have my lads check the system for any associates of Collins with blue cars and let me know what gives. Any uniform personnel at the barn yet?'

'Affirmative. No one inside the target vehicle, but there was evidence of drug use. They found a quad bike covered with a tarpaulin at the same location—'

'Yes!' Hank punched the air.

Kate was equally excited. 'Preserve the scene, Control.'

'They also found a ring in the back seat, ma'am. It's been identified by DCI Atkins as belonging to his daughter. We've requested the police helicopter.'

'Where exactly was the vehicle found?'

'Elishaw, just north of where the A68/A696 converge.'

It wasn't far away.

'Understood. Maintaining position and standing by.' Kate had a nervous feeling at the pit of her stomach. She clasped her hands together, elbows on the steering wheel. Beth had left them a clue. *Good girl.* With a bit of luck, she might leave more. But where the hell was she?

Beth pressed her body up against the car door, as far away as she could get from Collins, her body lurching from side to side as he raced down the road, ignoring her pleas to pull over and talk – at least slow down. It had been several minutes since they left Elishaw, even longer since he'd driven at her neighbour in Elsdon.

He'd have called the law by now . . .

So where were they?'

'Please stop,' she begged. 'I'm going to be sick.'

Collins kept on driving as if he hadn't heard her. Blind rage drove him on. Beth had seen it before, the night her father pushed her mum down the stairs when she was a kid. Her parents hadn't seen her standing at her bedroom door, woken by an argument that had spilled out of their room and onto the landing. Her mother had locked herself in the bathroom to get away from him. But he was as mad as hell and wouldn't leave it alone.

To the outside world, theirs was just another domestic dispute between two idiots who'd chosen badly and married the wrong people. Beth had grown up knowing that her mother could so easily have been one of those statistics she'd heard about on TV, murdered by an out-of-control spouse.

Was that where she was heading too?

Kate was right: abusive partners didn't stop.

Panicking, Beth saw her future in Technicolor. It was short, a deep shade of red seeping into the picture. She tried the door, prepared to fling herself from the moving car at sixty miles an hour. A crazy act, but she wanted rid of Collins at any cost. The door was locked.

*

Kate's radio crackled into life: 'Control to 7824. Pale-blue Ford Focus. Registration mark: November-Charlie-Five-Two-Papa-Delta-Romeo spotted by another road user travelling south on the A68. Driver, plus one. Vehicle was being driven erratically, according to the witness. Stand by.'

To hell with that, she thought. 'Control, does anyone on the ground have the eyeball?'

'Negative. You're the nearest car available. Units en route to your location from Byrness — ETA imminent – and dispatched from other points close to your location. Traffic car now travelling northwest on the A696.'

'Tell them all to get a move on! We can't let him reach a built-up area.'

Oh God! The car careered across the road. Collins was laughing one minute, weeping the next. Screaming at Beth for being unfaithful, even though she swore she'd never been. He was way worse than she'd ever seen him. On the day she told him of Gardner's behaviour in the car and Elliott coming to her rescue, he'd changed. In hindsight, she now recognized its significance. It was a turning point: what had begun with the occasional dig turned into out-and-out condemnation. His bitterness had escalated in recent weeks, a different lad emerging – like someone had flicked a switch.

His reaction to the assault was wholly unexpected, if not downright weird, a tone of distrust permeating every syllable. *What do you mean, assaulted?* He wasn't upset, he was furious. More than furious – and not with Gardner. Instead of offering support, he'd launched a ferocious attack on her, firing a succession of questions she didn't want to answer. No, not questions. Allegations. That's what they were . . .

What were you even doing in the cut? Who were you meeting? How come Elliott was there? And now Collins was goading her all over again, trying to trick her into submission. Beth was damned if she'd cough to something that wasn't true.

'You were screwing him,' he yelled.

'No, I swear I wasn't.'

'Don't lie to me!' He took a corner at high speed. 'I'm not blind or deaf. I've seen the looks between you. I've clocked the whispering behind my back. What do you think I am, stupid? I enjoyed seeing him swing for it anyway.'

72

Kate heard the panda car before she could see it. It flew over the brow of the hill and pulled into the lay-by behind her, sending a huge plume of dust high in the air. She didn't stop to chat, just engaged first gear and took off.

For a moment, there was a pause in communication.

Seconds later, Control came on the line. 'India 99 is in the air, ma'am. They've swept the major routes: A68/A696. No sign. Going round again.'

'That's received, Control.' Kate drove back to Elsdon and on through Otterburn, turning left onto the A68, travelling south. No sign of Collins. At The Steel, she pulled into a lay-by. Reaching into the back, she grabbed a larger-scale map from the pocket behind Hank's seat.

Sometimes satnav just wouldn't do.

Checking the index, she found the correct page and then looked up, southeast towards a small wind farm, scanning right towards a road she was familiar with. 'I know exactly where he is,' she said. 'He's steering clear of major routes. There are two minor roads that cut across country. The first is here. It runs from the A696 to the A68 via East Woodburn. I used to go fishing there as a kid with my dad. The other route is here' – she moved her finger higher up the page – 'from Knowesgate to Sweethope Lough. My nan called it the Wannies. Don't ask me why. It comes out there.'

She pointed to the horizon.

The words had hardly left her lips when they both saw a blue car shoot out of the road she'd just been talking about. It bolted across the A68 at a hell of a pace.

Dumping the map on Hank's knee, Kate engaged first gear and gave chase. 'Seven-Eight-Two-Four to Control: blue vehicle spotted. Too far away to make a positive ID. It just shot over the A68 travelling west, about half a mile south of The Steel on an unclassified road heading towards Redesdale, Riversdale and Bellingham. I'm in pursuit but I've lost the eyeball.'

'India 99.' The police helicopter pilot cut in. 'With you soonest.'

Kate was grateful to Cole. 'That's received, India 99.'

It took her a few minutes to spot Collins again.

'Control, I now have the eyeball. Target vehicle is totally out of control. Driver is ignoring slow signs, putting his female passenger in danger. He's screaming at her. He just reached into the back and punched her.' Kate ducked as something bounced off her windscreen. 'There's stuff being thrown from the windows, Control.'

Kate edged closer, then pulled off again as Collins swerved into the path of an oncoming tractor. He ploughed into the grass verge and bounced back onto the tarmac, ripping the sill from his vehicle. She needed to stop him. Not an easy task on a winding road with such a poor surface where, in places, it dropped steeply on either side.

Beth's safety was a priority.

Hank's was vital.

Changing down, she kept her foot on the gas. The view from this road was stunning but her eyes were on the vanishing point and nowhere else. Just as she caught up with Collins, he again veered into the path of oncoming traffic, missing it by a whisker. Taking a sharp bend at Buteland Farm, every now and then Kate caught sight of her target as the road dipped and twisted like a thin strip of grey ribbon through open countryside.

'Control, can you establish if there is any ambulance free in our location? If so, please make them aware of our pursuit. Keep them updated with our exact position. I don't think this is going to end well. The target is travelling in excess of seventy miles an hour. Any Traffic personnel in the area, please respond.'

Panic-stricken, Beth clung on to the grab strap as Collins hurtled round the bend on the opposite side of the road before raking the car onto the correct side again, fishtailing, almost tipping them over the edge, at grave risk of turning the car over. She stared at the back of his head, looking round for something to hit him with, but there was nothing.

Bizarrely, her father's voice arrived in her head: *Never leave anything loose on the backseat. If you hit something, it could fly forward and kill you.* Good advice, but it wasn't helping now. Collins looked over his shoulder, laughing at her pathetic attempt to stay calm, his eyes like black pools.

She couldn't pull her gaze away.

Every time she begged him to stop, he accelerated sharply, scaring her to death, pinning her to the seat, so far gone, he was unaware that they were now under police surveillance. Beth had spotted Kate's Audi as they tore along the road. She tried not to look in the wing mirror in case she drew the car to Collins' attention. Her father had formed roadblocks in pursuit of offenders. Maybe Kate would too. Chris would have to stop then. He'd have no choice.

Kate had lost him temporarily. As she passed the turn-off to Buteland Heights, she slowed down, scanning the surrounding countryside. Giving instructions to India 99 to check farm tracks left and right, she sped up, her eyes widening as she glimpsed Collins in the distance and, beyond him, a group of hikers.

Oh no!

'He's reached Redesmouth, Control. Pedestrians are jumping out of the way. I'm pulling off. Pulling off. No longer in pursuit. Any chance of a hard stop or stinger before he reaches Riversdale?'

'Negative, no one close enough.'

Dropping a gear, Kate negotiated a steep bank close to the river and over a bridge, losing sight of Collins again. The next voice they heard was from the air. Cole's helicopter was directly above them.

'India 99 to Control. I now have the eyeball. I'm recording this pursuit.'

Hanging on to the grab strap with his left hand, Hank stuck the fingers of his right hand down his throat, mimicking the pilot's voice. 'Ladies and gentlemen, this is your captain speaking. We'll shortly be arriving in Tenerife.' He winced as Kate slapped his chest with the back of her hand for taking the piss.

Once through Redesmouth, the DCI picked up speed, taking a really bad corner under a bridge, before a horrifying prospect presented itself via the radio.

'India 99: target vehicle is doing a reciprocal – Seven-Eight-Two-Four, be advised, he's travelling east at speed, heading towards you.'

'I see him.' Kate held her ground. 'He's driving at us deliberately. Brace! Brace!'

Collins screamed past her window, producing the most terrifying whoosh as he took out the Audi's offside wing mirror, glancing off the side panel of her car, sending metal debris flying everywhere. Swearing at no one in particular, Kate slammed her hand on the dash.

Hank blew out a breath. 'Could've been worse.'

'Oh yeah, in what way?'

'Might have been my motor.'

Kate swore at the top of her voice. Cars were her passion.

'Lighten up,' Hank said. 'It's a piece of tin.'

Unable to see the funny side, Kate turned the Audi around and put her foot down. As she completed the manoeuvre, Collins did the same and came back for a second run. 'He's coming at me again, Control. Heading back towards Riversdale and Bellingham. Brace yourself, Hank.' This time Collins missed them by inches.

Kate did a quick three-point turn and again gave chase. Cole had flown ahead. She could see India 99 hovering over the road. His words sent a chill down her spine. 'The schools are coming out, Control.'

73

Kate had visions of carnage on the road. As she began backing off on the outskirts of Riversdale, Hank didn't question
why she was slowing down. If they had been in open countryside, he knew she'd be on Collins like a rash but, in small
villages, she couldn't risk tracking him in case someone got
hurt. They couldn't afford the headlines that would surely
follow: *Cops' high-speed chase ends in tragedy for pregnant
teenager. Pedestrians killed.* Reckless driving charges weren't
exclusive to civilians. They were a reality for many police
officers too.

Collins was spaced out, enjoying himself, a line of coke
and a half-bottle of vodka having done its job. He hadn't
had this much fun in ages. He peered through the front
windscreen, the road ahead morphing into a psychedelic
highway. A car got louder as it approached, its horn blast-
ing, dying again as it flew by. He saw the whites of the
driver's eyes. A young woman, not much older than Beth,
terror on her face as she prepared herself for a collision.
Silly cow.

Beth was hysterical in the back, her throat sore from
screaming at Collins, imploring him to stop and think about

484

what he was doing. Then a terrifying thought occurred. It arrived like a time bomb in her head . . .

He was intending to kill them both.

Beth had never been surer of anything in her short life. Unable to hide her fear, her breathing came in short bursts. The pain in her head was blinding, blotting out logical thought. She couldn't stop him. The best she could hope for was to reason with him.

'Chris, pull over. We need to talk about this. You're not well. I see that. I can help you. It's not too late. You know how I feel about you. We can sort this.'

It was a lie. The words should have been formed in the past tense. Whatever feelings she'd had for him were long gone. The ear-splitting noise in her head was crushing her. Even when she threw up in the car, Collins continued to drive recklessly, putting her life and that of their child in danger. Holding on tight as they flew round the corner, she saw the flicker of a blue light in the distance. Kate had caught up with them.

India 99 picked up the commentary: 'Target vehicle is being driven at speeds in excess of seventy mph heading into Riversdale, driving on both sides of the road, causing absolute mayhem. Pedestrians at risk. I have a visual on police vehicle Hotel-Four-Seven west of my location. Make your way half a mile ahead and stop on Redesmouth Road preventing his exit through Bellingham.'

'Affirmative,' came the reply.

'Delta-Three-Two-Six. If you can stop at Boat Road in case he legs it towards the B6320. He's got nowhere else to go.'

'Roger that.'

Cole again: 'Target is going to have to bail, Control. Suggest the dog man alights his vehicle at the cricket club. Looks like he may head across country.'

Chris couldn't keep the car straight on the road. He was off his head with nowhere to go. Unwilling to listen to reason, he carried on, way past caring about Beth. He was yelling again, wanting details of the assault and Elliott's part in it, hell-bent on receiving an admission that she was meeting him, that they were more than friends.

'That's not right,' Beth yelled.

'Tell me the truth—'

'We were mates!'

He carried on baiting her, haranguing her. She was shaking violently. The shock of what happened in the cut would never leave her. The shock of what was happening now was almost worse. Collins' heartless reaction was why she'd failed to confide in her father, the police generally. She couldn't take the finger-pointing, accusations and disbelief. She'd told Kate she would stand up and tell her story to protect other girls from guys like Gardner – it's what her mother should have done – but Beth wasn't sure she could go there now.

Cole saw, rather than heard, the crash from the air. 'Target vehicle in collision with another car, Control. Driving recklessly. Children at risk. He's losing it. He's crashed. He's crashed. Ambulance required.'

'Roger that, India 99.'

Beth was unconscious; her body slumped across Collins as he came round. Dazed, he pushed her off, struggling to open the door and to get out, blood streaming down his face. He took off on foot as the Audi came into view.

'India 99 to Control: We have a runner. Seven-Eight-Two-Four arriving on scene.'

'That's received, India 99.'

Kate screamed to a stop, jumped out of her vehicle and ran towards Collins, shouting at nursery school teachers to move the children away. Hank ran the other way towards the car. Out of the corner of her eye, Kate could see him gathering Beth up in his arms, lifting her from danger. She was shocked and dazed, but coming round.

She was alive.

Relief flooded through Kate – and then the worst sight imaginable. Beyond a pile of rubble that used to be the wall of the Riverside Private Nursery School, toddlers had stopped playing and were running screaming to their teachers. A few feet away – to the left and in the foreground – Kate saw an upturned trike, its wheel still turning, next to a child's scuffed green shoe.

'Oh God!' A sob caught in her throat.

One of the teachers was staring at something Kate couldn't see. She didn't want to look, even though she was obliged to. Her imagination took over, macabre images flashing before her eyes: flowers, soft toys and teddies on the pavement. Distressed teachers. Inconsolable parents. Heartbroken kids. The noise of the helicopter hovering above drowned out the silent scream in her head.

'India 99 to Control: Please advise Seven-Eight-Two-Four that the child casualty is with an adult and has nothing more than a bloody knee. Breathe, Kate. The boy is OK. He's OK.'

He's OK.

Tears stung Kate's eyes. She was beginning to recover when Collins grabbed the one child who'd been left behind when the others were ushered into the nursery school yard. He gave the DCI a long hard stare, his crazy eyes full of malice.

He was desperate.

Kate was too.

Hank froze, Beth still in his arms.

'Don't do it,' he yelled. 'You're in enough trouble!'

'He's right,' Kate said. 'Chris, if you're going to make a run for it, you'll be a lot quicker without her. Let her go and I promise I'll do my very best for you. You have my word on that.'

Collins laughed.

He glanced at the little girl. Shoving her away, he staggered onto the bridge and leapt onto the parapet, swaying as he looked down at the North Tyne. The river was flowing fast over the weir after a period of heavy rain. Kate held her breath. Seconds later he was gone. Kate flinched, her whole body shuddering at the thought of him crashing onto the rocks below. Peering over the edge, she watched his body float downstream, turning the water red.

74

Whether Collins had leapt from the bridge to escape the law or commit suicide was unclear. He'd been spotted in the North Tyne, just south of Boat Road, by a K9 called Sophie – fished out by her handler – alive, fortunately. In time, he'd stand trial for murder, abduction and serious driving offences. Given his record, Kate suspected that he'd spend the rest of his life inside a secure unit of some kind, if not prison.

Beth's suffering went on . . .

In the few short hours since she'd been missing, a message had filtered through to MIT that her mother had died. When Kate gave her condolences, the teenager had been stoical. She was a gutsy kid, primed by palliative carers for the inevitable, able to draw comfort from the fact that Diane Casey's last hours were peaceful and that she'd passed away unaware of the drama taking place on a lonely stretch of road elsewhere in Northumberland.

Kate was less well prepared to deal with critical illness. Her father's coronary had come out of the blue. Back on intensive care, he'd come through the operation unscathed. Mr Rai, the surgeon, had assured her that the prognosis was favourable. He had every confidence that Ed Daniels would make a full recovery, although he still looked very poorly indeed. The next twenty-four hours would be tricky, she'd been warned.

It felt like déjà vu, watching over him in the small hours. The last time she'd done it, Jo had been by her side. This time Hank had come along to offer support. Taking hold of her hand, he squeezed it gently. They were both dog-tired.

'Did you know the name Elsdon is derived from Elli's Valley?' he asked.

'No, I didn't.' She turned to face him. 'Who told you that?'

'Lisa found a reference to it on the Internet.'

'Anglo-Saxon?'

'Apparently. A fitting tribute to Elliott, don't you think?'

She nodded. Whatever the story, the name Elli would always remind her of a gay Cumberland wrestler who'd died too young, caught up in one loser's savagery and another's psychosis.

How unlucky was it possible to be?

Sensitive to her sorrow, Hank changed the subject. 'Have you decided what to do about Atkins?' he asked.

'No.' Her eyes were back on her father: the tubes, the wires and the team of nurses fussing over him. Right now, she didn't want to think about anyone but him. Thunder rumbled overhead. Kate looked up at the ceiling as the lights flickered slightly. A nurse reassured her that backup generators would kick in should the power fail.

'Y'know, much as I hate his guts,' Hank said, 'there are two ways to play your hand with Atkins. I agree with Naylor. Beth is going to need him. More than that, she's going to need his money. Much as I'd love you to leave him without a bean to his name, there's an alternative.'

'Which is?' Kate could see him scheming.

'I know you'd like to pull his fingernails out one by one, but that's illegal and I'd advise against it. You could still call the shots and give him a chance of redemption.'

'Oh yeah? I'd like to know how.'

'You let him choose. Tell him you're going to expose him unless he steps down. He's got enough years in to take his pension and move on. That way he leaves quietly with his reputation intact.'

'What reputation?'

'Precisely. What use is he to the force anyhow? Who'd work with him? I wouldn't. Not one detective I've spoken to would. If you take up my suggestion, Beth doesn't have to suffer but he gets his comeuppance. It'll hurt him because he won't get the job he wants either.'

'That's your idea of a choice?'

'Put up or shut up works for me.' He pulled a crazy face.

Who knew that the voice of reason would come from Hank? Kate wasn't convinced that Bright would go for it. He wanted Atkins to suffer. A lot. And, if she were being honest, so did she. There were no guarantees that he'd help his daughter and his bullying would go unpunished, a thought she shared with Hank. 'Listen to yourself,' she added. 'You're acting like judge, jury and bloody executioner.'

'Someone has to.'

She gave him the evil eye.

'C'mon!' he said. 'It's not as if you haven't seen it before. Some arse walks rather than bringing the force into disrepute. It's everyday politics. The allegation you made as a rookie on its own will sink him. Wave it in front of his face and he'll be eating out of your hand in no time. You're in a strong position, Kate. Tell him the deal is off unless he signs a percentage of his commutation over to Beth.'

'That sounds like blackmail—'

'I prefer to call it a sensible solution.'

Put like that, it was tempting.

'I'm serious,' Hank said. 'If you shaft him it *might* stop him being a bully, but it'll *definitely* prevent him from helping Beth. She's already said she won't speak to him again unless he goes into therapy.'

'Good for her.'

'Can you see her pressing charges against Atkins?'

'Not really.'

'I can't either. Her mother went to her grave without ratting on him. Beth's a mixed-up, pregnant teenager. He's her father. The only one she's got. She cares for him deep down and wants his approval, just as you want it from him.' He head-pointed to her sleeping father. 'That's what we all want, isn't it? Validation from our parents.'

Ed Daniels appeared to stir.

'I'm here, Dad.' Sitting forward, Kate stroked his arm, wondering if he'd heard the conversation and was trying to respond. He'd kept his side of the bargain they had made at the door to the operating theatre. He'd come through to live another day. Maybe they would take that bike trip to Hartside and enjoy another sunset together. Things were set to improve between them. She'd make sure it stayed that way.

'Have you heard a word I said?'

'What?' Kate glanced sideways.

Hank returned her gaze, one eyebrow raised – a reprimand.

'OK, I wasn't listening. What did you say?'

'If you press ahead with a charge against Atkins, it may look like you're doing it for all the wrong reasons – for what he did to you – and I know you wouldn't want that. No matter which way you dress it up, people will believe it's some crazy-arsed revenge by someone on the wrong bus.' He raised his hand like a traffic policeman. 'Joke!'

She grinned at him.

'I'll give it some thought,' she said.

Hank took a hip flask from his pocket. 'Fancy a bevvy?'

'Tea, maybe.'

Hank glanced at his watch. 'You'll be lucky. It's one a.m. We shouldn't even be here.'

'Nice try,' Kate said. 'There's a machine on the wall outside the canteen. And you can stop sulking or I'm sending you home.'

They left the ward, telling the nurse in charge that they'd look in on the way out, reaching the canteen a few minutes later. Hank's smartphone bleeped an incoming voicemail as they arrived at the vending machine.

'Sit there.' He gestured to a nearby chair. 'I'll bring it over.'

Kate took a seat as he walked away, lifting the mobile to his ear. She watched him drop change into the slot, his back to her. Seconds later, he returned empty-handed, a haunted look in his eyes. Gone was the trademark smile, the witty routine. She stood up quickly, her eyes trained on the corridor, expecting Mr Rai to appear at any moment.

Hank was shaking his head, swallowing hard, temporarily speechless. 'It's not your dad, Kate.' It was almost a whisper.

She was confused. 'What then?'

His voice broke as he delivered the news. 'Jo's flight is missing.'

Acknowledgements

Thanks to the entire staff at Pan Macmillan; my editors Wayne Brookes and Anne O'Brien, whose patience is never-ending, not forgetting my publicist, Philippa McEwan. Thanks also to everyone at A.M. Heath Literary Agency, especially my wonderful agent, friend and collaborator, Oli Munson. Top man.

Gallows Drop is the sixth book in the Kate Daniels series. Appreciation must go to Daniel Nixon (Blake Friedmann, Literary, TV & Film Agency) who negotiated TV rights with Gina Carter at production company Sprout Pictures. Not forgetting the inimitable Stephen Fry for shouting loudly and enthusiastically on Twitter about my books. 'They're just great reads,' he said. Who am I to disagree?

I must acknowledge Barry Redfern, author of *The Gallows Tree – Crime and Punishment in the Eighteenth Century* (Tyne Bridge Publishing) – whose wonderful book was a source of historical and local information. A mention also for friend and ex-copper Alan Tailford, who appears in this book as himself; an enthusiastic follower of Kate Daniels I just happened to bump into during a research trip to Alwinton Show.

Big hugs and kisses to my family as always: Paul, Kate, Chris, Jodie, Max, Frances and Daisy – for love, laughs,

ACKNOWLEDGEMENTS

inspiration and support. Not forgetting Mo – partner, plotter, consultant and crime scene manager – who makes writing Kate Daniels so much fun.